SOLOMON vs. Lord

Paul Levine

BANTAM BOOKS

SOLOMON VS. LORD
A Bantam Book / October 2005

Published by Bantam Dell
A Division of Random House, Inc.
New York, New York

Grateful acknowledgment is given for permission
to reprint the following:

"But I Loved You," words and music by GORDON JENKINS.
Copyright © EMI ROBBINS CATALOG, INC. Used by permission
of Warner Bros. Publications. All rights reserved.

"Como Arrullo De Palmas," by Ernesto Lecuona. Copyright ©
1933, 1937 by Peer International Corporation. Copyright renewed.
International copyright secured. Used by permission.
All rights reserved.

Bantam Books and the rooster colophon are registered trademarks
of Random House, Inc.

ISBN 0-440-24273-8

Printed in the United States of America
Published simultaneously in Canada

www.bantamdell.com

OPM   10 9 8 7 6 5 4 3 2 1

For Renée, who lights the way.

ACKNOWLEDGMENTS

I am indebted to numerous individuals who have been generous with their time and expertise.

Randy Anderson—outstanding screenwriter, wily poker player, and wise friend—helped immeasurably in the creation of Steve Solomon and Victoria Lord.

Edward Shohat, top-flight defense lawyer, shared his encyclopedic knowledge of criminal law. Angel Castillo, Jr., a literate litigator, guided me through Little Havana and the civil courts.

Special thanks to comedic whiz Carmen Finestra; Miami-Dade County Circuit Judges Lester Langer and Stanford Blake and judicial assistant Terry Sullivan; Assistant State Attorney Christina Martyak, Assistant Public Defender Yvonne Colodny; Guardian Ad Litem volunteer Yolanda Berkowitz; and Voices for Children Foundation assistant director Martha Diaz.

Rick and Sue Newhauser kindly allowed me to borrow their Gables Estates home as a location. I have also used the resources of Grossman and Roth, PA, thanks to the continuing support of stellar trial lawyers Stuart Grossman and Neal Roth.

My editor Kate Miciak, who ushered me into this business, has an uncanny ear for dialogue, a laser eye for character, and a fiendish mind for plot. Thanks, too, to Bantam's Loyale Coles and Caitlin Alexander.

My agent Al Zuckerman, my personal publishing guru, has again provided me with sage advice and counsel as have Matthew Loze and Geoffrey Brandt at Course Management. Thanks, also, to Maya Rock at Writers House.

Finally, in these pages, Steve Solomon defines the difference between "success" and "excellence." I learned that personal philosophy from legendary football coach and friend Joe Paterno. Thank you, Joe.

Opposites attract, the wise men claim,
Still I wish that we had been a little more the
   same,
It might have been a shorter war.

"But I Loved You"
Written by Gordon Jenkins
Recorded by Frank Sinatra

One

CELL MATES

The man in the holding cell loosened his tie, tossed his rumpled suit coat into a corner, and stretched out on the hard plastic bench. The woman in the facing cell slipped out of her glen plaid jacket, folded it carefully across an arm, and began pacing.

"Relax, Vickie. We're gonna be here a while," the man said.

"*Victoria,*" the woman corrected. Her angry footsteps echoed off the bare concrete floor.

"Wild guess. You've never been held in contempt before."

"You treat it like a badge of honor."

"A lawyer who's afraid of jail is like a surgeon who's afraid of blood," Steve Solomon said.

"From what I hear, you spend more time behind bars than your clients," Victoria Lord said.

"Hey, thanks. Great tag line for my radio spots. 'You do the crime, Steve does the time.' "

"You're the most unethical lawyer I know."

"You're new at this. Give it time."

"Sleazy son-of-a-bitch," she muttered, turning away.

"I heard that," he said.

Nice profile, he thought. Attractive in that polished, cool-as-a-daiquiri way. Long legs, small bust, sculpted jaw, an angular, athletic look. Green eyes spiked with gray and a tousled, honey-blond bird's nest of hair. Ballsy and sexy, too. He'd never heard "sleazy son-of-a-bitch" sound so seductive.

"If you weren't so arrogant," he said, "I could teach you a few courtroom tricks."

"Save your breath for your inflatable doll."

"Cheap shot. That was a trial exhibit."

"Really? People have seen the doll in your car. Fully inflated."

"It rides shotgun so I can use the car-pool lane."

She walked toward the cell door. Shadows of the bars pin-striped her face. "I know your record, Solomon. I know all about you."

"If you've been stalking me, I'm gonna get a restraining order."

"You make a mockery of the law."

"I make up my own. Solomon's Laws. Rule Number One: 'When the law doesn't work, work the law.'"

"They should lock you up."

"Actually, they already have."

"You're a disgrace to the profession."

"Aw, c'mon. Where's your heart, Vickie?"

"*Victoria!* And I don't have one. I'm a prosecutor."

"I'll bet you think Jean Valjean belonged in prison."

"He stole the bread, didn't he?"

"You'd burn witches at the stake."

"Not until they exhausted all their appeals." She laughed, a sparkle of electricity.

Damn, she's good at this.

Fending off his *mishegoss,* trumping his insults with her own. Something else appealed to him, too. No wedding band and no engagement ring. Ms. Victoria Lord, rookie prosecutor, seemed to be unattached as well as argumentative. Maybe twenty-eight. Seven years younger than him.

"If you need any help around the courthouse," he said, "I'd be willing to mentor you."

"Is that what they're calling it these days?"

Touché. But she'd said it with a smile. Maybe this wasn't so much combat as foreplay. Another parry, another thrust, who knows? The more he thought about it, the more confident he became.

She likes me. She really likes me.

I hate him.

I really hate him, Victoria decided.

Dammit, she'd been warned about Solomon. He always tested new prosecutors, baited them into losing their cool, lured them into mistrials. And she wasn't totally "new." She'd handled arraignments and preliminary hearings for eight months. And hadn't she won her first two felony trials? Of course, neither one had involved Steve Slash-and-Burn Solomon.

"You gotta know, the contempt citation is all your fault," he said from the facing cell.

She wouldn't give him the pleasure of saying, *Why?*

Or, *How?*

Or, *Go screw yourself.*

"You should never call opposing counsel a 'total

fucking shark' in open court," he continued. "Save it for recess."

"You called *me* a 'persecutor.' "

"A slip of the tongue."

"You're incorrigible."

"Lose the big words. You'll confuse the jurors. Judges, too."

Victoria stopped pacing. It was stifling in the cell, and her feet were killing her. She wanted to pry off her ankle-strapped Prada pumps, but if she stood on this disgustingly sticky floor, she'd have to burn her panty hose. The plaid pencil skirt was uncomfortable, a tad too tight. Now she wished she'd taken the time to let it out before coming to court. Especially after catching Solomon, the pig, staring at her ass.

She saw him now, sprawled on the bench, hands behind his head, like a beach bum in a hammock. He had a dark shock of unruly hair, eyes filled with mischief, and a self-satisfied grin, like he'd just pinned a "Kick Me" note on her fanny. God, he was infuriating.

She couldn't wait to get back into the courtroom and convict his lowlife client. But just now, she felt exhausted. The adrenaline rush was ebbing, the lack of sleep was fogging her mind. All those hours practicing in front of the mirror.

"Ladies and gentlemen, you will hear the testimony of Customs and Wildlife Officers . . ."

Maybe she was going about this the wrong way. How many times had she had researched the legal issues, prepped her witnesses, rehearsed her opening statement?

". . . who will testify that the defendant, Amancio

Pedrosa, did unlawfully smuggle contraband, to wit, four parakeets, three parrots, two cockatoos . . ."

And a partridge in a pear tree.

Maybe she'd burned herself out. Maybe that's why she'd cracked today. Had she looked ridiculous pushing a grocery cart overflowing with boxes to the prosecution table? There was Solomon, holding a single yellow pad, and there she was, weighted down with books, research folders, and color-coded index cards bristling with notes.

Even though she despised Solomon, she did envy his brash confidence. The way he glided across the courtroom, skating to the clerk's table, flashing an easy smile at the jurors. He was lean and wiry and graceful, comfortable in his own skin. When she rose to speak, she felt stiff and mechanical. All those eyes staring at her, judging her. Would she ever have his self-assurance?

An hour earlier, she hadn't even realized she was being held in contempt. Judge Gridley never used the word. He just formed a T with his hands and drawled, "Time-out, y'all. This ain't gonna look good on the instant replay." It was only then that she remembered that the judge was a part-time college football official.

"Mr. Solomon, you oughta know better," Judge Gridley continued. "Miss Lord, you're gonna have to learn. When I say that's enough bickering, that's by-God enough. No hitting after the whistle in my courtroom. Bailiff, show these two squabblers to our finest accommodations."

How humiliating. What would she say to her boss? She remembered Ray Pincher's "two strikes" orientation lecture: "If you're held in contempt, you'll feel blue. If it happens again, you'll be through."

But she wouldn't let it happen again. When they got back into the courtroom, she'd . . .

Shit!

Something was stuck on the velvet toe of her pump.

A sheet of toilet paper!

Grimacing, she scraped it off with the bottom of her other shoe. What else could go wrong?

"Hey, Lord, we're gonna be in here a while." That aggravating voice from the other cell. "So here are the ground rules. When one person has to pee, the other turns around."

She shot a look at the seatless, metal toilet bowl.

Right. As if I'd squat over that fondue pot of festering bacteria.

When she didn't respond, he said: "You still there or you bust out?" Somewhere, deep inside the walls, the plumbing groaned and water gurgled. "Suit yourself, but I gotta take a leak."

What a jerk.

Solomon was one of those men you run into in bars and gyms, she thought, so clueless as to believe they're both witty and charming.

"No peeking," he said.

There was a plague of these men, with a sizable percentage becoming lawyers.

"Unzipping now . . ."

Dear God, scrunch his scrotum, zipper his balls.

"Ahhh," he sighed, the *tinkle-tinkle* sounding like hailstones on a tin roof. "Ninety-nine bottles of beer on the wall," he sang out. "Ninety-nine bottles of beer . . ."

"I didn't realize they still made men like you," Victoria Lord said.

I'm getting through to her, Steve thought. Sure, she was still playing that old *I am strong, I am invincible, I am wo-man* shtick, but he sensed a shift in her mood.

There seemed to be something different about the feisty Ms. Lord. Nothing like the court stenographers he usually dated. Quiet, rather submissive women who transcribed whatever they heard. And nothing like the SoBe models, whose brains must have been fried by exposure to so many strobe lights.

He remembered looking around the courtroom when Victoria rose to address the judge. All the players—from his shifty client to the sleepy bailiff—had been riveted. Jurors, witnesses, cops, probation officers, jailers, clerks, public defenders. Hell, everybody watched *her*, even when *he* was talking. Yeah, she was a natural, with the kind of pizzazz they can't teach in law school.

Maybe the best rookie I've ever seen.

Of course, she had a rigid prosecutorial mentality, but he could work on that, once she forgave him for suckering her into contempt. Not that he minded the downtime. To him, this eight-by-eight cell was a cozy second home, a pied-à-terre with a view of the Miami River from the barred window. Hell, they ought to put his name on the door, like a luxury suite at Pro Player Stadium. Failing that, he scribbled on the cell wall:

Stephen Solomon, Esq.
"Beating the state's butt for nine years"
Call UBE-FREE, 822–3733

Steve preferred to defend the truly innocent, but where would he find them? If people didn't lie, cheat, and steal, he figured he'd be starving, instead of clearing about the same as a longshoreman at the Port of Miami who worked overtime and stole an occasional crate of whiskey. Steve usually settled for what he called "honest criminals," felons who ran afoul of technicalities that would not be illegal in a live-and-let-live society. Bookies, hookers, or entrepreneurs like today's client, Amancio Pedrosa, who imported exotic animals with a blithe disregard of the law.

Steve glanced into Victoria's cell. She had resumed pacing, a tigress in a cage. Her tailored plaid jacket was draped over an arm. An expensive outfit, he was sure, but wrong for the jury. The high neck accentuated her—well, stiff-neckedness. She should ditch that Puritan look, get something open at the collar, a bright blouse underneath. The matching skirt was fine, a little tighter than he'd expect on the prim prosecutor. A nice ass for someone so flat on top.

"What do you say, after we get out, we hit Bayside, dive into a pitcher of margaritas?" he said.

"I'd rather drink from the toilet bowl."

Keeping her distance for now, he thought. Made sense as long as they were in trial. "Okay, let's wait till we get a verdict. Win or lose, I'll treat you to tapas."

"I'd die of starvation first."

"You might not be aware, but over the years, I've tutored several young women prosecutors."

"I'm aware you've bedded down a few. And rifled their briefcases in the middle of the night."

"Don't believe everything you hear in the cafeteria."

"You're one of those toxic bachelors, a serial seducer. The only thing that shocks me is that some women find you attractive."

Have I missed a signal? Shouldn't she be warming up by now?

"I'll bet any relationship you've had, the woman always ended it," she said.

"My nephew lives with me and scares most women off," Steve said.

"*He* scares them off?"

"He's kind of a reverse chick magnet."

"That sort of thing genetic?" she asked.

An hour later, her feet still ached and the toilet still gurgled, but at least Solomon had shut up. Victoria hoped he understood that she had no interest in him. You hit some men with a frying pan, they think you're going to make them an omelette.

But as annoying as she found him, the sparring did help pass the time. And if nothing else, jousting with Solomon might sharpen her courtroom tactics. The trick was not to let him provoke her once they were back in front of judge and jury. She made a vow. Even if he led a herd of elephants into the courtroom, she would maintain a Zen-like tranquillity.

If I get back into the courtroom.

She wondered if word had reached Ray Pincher

that she'd been sent to the slammer. A shudder went through her, and suddenly she felt both alone and afraid.

Awfully quiet over there, Steve thought, trying to see her through the shadows.

What was she thinking right now? Uptown girl inhaling the stale sweat and toxic cleansers of her own private Alcatraz. Probably planning what she'd tell her boss, that pious phony Ray Pincher. Scared he'd demote her to Traffic Court.

Had he gone too far, Steve wondered, baiting her into those outbursts? Judge Gridley's contempt citations were sort of like calling unsportsmanlike conduct on both teams. But would Pincher understand? Did he even recognize Lord's potential?

Dammit, Steve thought, beginning to feel regretful. He hadn't wanted to hurt her. He was just trying to have some fun while defending his client.

Another worry, too. His nephew, Bobby, barely eleven, was home alone. If Steve was late, who knows what might happen? One day last week, when he rushed through the door just after seven, the kid announced he'd already made dinner. Sure enough, Bobby had found a dead sparrow on the street, covered it with tomato sauce, zonked it in the microwave for an hour, and called it "roasted quail marinara." It had been easier to throw out the microwave than to clean it.

If he ever dated Victoria, he'd introduce her to Bobby, his relationship litmus test. If she responded to the boy's sweetness and warmth—if she saw past his disability—she might be a contender. But if she was repulsed by Bobby's semi-autistic behavior, Steve would toss her out with his empty bottles of tequila.

Now what the hell was going on? Did he just hear a sniffle?

I will not cry, Victoria told herself.

She didn't know what had come over her. A feeling of being totally inadequate. A loser and a failure and a fraud. Dammit, what baggage had spilled out of the closet without her even knowing it?

"You okay?" Steve Solomon called out.

Shit, what did he want now? A lone tear tracked down her face, and then another. Great. Her mascara would turn to mud.

"Hey, everything all right?" he asked.

"Just great."

"Look, I'm sorry if I—"

"Shut up, okay?"

The clatter of footsteps and the jangle of keys interrupted them. Moments later, a man's voice echoed down the dim passageway. "Ready to go back to work?"

"Go away, Woody," Steve said. "You're disturbing my nap."

Elwood Reed, the elderly bailiff, skinny as an axe blade in his baggy brown uniform, appeared in front of their cells. He hitched up his pants. "Mr. Pincher wants to see both of you, pronto."

A chill went through Victoria. Pincher could fire her in an instant.

"Tell Pincher I don't work for him," Steve said.

"Tell him yourself," Reed retorted, fishing for the

right key. "He's waiting in Judge Gridley's chambers and he ain't happy."

Reed unlocked their cells, and they headed down the passageway, Steve whistling a tune, jarringly off-key, and Victoria praying she still had a job.

SOLOMON'S LAWS

1. **When the law doesn't work . . . work the law.**

Two

HUMILIATIONS GREAT AND SMALL

No more tears, Victoria vowed as they approached the entrance to Judge Gridley's chambers. She would rather break a nail, tear her panty hose, and shear off a heel of her Prada pumps than cry in front of Steve Solomon.

Biting her lower lip, she tried to transport herself to more pleasant venues. A clay tennis court on Grove Isle, stretching high for an overhead smash, the solid *thwack* of racket on ball. Handling the wheel of her father's gaff schooner—the *Hail, Victoria*—when she was ten, the wind snapping against the mainsail. Anyplace but here, where her boss lay in wait, armed with the power to destroy her career.

"Something wrong?" Steve said, walking along-side.

Instincts like a coyote, she thought. The door was six steps away. She felt her insides tighten; her heart pitched like a boat in a squall.

"I've known Pincher for years," Steve persisted. "Why not let me handle him?"

"Does he like you?" she asked.

"Actually, he hates my guts."

"Thanks, anyway."

"Then a word of advice. Don't take any shit."

She stopped short. "What are you saying? That Pincher will respect me if I stand up to him?"

"Hell, no. He'll fire you. Then you can come over to my side."

Steve thought the chambers cannily reflected both of Judge Gridley's pursuits, misconstruing the law and bungling pass-interference calls. There were the required legal volumes, laminated gavels, and photos of the judge shaking hands with lawmakers and lobbyists. Then there were old leather football helmets and photos of the striped-shirted Gridley at work on Saturdays in various college football stadiums.

One wall was devoted to trophies and posters, evidencing the judge's fanatical devotion to his alma mater, the University of Florida. A plaque celebrated Gridley as a "Bull Gator Emeritus," and on his desk was a stuffed alligator head with its mouth open, teeth exposed, like a hungry lawyer. Only two things were missing, Steve thought: a bronzed jockstrap and Judge Gridley himself.

Standing on the orange-and-blue carpet was a scowling, trim, African-American man in his forties, wearing a three-piece burgundy suit. When he moved his arms, there was a soft clanging of metal. Raymond Pincher's dangling silver cuff links were miniature handcuffs.

Steve thought that Pincher, the duly elected State Attorney of Miami-Dade County, would have to loosen up considerably just to be called tight-assed.

Pincher billed himself as a crime fighter, and his campaign billboards pictured him bare-chested, wearing boxing gloves, a reminder of his days as a teenage middleweight in the Liberty City Police Athletic League. He'd won the championship two years running, once with a head butt, and once with a bolo punch to the groin, both overlooked by the referee, who by serendipitous coincidence was his uncle. Boxing had been excellent preparation for Florida politics, where both nepotism and hitting below the belt were prized assets. These days, when someone suggested he'd make a fine governor, Ray Pincher didn't disagree.

Pincher glared at Victoria, who was biting her lip so hard Steve thought she might draw blood. Suddenly, Steve was worried about her and wanted to save her job. But how to do it? How could he take the heat off her?

Victoria said a quick prayer. First that her voice wouldn't break when she was required to speak. Second, that Solomon would keep his big mouth shut.

"Hey, Sugar Ray," Steve called out. "Execute anyone today?"

Oh, Jesus.

"Good afternoon, Mr. Pincher." Victoria nodded stiffly, struggling to remain calm.

"Ms. Lord, I am disturbed by what I hear and concerned by what I see," Pincher chanted in a melodious singsong. Before attending law school, he had studied at a Baptist seminary. There, office gossips claimed, he'd been expelled for selling Bibles intended as gifts to Central American orphanages. "A prosecutor is the swift sword of justice, the mighty soldier in the war of good against evil."

"Amen," Steve said.

Victoria felt her cheeks heating up.

Dammit! Don't be such a girl.

"A prosecutor must never be held in contempt," Pincher said. "Contempt is for defense lawyers of the flamboyant persuasion." "Flam-boy-ant" sounding like a flaming French dessert. "Contempt is for the hired guns who sell their souls for filthy lucre."

"Or for peanuts," Steve said.

"Stay out of this, Solomon," Pincher said. "Ms. Lord, what is the most important attribute of any trial lawyer?"

"I'm not sure, sir," she said, afraid to venture a guess.

"The ability to lie while saying hello," Solomon volunteered.

"Dignity," Pincher fired back. "Ms. Lord, do you know what happens to prosecutors who bring disrespect to the office?"

She stood rigidly, unable to speak.

"Hellfire, damnation, transfer to hooker court," Steve enumerated.

"Termination," Pincher said.

"C'mon," Steve said. "Give her some room. She's gonna be really good if you don't squeeze the life out of her."

Great, Victoria thought, a compliment from Solomon, as helpful as a stock tip from Martha Stewart's broker.

Steve said: "She's already better than most of your

half-wits who want to plead everything out and go home at four o'clock."

"Not your business, Last Out."

Last Out. What was that all about? She'd have to ask around.

"My point, Ms. Lord, is that you cannot let Mr. Solomon badger, befuddle, or bedevil you." Pincher often employed the preacher's habit of alliteration and the lawyer's habit of using three words when one will do.

"Yes, sir," Victoria said.

"I myself have tried cases against Mr. Solomon," Pincher said.

"You're the best, Sugar Ray," Steve said. "Nobody suborns perjury from a cop like you do."

Cuff links jangling, Pincher wagged a finger in Steve's face. "I recall you bribing a bailiff to take two six-packs of beer to the jury in a drunk-driving case."

" 'Bribery' is an ugly word," Steve said.

"What do you call club seats for the Dolphins?"

"The way they're playing, torture."

"You're Satan in Armani," Pincher said.

"Men's Wearhouse," Steve corrected.

"You have raised contumacy to a high art."

"If I knew what it was, I'd be even better at it."

"We have a dossier on you. Contempt citations, frivolous motions, ludicrous legal arguments."

"Flatterer," Steve said.

"Any more circus tricks, I'll have the Florida Bar punch your ticket." Pincher shot his cuffs and flashed a hard, cold smile. "You don't watch your step, you're gonna end up like your old man."

"Leave him out of this." Steve's tone turned serious.

"Herbert Solomon felt he was above the law, too."

"He was the best damn judge in the county."

"Before your time, Ms. Lord," Pincher said, "Solomon's father was thrown off the bench."

"He resigned!"

"Before they could indict him. Bribery scandal, wasn't it?"

"You know goddamn well what it was. A phony story from a dirty lawyer."

"I was only a deputy then, but I saw the files. Your father's the dirty one."

The room had grown tense.

"What's the penalty for slugging the State Attorney?" Steve said. His hands were clenching and unclenching.

Pincher balanced on his toes like a prizefighter. "You don't have the balls."

The two men glared at each other a long moment.

"Boys, if you're through wagging your dicks," Victoria heard herself say, "I need to know whether to go back into court or look for a new job."

After a long moment, Steve laughed, the tension draining away. Now *she* was trying to help *him*. "Aw, fuck it, Sugar Ray."

"Never saw you back down before." Pincher sounded suspicious, like Steve might sucker punch him the second he dropped his guard.

"Vickie's influence."

"*Victoria,*" she corrected icily.

Pincher appraised each of them a moment, tugged at an earlobe, then said: "Ms. Lord, because I know of Mr. Solomon's predilection for provocation, I'm not firing you today."

"Thank you, sir." She exhaled and her shoulders lost their stiffness.

"For now, consider yourself on probation."

His good deed for the week, Steve thought, helping save her job. But what a prick, that Pincher, hacking away at the newbie. Steve felt embarrassed, like he'd been eavesdropping on another family's quarrel. Victoria tried so hard to be tough, but Steve had seen the tremble of her lower lip, the flush in her cheeks. She was scared, and it touched him.

A loud rush of water interrupted his thoughts, the unmistakable sound of an ancient toilet. A moment later, the door to Judge Erwin Gridley's personal rest room opened, and the judge walked out, carrying the sports section of the *Miami Herald*.

"What's all this caterwauling?" the judge drawled. He was in his mid-fifties and fighting a paunch but could still waddle down the sidelines after a wide receiver. Suffering bouts of double vision, he wore trifocals in court, but not on Saturdays, which Steve figured might explain some of his more egregious calls, including too many men on the field when replays clearly showed only eleven.

"Mr. Solomon and I were reminiscing about old cases," Pincher told the judge.

"Mr. Pincher remembers cases the way a wolf remembers lambs," Steve said.

"I was just about to tell counsel that I'll be sitting second chair to Ms. Lord for the rest of the Pedrosa trial," Pincher said.

"You, working for a living?" Steve said.

"It would be an honor to have you in my courtroom," the judge allowed.

"It's my new hands-on plan," Pincher said. "One week every month, I'll be in court."

"Then who's gonna shake down lobbyists for campaign money?" Steve asked.

"Keep it up, I'll sue you for slander, Solomon."

"Now, don't you two git started." The judge tossed the sports section onto his desk. "Mr. Solomon and Miss Lord wore me out this morning with their grousing." He turned to the two of them, squinting through his eyeglasses. "I'm hoping a few hours in the cooler settled your nerves."

"We're fine, Your Honor," Victoria said. "Thank you."

"Cell mates today, soul mates tomorrow," Steve vowed.

"Hah," Victoria said.

The judge said: "The clock's running down, so let's talk business."

"Yes, sir," Victoria said. "State of Florida versus Amancio Pedrosa."

"*University* of Florida versus Florida State," the judge corrected. "Gotta lay five points to take my dog-ass, butt-dragging Gators, for crying out loud."

"You don't want to touch that, Judge," Steve advised.

"Hell, no. Gator's QB got a stinger on the turf at South Carolina last week. I oughta know. I called roughing on the play."

As the three men continued to talk about football in grave tones, Victoria took stock of her career.

Humiliations great and small.

"Consider yourself on probation."

She had felt her face redden as Pincher berated her. Why did he have to do it in front of Solomon? It was doubly embarrassing when Solomon spoke up for her, though for a moment, it made him seem almost human. She wondered if the florid tint had faded from her neck and cheeks. Victoria could not remember a time when she didn't blush under pressure.

She dreaded going back into the courtroom with Pincher perched on her shoulder like one of Pedrosa's illegal birds. All she wanted now was to win and prove she had the chops to be a trial lawyer.

But what if she lost? Or worse, got fired? The legal market sucked, and her student loans weighed a ton. Each month she wrote a check for the interest, but the principal just sat there—eighty-five thousand dollars—taunting her. The only clothing she'd bought since law school came from Second Time Around, a consignment shop in Surfside.

Except for shoes. Shoes are as important as oxygen, and you don't want to breathe another person's oxygen, right?

If she lost her job, she'd have to start selling the jewelry The Queen had given her. Irene Lord, called The Queen for her regal bearing and lofty dreams. Even when her money was gone, she had maintained her dignity and grace. Victoria pictured her mother, dressed in a designer gown for the Vizcayans Ball, her Judith Leiber evening bag flecked with jewels but lacking cab fare inside. She remembered, too, her mother fussing about Victoria's decision to go to law school. A dirty business, she called it.

"You don't have that cutthroat personality."

Maybe The Queen was right. Maybe law school had been a mistake. She struggled to be strong, to

cover up her insecurities. But maybe she just didn't
have what it takes. Certainly Ray Pincher seemed to
doubt her abilities.

*What's this bullshit about Pincher sitting second
chair?* Steve hated the idea. There'd be no more fun
in the courtroom, that's for sure. And Pincher would
put even more pressure on Victoria. Steve wondered
if she could handle it.

Doing his pretrial homework, Steve had looked
her up in the State Attorney's Office newsletter, the
"Nolo Contendere." Princeton undergrad, summa
cum laude, Yale Law School, a prize-winning article
in the law journal. Nice pedigree, compared to his:
baseball scholarship at the University of Miami, night
division at Key West School of Law.

In addition to the ritzy academics, there was a little ditty in the newsletter: "We're hoping Victoria
joins us on the Sword of Justice tennis team. She won
the La Gorce Country Club girls' tennis championship three years running while in high school."

La Gorce. Old money, at least by Miami standards, where marijuana smugglers from the 1980's
were considered founding fathers. The La Gorce initi-
ation fee was more than Steve cleared in a year.
Thirty years ago, no one named Solomon could have
even joined.

So why was Victoria Lord slumming in the grimy
Justice Building, a teeming beehive of cops and
crooks, burned-out lawyers and civil service drudges,
embittered jurors and senile judges? A place where an
eight A.M. motion calendar—a chorus line of miscre-
ants on parade—could crush her spirit before her *café*

con leche grew cold. Steve felt a part of the place, enjoyed the interplay of cops and robbers, but Victoria Lord? Had she gotten lost on her way to one of the deep-carpet firms downtown? Stone crabs at noon, racquetball at five.

Now Steve tried to follow the conversation. Judge Gridley was spouting his views on a college football playoff—a grand idea, there'd be more games to bet on—when they were interrupted by a cell phone chiming the opening bars of Handel's "Hallelujah."

"Excuse me," Pincher told them, fishing out his phone. "State Attorney. What? Good heavens! When?" He listened a moment. "Call me when the autopsy's done."

Pincher clicked off and turned to the others. "Charles Barksdale is dead."

"Heart attack?" the judge asked, tapping his own chest.

"Strangled. By his wife."

"Katrina?" Victoria said. "Can't be."

"She probably had a good reason," said Steve, ever the defense lawyer.

"Claims it was an accident," Pincher said.

"How do you accidentally strangle someone?" the judge said.

"By having sex in a way God never intended," Pincher said. "They found Charles tied up in some kinky contraption."

"This is big," Steve said. "Larry King big."

"Charles was a dear friend," Pincher said, "not just a campaign contributor. To die like that . . ." He shook his head, sadly. "If the grand jury indicts, I'll prosecute it myself."

Pincher was not given to many honest emotions,

Steve thought, but the old fraud seemed genuinely upset.

"Charles was a gentle man, a charitable man, a good man," Pincher continued.

Now he sounded like he was rehearsing his closing argument.

"Boy, would I love to defend," Steve said.

"Widow'll end up with Ed Shohat or Roy Black," Judge Gridley predicted.

"I'm as good a lawyer as they are."

"This ain't a Saturday night stabbing in Liberty City," Pincher said. "This is high society."

Pincher was right, Steve knew. He'd had dozens of murder trials, but most were low pay or no pay. He never had a client with the resources of an O. J. Simpson or Klaus von Bulow. Or the looks and glamour of Katrina Barksdale. He didn't know the Barksdales, but he'd read about them. Charles had made millions building condos while collecting custom yachts and trophy wives. Katrina would have been number three or four. Wife, not yacht. Photos of the old hubby and young wifey were routinely plastered in *Ocean Drive* and the *Miami Herald*. You couldn't open a restaurant or hold a charity event without the glam couple. And when her husband stayed home, Katrina was on the arm of an artist or musician at younger, hipper parties.

The lawyer who got this case was gonna be famous.

Steve could picture the Justice Building surrounded by sound trucks, generators humming, a forest of satellite dishes, an army of reporters. A carnival in the parking lot, vendors hawking "Free Katrina" T-shirts, iced *granizados,* and grilled arepas. There'd be TV interviews, magazine profiles, analysts critiquing the defense lawyer's trial strategy and his haircut. It'd be a ton of publicity and a helluva lot of fun. And then there was the fee. Not that money juiced him. But Bobby's expenses were mounting, and he'd like to put some bucks away for the boy's care.

And wouldn't he love going mano a mano with Pincher? The bastard would try to ride that pony all the way to the governor's mansion. All the more reason Steve lusted after the case. He hated pretension and self-righteousness, but most of all, he hated bullies. And in Sugar Ray Pincher, he had all three.

"This one's out of your league, Solomon," Pincher said, hammering the nail home.

Out of his league.

God, how he hated that. Which prompted another disheartening thought.

Was Victoria Lord out of his league, too?

MIAMI-DADE POLICE DEPARTMENT
TRANSCRIPT OF EMERGENCY
FIRE AND RESCUE CALLS

Dispatch: Miami-Dade Police. One moment,
please.

Caller: 911? Goddammit, are you there? 911?

Dispatch: Miami-Dade Police. Is this an emergency?

Caller: My husband! My husband's not breathing.

Dispatch: Please remain calm, ma'am. Is his airway obstructed?

Caller: I don't know. He's not breathing!

Dispatch: Was he eating?

Caller: We were having sex. Oh, Charlie,
breathe!

Dispatch: What's your name and address, ma'am?

Caller: Katrina Barksdale, 480 Casuarina
Concourse, Gables Estates.

Dispatch: Have you tried CPR?

Caller: My husband's Charles Barksdale. *The*
Charles Barksdale! Jeb Bush has been
here for drinks.

Dispatch: CPR, ma'am?

Caller: I'll have to untie Charlie.

Dispatch: Untie him?

Caller: I've already taken off his mask.

Three

ZINK THE FINK

Pacing the corridor outside Judge Gridley's courtroom, Steve's mind drifted far from the bird-smuggling trial. He wanted to land the Barksdale case before a bigger, faster shark beat him to it. The case could change his life. And, more important, Bobby's.

Just last month, Steve had consulted a doctor specializing in central nervous system maladies. No one could pin a name on his nephew's condition, which combined acute developmental disorders with astounding mental feats. The boy could spend an hour sitting cross-legged on the sofa, rocking back and forth, lost in his own world, then suddenly erupt in a fit of crying. Five minutes later, he would recite lengthy passages from *The Aeneid*.

In Latin.

And then Greek.

The doctor tossed around bewildering phrases like "frontotemporal dementia" and "paradoxical functional facilitation" and "arrested neuronal firing." One phrase that Steve understood quite clearly was "five thousand dollars a month"—the cost of a private tutor and therapist.

So the more Steve thought about the Barksdale case, the more it took on mythic proportions. Sure, the money and the publicity would be great, but the real quest was for Bobby. The Barksdale case could be his ticket to a better life.

But how to get the client?

Because he did not run with the caviar-and-canapé crowd, Steve knew he needed an introduction to the widow. And quickly. Figuring he had five minutes before he had to plant his ass at the defense table in the Pedrosa trial, there was time for one phone call. On the move in the dimly lit corridor, he dialed his office on a cell phone.

"Hola. Stephen Solomon and Associates," answered Cecilia Santiago, even though there were no associates.

"Cece, you know who Charles Barksdale is?"

"Dead rich white guy. It's on the news."

"Who do we know who might know his wife, Katrina Barksdale?"

"Her maid?"

Cece wasn't the best secretary, but she worked cheap. A bodybuilder with a temper, she was grateful to Steve for keeping her out of jail a year earlier when she beat up her cheating boyfriend.

"You still go to clubs on the Beach?" Steve asked.

"Paranoia last night, Gangbang the night before."

"Katrina's supposed to be a big-time partier. You ever run into her?"

"You kidding? They don't let me in the VIP rooms."

A whiny voice came from behind him in the corridor. "Oh, Mr. Solomon . . ."

Steve turned, saw a human blob moving toward him. "Shit! Call you later."

Jack Zinkavich lumbered down the corridor. In his early forties, Zinkavich had a huge, shapeless torso and his suit coat bunched at his fleshy hips, as if covering a gun belt with two six-shooters. His skin was oyster gray, and he wore his spit-colored hair in a buzz cut that made his square head resemble a concrete block. Zinkavich worked for the Division of Family Services in Pincher's office and was, if possible, even more humorless than his boss. He ate alone in the cafeteria each day and was known as "Zink the Fink" for constantly welshing in settlement negotiations. In what Steve considered a lousy stroke of luck, Zinkavich represented the state in Bobby's guardianship case.

What Steve had thought would be a slam-dunk case—*I'm the uncle; I love Bobby; of course he belongs with me*—had turned instantly vicious. At the first hearing, Zinkavich called Steve an "untrained, unfit, undomesticated caregiver" and suggested that Bobby be made a ward of the state. Steve was baffled why a routine proceeding was becoming a balls-to-the-wall street fight.

Zinkavich huffed to a stop. "Is it true you were imprisoned again this morning?"

" 'Imprisoned' is a little strong. More like sent to the blackboard to clean erasers."

"Won't look good in the guardianship case." Zinkavich seemed happy as a hangman tying his knots.

"It's got nothing to do with Bobby."

"It reflects on your fitness as a parent. I'll have to bring it up with the judge."

"Do what you gotta do."

"I see a disturbing pattern here," Zinkavich said. "Your sister's a convicted felon, you're in and out of jail, your father's a disbarred lawyer—"

"He wasn't disbarred. He resigned."

"Whatever. My point is, your entire family seems spectacularly unfit to care for a special-needs child."

"That's bullshit, Fink, and you know it." Steve cursed himself for his own recklessness. With the guardianship hearing coming up, getting thrown in the can today hadn't been smart.

"The state only has Robert's interests at heart," Zinkavich said.

"The state has no heart."

"You have a real attitude problem. It's something else I intend to bring up with the judge."

"If that's it, I gotta go."

"Not until we schedule a home visit. You haven't allowed Dr. Kranchick her follow-up."

"She scares Bobby. I don't want her around."

"You don't have a choice. Either you give the doctor access or I'll have a body warrant issued and we'll seize Robert."

"The fuck you will."

Steve felt a wave of heat surge through him and struggled to control his rage. First that cheap shot at his father, now the threat to grab his nephew. The bastard just violated the unwritten rule that you could ridicule your adversary for anything from the cut of his suit to the size of his dick, but Family was off-limits.

Zinkavich smirked. "Maybe a few days in Juvenile Hall will change Robert's mind and yours."

"You son-of-a-bitch." Steve's hand flew up,

grabbed Zinkavich's tie, twisted it around a fist. "If your storm troopers ever lay a finger on my nephew, I will personally . . ."

Steve dug the knot into Zinkavich's flabby neck, increasing the pressure until his blowfish cheeks turned red. After a moment of staring into his bulging eyes, Steve released him.

"That's an assault!" Zinkavich squeaked. *Atthault.*

"Bring it up with the judge," Steve said, walking away.

That was smart, Steve thought, double-timing toward the courtroom. Real smart. Piss off the one guy who can wreck Bobby's life.

I would never lose my cool like that representing a client. But this is personal.

Halfway down the corridor, he overtook Victoria, her ear pressed to a cell phone.

"I'm so sorry, Kat," she said into a pink Nokia. "If there's anything I can do, please ask. . . ."

Kat? Holy shit. That wouldn't be short for Katrina, would it?

Steve slowed his pace, dropped back a half step.

"Of course I believe you. I know you wouldn't . . ." Victoria said. "You and Charlie always looked so happy together. God, I feel terrible for you."

Okay, makes sense. Miss La Gorce Tennis Champion would know the Barksdales.

"Please call if you need anything. I mean it."

Victoria clicked off, and Steve came alongside. "Are you friends with the grieving widow?"

"Were you eavesdropping?"

"C'mon, we only have a minute."

"I see Kat at the club. What's it to you?"

"Get me the case and there's a referral fee in it for you."

"It's illegal to solicit a case," she chided.

"You think Alan Dershowitz waits for the phone to ring?"

She stopped at the courtroom door. "Why on earth would I recommend *you* to anyone?"

He struggled for an answer, but didn't have one. She entered the courtroom with a smug look. As the door closed in his face, Steve's mind raced. How could he convince Victoria he had the stuff to help her newly widowed friend? And even if she believed he was the best lawyer in town, which he wasn't, why would she hustle the case for him?

Suddenly, the answers to both questions were obvious.

He'd change his approach. No more bickering, no more insults. When they resumed the Pedrosa trial, he'd show his kinder, gentler side. But he still had to win. She wouldn't send a case to a loser.

So I have to win nice.

It sounded good, he thought. Except for one little flaw. Maybe if his cockatoo-smuggling client were innocent, he could *win nice*. But as even a myopic judge or sleeping juror could see, Amancio Pedrosa was as dirty as a birdcage floor.

Four

AN ANGELFISH NAMED STEVE

The next morning was gray and cold, at least by Miami standards. Clouds the color of old nickels pushed down from the north, winds kicked up, palm fronds ripped loose from trees. Yesterday, the bird-smuggling trial had slogged along. Victoria had put on her case, Steve had minded his manners. He had even kept half his promise. He was playing nice; he just wasn't winning. Trial would resume at ten A.M. He should be spending the time preparing for court, but there were domestic duties to attend to first.

In his drafty bungalow on Kumquat Avenue in Coconut Grove, with Jimmy Buffet singing "License to Chill" on a CD, Steve grilled ham and cheese sandwiches and whipped up papaya smoothies. An unusual breakfast, but his nephew, Bobby, chose the menu. That was their deal; the kid would eat everything on the plate as long as he got to pick the food.

No matter the weather, Bobby wore baggy shorts and a Florida Marlins T-shirt. He was skinny, with pipe-stem arms and legs and sandy hair that stood straight up, as if he'd just stuck a finger in an electrical outlet. Rounding out the picture as the class *über*-nerd—if he actually went to Carver instead of homeschooling—was a double track of shiny braces and thick black glasses that were always smudged and cockeyed.

Bobby could not find his way home from the park three blocks away, but he could repeat everything he heard or read. Verbatim. As a result, Steve could never win an argument about current events, baseball statistics, or whether he had promised a trip to Disney World exactly seventy-eight days, fourteen hours, and twelve minutes ago. The doctors called it echolalia, the flip side of the boy's disability.

Recently, Bobby had found an Italian cooking site on the Internet and had become obsessed with grilled sandwiches. To accommodate his nephew, Steve bought a panini grill, which he used for breakfast, lunch, and dinner.

Now, as Steve constructed Bobby's sandwich with the care of Michelangelo sculpting a statue, the boy stood alongside, making sure he didn't take any shortcuts. If the cheese melted over the edge of the bread or if the ridged grill marks were uneven, Bobby would scream, bang his head against the counter, and wrist-flick the sandwich across the kitchen like a Frisbee.

"The ciabatta fresh?" Bobby asked.

"You bet."

"The ham Black Forest?"

"Nothing but."

"The cheese ricotta?"

"Sheep's milk. Just like you told me, kiddo."

From the intensity of Bobby's look, Steve might have been separating plutonium from uranium. Only when the sandwiches emerged from the press—ham and cheese blended into a luxurious melt, bread crusty with symmetrical grill marks—would the boy relax. While this was going on, with Jimmy Buffet advocating living for the weekend and jumping off the deep end, the phone rang. Fairly certain it wasn't the Key West troubadour inviting him fishing, Steve let the machine pick up:

"This is Herbert T. Solomon. Recovering lawyer." *Re-koven loy-yuh.*

Steve's father had been born in Savannah, and though Herbert Solomon had not lived in the Deep South for half a century, he still spoke in a mellifluous, musical drawl. The accent, Steve believed, was purposeful and exaggerated, Herbert's calling card. In his father's scrapbook was a faded newspaper clipping describing one of his closing arguments as a "melodic hymn to the angels, folksy as a farm, sweeter than molasses, soulful as a prayer." Steve's own courtroom style, should it ever be described at all, would be likened to a grenade exploding in a septic tank.

"Mah spies tell me you've been in the cooler again," said the voice into the machine. "Stephen, ah've taught you to win with style and grace, not shenanigans and tomfoolery. And when are you bringing mah grandson down here?"

Down here being Sugarloaf Key, just north of Key West, Herbert's own private gulag, though considerably warmer than Siberia.

"Somebody's gotta teach that boy to fish, and it sure as hell ain't you."

Granddad taking the boy fishing. Now there was a Norman Rockwell notion, Steve thought, not without some bitterness. Herbert Solomon was one of those men who became far better grandfathers than they ever were fathers. How much time did he ever spend with Steve? How many ball games? Track meets? Camping trips?

Steve knew he still resented his father for having placed career first, family a distant second. Herbert Solomon had become just what he wanted: a great lawyer and a great judge, before taking a great fall. Steve had other ambitions. Sure, he wanted to be successful, if he could do it his own way: no compromises, no political bullshit, no ass-kissing. So far, it hadn't exactly worked out.

"You couldn't hit a donkey in the fanny with a bass fiddle, much less outsmart a bonefish," Herbert continued.

Nothing like nurturing support, Steve thought, grabbing the phone. "Hey, Dad, chill, okay?"

"Why didn't you pick up?" his father demanded.

"Because I didn't want to fight at seven in the morning."

"Don't be such a pussy. What's this ah hear about Erwin Gridley tossing you in the pokey?"

"No big deal."

"The hell it's not. You're a damn embarrassment."

"*I'm* the embarrassment? I'm not the one whose picture was in the paper, cleaning out his office before he could be indicted."

"Your picture's never been in the paper 'cause you handle pissant cases."

"Gotta go now, Dad."

"Hang on. What are you wearing to court today?"

"Jeez, I'm not ten years old. You don't have to—"

"No sharkskin suits, no diamond pinky rings."

"Dad, nobody dresses like that anymore." He

already was in his uniform, a charcoal gray suit, straight off the rack, powder blue shirt, simple striped tie. Early on, he'd decided his actions drew enough attention without looking like a carnival barker.

"You got me on speaker, son?"

"No, why?"

Herbert lowered his voice as if he still might be overheard. "Your worthless sister called."

Meaning Janice. Herbert's worthless daughter, Bobby's worthless mother, Steve's worthless sister. "Worthless" not so much an adjective as a new first name.

"She's out of prison," Herbert continued.

"How'd that happen?" The last Steve had heard, his sister was doing a mandatory three years for a smorgasbord of drug and theft offenses. As for the boy's father? Spin the wheel of misfortune to figure out who that might be.

"She was evasive about it."

"Imagine that." Steve carried the handset into the living room so Bobby couldn't hear him. "How much money she ask you for?"

"Not a shekel."

"You sure it was her?"

"She said something about making a big move, changing her life. Mentioned New Zealand, but knowing her, she might have meant New Mexico."

Steve lowered his voice. "Did she say anything about wanting to see Bobby?"

"She did, but ah said you probably wouldn't let her."

"After what she did to him, you're goddamn right I wouldn't."

"That's what she figured. So you better stay on your toes."

"What are you getting at?" But even as Steve said it, he knew exactly what his father meant. "You think she'd try to snatch Bobby?"

"Ah don't trust her or that pokeweed religion crowd she runs with."

Steve couldn't disagree, so he didn't.

"You know what to look for," Herbert continued. "Hang-up calls, someone tailing you, strangers hanging around. And don't let Bobby wander off."

"Got it, Dad. Thanks. Sorry about before . . ."

Why the hell am I apologizing? He's the one who insulted me.

"Forget it. Let me talk to mah grandson."

Steve headed back into the kitchen, gave the phone to Bobby, and checked on the paninis. But something was gnawing at him.

An old green pickup truck with tinted windows and oversize tires.

He had seen it this morning, just after dawn. He'd walked outside to pick up the newspaper before it was pelted by red, squishy berries from a Brazilian pepper tree. A green Dodge pickup streaked with mud was parked catty-corner across the street. The truck had pulled away in what seemed like too much of a hurry for six A.M. He tried to summon up the image. There was something about the pickup that stuck in his mind.

The lovebug screen fastened to the front bumper.

Meaning the pickup wasn't local. Lovebugs were an upstate phenomenon, orange-and-black insects that mate in midair and get squashed in flagrante delicto all over your metallic finish. And now that he thought about it, wasn't the truck there the other night when he brought Bobby home from getting ice cream at Whip 'N Dip? He couldn't quite remember, maybe his mind was playing tricks on him.

Calm down. Don't get paranoid.

Okay, Janice is upstate; the truck's from upstate, which means . . .

Nothing. Nada. Gornisht. *But the old man's right. Be aware. Stay alert.*

Steve listened to Bobby chattering with his grandfather about fishing lures, and marveled at the progress he'd made. Ten months ago, when Steve rescued him—there was no other word for it—the boy would have been too timid to talk on the phone.

Steve had never told anyone precisely what happened that freezing night in Calhoun County. Not his father. Not Dr. Kranchick. And certainly not Zinkavich.

He wondered just how much Bobby remembered. They had never talked about it. Steve, though, recalled every moment, starting with the call from his sister.

Janice had been in one of those ecstatic states that always accompanied a change in her life, until she discovered she was the same old person without values, purpose, or goals. She'd just moved into a commune run by a whacked-out religious cult. The Universal Friends of Peace, or some burnout and loser name like that. They were tucked away in the woods somewhere in the Florida Panhandle. Best Steve could figure, the group believed that God resided in green leafy plants, especially cannabis. Orgies were believed to convey healing power, though Steve thought herpes was a more likely result.

In the beginning, Janice called every few weeks, usually to wheedle money out of him. Steve always spoke to Bobby, who seemed to be growing more withdrawn with each call. Steve was worried. Not about his sister, who, like a cockroach, could survive a nuclear blast. But there was Bobby, ten years old, shy and defenseless. Janice's mothering instincts, Steve knew, were on a par with rattlesnakes, and they eat their young.

Steve remembered the chill he felt the first time Janice refused to put Bobby on the phone. Doing chores, she claimed. The next time, Bobby had supposedly gone to town with her scuzzy friends. A week later, she said the boy just didn't feel like talking.

Steve had exploded at her: "Put him on the phone, goddammit!"

"Fuck you, little brother."

"Are you stoned?"

"What are you, a cop?"

"C'mon, Janice. Where is he?"

"He's my kid. Mind your own fucking business."

"I'm calling Child Welfare."

"Lots of luck. They're scared shitless to come out here."

"Then I'm coming up."

"Try it. We got a barbed-wire fence and some speed freaks with shotguns."

His imagination worked up one horrific image after another. Bobby lost or injured. Bobby sold for half-a-dozen rocks of crack. The next day, Steve flew to Tallahassee, rented a car, and drove west through the Apalachicola Forest, then down along the Ochlockonee River. It was January, and a cold front had roared south from Canada, dusting the Panhandle with snowflakes. He'd spent a day huddled in a blanket on a rise above the commune, where he watched through binoculars, looking for Bobby. Looking, but not seeing him.

He saw a barn with a sagging silo, a shed with a corrugated metal roof, and a farmhouse where black smoke curled from a chimney. A dozen scraggly-bearded men in filthy clothes worked the smudge pots in the marijuana patch. Scrawny women in sweaters and long dresses brought them steaming cups of coffee. New Age music played on a boom box.

After several hours, his feet were as cold as grave-stones. Finally, just before dark, he caught sight of Janice, wearing army boots and a tattered orange University of Miami sweatshirt she'd swiped from him years earlier. She was carrying a soup bowl from the farmhouse to the shed. Thinking back, he's not sure how he knew, but he did. She was taking food to her son, feeding him the way most people feed their dogs. Looking through the binoculars, Steve saw something he was sure he would remember until there were no more memories to be had.

There was no steam rising from the bowl.

On the year's coldest day, whatever slop Janice was delivering to her son was as cold as her own shriveled heart.

She disappeared into the shed, and he counted— *one one thousand, two one thousand*—until she reappeared without the bowl.

Twelve seconds.

Janice had spent twelve seconds with her son before returning to the farmhouse, where smoke puffed from the chimney. There was no smokestack on the shed, no power lines running in.

As a lawyer, there were only two categories of criminals Steve Solomon would not represent. Pedophiles and men who brutalize women. But at that moment if his own sister were within reach, he would have done her grievous harm. At that moment, it didn't matter that Janice was a lost soul herself, who'd gone seemingly overnight from her Bat Mitzvah to Jews for Jesus to pilfering money and drugs.

Steve waited until after midnight, watching the farmhouse, hearing laughter and music, catching sight of figures passing the windows, men urinating off the porch. He drifted into a restless, frozen sleep, awakened to the hooting of an owl in an icy rain. It was just after three A.M. The farmhouse was dark and silent as he made his way down the ridge to the shed, slipping on wet rocks, illuminated by a three-quarter moon. From somewhere in the compound, a dog howled.

The shed door was locked with a simple peg through a latch. The door creaked as Steve went inside, clicking on a flashlight. Pale and malnourished, Bobby lay curled in a metal dog cage, a bucket of urine and the empty soup bowl at his side. He wore only underpants and a sweatshirt. He was barefoot. His feet were filthy and covered with sores.

"Bobby, it's your uncle Steve."

The boy scuttled to the far corner of the cage, eyes wide with fear.

"Don't be scared."

Bobby rocked back and forth.

"Do you remember me?"

The rocking grew faster.

A padlock secured the cage, and Steve began working at the hinges with his bare hands, trying to lift the pin. Just then, the door to the shed flew open and a broad-shouldered man with a tangled beard stepped inside. The man could have been thirty or sixty or anywhere in between. He wore a dirty red Mackinaw and a winter hat with fur earflaps, and his face was smudged with black splotches that looked like charcoal dust. He gripped a stick as thick as a man's forearm. Probably carved from an oak tree, the stick was curved at the top like a shepherd's staff.

"I'm the boy's uncle," Steve said. "He's coming with me."

"He ain't going nowhere," the man said.

Bobby continued rocking.

The man closed the distance between them and drew back the curved stick. His voice rumbled, " 'Heal the sick, cleanse the lepers, raise the dead, cast out devils.' Matthew, Chapter Ten, Verse Eight."

"Get the fuck out of my way. Solomon. Chapter One. You don't want to hear Chapter Two."

"Be gone!" The man swung the stick, and Steve took the impact on the shoulder and staggered backward. The man swung again and Steve stopped the stick with both hands and shoved back, hard. He slammed the man against the shed wall and pushed the stick to his neck. Steve's face was buried in the collar of the soggy Mackinaw, and a mangy smell like a wet dog made him gag. The man squirmed and gasped for air and tried to knee Steve in the groin. Steve kept up the pressure, jamming the stick hard into the man's Adam's apple. When his attacker's face turned crimson, a gurgle coming from his throat, Steve released him, and the man dropped to the floor.

Still holding the stick, Steve turned to Bobby. "The padlock. Where's the key?"

The boy stopped rocking, but he still hadn't said a word.

"Bobby, do you understand what I'm saying?"

"Uncle Steve, look out!"

Steve pivoted and swung the stick like a baseball bat even before he saw the man coming up from the floor, a hunting knife in his hand. Head down, hips turning, it was a compact but powerful swing.

The stick caught the man squarely above the temple with a *crunch* of bone: he dropped like a mallard felled by a hunter. Steve stood over him, breathing hard, aware of his own pounding heart. Frozen in place, filled with fear. Had he killed him?

"We better go, Uncle Steve."

The voice was so close it startled him. Bobby was outside the cage, the back panel removed. "Mom doesn't know I can do this."

The man on the floor was moaning, trying to get to his feet. Thank God he wasn't dead. Steve grabbed Bobby and swung him into his arms, stunned by how light he was. All elbows and knees, no meat on his bones.

They ducked out of the shed. Dogs barked. Lights flicked on in the farmhouse. Steve could make out a shadowy figure on the porch and the silhouette of what looked like a rifle or a shotgun.

"You! Stop!"

Carrying Bobby, Steve took off. He headed for the tree line, heard shouts from behind, looked back over his shoulder, caught glimpses of men with torches. A shotgun roared. Then another blast, echoing across the valley. He ran through the woods, leaping over fallen trees, slipping on wet rocks, crossing a stream, chugging hard up a hill and down the other side, through a strand of mahogany trees, running hard and not stopping until there were no more torches, no more gunshots, and no more men.

They were in the car headed toward Tallahassee before Steve spoke again. "I didn't think you remembered me."

"You took me snorkeling," Bobby said.

"That's right. I did. You must have been about five or six."

"It was September eleventh. I was five plus eight months and three days. We saw lots of green-and-yellow fish with blue spots that sparkled."

"Angelfish."

"*Holacanthus ciliaris*. I gave one a name."

"Really?"

"You told me not to touch the coral because it'll break and it takes hundreds of years to grow back. I liked the sea fans best because they wave at you like they're friendly. And the parrotfish. *Sparisoma viride*. They look like parrots but they don't talk."

"How do you remember all that? How do you know their Latin names?"

The boy's thin shoulders shrugged.

"Do you want to go to my house?"

"Eleven white stones from the driveway to the front door."

"I guess there are. Would you like to go there?"

"I named the angelfish 'Steve,' " Bobby said.

———

Now, ten months later, Bobby was putting on weight—thanks to the paninis—and becoming more comfortable around people. He said good-bye to his grandfather, hung up the phone, and came over to the counter just as Steve opened the lid of the grill.

"Turn them a hundred eighty degrees," Bobby said.

"That's what I'm doing." Steve slid the sandwiches around to cross-hatch the bread with grill marks.

"Not a hundred ninety," Bobby ordered. "The marks won't be even."

"Got it."

The melting cheese sizzled seductively, and an aroma of salty sweetness filled the kitchen. "How come you and Pop always argue?" Bobby asked.

"I guess because we've each done things that disappoint the other."

Bobby used his tongue to snap a rubber band on his braces. "Do I disappoint you?"

"Never. Not once."

The boy's smile was all orthodonture. "Don't burn the sandwiches, Uncle Steve."

"Have I told you today how much I love you, kiddo?"

"You tell me every day, Uncle Steve."

"Well, today, I'm telling you twice."

Five

MONEY, SEX, AND MURDER

Inside the Justice Building, Steve was feeling as gray as the weather outside. The morning session ended with a Customs Officer testifying that Amancio Pedrosa was harboring a menagerie of smuggled birds, including a foulmouthed cockatoo.

A beaming Victoria then crowed: "Having established a prima facie case, we rest, Your Honor."

Steve made his obligatory motion for a directed verdict. Judge Gridley called a sidebar conference and asked his advice: Should he take the over or the under on the Michigan State–Penn State game? The under, Steve said. The weather forecast for central Pennsylvania was wind and rain. The judge agreed, then denied Steve's motion.

With no pyrotechnics to ignite, Steve had spent considerable time studying his opponent. Today Victoria wore a dark, tweedy jacket with a matching skirt. She looked professional and businesslike—and, given the conservative wool, unaccountably sexy. Next to her at the prosecution table, Ray Pincher whispered to a variety of aides, who brought him messages and kneeled at his feet like supplicants to a king.

Now, returning from lunch, Steve hurried along the crowded corridor, weaving past sheriff's deputies, touring schoolchildren, and lawyers soliciting clients. A courtroom door opened and an elderly man toddled out; Steve braked but still bumped the man. "Whoops. Sorry, Marvin," he apologized.

"Watch out, boychik, or I'll sue you for whiplash," Marvin Mendelsohn said.

Marvin the Maven was the unofficial chief of the Courthouse Gang, a posse of retirees who moseyed from courtroom to courtroom, observing the juiciest trials. The Maven was a dapper little man, almost eighty, with a pencil mustache, oversize black-framed glasses, and a bald head that shone under the fluorescent lights. Today he wore gray wool slacks and a double-breasted blue blazer with gold buttons. A paisley cravat of shimmering silk blossomed like a colorful bouquet at his neck.

"Looking good, Marvin."

"Horseshit. My sciatica's killing me. You wanna sue my chiropractor?"

To most lawyers, Marvin and his Gang were either invisible or bothersome. *Alter kockers*. Old farts who clogged the cafeteria line and kibitzed in the corridors. Steve enjoyed their company. He lunched with them, listened to their stories, took their advice. Marvin the Maven had uncanny instincts about jury selection, particularly with women, where Steve needed the most help. Marvin had owned a women's shoe store in Buffalo for forty years before fleeing the winters. Maybe it was selling thousands of pumps and slingbacks, stilettos and sandals over the years that gave Marvin insights most men lack. Or maybe it was just listening to the women themselves.

"So what you got going besides your *farshtinkener* bird trial?" Marvin asked, as they made their way down the corridor.

"I'm trying to hustle Katrina Barksdale."

"The woman who *shtupped* her husband to death?"

"Can you imagine the trial? Money, sex, and murder."

"Save me a seat in the front row."

"If I got that case, I could pay my bills, get a new car, hire a tutor for Bobby."

"I love you like a grandson, Steve, but why would this woman hire a low-rent lawyer like you?"

"Because Victoria Lord's going to recommend me."

"You romancing that fancy lady prosecutor? That your way in?"

"All business, Marvin."

"What happened to that nice Jewish girl you were going out with?"

"Sally Panther? She's a Miccosukee."

"So? Indians are the lost tribes of Israel."

"Whatever she is, she dumped me."

"Okay, so sniff around after Miss Lord. But if you ask me, she'll buy her pumps at Wal-Mart before she brings you a case."

As they walked, Steve told Marvin his game plan. He was about to put on the defense case in the Pedrosa trial. He'd dazzle Victoria with his footwork and hypnotize her with his words. He'd win, but he'd win nice.

Marvin gave him a skeptical look. "You're playing by the rules?"

"Strictly Marquis of Queensberry."

"This I gotta see."

"You don't think I can do it?"

Marvin shrugged. "Why do you think the Gang watches your trials?"

"Because I'm the only lawyer who'll talk to you."

"Because you're Barnum and Bailey. You try a case, there's always a dozen clowns crawling out of a little car."

"Not today."

Marvin was quiet a moment. Then he said: "Sometimes a woman who needs a size nine will lie to herself. Try to squeeze into an eight-and-a-half."

"What's that supposed to mean?"

"Maybe you don't know it, boychik, but getting the Barksdale case is your alibi. It's the girl you're after."

"Absolutely not."

"Good, because this one's not your type."

"Meaning what?"

"She's classy, is all. No offense."

"Jeez, Marvin. I thought you loved me like one of your grandsons."

"They never visit," the old man said.

The corridor was jammed with the usual flotsam and jetsam. Sheriff's deputies herded shackled prisoners from holding cells to courtrooms, bail bondsmen trailing in their wake like rudderfish after sharks. The prisoners' girlfriends and wives lined the walls, yelling encouragement or insults at their men, depending on the current state of their relationships.

The elevator door opened, and an attractive, trim woman in her seventies walked out. "*Hola,* Marvin. Stephen."

Teresa Toraño wore a stylish two-button herringbone jacket with a matching camel skirt. Her dark hair was tied back in a bun with what looked like ivory chopsticks.

"Teresa," the men said in unison.

Teresa's husband, Oscar, had owned a chain of funeral homes in Havana but lost the business—and his life—when he opposed Fidel Castro. In the early 1960's, Teresa brought their children to Miami and worked for minimum wage as a mortician's assistant. Within five years, she had her own license and opened Funeraria Toraño on Calle Ocho. By the time she turned the businesses over to her children, Teresa owned seven funeral homes, a jai-alai fronton, and a Chevrolet dealership.

In Steve's accounting ledger—a ragged notebook where he recorded his income, when he had any— Teresa Toraño was listed as Client 001. Looking back, he wondered if he could have made it that first year if she hadn't hired him to represent her companies. Since then, they had grown close. Teresa adored Bobby, taking him to the Seaquarium and baking him *pastelitos de guayaba.* It was almost time for her homemade *crema de vie,* the anise Christmas drink that makes eggnog seem like Slim-Fast.

At about the time Teresa became Steve's client *numero uno,* she became Marvin's second love—the only woman he'd been with since the death of his beloved Bess. Now Marvin spent every Friday night at Teresa's Coral Gables villa. Neither ever acknowledged the relationship, not even when Steve ran into them holding hands and drinking mimosas at brunch one recent Saturday morning.

"Stephen, what did you do to Jack Zinkavich?" Teresa demanded as they approached Judge Gridley's courtroom.

"Nothing. Why?"

"I hear things."

"Yeah?"

"The receptionist in Family Services is a cousin of my late Oscar's grandniece," Teresa said, "and she eats lunch with an investigator who works with Zinkavich."

"What's that gotta do with me?" Steve asked.

"Zinkavich told his investigator he's gonna kick your *culo*."

"The *momzer*," Marvin said.

"Zinkavich wants to take Bobby away from me," Steve said.

"That's not it," Teresa said. "He's talking about criminal charges."

Steve stopped dead. "For what?"

"All I know, he took a trip to Blountstown to look into it."

Calhoun County, Steve thought. In the Panhandle. Where he'd busted Bobby out of the commune. And busted the bearded guy's skull.

A feeling of dread swept over him. Criminal charges?

Why's the Fink coming after me? All I want is to protect Bobby, give him a life.

"You watch out for Zinkavich," Marvin warned. "He may look like a schlub, but he's mean as a Cossack."

"Even worse," Teresa said. "Mean as a *comunista.*"

Six

VICTORIA'S SECRET

Walking into Judge Gridley's courtroom with Marvin and Teresa at his side, Steve took a quick inventory of his life. Zinkavich was gunning for him; his crazed sister was on the loose; and a mysterious pickup truck might be tailing him. Not only that, a case he lusted after seemed beyond his reach. Maybe a woman, too.

Could it be, he wondered, that the high point of the last couple days was spending time in jail with Victoria Lord?

The jurors were in their box. Reading, knitting, staring into space. Ray Pincher was in the gallery, pumping constituents' hands. Judge Gridley was in his chambers, probably on the phone with his bookie.

At the prosecution table, Victoria was shuffling through her neatly arranged note cards. Steve nodded in her direction. "Marvin, give me your quick read."

The old man squinted through his thick glasses. "Gucci pumps, snakeskin. And that woven leather handbag. Bottega Veneta. Fancy-schmancy."

"I figure she's an heiress."

"Not just expensive," Teresa said. "Good taste, too."

Steve headed toward her. "Wish me luck."

"Gai shlog dein kup en vant," Marvin said. "Go bang your head against the wall."

Steve sized up Victoria's miniature war room. Her table was ringed with a Maginot Line of law books stacked six high. At her feet were boxes filled with files. On the table were cross-indexed depositions, fat pleadings binders, a box of index cards, and a dozen yellow pads. Lined up alongside were colored pens, Magic Markers, a ruler, and a pair of scissors. A plastic salad container held her uneaten lunch.

As Steve approached, he noticed that her skirt was hiked several inches above the knee. He'd known women lawyers who intentionally gave the jury a peek. Not Victoria. Any show of thigh would be totally accidental. But still appreciated.

He watched her drum her fingers on the table. Rookie jitters. The nails were painted a light pink. He pictured her at an expensive spa. Massage, facial, body wrapped in seaweed. Marvin was right. Fancy-schmancy.

At that moment, Victoria was also looking at her nails. Before racing to court, she had clipped, filed, and painted them a color called "Alaskan Dusk." They'd been in terrible shape, the polish chipped, cuticles ragged. Now she used a fingernail to scrape some excess polish from a cuticle. Damn, she'd been rushed. When was the last time she spent the money for a manicure, much less a pedicure? These days, she did all her own grooming, including the blond highlights in her hair. Number eight Winter Blonde mixed with twenty volume peroxide. Her mother, who spent endless hours in the best salons, was appalled and let her know about it.

Victoria heard her stomach growling. There'd been no time for lunch. Not when she had to prepare for Solomon's stunts. While she had put on the state's case, he'd been unexpectedly well behaved. What was he planning? Pincher had it right when he advised her: "Keep your cool while he plays the fool."

Don't worry, boss. Nothing Solomon can say or do will frazzle me.

She made another vow, too.

I'm going to win.

She had the evidence; she had the law; and she was smarter than Solomon.

Victoria imagined herself an architect, drawing up precise plans for a solid house. Solomon was a vandal, tearing down pillars, spray-painting graffiti. To him, laws were meant to be twisted, judges manipulated, jurors confused. He didn't even do research, for God's sake. She indexed every deposition by subject matter and cross-indexed by keyword. Every relevant appellate case was Shepardized, summarized, and yellow-lined. Her closing argument had been prepared for weeks. When Solomon came to court, carrying nothing but a cup of coffee, his hair was still wet from the shower and he was shaving in the elevator.

And here he came now, with that annoying grin on his face. Was he staring at her legs again?

"Got some trial tips for you." Steve parked his butt on the corner of her table.

She covered up her index cards so he couldn't steal her closing argument.

"Never skip lunch," he said, pointing at the unopened salad container. "Trials are draining. You need your energy."

"What do you want, Solomon?"

He picked up a pair of scissors from her table, folded an index card twice, began snipping. "Look at my table. What do you see?"

"Your client. Sound asleep."

True. Slumped in his chair, bird smuggler Amancio Pedrosa was snoring, drool dripping into a rectangular patch of whiskers just south of his lower lip. He was a stocky man in his forties in a rumpled guayabera.

Steve continued snipping at the card. "What else you see?"

"Nothing. There's nothing on your table except a blank legal pad."

"Almost blank," he agreed. "Sofia wrote her home number there while we were at lunch."

"Sofia?"

"The court reporter."

He nodded toward the attractive, dark-haired woman slipping a new roll of paper into her stenograph machine. Sofia Hernandez smiled back.

The woman's see-through orange blouse seemed inappropriate for court, Victoria thought. It was also a trifle small, or were her breasts simply a trifle large?

"What do you and Sofia do for fun?" Victoria asked. "Have her read back your best objections?"

"C'mon, this for your own good. What do the jurors think when they look at my table?"

"That you're not prepared."

"That I'm not worried." He gestured with the scissors toward the wall of law books on Victoria's table. "This little fortress seals you off. Unfriendly. Offputting. The jury's thinking, 'If she had to do all that work, she's got a weak case.' So, tip two, come into court lean and mean."

"You practice your way, I'll practice mine."

Steve unfolded the scissored index card and handed her the cutout of a long-winged bird. "For you. To remember this day."

The courtroom door opened, and in walked a tall, handsome man with a great head of silvery blond hair.

"Oh, no," Victoria groaned. She scooped up her salad container and tossed it into an open trial bag.

The handsome man walked toward them with long strides. He wore gray slacks, a blue blazer, and a white shirt with a club tie. His tie tack was a Phi Beta Kappa key. He looked Steve in the eye and extended a hand. "I'm Bruce Bigby," he boomed so cheerily he might have been running for County Commissioner. "Are you Steve Solomon?"

"I am, unless you're a process server."

Bruce Bigby? The name was familiar, but Steve couldn't get a handle on it.

"Heard all about you." Bigby shook Steve's hand hard enough to crack walnuts. He leaned over and kissed Victoria on the cheek. "Hello, sweetie."

Sweetie?

"Bruce, what are you doing here?"

"Zoning Commission meets downstairs. How was the avocado salad?"

"Delicious," she said, shooting a look, sharp as a dagger, at Steve, who judiciously kept quiet. "So thoughtful of you to make it."

Who the hell is this guy? Boyfriend or personal chef?

"Sweetie!" Bruce Bigby sounded alarmed. "Where's your ring?"

Victoria glanced toward the jury box, then whispered: "It's a little ostentatious in front of the jurors."

"Nonsense. They'll understand. You've got a man who loves you enough to go whole hog."

Victoria smiled wanly, dug into her Italian handbag, brought out a small velvet box, and opened it.

"Holy shit." Steve peered at a hefty slab of a diamond, held up by four pedestals, like one of those houses built on stilts in Biscayne Bay. Running up each side were two rows of smaller yet still chubby diamonds.

Victoria slipped the ring on. It looked heavy enough to give her a case of carpal tunnel.

"You're engaged?" Steve felt like someone had slugged him in the gut.

"Say, Steve, you like avocados?" Bigby said.

"I don't spend a lot time thinking about them." He was still processing the information.

Victoria Lord was engaged!

"Because Monday, I could bring two salads," Bigby said. "Baby lettuce, beefsteak tomatoes, and fresh avocados from Bigby Farms."

Bigby Farms. Bingo. Thousands of acres between Homestead and the Everglades. Agriculture, real estate, land development . . .

Bigby said: "Nothing like six grams of fiber to flush you out."

"Or a thousand grams of beef burrito," Steve said, sinking deep into depression.

"Those nitrites will kill you, my friend. Thank God I got Victoria to become a vegan."

Steve could have sworn he'd seen Victoria at the Sweet Potato Pie the other day, sucking on a short rib.

"Lips that touch pork chops shall never touch mine," Bigby said.

Dammit, why hadn't she told me?

A beautiful woman without her engagement ring is like a handgun without a safety. She'd known he was interested. He'd offered her margaritas and tapas and his own personal mentoring. But she wasn't available. And still she let him go on. Had she told Bigby about the schmuck who kept hitting on her? Had they laughed at him over guacamole?

The more Steve thought about it, the hotter the fire burned. What was he doing giving her trial tips? Using kid gloves instead of brass knuckles? Didn't he have an obligation to zealously represent his client?

Damn right. You could look it up. The preamble to Rule Four of the ethical rules.

Zealous advocacy. It's required. Wimps need not apply.

To hell with winning nice. It was time to take Victoria Lord to school and steal her lunch money. He'd slash and burn, scorch the earth, leave bomb craters in the courtroom. When he was done with her, she'd never set foot in the Justice Building again.

Another thought crept into his mind, a searing realization of blinding truth. What he was planning was not so much *zealous* advocacy as *jealous* advocacy. Was Marvin right?

"Getting the Barksdale case is your alibi. It's the girl you're after."

Not anymore. As for his plan to hustle the Barksdale case, forget it. He pictured Victoria down on the farm with Diamond Bruce Bigby, ridiculing Steve. *"Solomon is so deluded, he thinks I'd send him Kat Barksdale as a client."*

"Say, Steve, mind if I say something out of school?"

Bigby talking. What the hell did he want?

"Shoot," Steve said.

Bruce laid a protective hand on Victoria's shoulder. "My sweetie tells me you're one heck of a wily competitor."

"She said that?"

Bruce laughed like a man who didn't owe anyone a dime. "Actually, she said you're a sleazy son-of-a-bitch who should be disbarred, flogged, and run out of town."

"She's an excellent judge of character."

"Isn't your hearing about to start, hon?" Victoria said.

Bigby plowed ahead, looking Steve squarely in the eyes. "I told Victoria you were her baptism of fire." He stopped, caught himself. "That's not offensive to you, is it, Steve, the word 'baptism'? I mean, I assume you're Jewish."

"No problem. It's probably better than 'Bar Mitzvah of fire.' "

"Anyway, I told her that crossing swords with you would be good training for coming in-house."

"Not following you, Bruce."

"After we're married, I want Victoria to come aboard. General counsel of Bigby Resort and Villas. We're converting farmland to vacation ownership units. More than eight thousand potential owners. Can you imagine the paperwork?"

"Time-shares?" Steve asked. "You're selling time-shares in the Everglades?"

Bigby held up a hand. "Please. Time-share is old school, used-car salesmen in cheesy sport coats giving away steak knives. Vacation ownership reflects modern sensibilities."

"Like calling a garbage dump a sanitary landfill?"

"I can give you a heckuva deal on a unit right on the lake. Throw in upgraded cabinets, too."

A *beep* interrupted them. Pulling out his pager, Bigby checked the digital display. "Whoops. Zoning Board's back. Gotta go."

He brush-kissed Victoria, slapped Steve heartily on the back, and hustled out of the courtroom.

Victoria pretended to study her notes. "Don't say a word."

"Real estate contracts? You, a paper pusher? And what's that bit with the salad?"

"I'm allergic to avocados."

"And you've never told your fiancé?"

"It would hurt his feelings."

"Why aren't you that nice to me?"

"You don't have feelings."

"So, you can be honest with a guy you call a sleazy son-of-a-bitch but you have to lie to the man you allegedly love?"

"This doesn't concern you."

"May I ask a personal question?"

"No."

"This Bigby. Does he have a foot-long shlong?"

"You are such a vulgarian."

"Because I don't know what you see in him."

"Go back to your table."

"He's not right for you. He's got no poetry in his soul."

"And you do?"

"Maybe not," Steve said. "But at least I wish I did."

"All rise! Court for the Eleventh Judicial Circuit in and for Miami-Dade County is now in session!" Elwood Reed, the elderly bailiff, announced His Honor's arrival as if the judge were Charles the Second ascending the throne. "All those having business before this honorable court, draw near!"

Judge Gridley strode in, robes flowing, and with a wave commanded all to sit. "Are counsel ready to proceed?"

"State's ready, Your Honor," Victoria said.

"Defense is ready, willing, and able, Your Honor," Steve said, sliding off the prosecution table.

"Mr. Solomon, call your first witness," the judge ordered.

"The defense calls Mr. Ruffles," Steve said.

"Objection!" Victoria leapt from her chair and knocked over a stack of books.

"On what grounds?" the judge asked.

"Mr. Ruffles is a bird," she said.

SOLOMON'S LAWS

2. In law and in life, sometimes you have to wing it.

Seven

TWO BEAGLES IN THE BARN

A white cockatoo named Mr. Ruffles sat on the limb of a plastic tree, swiveling its head left and right, one blue-rimmed eye locked on Victoria. The fluffy bird, its feathers the color of sugar, resembled some dazzling sweet confection, she thought, a coconut cake maybe. The bird had a curved beak the color of blue curaçao and intelligent, liquid eyes. On its head, a flaring sulfur crest added a punctuation mark, like a sapphire brooch on a gown.

"Hello there, fellow," Judge Gridley said. "What's your name?"

"Feed me, dickwad," Mr. Ruffles said.

Scowling, the judge turned to Steve. "Counsel, control your bird."

Steve signaled Marvin the Maven in the front row. "My associate may be able to help."

Marvin toddled through the swinging gate, opened a small deli bag, and began feeding the bird a prune Danish, one nibble at a time.

Victoria quickly decided that her job was to keep Solomon from turning the courtroom into a zoo and herself into a laughingstock. The judge had sent the jurors back into their little room to bitch and moan in private while the lawyers argued whether a cockatoo could testify, or at least talk a bit.

"Birds represent love in mythology," Steve began.

Victoria felt Pincher's eyes on her back, heard his pen scratching on his notepad. "What's love got to do with anything?" she demanded.

"A revealing question," Steve shot back, "considering the unfortunate choice you've made in your personal life."

"That's totally improper. Your Honor, defense counsel should be admonished for the ad hominem attack."

"Settle down, both of you." Judge Gridley tossed aside *Lou's Sure Picks,* a betting tip sheet. "Mr. Solomon, just what the heck are you saying?"

"Every bird must be heard," Steve said. "It's in the Constitution."

"Where?" Victoria demanded.

"It was implied when the Founding Fathers chose the bald eagle as the symbol of the country."

"That's ridiculous. In the history of the Republic, no bird has borne witness in a court of law."

"Ms. Lord overlooks *The Case of the Perjured Parrot.*"

"Don't think I know that precedent," the judge said.

"One of the early Perry Masons," Steve said. "A parrot named Casanova witnessed a murder."

"Your Honor, this is ludicrous," Victoria said. "A bird can't swear to tell the truth."

"Tell the truth!" Mr. Ruffles said, spitting crumbs of prune Danish.

"Shut up!" Victoria said. Startled, the bird hopped from its tree to Steve's shoulder.

"Your Honor, Ms. Lord is harassing my bird," Steve said.

The judge's gavel cracked like a rifle shot. "C'mon up here, both of you."

As she approached the bench, Victoria felt her pulse racing. But just look at Solomon. A bird on his shoulder, a shit-eating smirk on his face. The judge was going to ream them both, and the idiot didn't even seem to care.

"Y'all want to have your dinner tonight in the stockade?" the judge asked.

"Certainly not, Your Honor," she said respectfully.

"Chipped beef on toast again?" Steve inquired.

"My outburst was provoked by Mr. Solomon, Your Honor. And his friend, Ruffles."

"*Mister* Ruffles," protested Mr. Ruffles, flapping his wings.

"Ms. Lord doesn't understand creative lawyering," Steve said.

"Mr. Solomon doesn't understand *ethics*."

Judge Gridley exhaled a long sigh. "When I checked my calendar this morning, it said, 'State versus Pedrosa,' not 'Solomon versus Lord.' " He leaned back in his leather chair. "You two remind me of a couple beagles I have on my farm outside Ocala. One male, one female, always yapping and nipping, raising general hell. Tried keeping those two apart, but they'd just yowl. See, they couldn't stand each other, but couldn't stand to be apart. They just loved the fight."

"Loved the fight!" Mr. Ruffles said.

"Then one day, it all stopped."

"Did the female kill the male?" Victoria asked, hopefully.

The judge cleaned his trifocals on the sleeve of his black robe. "I came out to the barn and found the male humping the bitch, just pumping away on a bale of straw."

"Humping the bitch," Mr. Ruffles said.

"If that's the court's order," Steve said, "we have no choice but to comply."

"You see what I have to put up with." Victoria felt her face redden.

"After that, those two dogs stayed as close as hog jowls and black-eyed peas," the judge said. "Now, I'm not gonna referee you. Y'all want to rut around, find your own barn on your own time."

"Six o'clock works for me," Steve said.

He's a juvenile delinquent, Victoria thought. A spoiled brat. She turned her back on him.

"As for the pending issue," the judge continued, "no dad-gum animal's gonna testify in my courtroom. I'm warning you both. Any attempt to elicit information from the bird will be considered a contempt of court."

Victoria felt herself exhale. *Ye-ssss!* Solomon wanted to give her trial tips? *Here's a tip for you. Don't mess with Victoria Lord.*

"Now, git on back to your places and let's hang the ham in the smokehouse," the judge said, then gestured for the bailiff to bring in the jury.

On the way to her table, Victoria smiled at Pincher, letting him know she'd won the motion. He nodded his appreciation. Then she felt Steve alongside her.

"Another trial tip, Lord," he whispered. "In law and in life, sometimes you have to wing it."

"Thanks a bunch," she said.

"I have to wing it right now. You know why?"

"I don't care."

"My client's guilty."

She stopped short. "What?"

"He imports illegal birds, snakes, big cats. Sells them to zoos and collectors."

Now she was confused. "You want to plead him out?"

"No way. Pedrosa gives people work, and the animals are healthy and happy."

"What he does is a crime."

"A victimless crime," Steve said. "Pedrosa came to this country with nothing. He's put two kids through college. He's good people."

"Why are you telling me this?"

"So you can dismiss the case and spare yourself embarrassment."

"Forget it."

"Then I'm not responsible for what happens."

"Are you threatening me?"

"You're going to be a fine lawyer someday, Lord. But not until you find your heart."

Victoria felt dizzy as she sat down, as if she had plunged through the rabbit hole and just kept falling. Hoping to stem the vertigo, she tried focusing on the sign above the judge's head. *We Who Labor Here Seek Only Truth*.

Sure. Solomon seeks to beat her brains in, the judge to beat the point spread, and the jurors to beat the traffic home.

Amancio Pedrosa swore to tell the truth and Steve started asking questions.

"What's your occupation, sir?"

"I run an animal shelter for poor, injured creatures," Pedrosa said.

And Fidel Castro runs Club Med, Victoria thought.

"So you have birds on your property?" Steve asked.

Pedrosa's eyes welled with tears. "Flamingos with broken legs. Pelicans with fishhooks in their beaks. Egrets that swallow beer-can tabs."

The jurors seemed stricken, Victoria thought. Could they be buying this shit?

"Do you recognize the bird sitting on my shoulder?"

"Looks like a Brazilian white cockatoo with a sulfur crest," Pedrosa said.

"Cockatoo!" Mr. Ruffles said, as Steve hand-fed him another prune Danish.

"Did you smuggle this bird into the country?"

"No, sir."

"Then how do you explain how Wildlife Officers found the bird on your property?"

"Hurricane Brenda," Pedrosa said. "You remember? The storm came up the coast from South America."

"So the hurricane blew our feathered friend north and deposited him on your property," Steve said.

No one laughed, no one screamed, and Solomon's pants didn't catch fire.

Just wait till cross-examination. I'll show you a hurricane.

"That's about it," Pedrosa said. "One day just after the storm, I saw that bird perched in a gumbo-limbo tree."

"Gumbo-limbo," Mr. Ruffles said.

"The same day, the Wildlife people showed up and arrested me."

"For saving this bird's life, you were arrested," Steve said sadly. He gave Mr. Ruffles a nudge, and the bird flapped his wings and hopped to Pedrosa's shoulder.

Victoria leapt to her feet. "Your Honor, let the record reflect that the bird has just landed on the defendant, Amancio Pedrosa."

"Objection," Steve said. "It's irrelevant where Mr. Ruffles sits."

The bird was nuzzling Pedrosa's neck. Victoria felt her excitement rise.

You think I can't wing it? Just watch, Solomon.

"It's highly relevant, Your Honor," she said. "It proves that Mr. Ruffles knows Mr. Pedrosa. Just look at them. They're practically cuddling."

"It's a case of mistaken identity," Steve said. "By zoological malfeasance and misleading suggestion, the state has planted false evidence."

Solomon's babbling, Victoria thought. He's scared. She had him right where she wanted him.

Hoisted on his own gumbo-limbo.

"Ms. Lord has employed trickery to dupe this innocent bird," Steve railed. "To Mr. Ruffles, all people look alike."

"Then why," Victoria retorted, "of all the people in the courtroom, did Mr. Ruffles choose Mr. Pedrosa? There's only one reason. Because it's Mr. Pedrosa's bird!"

Mr. Ruffles said: "Mr. Pedrosa's bird."

"Objection!" Steve yelled. "Ms. Lord has tainted these proceedings with prejudice."

"Mr. Pedrosa's bird," Mr. Ruffles repeated.

"Stifle that bird," the judge demanded, then turned to Victoria. "Ms. Lord, you think I was born tired and raised lazy?"

"No, sir."

"Then why did you elicit testimony from that flea-bitten bird?"

She felt the first sharp dagger of panic.

The judge's order. Have I violated the judge's order?

Next to her, Pincher cleared his throat with the sound of a truck dumping gravel. She could feel Solomon's presence, gliding into the well of the courtroom, circling like a hungry shark.

"It's Mr. Solomon's fault," she said. "He planned this. I don't know how exactly, but I know he did."

"That doesn't cut it, Judge," Steve said. "Ms. Lord has shamefully induced Mr. Ruffles to incriminate the defendant. I reluctantly move for a mistrial."

The word "mistrial" sent a shiver of fear through her. She groped for the right response, not daring to risk a glance at Pincher.

"But Pedrosa's guilty! Solomon told me so." The words just poured out. "That's why he's winging it. Solomon's diabolical, unbalanced, dangerous. He should be locked up along with his guilty client."

The courtroom was hushed. Everyone was staring at her. Victoria looked down. She was pointing her scissors at Solomon, her hand shaking.

"Bailiff, disarm counsel," the judge said, gravely.

Elwood Reed hitched up his belt, walked purposefully to the prosecution table, and took the scissors from Victoria.

"Mistrial granted," Judge Gridley said. He turned to the jurors and thanked them for their service, explaining that their duties were over, and isn't it wonderful to live in a country where the rule of law prevails?

Victoria slumped into her chair, dazed. She was vaguely aware of Pedrosa hugging Steve Solomon at the defense table. There was a flapping of wings. The damned bird was celebrating, too. Next to her, Pincher stirred uncomfortably.

"I'm sorry, sir." Her voice was as dry as the rustle of dead leaves.

"Some lawyers aren't cut out for the courtroom," Pincher told her. "Maybe you can be a back-office scrivener somewhere, but trial work's not for you."

She must have been shaking her head, because he said, "Do you understand?"

"No, sir."

"Do I need Donald Trump to deliver the news? You're fired."

Pincher got up and left her there, alone. A loser. A leper in a colony of one.

Her throat felt constricted, and her heart, which had been beating like a hummingbird's wings, seemed to stop. The courtroom became unbearably hot, the lights excruciatingly bright. Footsteps of departing spectators echoed like thunderclaps, whispers cackled like derisive laughter.

She tried to compose herself, knowing her cheeks were crimson, her makeup melting. And then it came. The first salty tear.

At the defense table, Steve looked at Victoria sitting alone and forlorn. Only another trial lawyer could understand what she was going through, her blood pooling on the courtroom floor. Steve had lost cases—though perhaps none so spectacularly—and he knew the shame. He'd heard Pincher fire her. The prick hadn't even waited until they were back in the office.

And now what?

Oh, jeez, she's crying.

Steve felt an emotion that seldom wormed itself into his consciousness: guilt. He hadn't meant to get her fired. He wanted to tell her that the only lawyers who never get humiliated in court are those too chickenshit to venture there. He wanted to tell her that she had more potential than any young lawyer he knew. She was a gladiator who'd gone down swinging her sword. Nothing to be ashamed of, not her fault her boss was a jerk.

Steve watched Victoria unstrap her expensive Italian shoes and toss them into a plastic bag, slipping on white Nikes for the trek to the parking lot. The Warrior Princess stripped of her armor. He told himself that someday she'd look back and realize it was for the best. Why should she waste her time with Sugar Ray Pincher? He'd do nothing but stunt her growth. She should be in private practice. Like him.

An idea was forming.

He could groom her, teach her all his tricks.

We could handle the Barksdale case together.

He wondered just how furious she was. Would she even listen to his offer? Would she help him—help *them*—land Katrina Barksdale as a client? He gathered up Mr. Ruffles and walked to the prosecution table.

"I'm sorry," he said.

"No you're not."

"I am. Really. But try to look at it as an opportunity."

"I hate you, you know."

"I hate you," Mr. Ruffles said, then hopped from Steve's shoulder to Victoria's. She was too numb to even care.

"What are you going to do now?" Steve asked.

"I don't know."

"Maybe I can help."

"You've done quite enough."

"I have a proposition for you."

"Shit!" she screamed.

"Don't say that till you hear me out," he said.

"Dammit! Your bird."

Mr. Ruffles flapped his wings and flew away. Eyes filling with tears, Victoria stared at the arm of her tweedy jacket where Mr. Ruffles had just left the molten aftermath of what had been prune Danish.

"They say it's good luck," Steve said.

GRAND JURY CONSIDERS BARKSDALE DEATH

By Joan Fleischman
Herald *Staff Writer*

The Miami-Dade Grand Jury will hear evidence Monday in the strangulation death of construction magnate and philanthropist Charles Barksdale, 60.

County Coroner Wu-Chi Yang reportedly will tell the Grand Jury that Barksdale died from "erotic asphyxia," death from cutting off the air supply during sex. The issue before the Grand Jury is whether there is probable cause that the death resulted from a homicide, rather than an accident.

Dr. Yang would not comment on these reports, and all proceedings before the Grand Jury are confidential. The sole suspect in the inquiry is Barksdale's widow, Katrina Barksdale, 33, who reportedly was with her husband in the bedroom of their luxurious bayfront home when the incident occurred last Wednesday night. The couple had been married four years.

Barksdale was best known for his waterfront condominium projects and as a sponsor of book fairs and poetry seminars.

Asked for a comment, State Attorney Raymond Pincher said, "We will present the Grand Jury with evidence that Mrs. Barksdale had ample motive, opportunity, and means to commit this heinous crime, and that she did so with premeditation and malice aforethought."

The State Attorney then added, "Not that I'm prejudging her."

Eight

THE OLD MAN
AND THE SEA BREEZE

What the hell did his father want?

What was so important that Steve had to fill the mammoth tank of his 1976 Cadillac Eldorado for the drive down Useless 1, the old highway that runs from Maine to Key West?

And why did the old man say to leave his grandson behind? Strange, because Bobby's the one Herbert Solomon enjoyed seeing.

These were the questions plaguing Steve as the old Caddy powered past the mango groves and vegetable farms of South Dade. Not that he had anything better to do. With the bird trial ended and his office empty of clients—*customers*, Cece called them—he had time for a quick trip to the Keys.

Or a long trip.

He felt a stab of pain when he saw the billboard with a drawing of pastel-colored low-rise buildings around a lake ringed by avocado trees.

BIGBY RESORT & VILLAS
Your Forever Getaway

Sounded like Menorah Gardens Cemetery, he thought. He had tried calling Victoria last night, but she wasn't picking up the phone, even though he'd dangled irresistible bait.

"Your Prince Charming here," he said to her answering machine, "and if you ever want to see your size eight-and-a-half Guccis again, you'll return my call."

In Victoria's haste to flee the courtroom, bird crud on her sleeve, Nikes on her feet, she had left her shoes behind. The snakeskin pumps, greatly admired by Marvin the Maven, now sat on the cracked white leather of the passenger seat, like a pair of miniature schnauzers.

When the phone rang just before midnight, he hoped it was Cinderella calling back. No luck.

"You stepped in the deep shit this time," Herbert Solomon had drawled, sounding semi-blitzed, "and ah'm gonna pull you out."

Steve heard the soft sound of water splashing. "You in the bathtub, Dad?"

"Pirates Cove, flashlight in one hand, shrimp net in the other."

"Where's the bottle of bourbon?"

"Shrimp are fat and juicy. Ah'll bring you some."

"You okay to drive home?"

"Drive? Ah'm in the kayak."

"Great. I'll alert the Coast Guard."

"Just git on down here tomorrow. It's important."

"Just what shit did I step in?"

"Not on the phone, son. Don't be such a dimwit."

They spent a few minutes negotiating a meeting place like two lawyers haggling over an insurance settlement. His father argued that Steve had the benefit of turnpike speeds all the way to Homestead, while he'd be stuck in traffic in the Lower Keys, so they should meet somewhere south of the halfway point. In rebuttal, Steve claimed that he actually worked for a living, while his father sipped hootch from Mason jars, so how about driving farther north? They settled on Tortugas Tavern, an open-air guzzlery just south of Islamorada on Lower Matecumbe Key.

It was cloudless, the Eldo's top was down, the steering wheel was warmed by the sun. Once a fiery red, the Caddy was now a faded dingy orange, but its fuel-injected engine still managed a throaty roar. On the reggae station, Bob Marley was confessing that he'd shot the sheriff, though apparently not the deputy.

The drive gave Steve an uncomfortable ninety minutes to think about his upcoming sparring match. He wasn't in the mood to hear about his own failings for the zillionth time. Long ago, he figured that his father's parenting was divided between the schools of benign neglect and don't-be-such. As in, *Don't be such a wimp; Don't be such a whiner;* and the classic ego-booster for an adolescent boy: *Don't be such a loser.*

Traffic slowed near Key Largo as he passed a collection of trailer parks, bait shops, souvenir stands, and ticky-tack apartment buildings on stilts. South of Plantation Key, the land fell away in spectacular fashion, leaving nothing but the two-lane roadway, slender beaches, and a series of bridges. Zipping past utility poles topped by osprey nests, Steve inhaled the rich, earthy smells of low tide along with the exhaust from a Hummer hauling a power boat. To the left was the turquoise water of the Florida Straits, to the right, the placid Gulf of Mexico, patches of red coral visible just beneath the surface.

Along the bridges, fathers and sons fished from catwalks and brown pelicans dive-bombed the shallows. Rec vehicles were parked in the white sand, kids piling out, splashing through the shallow water, their dogs yapping after them.

Regular families.

Unlike his, Steve thought. His mother deceased, his father in exile, his sister a habitual criminal. And what about him?

Just who the hell was Steve Solomon, anyway?

Pulling into the beachfront parking lot of crushed shells, the Eldo stirred up puffs of limestone dust. Steve spotted his father's old Chrysler Imperial, a kayak tied to a roof rack, rust spots on the hood and trunk where salt water had dripped. In his forced retirement, Herbert had taken to paddling across Florida Bay, exploring the Everglades, and camping on uninhabited islands.

The Tortugas Tavern was not much more than an open tiki hut with a thatched roof and a four-sided bar with mounted stools. The temperature hovered around eighty, and the air smelled of salt mixed with tangy smoke from the open kitchen. As he approached, Steve caught sight of his father, perched on a bar stool, a martini glass in front of him. Tanned the color of a richly brewed tea, Herbert wore khaki shorts and a T-shirt from a Key West oyster stand with the logo "Eat 'Em Raw." His long, shimmering white hair was combed straight back and curled up at the neck.

The image was jarringly at odds with what Steve remembered of his father, the neatly groomed downtown lawyer, and later the respected judge. Some of Steve's earliest memories were of his father's crinkly seersucker suits, a countrified Southern tradition. When Miami became more sophisticated, so did Herbert. As senior partner of his own law firm, he switched to Saville Row suits and advised younger lawyers to "think Yiddish, dress British."

Moving closer, Steve heard his father's voice, carried on the easterly breeze. He seemed to be entertaining a fortyish female bartender.

"So ah'm presiding over this sexual harassment case, and this pretty little lady testifies that her boss browbeat her into putting out for him." Herbert's voice was so musical you could dance to it. "Her lawyer asks her to tell the jury exactly what her boss said, but she cain't 'cause she's just too proper. Ah say, 'Write it down, missy, and ah'll show it to the jury.' So she writes on a slip of paper—'Ah want to fuck you so bad'—and ah give it to the jury. Jurors One and Two read it and pass it on, but Juror Three is sound asleep."

"I think I see this coming," the lady bartender said.

"Hang on, Ginger. Did ah mention that Juror Two is a cute gal and Juror Three is a middle-aged guy? Anyway, the gal elbows the guy, wakes him up, and hands him the note. He reads it, grins like he's won the lottery, winks at her, and tucks the note into his pocket."

The bartender laughed. "I knew it!"

"Never happened," Steve said, slipping onto the adjacent bar stool. A sailboard, dented with shark bites, was mounted on the back wall, and a paddle fan made lazy circles over their heads.

"Hey, son. It's the *emmis*. Every word."

"A courthouse myth."

"Dammit, ah was there." He turned to the bartender. "Ginger, this is mah boy. Stephen, the smart-ass."

Ginger had a pile of blond hair and wore white shorts with a floral top that was nothing more than a scarf tied behind her back. Her shoulders were slumped and her suntanned midriff was starting to sag. She had the tired look of a woman who'd spent too much time with too many wrong men and took too long to do something about it. "Getcha something, smart-ass?"

"Beer. Whatever's on tap."

"Something to eat?"

"You have conch chowder?"

"Do gators shit in the swamp?"

"Bowl. A little sherry in it. Basket of crab fritters."

"You got it."

She left and the two men appraised each other. Herbert's still-handsome face was lined and flecked with age spots, but his eyes were clear, dark, and bright, the same eyes as his son. His deep tan made his smile seem almost too bright.

"How's Bobby?" Herbert said.

"Making progress. Fewer nightmares, fewer fits."

"You give him a hug for me, tell him his Pop loves him."

"Sure thing." It was easier for his old man to send I-love-you messages by courier than deliver them personally, Steve figured. "He's at the Seaquarium today with Teresa and Marvin. They're crazy about him."

"Nice people. Used to pass me notes on the bench, tell me who was lying."

Steve already had taken Bobby to the Seaquarium five times in the last month. It would have been thirty times if the boy had his way. Whatever grabbed Bobby's attention quickly became an obsession, and currently he was fascinated with trained seals. Steve could picture him now, expertly mimicking the seals' mating calls, luring them off their platforms, wreaking havoc with the show.

"So what's up, Dad? What's the emergency?"

"In due time, son." Herbert sipped at his martini, straight up. "You seeing anyone special?"

"You mean a woman?"

"No, a Saint Bernard. Of course a woman."

"I don't have the time."

"That it? Or you don't have anything to offer?"

Aw, jeez. Not this again, Steve thought. Ginger delivered his beer and a steaming bowl of chowder. "C'mon, Dad. Just tell me why you hauled me down here."

"Women want a man of substance," Herbert declared, not easing up.

"You mean money."

"Status. Prestige. Money, too."

"False gods, every one," Steve said.

"What happened to that TV anchorwoman? Diane something-or-other."

Steve took a long hit on his beer. "She dumped me for a partner at Morgan Lewis."

Herbert nodded knowingly. "So now I can ask. Her boobs real?"

"As real as her smile." Steve remembered the first time Diane came to his house. She took one look around and suggested he sell all his furnishings on eBay.

"And that card shark," Herbert said. "What happened to her?"

"Sally Panther wasn't a card shark. She dealt Texas Hold 'Em at the Miccosukee casino." Steve spooned the spicy chowder, thick with conch meat. "She found a high roller, moved to Palm Beach."

"Uh-huh. See a pattern here?"

"Yeah. The women I meet are shallow."

"They trade up, is all."

Ginger slid a basket of crab fritters toward Steve. "You drag me down here just to bust my balls?"

"Enjoy your lunch first," Herbert said.

"Enjoy" was not a word that Steve usually associated with his father's company. But he had no choice. Herbert Solomon always had to be in control. He would play his poker hand when he damn well felt like it. Steve vowed to get through the meal peacefully, even if it gave him heartburn.

"You hear anything from Janice?" Herbert asked.

"Not a word." Steve chose not to mention the dirty green pickup truck. He thought he'd seen it again on South Dixie Highway, but he'd been looking through the rearview mirror, and it was impossible to tell. "Maybe she already left for her magical mystery tour."

"Little Janice," Herbert murmured, looking toward the water, where a gull was circling. "Ah remember putting the training wheels on her first bike. What the hell happened?"

"What happened was you didn't pay any attention to her after you put the wheels on."

"You laying her shit on *me*?"

Steve dipped a fritter in the creamy lime sauce, popped it into his mouth. The smoky crabmeat had the bite of jalapeño peppers. "Doing drugs. Stealing stuff. Running with punks. It was all to get your attention."

"And ah suppose you're screwed up because ah didn't come to your T-ball games."

"I skipped T-ball, went straight to Little League. Those were the games you missed. Plus Sunday school basketball, Beach High track, and U of M baseball. You were late for my confirmation because you were giving a lecture to a lawyers' convention, and you missed high school graduation when you were in trial upstate."

"Jesus. A junkie daughter and a grumble guts son. Maybe ah should get your DNA, see if you two got the milkman's genes instead of mine."

"What gets me is that you're so smart about complex stuff and so dumb about simple stuff. Spending time with your kids is good for them. Ignoring them isn't."

"Aw, don't be such a pantywaist."

Pantywaist? Now, there's one he hadn't heard in years. "Dammit, just tell me what I'm doing here or I'm getting back in the car and you can pick up the check."

Herbert ignored him and signaled Ginger for a refill, but she was mixing drinks for a couple of sunburned Yuppies at the end of the bar.

"Dad, I mean it. What'd I do now?"

Steve dipped his spoon into the chowder. His father put a hand on his arm and spoke softly. "The way ah hear it, you split open a man's skull."

The spoon stopped halfway to Steve's mouth.

"The night you grabbed Bobby," Herbert continued.

"Who told you that?"

"Jack Zinkavich. He drove all the way to Sugarloaf. Which ah might add is more than mah own son will do."

"You like the Fink so much, adopt him."

"Too late. Abe and Elaine Zinkavich already did. Thirty-some years ago."

"You mean somebody wanted the Fink?"

"Don't be such a shit. It's gonna come back to haunt you."

"Okay, I apologize to the prick. Tell him the next time he comes for a visit."

"Didn't ah teach you to always know your opponent? Know what they drink and who they screw, and sure as hell, where they came from. A man's past sticks to him like mud on cleated boots."

"You oughta know. Now, why did Zinkavich come all the way—"

"What do you know about him, smart-ass?"

Steve guzzled his beer. He'd have to play by his father's rules, answer his questions, take his abuse. "The Fink's a lifer at Family Services. Typical civil service drone."

"Nothing typical about him. If you'd done your homework, you'd know that. You'd know that as a little kid, he lived in a trailer park out on Tamiami Trail. His father was a mean drunk who abused his mother, took a leather strap to the boy. When Jack was seven or eight, he watched his father slit his mother's throat. She died in his arms."

"Jesus. I didn't know."

"Jack goes to a state shelter for a year. A shelter

run by Family Services. He bounced around in foster homes for a while, but it was hard as hell to place him. Too old, too angry, and not exactly a cute little teddy bear. But this social worker at Family Services wouldn't give up. You see where I'm heading?"

"I'm not sure."

"The social worker found Abe and Elaine. Now, what do you suppose Abe Zinkavich did for a living?"

"How should I know?"

"Juvie Court judge up in Lauderdale. That's how the social worker knew him. Abe provided a good education, taught the boy the importance of protecting children. Not that Jack needed much instruction. So the guy you call a drone is anything but. Jack's a crusader, a true believer, a zealot who hates violence. And you're the guy who kidnapped your nephew and nearly killed a man doing it."

"It was self-defense."

"So you say. What about choking Zinkavich in the courthouse?"

"I was straightening his tie and got carried away."

"You called him a Nazi storm trooper, for chrissakes."

"He sent investigators to the house at night. Scared the shit out of Bobby."

"And you told him Family Services was run by incompetent fools who should go to prison."

"Didn't you read about them losing a little girl in the system?"

"So write an op-ed piece, but stop sticking your thumb in Jack's eye."

"Look, I'm sorry about what happened to him, but he's still an asshole."

"Ah'm sure he can be a bigger shit than a ton of

manure, especially when provoked by the likes of you."

"Didn't you ever run up against someone who hates you right off the bat?"

"Not as much as you seem to, smart-ass. But you're missing the point. Family Services isn't just Zinkavich's employer. It's his family. It's his home. And you've crapped all over his front stoop. Now he's coming after you with everything he's got."

"So what's he got?" Steve asked.

"He's looking for the guy you clobbered the night you grabbed Bobby."

Steve felt his stomach tighten. The shepherd in the shed, the guy who smelled like a wet dog. Steve believed he had lawfully used self-defense when he hit the guy with the staff. The guy had a knife, right? But you can only fight back with reasonably necessary force. Had he? That's what they call a jury question, and Steve didn't want to hear a judge asking if the jury had reached a verdict.

"I assume you told Zinkavich you didn't know anything."

"Ah told him he could kiss mah kosher butt."

Steve thought about it a moment. "I don't get it. Why would the Fink think you'd rat me out?"

"Excellent question." Herbert waved at the bartender, who was working on a tray of colorful drinks. "Ginger, what the hell's that disgusting thing that looks like toilet bowl cleaner?"

"Apple martini, Herb." She dropped a slice of a Granny Smith into the green drink.

"Apple martini, now there's an oxymoron. Gin plus vermouth equals martini. An olive's okay. Onion's okay. Fruit is not okay."

"Dad . . ."

"A martini should taste like liquid steel."

"Dad, why did Zinkavich—"

"And what's that red one?" Herbert gestured at her tray.

"Sea breeze. Vodka, cranberry juice, and grapefruit juice." She pointed to the other drinks. "This one's a sex on the beach, and the tall one, that's a Long Island iced tea. Vodka, gin, rum, tequila, cointreau, and Coke."

Herbert made a face. "That's not a drink, it's a frat party. When the circus is over, can you fix me another martini?"

"Why'd Zinkavich think you'd help him?" Steve persisted.

"He said if ah cooperate, he'd put in a good word in Tallahassee, maybe get me reinstated with the Bar."

"Lousy deal. Hold out for the governorship."

"So ah figure ah'm not the only member of our *mishpoche* that Zinkavich is talking to," Herbert said.

"Meaning?"

Ginger delivered the martini, and Herbert nodded his thanks. "Think about it. Who gave Janice a get-out-of-jail-free card? And why?"

"You're saying my worthless sister's helping Zinkavich nail me."

"Ah'm saying it's possible."

Teresa Toraño had been right. From the Panhandle to the Keys, Zinkavich was covering a helluva lot of ground. And why?

To bury me. All I want is to raise Bobby, and the state unleashes this vengeful fuck on me.

"This much ah know for sure." Herbert twirled the martini glass by the stem. "Zinkavich wants to squash you like a palmetto bug. He was tossing around words like 'aggravated assault' and 'attempted murder.' "

The tightness in Steve's stomach had become a thudding pain. So many questions, so many fears. How much did they have on him? Had Janice led Zinkavich to the guy in the shed? Would there be a knock on his door, cops dragging him away, social workers grabbing Bobby?

"Let me in, son," Herbert said.

"In where?"

"Your life." Herbert drained the martini. One long, silvery river of liquid steel, just as he liked it. "Ah'm still your father, and ah want to help."

So that's what this was all about, Steve thought. Some buried paternal instincts had been unearthed like fossils after a flood. Maybe some guilt, too. Is this what happened to inattentive fathers as they aged? For a moment, Steve felt sorry for his old man. At forty, he'd been one of the leaders of his profession. And at sixty? Widowed, disgraced, living alone. Two grown kids, both alienated in varying degrees.

Were his own troubles a boon to his father, a way to reconnect? The thought angered him. What did his old man expect him to do? Pull up a chair, pour some bourbon, and ask for advice? The lyrics of Warren Zevon's "Lawyers, Guns, and Money" floated into his head: *Dad, get me out of this.*

But that had never been their relationship, and it wasn't going to start now. Too much emotional overload. His father helping now would only stir up old resentments by reminding Steve of his earlier absence.

"I appreciate the gesture, Dad, but it's a little late to start tossing the ball in the backyard."

"Ah know ah wasn't always there for you. But anybody wants to do you harm, they're gonna have to deal with me."

Herbert blinked, his eyes watery. From the gin or something deeper, Steve didn't know.

Nine

MINIMUM HUSBAND
STANDARDS

What more could go wrong? Victoria wondered.

In one lousy day, she'd been jailed, fired, shit on . . . and she'd lost her shoes.

Now, two days later, the dry cleaner said it would take a nuclear weapon to purge the bird poop from her Ralph Lauren tweed; she couldn't get her résumés to print out; and that lunatic Solomon was holding her snakeskin Gucci pumps for ransom. Not only that, she was irritated with Bruce.

He could have been more supportive.

He could have said: "You're a terrific lawyer with awesome talents. You'll overcome this."

But he didn't say that.

Or he could have said: "Pincher's a jerk, and someday you'll go into court and kick his butt. Solomon's, too."

But he didn't say that, either.

Bruce, her betrothed, had said: "Maybe getting sacked is for the best. Now you can come to BRV with a clear head, make a fresh start."

BRV being Bigby Resort & Villas. Drafting real estate documents. Deeds and mortgages, liens and affidavits. Yawn, yawn, yawn . . . and yuck.

He just didn't get it, she thought. But how could he? His father bequeathed him thousands of acres and several thriving businesses. Bruce didn't know what it was like to stand alone in the Colosseum, surrounded by lions, armed only with your wits.

She was thinking all this while staring into the open maw of her printer, which had been chewing up copies of her résumé and spitting out confetti. Wearing an old pair of corduroy jeans with one of Bruce's Oxford-cloth blue shirts, she sat at her desk in the spare-bedroom-turned-study of her condo. She closed the lid of the printer and hit the RESET button.

Nothing but a message: Error 31, whatever the hell that meant.

She looked out the window at cars crossing the Rickenbacker Causeway, headed for the beaches of Key Biscayne. Across the bay, she could see a dozen white sails, a boat race forming up. She pictured the people on board, enjoying the breeze, the sunshine, the company. Enjoying *life*, while she sat here, cursing her computer, mourning her shattered career.

If she went to work for Bruce, wouldn't it all be so much easier? She'd have time to sail and learn French cooking and play tennis at the club . . . like Katrina Barksdale. Maybe she should call Katrina, ask if she'd found a lawyer, offer her services. No, that would be unseemly, like inviting yourself to a party.

Her mind drifted back to the previous evening. Bruce wasn't being mean. He was just trying to cheer her up. First, his personal chef had cooked another of those tasteless vegan meals, some greens sizzling in a wok with tofu the consistency of snot. She longed for filet mignon, rare, *pommes frites* . . . and another chance in the courtroom.

Over herbal tea and sugar-free rice pudding, Bruce had said: "General counsel and executive vice president of BRV. How does that sound, sweetie?"

Like a sellout, that's how.

Maybe Bruce was trying to tell her something in a roundabout way. Maybe he thought she didn't have the chops to be a trial lawyer. What if he was right? Maybe she'd get shit on in every trial, one way or another. Maybe she should just do what Bruce wanted. Which meant relying on him, being totally dependent, emotionally and financially. And that meant, she realized, violating a promise she had made to herself when she was twelve years old, just after her father died.

I will never depend on any man. I swear I won't.

She remembered the very first to-do list she'd written on her very first note card.

1. Study hard.
2. Stay away from boys.
3. Make lots of money.

Okay, so she'd only gone one for three. She'd pocketed a summa cum laude parchment. As for the boys, a girl's gotta have fun, right? And her net worth, well, that was printed in red ink.

Still, she had her membership card in the Florida Bar. She would rebound from getting fired. She wouldn't be like her mother, who had relied so totally on Victoria's father and had been let down so hard. A man who spent lavishly on his wife and only child. A man who could, on a moment's notice, swoop up the family for an impromptu cruise, his valet racing aboard with their bags while the ship's horn bleated visitors ashore.

Victoria remembered her father as a barrel-chested man with a mane of wavy, silver hair and a joyous, rippling laugh like a stream pouring over boulders. Even now, she could smell the rich leather of his handmade Italian shoes, the tang of his cologne, the worsted wools of his tailored suits, laced with cigar smoke.

"What's Daddy's little girl want for her birthday?" he once asked.

"A horse," she answered.

Poof. Like magic. A Shetland pony with a silky white mane.

A dollhouse? *Poof.* The size of a bungalow, it was fit for a princess, the daughter of a king.

Fireworks? *Poof.* Rockets soaring from the front lawn, turning the neighborhood into a carnival.

Until it all went to hell, to use her mother's expression.

How could it have happened? Lord-Griffin Construction Company was booming. Her father and his partner, Harold Griffin, were building high-rise condos on both coasts of Florida, making tons of money, living in a paté and white wine world. The two couples—Harold and Phyllis Griffin, Nelson and Irene Lord—were best friends. Their two children—Hal, Jr., and Victoria—were inseparable from the time they were toddlers. The future seemed preordained. Private jets, Caribbean villas, a life of privilege and comfort.

"Until your father cracked."

Another one of her mother's expressions.

There had been a grand jury investigation. A scandal in the Broward County Building and Zoning Department. Allegations of code violations and payoffs, bribery and extortion. Nelson was subpoenaed to testify.

Then, one horrible night, the call to Victoria at boarding school. Her mother's voice: "Your father's gone."

Gone where? For how long?

Gone forever.

The fall was twenty-two stories from the roof of a condo under construction in Lauderdale-by-the-Sea.

Now, thinking back, Victoria realized how those experiences pushed her toward a man of moderate sensibilities. A clearheaded man, and if he was a tad boring, well, that was the trade-off. We don't get to choose our fathers, but we can learn from them in choosing our husbands, she believed. Of one thing she was certain: Bruce would never bail on her or himself. He was as safe and comfy as a terry-cloth bathrobe. She didn't need fireworks on the lawn, and as for fireworks in the bedroom, that never lasted, anyway, right?

In Bruce, she had a man of solid normalcy. A straight-arrow of a man who adored her. So even if he didn't comprehend how getting fired had crushed her self-confidence and wounded her pride, even if he didn't say precisely the right things, she forgave him.

Victoria banged the palm of her hand against the side of the printer. It didn't say "Ouch," and the green light still didn't come on. Dammit, she had to get her résumés out. How long could she go without a paycheck? She was afraid to look at the monthly statement from the bank.

No problem. I can always find the hidden diamonds.

The thought brought a rueful smile to Victoria's face. It's what her mother always said when money was tight. The "hidden diamonds" reflected The Queen's dreamy personality, Victoria thought. Her apartment—now Victoria's—was on an upper floor of the first high-rise built on Brickell Avenue, overlooking Biscayne Bay. Victoria remembered her mother telling her tales about the apartment's first tenant, long before the building converted to condo and the street turned into a forest of ritzy skyscrapers.

"Murph the Surf lived here," her mother had said, with a tone of awe.

She explained that Jack Murphy was a surfer, violinist, tennis pro . . . and amateur jewel thief. Victoria listened with wide eyes to the tale of Murph pulling a massive heist—breaking into a New York museum and spiriting away the Star of India, the world's largest sapphire, plus a bunch of diamonds.

"They caught Murph, got back the Star of India and most of the other jewels," her mother told her. "*Most*, but not all." This is where The Queen would lower her voice, as if people in the next apartment were listening through the walls. "He hid the rest of the diamonds right here, right in this building. If things get tough, no problem. I can always find the hidden diamonds."

From time to time, usually after a bit of sherry,

The Queen would chisel holes in the stucco walls, pop open recessed ceilings, and pry the covers off old light fixtures. But the diamonds, if they existed at all, seemed destined to be hidden longer than the treasures of King Tut.

These days, Irene Lord's diamonds came from a succession of wealthy, older suitors. She chose not to marry any of them, content to be escorted to various glam spots around the world. The last time she had called, The Queen was happily ensconced in a fancy spa in Johannesburg, recovering from her latest installments of plastic surgery. She informed Victoria she wouldn't be home for Christmas, something about a side trip to Zurich for injections of sheep hormones.

Victoria believed she had a more practical streak than her mother. At least, that's what she told herself as the TROUBLE light on the printer flashed red.

Damn the printer and damn the legal profession and damn Steve Solomon.

Yep, thoughts of Murph the Surf had morphed into thoughts of Steve the Sleaze. He'd gotten her fired.

No. Strike that. It wasn't Solomon's fault. He had warned her, even while he taunted her for her inability to act spontaneously.

"Sometimes you have to wing it."

And he'd been right, damn him. If only she had a second chance, she could handle it. She would slough off his stunts with a patient smile and a wry comment. The judge would admire her aplomb. The jury would sympathize, poor girl having to put up with such an obnoxious prick. But there would be no second chance. What was it about Solomon that so provoked her?

The ringing doorbell interrupted her thoughts.

"Who is it?"

"George Clooney!" cried a woman's voice. "Naked and bearing gifts."

Victoria unlatched the door. "With a three-day beard?"

"Just enough to chafe your inner thighs." Jacqueline Tuttle laughed and breezed in, carrying a cardboard tray from Starbucks. "Which reminds me, do you have any Monistat in the medicine chest?"

"I don't think so."

"Damn. Last time I sit in the Jacuzzi for three hours." Jacqueline placed the tray on the kitchen table. "Frappuccinos, extra whipped cream, carrot cake with double icing."

"You're a godsend, Jackie. I'm starving."

"I was in the neighborhood. Got the listing on a penthouse at the Santa Maria. Two million five."

"Great."

"Plus I'm showing a three-bedroom at Bristol Tower at noon and checking an open house at Espirito Santo at one. Ever notice that the way Bristol Tower tapers at the top, it looks like a forty-story penis?"

"No, but now that you mention it . . ."

"Circumcised, of course." Jackie's laugh crackled like kindling on a fire. She looked around the apartment, which was unusually dark for a bayfront condo. "You ever think about updating this place?"

"I can't afford to update my manicure, and if I don't get my résumés out—"

"That's what we need to talk about. I've got some advice for you."

Uh-oh, Victoria thought. Jackie Tuttle might be her best friend, but sometimes Victoria wondered what the two of them had in common. Jackie was uninhibited and bawdy and laughed loud and often. Victoria had never seen her depressed, not even when her slime of an ex-boyfriend, Carlos, wrecked her BMW convertible on the Don Shula Expressway while getting head from a Hooters girl he'd picked up at an airport bar.

"No problem," Jackie had told Victoria. "I get a new car from the insurance. The cop who investigated the accident asked me out. And Carlos' reattachment surgery didn't take."

That was Jackie, making a Prada purse out of a sow's ear.

She was five-foot-ten and had a wild mane of dyed red hair. She owned a collection of immense dangling earrings, some of which reached her shoulders and enough Blahnik, Choos, and Chanel shoes, boots, sandals, stilettos, flats, pumps, and Mary Janes to make Sarah Jessica Parker jealous.

Today she wore a leather mini with a cropped tank top and knee-high Stephanie Kelian boots in a soft, buttery suede. Most women Jackie's size would have shied away from such an outfit. Jackie didn't care. She was happily, gloriously plump, with natural breasts she called her "bazooms," which jiggled when she laughed and popped out of her top when she water-skied. Just above her left breast was a small tattoo of Cupid, firing an arrow at whoever happened to be in close proximity.

Jackie was a real estate broker, specializing in what

she called the "king-of-the-jungle market," high-end, waterfront condos that appealed to rich, single men. The real estate license allowed her to run a credit check on any potential buyer or potential spouse in about thirty seconds. This was useful, given all the poseurs, phonies, and outright felons masquerading as legitimate candidates for matrimony. She told Victoria she'd never known how many deadbeats leased Porsches until she logged onto the credit data-bases. Jackie's own credit report would show that she made lots of money and spent even more.

Now, just what crazy advice did Jackie have?

"Don't send out your résumé," Jackie said, slurping her Frappuccino through the straw. "Go out on your own. Open your own shop."

"And where do I get my clients?"

"Katrina Barksdale, for starters. She likes you."

"She likes to play tennis with me. We've never even talked about law."

Jackie tore off a chunk of carrot cake. "Look, if I killed my husband, should I ever be so lucky to have one, I'd hire you in a minute."

"I'd have to rent an office, print stationery, hire a secretary. . . ."

"Whatev," Jackie said. "How much do you have in the bank?"

"In round numbers?"

"Yeah.

"Overdrawn."

"I could lend you some money."

"You? You have money?"

Jackie licked icing from her upper lip. "If I sell all my Jimmy Choos on eBay." She laughed, and then, as great friends sometimes do, she seemed to read Victoria's mind. "You could always work for Bruce."

"I've thought about it."

"But . . . ?"

"Wouldn't that be cowardly? I get smacked around in court, so I hide in a back office?"

"C'mon, Vic. You don't have to prove anything. You're marrying Mr. Perfect. Let him pay the freight."

Sure, it would be so easy, Victoria thought. Take the pressure off, slide papers from the in-box to the out-box. What's the most stress she'd face?

"There's a problem, Ms. Lord. That signature from the bank isn't notarized."

Maybe she should just say yes. Who could blame her?

But she said: "Can't do it."

"Okay, but if I were marrying a guy like Bruce, I'd never work another day in my life. 'Course, you don't know what it's like in the husband hunt these days."

"You'll find someone."

"Easy for you to say. You've bagged your big game. Nothing out there but Peter Pans, commitment phobes, momma's boys, and brats. Sometimes all in the same package."

"Just take your time," Victoria said.

"Did I mention guys who don't know they're gay?"

"Is that possible?"

"Or guys who expect blow jobs if they splurge for stone crabs?"

"No way."

"It's true. Right after the key lime pie."

"I'm lucky to have Bruce," Victoria said. "I know that."

"Lucky? I'm so jealous, my contacts are turning green."

Relationships were based on good fortune—or bad—Victoria thought. What were the odds she'd be reaching toward a high shelf for Lisa Scottoline's latest courtroom novel just as a tall, blond man walked by? Bruce had plucked *Killer Smile* from the shelf, insisted on paying for it, and invited her for coffee. Books & Books, she now figured, was a better place to meet a guy than a South Beach club.

Jackie was right. Bruce was a prize. Handsome and stable, kind and giving. And literate, even if his reading habits gravitated toward *Saving Taxes Through Offshore Trusts*.

"I'll bet you don't even have a punch list for Bruce," Jackie said.

"What do you mean?"

"Change orders. Every guy I meet, I write down all the changes he needs to make to meet Minimum Husband Standards. Say a guy's favorite music is the theme from Monday Night Football."

"You're making this up."

"Last Friday. Blind date at the Blue Door. It's gotten so bad I'm gonna stay home and pet the kitty."

"I give it a week."

"I mean it, Vic. No more dating. Just me and my . . ." She made a buzzing sound. "*Leetle* friend."

Again, the doorbell rang, and Victoria headed for the foyer. "Maybe *that's* George Clooney."

This time, it was a deliveryman bearing gifts: a tropical bouquet, a bottle of Cristal, and a mystery box wrapped in silver foil. Victoria carried the good-ies back to the dining table.

"Bruce is the most thoughtful man in the world," Jackie said.

"True," Victoria said, fishing the plastic spear out of the flowers and examining the envelope. "But it's not from him."

"Who, then? Open, open!"

Victoria tore open the envelope, pulled out the card. "The most irritating man in the world."

"Solomon? That defense lawyer?"

"He's been leaving messages, asking me out to lunch. He says he's going to help me find a job, but what he really wants is for me to get him the Barksdale case."

"All the more reason to get it for yourself."

Could she do it? Victoria wondered. Grab the phone and solicit the case? It would be so unlike her. . . .

"So what's in the box?" Jackie demanded.

Victoria removed the foil, opened the box, and pulled out a single Gucci snakeskin pump. "My left shoe," she said.

"If the right one's under that bad boy's bed, I'm gonna tell Bruce."

"I left the shoes in court. Solomon won't give me the other one unless I return his calls."

"Does he have a foot fetish?" Jackie examined the two-and-a-half-inch heel with a critical eye. "And more important, is he cute?"

"I suppose, if you like that kind of look."

"What kind?"

"Like a fox. A dangerous, bushy-tailed fox—"

"Ooh."

"With this look in his eyes, like he's playing some trick on the world."

"He sounds divine. Maybe you should introduce us."

"What happened to staying home and petting the kitty?"

"Dead batteries."

"Believe me, you don't want to get mixed up with Solomon."

"I'm not talking about forever. I'm talking about a horny Tuesday night."

"Jac-kie," Victoria chastised her in a tone reminiscent of The Queen. "You can do a lot better than Steve Solomon."

"Are you keeping that bad boy for yourself?"

"Are you crazy? I'm marrying Bruce in a month."

"One last fling with a wholly inappropriate man. It's de rigueur."

"Says who?"

"*Cosmo.*" Jackie grabbed the rest of the carrot cake, and with a mouth full of icing said: "Wouldn't you love to see Solomon's face if you got Katrina as a client?"

It was a tantalizing thought, but could she do it? "I've never handled a murder case."

"C'mon. Go for it."

Maybe Jackie was right. Maybe she should be more aggressive, not worry about appearances. As Victoria thought about it, a realization dawned. There were no hidden diamonds. At least none buried in the stucco or tucked inside light fixtures.

The only diamonds we'll ever find are the ones we make ourselves.

She should probably plan what to say, scribble

notes on index cards, but to hell with it. She'd do it the way Solomon would.

Moving quickly so she couldn't change her mind, Victoria flipped open her cell phone.

"What are you doing?" Jackie asked.

"Winging it," Victoria said.

Ten

AMBUSH ON KUMQUAT STREET

Victoria hit the brakes, and her aging Ford Taurus swerved into the oncoming lane, barely missing a two-foot-long green iguana wiggling across the asphalt. It made her think of that other lizard, the shoe-stealing Steve Solomon. Except, had he been slithering by, she would have floored it. *Squish.*

There was Loquat Avenue. Where the hell was Kumquat? The streets were not well lighted, and Victoria was lost after dark somewhere in Coconut Grove. She'd been distracted, practicing what she would say to Solomon if she could ever find his house.

I don't want your champagne. I don't want your flowers. I don't want to see your face or ever hear your name.

Then she corrected herself. She *did* want to see his face. She wanted to watch him suffer. *Lord* it over him, as her mother used to quip.

"Katrina Barksdale hired me. So go back to your fender benders and birdshit cases. And give me back my damn shoe."

It sounded good to her. Strong. Defiant.

But now she was adrift in a neighborhood where hibiscus hedges burst from front yards and crept, untamed and unshorn, to the street, where live oaks eclipsed the moon, erasing shadows and turning everything a poisonous greenish black. The windows on the Taurus were down—the A/C needed freon—and the intoxicating fragrance of jasmine washed over her in the humid night. She was starting to perspire. Why did she wear the white satin blouse and worsted wool slacks?

It was the second outfit she'd tried on. First the white jeans with the sleeveless silver nylon net top, flecked with confetti beads. A little too sexy for an unannounced visit to a man's home after dark. And altogether too frivolous for this mission. She could have covered up with her little silver leather jacket with the snap buttons, but the night was too warm. Not only that, she'd promised Bruce she'd throw out all her leather, as it offended his PETA principles. So far, she hadn't done it, and she wished he would lighten up.

Just as she was thinking about her other broken promise—to stop eating meat—she caught a whiff of someone's backyard barbecue. It smelled like ribs being smoked, the tang of a vinegary sauce in the evening air. God, could she help it if she was a born carnivore? If she joined PETA, she'd change the name to People for Especially Tasty Animals. But when you love someone, you make compromises, right? Giving up meat in return for Bruce—well, that was a no-brainer, wasn't it?

One hand on the steering wheel, she absentmindedly ran a finger over her blouse's twisted cording. The satin braids twirled in a floral pattern, and the sleeves puffed out with elaborate scalloped cuffs. The slacks were nothing fancy, plain black with straight legs. A trick from her mother. "Basic bottoms with a glamorous top. Simple but elegant."

Now where was she? She'd passed Palmetto Street, Royal Palm, and Poinciana. She figured she'd gone too far. She hung a U-turn and backtracked, and there it was. Kumquat Avenue. Which house was it?

Shit!

She slammed on the brakes and barely missed hitting a pickup truck head-on. An old green pickup with no lights and a bug screen on its front bumper. It must have pulled out from the curb in the darkness. She flashed her lights, but the truck sped away with its lights still off. *Asshole.*

The bungalow was just as she'd imagined it. Concrete block and stucco. Needing a paint job. Lightbulbs missing on a lantern near the front door. Dead fronds from a sabal palm littering the front yard. Solomon's car, an ancient Cadillac convertible the size of an aircraft carrier, sat in the gravel driveway. She knew it was his from the vanity plate: I-OBJECT. Rust spots sprouted on the fenders like cancerous growths, and the white canvas top was freckled with mildew and patched with duct tape. The overall impression was that the car had been pulled from the bottom of a canal with a mobster stuffed in the trunk.

Carrying Solomon's bribes—the bottle of champagne and a wilting bouquet of birds of paradise— she followed a path of chipped flagstone to the front door, avoiding the red berries of a Brazilian pepper tree that could send her blouse to dry-cleaner hell. She stepped around a dead frog, careful not to let her high-heeled sandals touch the gray cadaver being autopsied by a phalanx of carpenter ants. A plant with drooping white flowers overhung the path. Like the entire neighborhood of overgrown vegetation, like Solomon himself, the huge plant needed trimming back. What was it called?

Ouch. She stopped short. A sharp, pointed leaf had snagged her puffy sleeve. She gently extricated herself. Too late. A ragged hole appeared in the blouse, a swirling soutache braid torn loose.

Damn you, Solomon, and damn your shrubbery, too.

Of course, the doorbell didn't work. She pounded on the door, and the name of the plant came to her. Spanish dagger.

Suddenly, a startling sensation. Something cold on the back of her neck. She wheeled around and caught a blast of water in the face.

Shit! Did a sprinkler turn on? Why did every encounter with Solomon turn into a disaster?

"Oppugnatio!"

The yell came with a green-and-brown blur, a figure leaping out of the pepper tree, landing three feet away. A skinny boy, maybe eleven or twelve years old, in camouflage gear.

"Capitis damnare!" he bellowed, then raised a red plastic rifle and hit her with a powerful blast of water. She stumbled backward, snagging herself again on a Spanish dagger leaf. She dropped the flowers and Cristal. The bottle shattered and sprayed her sandals and bare toes with champagne. Her attacker

dashed past her, flinging open the door and running into the house.

A bare-chested man appeared in the open doorway. "What the hell's going on?" Solomon was wearing nothing but a towel around his waist.

"Some little monster just—"

"Bobby. My nephew. You scared him."

"*I* scared *him?*" The nephew, she thought. Back in the jail cell, Solomon called him a reverse chick magnet but failed to mention he was a serial killer in training. "If I remember my Latin, I think he just condemned me to death."

"He must have thought you were a social worker."

She stuck a finger through the hole in her blouse. Ruined.

"Family Services is checking out my parenting skills," Steve continued.

"Is there a grade below F?"

"So why are you here? Wait. Don't tell me. You're taking me up on my offer?"

"That what you think?"

"Or you're hitting on me." He gave her that infuriating grin. "I haven't been to a wet T-shirt contest in years."

She looked down at her blouse, her breasts and nipples silhouetted by the wet fabric.

Oh, great. The one time I don't wear a bra.

"You're disgusting," she said.

"Hey, I'm not the one who's aroused. Yet."

"I'm leaving."

"C'mon, all in fun. You're bringing me the Barksdale case, right?"

How could any man be so clueless?

"You are so perceptive," she said.

"I'm sorry about your blouse," he continued, not sounding a bit sorry. "If you want to come in and take it off . . ."

"In your dreams. Just give me my shoe." She'd lost the desire to taunt him. Let him learn about her new client, her new life, from the newspaper.

"Come on in," he said, "and we'll talk about our case."

"Not *our* case. *My* case!"

"I get it. You're playing hardball on fees. Fine, everything's negotiable."

"You're unbelievable."

"You'll sit second chair, and I'll give you thirty percent of the fee."

"I have a counteroffer. I'll sit first chair and take all the fee. You sit on the sofa and watch on Court TV."

He looked baffled.

To hell with running home. Rub his nose in it first.

"I'm going out on my own. And Katrina Barksdale is my first client."

"C'mon. She didn't hire you."

Look at him. He couldn't believe it. "Wanna bet? Kat and I have already talked."

"What'd you talk about, shopping?"

"It's a done deal. She wants a female lawyer and thinks I'd be perfect. She's signing a retainer tomorrow morning."

"You tell her you've never tried a capital case?"

"I did what you would have done." Victorious now, smile as sharp as a razor.

"You lied? Mother Teresa of the courthouse lied?"

"She never asked and I never said."

"Barksdale's too big. You don't start with this one."

"Watch me," she taunted, luxuriating in his pain.

"Do you even know what the pressure's like in a celebrity murder trial? Everyone's watching. The media, big-time lawyers, Oprah."

He was sputtering now. This might even be worth a torn blouse. "I love seeing you like this, Solomon."

"The case involves kinky sex. You'll blush during opening statement."

"Now you're an expert on my sex life?"

"You and Bruce, white bread and mayonnaise. Maybe a slice of avocado on the side."

"You can't push my buttons. Not anymore."

"You probably do it watching Lou Dobbs. Amazon's up three bucks, Bruce is up three inches."

"You don't know the half of it."

"C'mon, I know guys like Bigby. No reverse cowgirl, no doggie-daddy, straight mish all the way."

"If you were capable of a human emotion, I'd think you were jealous."

"You need me, Lord."

"I need my right shoe. Give it to me, and I'm out of here."

"I can make you into a great lawyer."

"My shoe. Now!"

"You've got guts. You've got presence. But you're unmolded clay."

"And you'd like to mold me? Forget it."

God, this was fun. It reminded her of something. What? Of course . . .

Bickering and bantering in the holding cells.

That had charged her batteries, too. Squabbling

with Solomon was like a competitive tennis match, two hard-hitters going all out.

"All right. I surrender." Solomon threw up his hands, the towel slipping lower on his hips.

"What?"

"Good luck on the Barksdale case."

"That's it? No last-ditch effort?"

"It's all yours, Lord. I'll sit in the front row and cheer."

She was disappointed. Here they were, just getting warmed up, and he defaulted.

"Come on in," he said. "I'll get your shoe."

"I'll wait here."

"It's important. For Bobby. If he thinks you came to take him away, he won't sleep tonight."

"If this is one of your tricks . . ."

"Not about Bobby," he said, subdued. "Never about Bobby."

Eleven

THE RUDNICK RACK

Steve had just lied. And told the truth.

The bit about Bobby, one hundred percent true. Bobby came first, and there were no games or tricks where his welfare was concerned. But the other stuff: *"Good luck. It's all yours."*

Now, that was a big fat fib.

Not that it was his fault, Steve told himself. Like a nervous witness on the stand, Victoria had disclosed too much.

"It's a done deal. . . . She's signing a retainer tomorrow morning."

Leading Victoria into his home, Steve did not bother to correct her.

"No, Vickie, it ain't a done deal till the thin lady signs."

Which meant he had until sometime tomorrow morning to steal the case, just like he once stole home against Florida State. He hadn't pranced up and down the baseline, as if he might make take off. He'd scratched his ass, feigned a limp, lulled the pitcher to sleep . . . then raced for home.

"So where's your new office?" Steve said, as casually as possible.

"Don't have one yet."

Which meant they were meeting at the Barksdale home, he figured. A restaurant would be too public. Okay, he had half a plan now. He'd get to Gables Estates before Victoria. What he'd say when he got there—well, that would have to come later, because he didn't have a clue.

"Where's my Bobby?" Steve called out as they walked inside.

No answer.

"C'mon, kiddo. I want you to meet someone."

Still no answer.

Steve wondered how Victoria would react to the boy. Some women tensed up. Others ignored him. A few were frightened, but who could blame them? A romantic evening does not usually end with an eleven-year-old boy crouched at the foot of your bed, barking like a dog.

Victoria took inventory of Steve's living room, decorated in Early Fraternity House. A coffee table made from a surfboard. A poster of quarterback Dan Marino. A sculpture, if that's what you call it when you crush several hundred beer cans and shape them into the torso of a naked woman. Newspapers and magazines littered a black leather sofa that looked like it had been left out in the rain. All in all, the home of an overgrown adolescent, she decided.

Without warning, a flash of movement, and a small thin figure dashed from behind window drapes and dived onto the sofa. The camouflage gear was gone, and the boy wore only undershorts.

"There you are," Steve said.

Bobby tucked his knees under his chin, scrunched into a corner of the sofa, and rocked back and forth. He was so skinny that his protruding ribs looked like the struts of a sailboat under construction. His long hair needed cutting, and his black glasses were smudged. His feet were bare, and his head was tilted sideways so that one ear nearly touched a shoulder. A sudden pang struck Victoria. The boy seemed mentally disabled. Maybe physically, too.

"Bobby, this is Victoria Lord," Steve said.

"Hello, Bobby," Victoria said cheerfully, trying to put the boy at ease. She walked to the sofa and extended a hand, but the boy shrank farther into the cushions.

"Bobby doesn't like to be touched," Steve said, tightening the towel around his waist. In the light, Victoria noticed he kept in shape. Good pecs and shoulders. She looked away, wishing he'd get dressed.

"Victoria's my friend," Steve said.

For the sake of the child, she decided not to contradict him.

"She's not going to take you away," Steve continued in a gentle voice he never employed in court. "You remember what I told you about her?"

"She's a rich bitch-kitty with a wicked tongue," Bobby said, matter-of-factly.

"Isn't that sweet?" Victoria said, forcing a smile.

"Uncle Steve said something else, too." The boy's voice grew deeper: "She's pretty and smart and the best rookie lawyer I've ever seen."

Surprised, Victoria turned to Steve. "You said that?"

"Bobby only speaks the truth. He couldn't tell a lie if he wanted to."

"What an odd couple you make."

"And he said you don't have Rudnicks," the boy added.

"That's enough, Bobby," Steve said.

"Rudnicks?" She'd never heard the word.

"Sneakers," Steve said. "Like Reeboks."

"No they're not," Bobby said.

Victoria shot Steve a look, but he wouldn't give anything away. "Bobby's a very special kid," he said, pride in his voice.

"I'm just a spaz who's good at stuff nobody cares about."

"I'm sure you're much more than that," Victoria said.

A voice interrupted them. "You coming back to bed, Steve?"

Coming from a hallway was a young woman with long, dark hair. She looked familiar to Victoria, who was distracted, perhaps because the woman wore nothing but gold hoop earrings and a black beaded thong. Her breasts were round and full, her nipples pointed inward, like slightly crossed eyes. Now Victoria had two chests not to stare at.

"Oops," the woman said, trying to cover her breasts with hands too small for the task.

"*Those* are Rudnicks," Bobby said, pointing at the woman's chest.

"Oh, Ms. Lord," the woman said. "I didn't know . . ."

Of course. Sofia Hernandez. The court reporter

with the peekaboo blouse, the available phone number . . . and the large boobs.

"Hello, Sofia," Victoria said, then turned to Steve. "Maybe I should go."

"Hang on a second." He was headed down the hallway toward the bedroom.

Again Bobby dropped his voice into a perfect impersonation of his uncle's: "Dr. Harold Rudnick is a skilled plastic surgeon, a diplomat in the Academy. His trademark is a full contour of the breast, rotund without being pendulous. If the plaintiff wanted anything but the traditional Rudnick rack, she should have informed the doctor."

"Word for word from Steve's closing argument," Sofia told Victoria, her arms folded under her own rotund Rudnicks. "He got me a free boob job just for being the court reporter. You want, I bet Steve could get you a discount."

What was the polite reply to such an offer? Victoria didn't know.

"I mean, yours got a nice shape," Sofia continued. "You just need some size."

I'm on a strange planet in a distant galaxy. How did I get here?

Steve came back into the room, carrying Victoria's missing shoe and wearing sweatpants, thank God. He tossed a man's shirt to Sofia.

"The old Rudnicks were silicone," Bobby said. "Some funky chunky neurotoxins."

Victoria wished they would change the subject. Sofia slipped into the shirt but didn't button it. She looked like one of those magazine ads that seemed to suggest: *Sex was grand, let's drink some vodka.*

"Methyl ethyl ketone," Bobby continued. "Cyclohexanone, acetone, polyvinyl chloride, xylene, ethyl acetate, benzene—"

"Stop showing off," Steve said.

"Kid's brilliant," Sofia said. "Sometimes I wish I was an idiot savant."

"I'm not an idiot, you twat," Bobby said.

"Bobby! That's an ugly, ugly word," Sofia said.

"No it's not," Bobby said. " 'Twat. Noun, seventeenth century. Slang for vulva, related to *thwaite*, meaning forest clearing.' "

"You've memorized the dictionary?" Victoria asked.

"Not all of it. Wanna play the name game?"

"I don't know how."

"Give him a famous name," Steve said.

"George W. Bush," Victoria said.

The boy squinted behind his thick lenses and chewed his lip. Then he smiled for the first time, revealing two rows of shiny braces. "HE GREW BOGUS!"

"Good one," Steve said.

"It's called an angiogram," Sofia said.

"Anagram," Bobby corrected.

"How did you do that?" Victoria asked.

"Letters float around in my head, and I catch them. Give me another name."

"Monica Lewinsky," Victoria said.

Bobby fidgeted a moment, then said, "INSANE MILKY COW."

"Wow," Victoria said.

Steve sat down on the sofa. "Bobby suffered sensory deprivation—"

"When Mom locked me in a dog cage for, like, a year," Bobby said.

"Oh, God," Victoria said.

"Bobby's left brain sort of shut down," Steve said. "Limbic memory, logical and sequential thinking. But his right brain took off. Striatal memory, habit and procedural thinking."

"I can memorize stuff," Bobby said.

"We've been reading a lot of medical journals together," Steve said.

"We're best buds," Bobby said. "I'm gonna live with Uncle Steve until I'm old enough to hook up with Jenna Jameson."

"Is she from the neighborhood?" Victoria asked.

"Duh."

"She's an actress," Steve said.

"I don't think I've seen her movies," Victoria said.

"*Jennatilia,*" Bobby said. "*Lip Service. Cum One, Cum All.*"

"I should be going," Victoria said.

"Will you come back?" Bobby asked.

"Now, there's a first." Steve tousled Bobby's hair and looked at the boy with genuine warmth. Gone was the smart-ass grin, the wiseguy guile. At home, with his nephew, Solomon was a different man, Victoria thought.

On the sofa, the boy swiveled up onto his knees and held up his right hand toward Victoria, fanning out his fingers.

"Son-of-a-gun," Steve said. "He wants to touch hands."

Victoria raised her right hand and they touched palms and fingers.

"Like with Mom," Bobby said. "Except no window."

"Window?" Victoria asked, bewildered.

"Jail visitors' room," Steve interpreted. "When

Bobby was little and his mom was doing time, they'd touch each side of the glass."

Victoria didn't want to embarrass Bobby by asking about his mother's incarceration. Behind his glasses, there was a sadness and vulnerability in his eyes.

"Please come back," Bobby said.

"If it's okay with your uncle," she said.

"Anytime."

"So long, Solomon," Victoria said. "Bobby, you're a wonderful kid. Sofia, nice seeing you and your Rudnicks."

"You bet," Sofia said.

Steve walked Victoria to the door. "Good luck on the case. If you need any advice, just call."

Solomon seemed sincere, Victoria thought, stepping into the humid night, heading for her car. What was that she was feeling, her emotions as tangled as raveled wool? A tinge of disappointment, maybe. She was going to miss the sparks that crackled off their crossed swords. She had the strange sense of something ending without ever having begun.

"Victoria, wait," Steve called out, hurrying down the flagstone path after her.

For a reason she couldn't fathom, excitement buzzed inside her like a bee against a windowpane. What did he want?

Steve handed her a snakeskin Gucci pump. "You forgot this," he said, then walked back into his house and closed the door.

SOLOMON'S LAWS

3.   I will never take a drink until ~~sundown~~ . . .
     ~~two o'clock~~ . . . ~~noon~~ . . . I'm thirsty.

Twelve

THE BIRD-DOGGING, CLIENT-RUSTLING CASE POACHER

Maybe she'd judged him too quickly, Victoria thought the morning after her visit to Solomon's house. Sure, in court, he was a gunslinger, taking potshots at anything that moved. But at home, he displayed something else altogether. Besides his pecs, she meant.

For all Solomon's flaws, he clearly loved his nephew, and the boy adored him. So few men these days were good candidates for fatherhood. If Solomon could only cure several dozen obnoxious traits, maybe he'd be a decent catch for someone.

Victoria was thinking these thoughts as she drove under a canopy of banyan trees along Old Cutler Road on her way to Katrina Barksdale's house. Giving it some gas, she passed a Gulliver Prep bus, a reckless maneuver on the two-lane road that meandered along the coastline. But time was of the essence, as lawyers were inclined to say. The Grand Jury was in session this morning. Word had leaked out that Katrina would be indicted for murder by Happy Hour. Victoria needed to sign her up and prep her for the forthcoming arrest and booking.

Still rehashing last night, she realized that Solomon had surprised her with something else, too. He'd graciously backed off the Barksdale case. Maybe he wasn't a total shark, after all. Now that she thought of it, there had been other moments when he showed a human side. Hadn't he defended her to Ray Pincher? *"She's gonna be really good if you don't squeeze the life out of her."*

And there was Bobby repeating what his uncle had said. *"She's pretty and smart and the best rookie lawyer I've ever seen."*

So, upon rehearing, she reconsidered the case of Stephen Solomon, Esq. She'd been too harsh with him. She knew she could be abrasive. Maybe she brought out his worst behavior with her own. Next time she ran into Solomon, she promised herself, she'd apologize and make amends.

As she turned on Casuarina Concourse, her mind settled on the business of the day—*State v. Barksdale*—and Solomon had no part in it. Would the indictment be for first-degree murder? What was the evidence of premeditation? What was the motive? Which led to another thought, more philosophical than legal. Just why do spouses kill, anyway? It all seemed so foreign to her. Solomon said he had tried more than two dozen murder cases, and now, for a moment, she wished she had handled at least one.

She wanted to appear confident with Katrina, but tension started to creep up her spine. She pictured Ray Pincher holding a press conference just in time for the evening news. Whipping up the media like a lion tamer at the circus. Maybe she should hire a PR firm. Hold her own press conference. Would that even be ethical? She had no framework for a high-publicity trial.

As she headed toward the bay, a soft breeze rustled the fronds on the towering Royal Palms in the grassy median. She passed a dozen postmodern houses, asymmetric concrete boxes gleaming in the morning sun. At the end of the block, sitting on a promontory surrounded on three sides by water, was Casa Barksdale. Victoria drove through an open wrought-iron gate, wended past bubbling bronze fountains, and stopped in front of a seventeenth-century Italian palazzo . . . built in 1998. Her mother, who always fancied ruffles and flourishes, would love this place. A sprawling estate of courtyards and loggias, arches and gazebos, curlicues and ornate designs. Inside were marble stairwells and terrazzo floors, dark wood wainscoting and plaster crown molding. Behind the main house, facing the waterway that opened directly to the bay, a lap pool with a mosaic pattern floor, and a keystone deck. At the tiled dock, the *Kat's Meow,* a custom Bluewater yacht.

Victoria had been here for several charity events—cocktails and canapés on the deck under an air-conditioned tent. At each, Charles and Katrina had walked hand in hand, moving from guest to guest, offering small talk and thank-yous for helping the zoo or symphony or book fair. Had they gone upstairs later, stripped out of their party duds, and hauled out the kinky paraphernalia?

She'd come to the parties with Bruce, of course. Funny, thinking of him just now. Bruce and kinky paraphernalia didn't usually occupy the same thoughts. Solomon hadn't been far off. Sex with Bruce was fine, though predictable. If they didn't swing from a trapeze, so what? She had no complaints, even if the word that sometimes came to her mind during Bruce's exertions was "workmanlike." He expelled his breaths in short and steady puffs, as though running the marathon. And like a distance runner, he had stamina. So much, she was often sore by the ten-mile mark.

She had tried a few tactics to speed him up. A tongue in the ear merely tickled him and slowed him down. Changing positions, searching for a new friction point, didn't work either. But marathon runners were preferable to sprinters, to say nothing of guys who couldn't get out of the blocks. Besides, she could teach him, could harness that engine. Bruce so far exceeded Minimum Husband Standards in every other respect, sex was simply not a problem.

As Victoria approached the front door, she straightened her skirt. She'd dressed in one of her favorite work outfits. A Zanella double-breasted, wide-collared brown pinstripe jacket with a matching A-line skirt that fell below the knee. A simple dark brown silk blouse underneath with sensible—if obscenely costly—Prada pumps, a single strap at the ankle. Only the shoes had been purchased new. The rest, which would have cost at least twelve hundred dollars retail, she'd bought for a fifth of that at the consignment shop in Surfside.

She carried a suede briefcase that held a Retainer Agreement she had typed herself. It would formalize her hiring and set her fee. She'd left the amount blank. How much should it be? Enough to pay off the student loans, rent an office, print stationery and business cards, pay a secretary, and still have something left in the bank.

She approached a ten-foot-high door with a scroll design that made her think of a Spanish monastery. She rang the doorbell, and in a moment a Honduran housekeeper, a short squat woman in a white uniform, opened the door. *"Te están esperando, señorita."*

They're waiting for you. Victoria's Spanish was passable. In Miami, it had to be. But is that what the housekeeper had said? *They?*

Her pumps clicking on the mosaic terrazzo of the foyer, Victoria followed the woman. They passed a library with thousands of books, many rare first editions. Charles Barksdale had been both a serious collector and a serious reader and often quoted the classics. Next came the billiard room, and the living room, with its huge Italian stone fireplace. Then out through double doors and into a landscaped courtyard with a covered loggia. She heard the soft gurgle of water from a fountain of spitting cherubs. But another sound, too. A man's laugh. The robust, jovial laugh of a car salesman who's just talked you into that options package you didn't really need. The laugh sounded just like . . .

No, it couldn't be.

They rounded the fountain, and there he was, sitting at a redwood table. Steve Solomon, the sleazy, conniving son-of-a-bitch. He wore a blue sport coat with gold buttons over a pink polo shirt and white slacks.

Gold buttons, pink shirt, white slacks!

Like some banker from Greenwich at the yacht club. Sitting next to him was Katrina Barksdale, laughing with the trill of a mockingbird. Having too damn much fun for a woman about to be indicted.

And check out the lipstick-red, low-cut, one-shoulder spandex halter. The slit skirt was white and low on the hips, exposing her bare, tanned midriff at the top and a lot of thigh below. The shoes were strappy slingbacks, and the toenails were the same color as the halter. No, this would not do for booking.

"Vic-tor-ia," Katrina sang out. "Join us!"

Katrina's makeup was a little heavy for a Monday morning. Her raven hair cascaded over her shoulders and stopped at the top of her creamy white breasts. It gave her the overall look of a hot fudge sundae.

As Victoria approached, Katrina crossed her long legs, and the slit slid higher up her thigh. "Victoria, we were just talking about you."

"Oh, really?" Victoria forced a smile that stopped before it got to her eyes.

She knew that Katrina had started life as Margaret Katherine Gustafson in Coon Rapids, Minnesota. Not that she hid her background. On the contrary, Katrina bragged about each step up. She had twirled flaming batons at halftime at St. Cloud State football games, then took a snow princess act onto skates in a traveling Ice Capades show. According to the bitchy set at La Gorce Country Club, Katrina had supplemented her wages by twirling other batons at night in various hotel rooms along the tour. Then a feathers-and-boobs skating show in Las Vegas, where she met the newly widowed Charles Barksdale, and it was love at first double axel. For him, at least. Victoria preferred to believe that Katrina loved Charles, too, but when a hardscrabble young woman marries an older, wealthier man, questions are raised. Pincher would certainly raise them.

"How clever of you to team up with Stephen,"

Katrina said. "He was just telling me about all his exciting trials."

This couldn't be happening, Victoria thought. She half expected a low-flying gull to drop another load of shit on her.

"Hello, partner." Steve popped up and pulled out a chair. The perfect gentleman. The perfect, bird-dogging, client-rustling, case-poaching gentleman. Just when she was starting to feel all warm and fuzzy, he had sandbagged her.

Dammit, how could I have been so stupid!

"Iced tea?" Steve asked, reaching for the pitcher even as he slid the chair beneath her. "If my taste buds are in tune, it's passion fruit."

"Passion fruit it is," Katrina said. "You have a good tongue, Stephen."

Good tongue? Did she really say that?

"But perhaps you both want something stronger," Katrina said.

Even on the precipice of jail, she hadn't forgotten her Gables Estates etiquette. Victoria forced herself to remain calm. "Iced tea's fine."

"Stephen?" Katrina asked.

"I usually don't imbibe until sundown," he said. Putting on airs.

"Somewhere in the world, it's got to be dark." Katrina's voice swirled like wine in crystal.

"In that case, a single-malt Scotch, if you've got it."

"How's a twenty-year-old Glenmorangie?"

"Like a Sunday stroll through the heather," he purred. "Three fingers neat ought to do me."

Katrina smiled coquettishly and called for the housekeeper. Victoria gave Steve a look that could leave second-degree burns, then asked: "So what have I missed?"

"Stephen was telling me about your new partnership," Katrina said.

"Was he now?"

"Solomon and Lord," Katrina said. "It has cachet, no?"

"Cachet, yes," Steve said, and Katrina giggled like a schoolgirl.

"And what have you told Stephen?" Victoria asked her, trying not to exhale the steam she felt rising from deep inside.

"Everything. What happened that night. And other nights. He'll fill you in."

"I can hardly wait."

"Believe me," Katrina said, "some of the details make me blush."

How could we tell through all that Deep Cover Number Nine?

"For a guy his age, Charlie had some appetite." Katrina's laugh jangled like a pocketful of coins.

The widow Barksdale seemed to be handling her bereavement quite well, Victoria thought.

"The night it happened," Katrina continued, "Charlie had this stomach virus, and I thought no way he'd want to fool around. But he hauled out the latex and leather and popped a hundred milligrams of Viagra. I mean, there was no stopping the guy."

"I wonder if I could talk to my partner for a moment," Victoria said, resting her hand on Steve's, then digging her fingernails deep into the underside of his wrist.

"Don't be long," Katrina said, winking at Steve.

Victoria dragged Steve to his feet and led him to

the dock. They stopped in the shadow cast by the flying bridge of the *Kat's Meow*.

"What do you think you're doing?" Victoria meant to whisper but it came out like a hiss from a punctured tire.

"Interviewing our client."

"*My* client."

"I think she likes me."

"She'd like a Great Dane if it had balls."

"This is for your own good, Victoria. You need me on this."

"You lied to me! Last night you said, 'It's all yours.' "

"I semi-lied. It's half yours."

"Just when I was starting to think you were almost human."

"Really? Thanks."

He seemed genuinely moved, like the nicest thing anyone ever said to him was that he wasn't just a lump of useless protoplasm.

"I'm sure we'll work great together," he said.

"Forget it. I'm reporting you to the Bar."

"Be sure to tell them you misled Katrina about your trial experience. Naughty. Very naughty."

"Are you threatening me?"

"I'm trying to get you to redirect your anger. Think how good it would feel to beat Pincher in court."

"Almost as good as it would feel to see you disbarred."

"When I said you had the makings of a great lawyer—"

"It was a con, a pickup line."

"It was the truth."

"Forget it. I can't work with you."

"Too late. Katrina already wrote a check. Payable to Solomon and Lord."

"There's no such firm. Never will be."

Steve looked back toward the courtyard and gave Katrina a little wave. "Okay. We're a one-case firm. Win, lose, or draw, we split up. But for now . . ."

"No way. I'll tell Kat you're an impostor and a shyster."

"We'll look like clowns. Neither of us will get the case."

"You bastard. You low-life, bullshit-slinging bastard!"

"Go ahead. Get it out of your system."

They were at the edge of the dock, the huge yacht looming over them. A three-foot metal gaff was mounted on hooks attached to a piling. She could grab it, bash his skull, and push him into the water. When he tried to crawl out, she'd clobber him. Again and again. Watch him slip under in a mess of splintered bone and bubbling blood. Justifiable homicide. No jury would convict her.

"Trust me," he said. "Someday you'll thank me."

"Someday I'll kill you."

"Like it or not, we're attached at the hip."

Furious, she spun around so she wouldn't have to look at him. She needed a plan. She could torpedo him, no doubt about it. But what would Katrina think? That she didn't have her shit together. Solomon was right, damn him. If she opened her mouth, they'd both lose the case.

She wheeled back and faced him. "Katrina really wrote a check?"

Smiling like a lizard on a sunny rock, Steve patted

his jacket pocket. "It's right here. Ten thousand dollars."

"Ten thousand? For a murder case? Are you kidding? It's got to be six figures."

"Sure, it should be. But Barksdale's kids have filed suit against Katrina for wrongful death, tied up all the money. She's got hardly anything in her own name."

"She's got more than ten thousand."

"Jeez, one day in private practice, you're greedy already. Look, we'll get a million dollars' worth of publicity, and if we win, the money gets freed up and we get paid."

"I can't buy groceries with publicity."

"Why do you rich people worry so much about money?"

"I'm not rich, you jerk."

"But your clothes."

"Consignment shops."

"And jewelry?"

"My mother's castoffs."

"Princeton? Yale?"

"Scholarships and loans."

"Oh," he said, downcast. "And I was hoping you could front the expenses for expert witnesses, lab tests, consultant fees."

"You are so totally dim. I'm broke."

"All the more reason for you to tag along."

"I don't tag along."

"Okay, you take the law, I take the facts."

"I'll consider it if we split fees, sixty-forty my way," she said.

"Sixty-forty, *my* way. I'm providing you with free space in my penthouse office."

"You have a penthouse?"

"Top floor. Of a two-story building."

"I'll bet it's a real showplace," she said. "Fifty-five, forty-five, my way."

"Fifty-fifty. You can use my secretary. She types a hundred words a minute. In Spanish. In English, she spells everything phonetically, so you gotta really proof it."

"She won't mind the extra work?"

"Doesn't matter. It's a term of her parole that she have a job."

"Great," she said, feeling her temples beginning to throb. "Just great."

"So, we have a deal?"

She thought a moment before saying: "Not until you agree to some ground rules."

"Whatever you say."

"None of your macho bullshit. You treat me as an equal."

"You got it."

"We don't do anything unethical."

"Of course not."

"And none of your sophomoric cracks about my sex life."

"Or lack thereof?"

"That's what I'm talking about," she said.

"Just testing the boundaries. So—partners?"

"For one case."

"Fine. Let's shake."

She extended a hand, but he didn't shake. Instead, he fanned out his fingers, just as Bobby had done. She paused another moment—dammit, this sucked, but what choice did she have?—raised her hand, and pressed it against his.

Steve looked into her eyes as their hands pressed together, wondering just how long she would hold the position. First time they'd ever touched, and he sure as hell wasn't going to be the one to break away.

She caught the look in his eyes and pulled her hand back.

Suddenly, a churning noise in the water startled them both. The engines on the *Kat's Meow* were firing up, and water churned at the stern.

"Hey there!" a voice came from above. "Sorry if I spooked you."

On the flying bridge, a sun-baked man in a white shirt with epaulets stood at the wheel. In his midthirties, he sported a mustache and wore aviator sunglasses and a blue ball cap. "Wanna give me a hand with the lines?"

"No problem," Steve said. He walked to the front cleat, unwrapped the bow line, and tossed it aboard.

Katrina called from the courtyard: "Where you going, Chet?"

"The marina. Carbon monoxide gauge is on the fritz. Be back before sundown." He looked down at Steve, who was untying the stern line. "She's a beauty, huh?"

For a second, Steve thought he was talking about Katrina.

"Sixty-four feet with a hull draft of only twenty-three inches," the man said.

Oh.

"Sleeps eight. Or twelve if you're *real* good friends." The man laughed, and Steve tossed the stern line onto the deck.

"You live aboard?" Victoria asked, and Steve smiled. He was about to ask the same thing.

"Captain's quarters," Chet said.

"Were you here the night Charles died?" she asked. That was Steve's next question, too. He'd been right about Victoria. She had great instincts. "Mr. . . . ?"

"Manko. Call me Chet. I was sleeping in my state-room. Mrs. B called me right away. I got there even before the paramedics, but Mr. B was already dead."

"We're going to need to talk to you, Mr. Manko," Victoria said.

Steve smiled, liking the sound of the "we."

"Not a problem," Manko said. "I'm always around." Then he waved to Katrina, gave the throttle some juice, expertly pulled away from the dock, and headed toward the open bay.

"You're thinking he's a corroborating witness?" Steve asked.

"I'm hoping," she said.

"Me, too. Because the other choice is accomplice."

On the loggia, the Honduran housekeeper was back with their drinks and three uninvited guests. Two plainclothes detectives and Ray Pincher.

"Already," Victoria said.

"Let's go to work, partner," Steve said.

They hurried back just as Pincher was telling Katrina that the Grand Jury had indicted her for first-degree murder, and she had the right to remain silent.

"Our client invokes all her rights," Steve called out.

"Solomon and Lord. On the same side?" Pincher said, a twinkle in his eye. "This is going to be fun."

"What does he mean by that?" Katrina asked.

"Shh," Steve said. "You're remaining silent."

"We'll want a private entrance to the jail for booking," Victoria said to Pincher.

"Not necessary," Steve said.

"No advance word to the media," Victoria said. "We don't want a circus."

"Circus is fine," Steve said. "Cirque du Soleil even better."

"Mrs. Barksdale will need twenty minutes to get dressed," Victoria said.

"Make it an hour," Steve said.

Pincher beamed and turned to one of the detectives. "Del, I think we could charge admission to this one."

Looking worried but retaining her composure, Katrina stood and started toward the house. "I'd excuse myself," she said to Pincher, "but my lawyers instructed me to remain silent."

Steve pulled Victoria aside and whispered, "Go help her. You know what clothes to pick out?"

"Something subdued," Victoria said. "Maybe a Carolina Herrera pantsuit."

"Wrong," he said. "A slinky dress, maybe one of those leopard prints, something off the shoulder. Show some boobs. And those stockings with holes."

"Fishnets?" Victoria was shocked.

"Yeah. And red lipstick, really red."

"You want our client to look like a hooker?"

"I want her to look like a farm girl, an innocent naif from the Midwest who was corrupted by the dirty old man she married. He twisted her into his perverted sex slave."

"You think we can sell that?"

Steve's tone of righteous indignation was a rehearsal for the jury. "How dare the state accuse this woman of murder when all she did was try to satisfy her husband's deviant demands? What is she guilty of, besides giving too much of herself, unaware of the dangers?"

"That's our defense?"

"For now, it's all we've got," Steve said.

IN THE CIRCUIT COURT OF THE ELEVENTH JUDICIAL CIRCUIT IN AND FOR MIAMI-DADE COUNTY, FLORIDA—FALL TERM, 2005

INDICTMENT
MURDER FIRST DEGREE
FLA. STAT 782.04(1) & 775.087

STATE OF FLORIDA
VS.
KATRINA BARKSDALE

IN THE NAME AND BY THE AUTHORITY OF THE STATE OF FLORIDA:

The Grand Jurors of the State of Florida, duly called, impaneled and sworn to inquire and true presentment make in and for the body of the County of Miami-Dade, upon their oaths, present that on or about the 16th day of November 2005, within the County of Miami-Dade, State of Florida, KATRINA BARKSDALE did unlawfully and feloniously kill a human being, to wit: CHARLES BARKSDALE, from a premeditated design to effect the death of the person killed, by strangling the said CHARLES BARKSDALE with a weapon, to wit: a leather device, in violation of Fla. Stat. 782.04(1) and 775.087, to the evil example of all others in like cases, offending and against the peace and dignity of the State of Florida.

Mitchell Kaplan
Foreperson of the Grand Jury

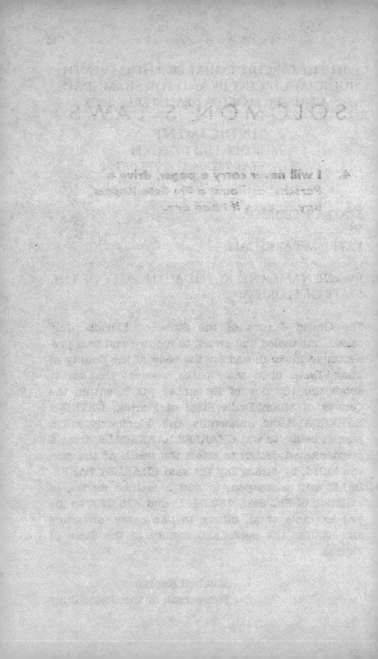

SOLOMON'S LAWS

4. I will never carry a pager, drive a
    Porsche, or flaunt a Phi Beta Kappa
    key . . . *even if I had one.*

Thirteen

DOODADS AND DILDOS

"You're saying Charles Barksdale forced Katrina to have kinky sex?" Victoria shouted above the wind.

"Not physical coercion," Steve answered. "More like emotional pressure. 'If you love me, you'll do this.' And financial pressure. 'Look at everything I've given you.' Plus the trump card: 'If you won't wear a strap-on, if you won't whip my ass, if you won't do bondage, I'll dump you and find someone who will.' "

Victoria was dubious. "Kat told you all that?"

"What?" Steve was dialing through the static, searching for a radio station. Top down on his ancient Cadillac, they were headed across the MacArthur Causeway from Miami to South Beach, the car spewing contrails of oily smoke. In the backseat, Bobby was speed-reading a coroner's textbook, *Medicolegal Investigation of Death*. Victoria had glanced at an autopsy photo and turned away.

The Solomon Boys, as she'd started thinking of them, had picked her up at her condo, Steve saying they could work on the drive to the office. Taking one look at the convertible, she knew her hair would be wrecked in two minutes. Always a good soldier, she didn't complain.

It was the day after they'd signed up Katrina, who was immediately booked, fingerprinted, and jailed for first-degree murder. There were a hundred things to do, starting with prepping for the bail hearing. Victoria had not had time to interview their new client, so she was forced to rely on Steve's recitation of what Katrina had told him. Naturally, he'd taken no notes. Had she been running the show, they'd have tape-recorded every syllable, and by now they'd have the transcripts indexed and color-coded. When she told Steve this, he smiled tolerantly and said that at the beginning of a case it was better to keep a client's memory flexible.

"Flexible," she thought. A slippery lawyer's word.

She questioned whether this shotgun marriage was going to work. Sure, Solomon had all that experience. But he was so aggressive, so reckless, he would lead them into untold disasters. She was still furious at him for stealing her client, but she had vowed to put up with him. She needed this case to get on her feet, start building her practice. As far as learning trial tactics from Solomon, she'd study his every move, then do the exact opposite.

He must have found the radio station he wanted, because he stopped fiddling with the dial, and Robert Palmer was singing that a woman was simply irresistible. Victoria yelled over the music and the wind: "Did Kat tell you Charles would dump her if she didn't do what he wanted?"

"Not in those words. I filled in a few gaps for her."

"You coached her?"

"I amplified her responses."

"You make fine distinctions."

"That's what lawyers do, Victoria."

Victoria, she thought. No more "Vickie." At least he was starting to show her respect. Crossing the causeway, she looked enviously at a cruise ship steaming out Government Cut toward the Atlantic. The passengers were waving at a party fishing boat following in their wake. The air tasted of salt, and the wind whipped at her hair.

"You're saying Charles pressured Kat into choking him as part of their marital relations," she said.

"Marital relations? Who talks like that?"

Victoria motioned toward the backseat. "I do, in front of a child."

Bobby said: "So they had a freaky way of doing the bone dance. Big deal."

The light turned red at the entrance to the Fisher Island ferry, and Steve pulled to a stop, the Eldo's brakes screeching like the call of a pelican. The morning sun was still low in the southeastern sky but warm as a mitten on their faces. Just across the channel rose hundreds of multimillion-dollar condos protected by a moat from the real world. Directly in front of them was a Metro bus, its rear billboard advertising free consultations with a smiling, mustachioed lawyer. *Hablamos Español.*

Victoria fanned away the diesel fumes. "Could you put the top up?"

"A/C doesn't work," Steve said.

She made a face but didn't say a word.

"Sorry if I don't drive a Porsche like Bigby," Steve said.

"Don't start."

"I also don't carry a pager or wear a Phi Beta Kappa key like the Bigster."

"You don't have a Phi Beta Kappa key," Bobby piped up.

"Thanks for the support, kiddo," Steve said.

He fooled with the radio again, picked up what sounded like a bugle playing reveille, and Bobby yelled happily: "Long Shot Kick De Bucket!"

"A classic," Steve said as the song began.

Victoria listened a moment, something about weeping and wailing and getting in the race, but it made no sense to her.

"Don't you like reggae?" Steve asked.

"I can never understand the patois."

"I could teach you. It's the language of sugarcane fields, the music of repression and rebellion."

"You see yourself as a rebel? A lawyer with a machete?"

He shrugged. "I just like the music."

The light turned green, Steve gunned the engine, and the old Cadillac coughed and sputtered but managed to pull around the bus.

"Now, where was I?" Steve said.

"Sex," Bobby reminded him.

Victoria said: "Really, is this proper conversation for a young—"

"Bobby's cool with it," Steve interrupted. "So Katrina's dressed in leather chaps and a laced corset, and she ties Charlie spread-eagle on the bed. He's wearing a collar around his neck with two leather straps fastened to the bedposts. He increases the pressure on his neck by leaning back, decreases by leaning forward. The idea was to cut off his oxygen, increase the power of his orgasm."

"Asphyxiophilia," Bobby said. "I read about this guy who wrapped a wire around his willy, tied it to two teaspoons, put one in his butt, another in his mouth, all plugged to an electrical outlet. Guess what happened?"

"He caused the Northeast blackout of 2003," Steve said.

Bobby made a sound like bacon sizzling in a pan. "Elec-tro-cuted."

"Barksdale had something in his mouth, too. A latex dick."

"That's disgusting." Victoria wrinkled her nose.

"But relevant to our defense. Why?"

"Because he couldn't cry out with that doodad in his mouth," she answered.

"You mean dildo."

"Some female jurors might be offended by the word. I thought I'd soften it."

Soften it? God, did I really say that?

Steve laughed. "We're gonna be in Criminal Court, not on *Sesame Street.* Do you know how many words there are for 'penis'?"

"I know twenty-six," Bobby said. "One for every letter of the alphabet."

"Cool it, kiddo," Steve said.

"Anaconda. Beaver Buster. Corn Dog."

"Not now, Bobby."

"Dipstick. Earthworm. Frankfurter."

"Put a lid on it."

"Gherkin. Hose. Iron Rod. Joystick."

"I said that's enough," Steve ordered.

"And to think," Victoria said, "when I was in school, we only memorized the Gettysburg Address."

"Don't look at me," Steve said. "I didn't teach him that stuff."

"Kosher Pickle," Bobby said. "You taught me that one."

"That's part of your ethnic heritage. Look, it's okay if you screw around with us, but if you try that stuff with Dr. Kranchick, she's gonna think I'm a pervert, and you're gonna be bunking at the state hospital."

"Who's Dr. Kranchick?" Victoria said.

"Doris Kranchick," Bobby said. "RAKISH CORN DICK."

"I'm warning you," Steve said, then turned to Victoria. "Kranchick works for Family Services. She wants to take Bobby from me."

"Uncle Steve says we'll go to some desert island if the judge rules against us."

"What about just filing an appeal?" Victoria said.

"C'mon, let's stay focused," Steve said. "Barksdale is sprawled on the bed. Katrina performs her magic and gets him off. She unties his hands but leaves the collar on. Then she crawls out of bed and walks over to the wet bar."

"Why didn't she untie him then?"

"She says he was good for a second pop after a time-out. So she's pouring herself a drink at the bar when she hears something back on the bed. Charlie's thrashing around, this gurgling sound coming from his throat. She runs to him, sees the collar digging into his neck. It takes her a while to loosen the straps, and by the time she gets the collar off, he's not breathing. She calls nine-one-one. End of story."

Victoria processed the information as they headed east on Fifth Street, three blocks from the ocean.

They had left downtown Miami behind, its skyscrapers honeycombed with lawyers and bankers in their light winter wools, the streets in cool shadows from the buildings themselves. Everything was brighter here, the colors of the low-rise stucco buildings, the shorts and shirts of the people hauling coolers and lawn chairs to the beach. She was unexpectedly happy to be with the Solomon Boys, working together, a world away from the stifling confines of the Justice Building.

"Accidental strangulation following kinky sex?" she said. "You think the jury will swallow that?"

"I don't know, but I'm gonna rephrase your question for voir dire."

"You know what I mean. It sounds pretty far-fetched."

"Just because you and Bruce never try anything exotic—"

"Don't go there," she said sternly. "You have no idea what Bruce and I do."

"Give me all the details. I've got thirty seconds."

"Stop this car!"

"Aw, I'm just joking around."

"Stop right now!"

He pulled to the curb. A gray tern swooped close, bleating, *kerri, kerri, kerri,* sounding like a lovelorn suitor.

"What is it with you?" Victoria demanded, but didn't wait for an answer. "We were just starting to get along and you pull that shit. Sorry, Bobby."

"No problem," came the voice from the backseat.

"If we're going to work together, you've got to stop doing this."

"Okay. Okay."

"You have to control your Inner Jerk."

"I apologize. Now, let's move on."

"Not so quick," Victoria said. "Let's get to the root of this."

"There's no root."

"Let's look inside Steve Solomon."

"There's nothing there," he shot back.

"Be honest now." She leveled a gaze at him, detected a hint of fear in his eyes. Now, that was something new, she thought. Maybe he can handle an assertive woman in court, but get inside his personal space, he breaks out in hives. "Be honest, Solomon. Do you have a thing for me?"

"What!"

"Do you drift off to sleep with little fantasies? The two of us in the stacks at the law library?"

"I've never been in the law library."

"Are you writing my name on your legal pad, drawing hearts around it?"

"You're not my type, Lord."

"Why not? All brains and no Rudnicks?"

"Exactly. Go marry the Avocado King."

"Why shoot spitballs at me? What are the feelings you're not expressing?"

"At first I thought you were a royal pain. Rigid, arrogant, self-righteous. But with great legs. Thought I expressed all that pretty clearly."

"And now?"

"Now that we have to work together, I tolerate you."

"As long as that's all it is," she said.

"That's all."

"Good, then it's mutual," Victoria said.

Ten minutes later, Steve parked the car in an open lot, and they walked along Ocean Drive past the usual collection of sunburned tourists and skateboarding teens. It was a sunny day, with a steady breeze off the Atlantic. As they headed to his office, Steve tried to figure out what had just happened. Why *had* he taken those cheap shots? Why couldn't he just say what he felt?

Because you don't tell another man's fiancée that the air sizzles when she walks into the room and fizzles when she leaves.

Now, there was the painful truth. Even though he knew he was lousy at introspection, he dug deeper. Ever since learning Victoria was engaged, he'd been trying to convince himself that he wasn't attracted to her. Now he was going out of his way to piss her off. He felt like the awkward sixth grader, who, unable to talk to the prettiest girl in class, yanks her pigtails instead. And she'd just busted him on it.

"Be honest, Solomon. Do you have a thing for me?"

Nolo contendere. He would cop a plea, but only to himself. To Victoria, he would keep up the front, pretending he could barely tolerate her. He would never mention his feelings, and he surely wouldn't act on them. First, because it would be damaging to their working together. And second, because in an uncertain world, he was quite certain of one thing: Whatever he felt for Victoria Lord, she did not feel for him.

SOLOMON'S LAWS

5. I will never compromise my ideals to achieve someone else's definition of success.

Fourteen

SUCCESS VERSUS EXCELLENCE

"Me first," Bobby shouted, running ahead and ducking into a pink, two-story stucco building. It had been built in the 1930's but had none of the charm of Art Deco. No graceful curves or ornamental friezes. No oak floors or cathedral ceilings. The walls were made of plaster mixed with beach sand, and the caustic effect of the salt corroded the plumbing and wiring. As a result, the building was subject to power outages and overflowing toilets. A sign on the exterior read, "Les Mannequins."

Three young women, impossibly tall, impossibly thin, high-stepped out the front door. All three wore short shorts, cropped tees, and open-toed sandals with four-inch heels. "Hi, Steve," they cooed.

"Let me guess," Victoria said. "Your law clerks?"

"It's a modeling agency," Steve admitted.

"Really? And I thought it was the Supreme Court."

"All right, listen up, Lord. Getting to my office is like walking over hot coals. So whatever happens, just keep moving."

"Why?"

"You'll see." Steve took Victoria by the arm and hurried her through the door. In the lobby, two more young women—six-foot-tall twins with long, flaxen hair—stood at a counter studying contact sheets of headshots.

"Hey, Steve," they said in unison. "When are you—"

"Lexy. Rexy," Steve said, still on the move. "Not now."

"But you promised," Lexy said. Or maybe it was Rexy.

"You owe us," the other one said. "Remember?"

"I'm busy." He tried to hustle past them, but the two women, slender as straws, spun gracefully, despite their high-heeled slingbacks, and blocked his path. In spandex tube minidresses, one Day-Glo red, the other Day-Glo green, with long legs spread, the pair looked like twin Eiffel Towers decorated for Christmas.

"Do you know what parking's like on Ocean Drive?" Lexy asked.

"I know, I know," Steve said.

"So where are our handicap stickers?" Lexy asked.

"We had to walk three blocks today," Rexy said.

"In our Jimmy Choos," Lexy said.

"You're not handicapped." Steve pushed past the two women.

"Anorexia doesn't count?" Victoria said.

"Come on. My office—*our* office—is on the second floor." Steve tried to hurry her along. Bobby was already at the stairs.

"The penthouse," Victoria said. "I remember."

"Don't bust my chops, okay? I get free rent in exchange for handling the agency's legal problems.

Gotta do some work for the models, too. The trick is to get upstairs before they—"

"Steve, wait up!" A suntanned young woman in Lycra bicycle shorts and a sport bra approached.

"Later, Gina," Steve said. "I've got law business."

"So do I." Pouty-lipped and big-busted—Rudnicks, Victoria guessed—Gina had a China chop of coppery hair as bright as a new penny. She stuck out her left hand and showed off a diamond the size of an eyeball. "Paco asked me to marry him."

"Looks like you accepted," Steve said.

"For one night. Then I changed my mind. He's just another Euro-rich model-humper. Now the creep wants the ring back."

"Imagine the nerve."

"I don't have to give it back, do I?"

"How should I know?" Steve said.

Victoria interceded. "The general rule is that an engagement ring is a gift. So, even if there's no wedding, the woman keeps the ring."

"Look who got the book award in Contracts One," Steve said with mock admiration. "Gina, this is Victoria, my new law partner."

"Great," Gina said. "Will you be my lawyer if the prick sues me?"

"I should caution you, Gina," Victoria said in her lawyerly voice, "if you intended to break up ab initio, your fiancé could claim fraud and get the ring back."

"Ab what?" Gina asked.

Bobby said: "Ab initio. From the beginning. Like, did you always plan to rip off the guy like you did the fertilizer salesman who paid for your boobs?"

"You have a big mouth, Bobby," Gina said. Then she let out a little gasp and grabbed Victoria's left hand. "Omigod! Look at yours. It's gorgeous." She practically drooled on Victoria's emerald-cut diamond, propped up on four pedestals, with smaller diamonds running up two side channels. "I love the design. The baguettes are, like, I don't know, a shiny staircase, a pathway to heaven."

"Why would a man give a woman a ring like that," Steve asked, "when for a fraction of the money, he could buy a plasma TV?"

"Don't listen to him," Gina said. "He's the least romantic man I've ever slept with. And I've shagged some real turkeys."

"But look who's the biggest giblet of them all." Victoria's smile was as shiny as her diamond.

"Victoria, if you broke up with your fiancé, would you give the ring back?" Gina asked.

"I'm definitely going to marry Bruce, so it's a moot question."

"But what if something happened," Gina persisted, following them halfway up the stairs. "What if you caught him cheating?"

"I can't imagine Bruce doing anything like that," Victoria said.

"I can," Steve said. "In flagrante delicto with a curvaceous avocado."

"Or what if you got tired of him or found someone else?" Gina said.

"That," Victoria said, sounding profoundly confident, "would never, ever happen."

Victoria checked out Steve's waiting room like a detective at a crime scene. Faded plaster walls and flickering fluorescent lights. Client chairs covered in cracked vinyl but missing clients. A receptionist sat at her desk, and it was a good thing the phone wasn't ringing, because she wouldn't have answered it. The receptionist was a life-size inflatable doll that bore a striking resemblance to Pamela Anderson in a bikini. Her desk was littered with empty cartons of Chinese takeout and stacks of unopened mail. Most looked like bills.

Victoria had never seen a law office—or any office—quite like it. The carpet, which must have been an industrial gray when new, was spotted with coffee stains, and the few clean spots were threadbare. The air smelled of dust and mildew.

Okay, so she hadn't expected teak wainscoting, but this . . .

What a dump.

She tried to suppress what she was feeling. That she'd been conned. That Solomon was a small-time shyster, a low-rent—strike that—a *no*-rent, flimflam man.

Steve tried to look at his waiting room through Victoria's eyes. He had always thought of his office as understated, but now it seemed downright shabby. But dammit, material things weren't important to him. How could he explain that without sounding like a total loser? He wanted to tell her about his pro bono cases—clients with just causes and thin wallets—but it would sound so self-serving, so defensive, he just kept quiet.

From somewhere Victoria heard a grunt, then the clang of metal on metal.

"That you, Cece?" Steve asked.

A woman's voice rose from behind Pamela Anderson. "No, *jefe,* it's Sandra Day O'Connor."

In the space between Pamela Anderson's chair and the wall, a thickset woman in her early twenties lay flat on her back on a workout bench. As she raised a barbell, straining against the weight, cursing in Spanish—"*Ay, mierda!*"—the tattoo of a cobra on her beefy upper arm coiled and uncoiled.

She wore a sleeveless cropped tee and low-slung tattered jeans and had a cream-of-caramel complexion. Her neck seemed to be connected to her shoulders with thick steel cables, and her shoulders rippled with muscles. Her eyebrows had been plucked into diagonal slashes, one pierced by three metal studs, and she had a crown of curly, reddish-brown hair.

"*Maldito!*" the woman exhaled as she lowered the bar. "Who's gonna spot me?" Her accent was pure Little Havana.

Bobby hustled over to her. "Me, Cece."

"*Gracias,* brainiac."

Bobby kept his hands on the bar as the woman did two more reps, then, with a grunt, eased the bar down into its brackets. Still on her back, Cece looked up at Victoria and said: "*El Jefe*'s got no manners. I'm Cecilia Santiago."

"My personal assistant," Steve said.

"Personal slave is more like it. You that persecutor?"

"Ex-persecutor," she said. "Victoria Lord. Hello, Cecilia."

"Yeah, whatever."

"Hey, Cece," Steve said, "when you're done working on your pecs, could you schedule a press conference on the Barksdale case?"

"Is that ethical?" Victoria asked.

"Would F. Lee Bailey ask that question?"

"Probably not. He's been disbarred."

Cece vaulted to her feet. A printed message was visible on her cropped tee: *All Men Are Animals. Some Just Make Better Pets.* She had a second tattoo, a green sailfish, which seemed to burst from the top of her low-slung jeans and leap over her navel. "Yo, Lord. King Solomon tell you anything about me?"

"Not in any detail," Victoria replied, diplomatically.

"What I done was no big deal. Sort of like *choplifting.*"

"Right," Steve said. "You *choplifted* Enrique's Toyota."

"My boyfriend. He was screwing my cousin, Lourdes, behind my back. So I borrowed his car."

"You beat him up, then you drove his car off the boat ramp at Matheson Hammock."

"Not gonna 'criminate myself." Cece looked at Victoria with suspicion. "So now I gotta slave for two of you?"

"I'm sure we'll all get along fine," Victoria said, not believing it for a moment.

Cece ran her bloodred fingernails over her abs, contracted and relaxed the muscles. The sailfish wagged its tail. "Look, Lord, I don't make coffee. I don't take your Needless Markup designer shit to the cleaners, and I don't type. We cool?"

"Cece types," Steve contributed. "She just can't spell."

"It's my lexus," Gina said. "You fire me, I'll sue your ass off."

"You don't have dyslexia. You're just too lazy to use the spell check."

"Hey, Lord, hear that? He's saying Hispanics are lazy. I'm calling the EEOC."

"And I'm calling your probation officer," Steve said.

Victoria watched in amazement. She'd never seen such a lack of professionalism. How could she work in a place like this?

Cece laughed. "Good one, *jefe*."

"You, too, Cece."

They exchanged high fives, then bumped chests, like football players celebrating a touchdown.

Okay, so this was their routine, Victoria thought. First they trade barbs, then display affection. So now there were four people who seemed to care for Solomon. There was that old couple, Marvin and Teresa, who followed him around the courthouse; there was sweet, needy Bobby; and now this felonious, steroid-juiced secretary. What was his appeal, anyway?

Am I missing something? Or am I just too normal to belong to the Steve Solomon Fan Club?

"Okay, everyone to the inner sanctum," Steve said. "Let's talk about how to win a murder trial."

As Steve led his crew through a door into his private office, Victoria was aware of two sensations: the smell of rotten vegetables and what sounded like metal garbage cans banging against each other. Just below the grimy window, in a narrow alley, was a green Dumpster, horseflies buzzing around its open lid. Across the alley was a three-story apartment building, and on the nearest balcony, five bare-chested men beat sticks against metal pans and what looked like fifty-five-gallon oil drums.

"Trinidad steel band," Steve said.

"That's reassuring," she said. "I thought it was a prison riot."

To escape the stench and the percussion, Victoria moved toward a corner of the room where a bub-bling fish tank housed half a dozen rust-colored crus-taceans. "Let me guess. You poach lobsters in your spare time."

"You think too small."

"His client hijacks refrigerated trucks coming up from the Keys," Cece said.

Victoria scoped out the rest of the place. On one wall was a framed cartoon of a courtroom filled with water. The fins of two sharks were visible, cutting smoothly through the water, headed toward the judge. The caption read: "Counsel Approaching the Bench."

Sure, Solomon would relate to that.

Victoria was in purgatory. What had happened to her master plan? Five years of public service parlayed into a job in a prestigious firm, all leading to partner-ship and lifetime tenure. Or maybe a judgeship.

Judge Lord.

But here she was, inhaling the fumes from a Dumpster, her plans dashed, her career in shambles.

Looking at the cracked and soiled plaster walls, feeling a mixture of anger and regret, Victoria said:

"For a hotshot lawyer, Solomon, your office is . . ."
How could she put this delicately? "A real shit hole."

So there it was, Steve thought. Being compared to
the deep-carpet types downtown. Being compared to
Bigby, too, he supposed, with all that inherited
money. What were her values, anyway? If wealth and
status were her turn-ons, maybe it was better that she
was taken.

"That stuff important to you, Victoria? Marble on
the floor, mahogany on the walls?"

"For better or worse, that's how we measure success."

"Success should never be confused with excellence."

"Here we go again," Cece said. "He always uses
this shit to explain why my paycheck's late."

Steve walked to the lobster tank, picked up a stale
bagel from a dish, crumbled it, and dropped the
pieces into the water. He watched the crustaceans
crawl over each other, like fans after a Barry Bonds
home run. "Success is how other people judge you,"
he said. "Are you driving that Ferrari, buying that
house in Aspen? Excellence can't be measured in dollars. Ideals don't fit into a bank account. It's about
judging yourself. Have you lived up to your principles or have you sold out?"

"You have principles?" Victoria asked.

"I make up my own."

"Solomon's Laws," Cece said. "Every time he gets
a bright idea, I gotta write it down for *posteridad*."

"Write this down, Cece. 'I will never compromise

my ideals to achieve someone else's definition of success.' "

"Yeah, yeah, I got it."

"Sounds like you're making excuses for not earning enough money to buy a decent car and clean the carpets," Victoria said.

"He could make a shitload," Cece said, "if he wasn't the *santo patrón* of lost cases. You got a lousy case and no money, come on down. Haitian refugees want green cards, Miccosukees want their burial ground, migrant workers want fair pay. We take 'em all."

"I didn't know you did pro bono work," Victoria said.

Steve shrugged. "I do my share."

"And everybody else's," Cece said. "I don't let him advertise it, or every deadbeat in town would be in our waiting room."

"Solomon, you are full of surprises," Victoria said.

"Don't make a big deal out of it," he said.

"No, I mean it. I'm sorry."

"Yo, *jefe*," Cece said. "We gonna talk about the case or what? I gotta do my speed reps."

Steve sat on the edge of his desk. "Let's start with Charles Barksdale. Victoria, paint us a picture."

She took a breath. "He had a lot of interests," she began. "Art, literature, poetry. He was proud of his first editions. He was extremely well read. And he let everybody know it."

"How?"

She seemed reluctant to go on. Was Victoria Lord too refined, Steve wondered, to speak ill of the dead? That never troubled him. The deceased were the only people who couldn't sue you for slander.

"Sometimes, at a dinner party," she continued apologetically, "Charles would bring up some book by Proust or a Sylvia Plath poem, and you got the idea he'd just read it that day and shoehorned it into the conversation."

"So Barksdale was a phony? A pseudo-intellectual?"

"More like he had to show everybody he was the smartest guy at the table."

"Who cares what he read?" Cece said. "Did his bony-assed wife kill him?"

"Let's take a vote," Steve said. "Gut impressions. Who thinks Katrina murdered her husband?"

"Cooch wouldn't have the balls," Cece said.

"Okay, that's a not guilty. Bobby."

"*Ubi mel, ibi apes.*"

"Meaning?"

"Honey attracts bees."

"Meaning?" he repeated.

"She killed him for the money."

"One not guilty. One guilty." Steve turned to Victoria. "Partner?"

"I don't think we have enough facts," she said.

"Facts shmacks. What's your gut say?"

"I try not to go with my gut."

"I know. If you did, you wouldn't be marrying Mr. Guacamole."

"Don't take that shit from him," Cece said. "He talk that way to me, he wouldn't be able to feed himself."

"C'mon," Steve said. "There's a question pending. Guilty or innocent?"

After a moment, Victoria said: "I just don't see how Katrina could have done it. How do you live with a man, have breakfast with him every day, kiss him before he goes to the office, sleep with him every night, then kill him?"

"A vote for the goodness of human nature, a vote for innocence," Steve said.

"I'm hoping," Victoria said. "And what do you think?"

"She's our client," Steve said, "and she's relying on us for every breath she takes. If a hundred witnesses saw her shoot a man on Flagler Street at high noon, they're lying or nearsighted or insane. If the polygraph goes off the Richter when she professes love for old Charlie, the machine is on the fritz. If the forensics all point to her, they've been tainted by mendacity or incompetence. She's our client, which means she's wrongfully accused, an innocent victim of a system run amuck. We hold her key to the jailhouse door, and we, my friends, shall swing that door open and set her free."

SOLOMON'S LAWS

6. **Lie to your priest, your spouse, and the
    IRS, but always tell your lawyer the truth.**

Fifteen

SKELETONS IN THE CABANA

Victoria was trying to decipher the first autopsy report she'd ever read in the first murder case she'd ever handled.

"What are Tardieu's spots?" she asked.

"Pinpoint hemorrhages on the face," Steve said. "Common in strangulation." He was leaning back in his chair, flipping the pages of a magazine.

"Charles Barksdale's thyroid cartilage was intact. Shouldn't it have been fractured?"

Steve didn't look up from the magazine. "Maybe in a hanging, but not a slow, steady pressure like we've got here."

Victoria was starting to wonder about Steve's work ethic. He'd spent half an hour drinking Cuban coffee, eating guava pastries, and reading the *Miami Herald*, laughing out loud at Carl Hiaasen's column. He'd spoken on the phone with a man he called Fat Louie, saying, "Gimme the over for a nickel on the Dolphins–Jets." And for the past twenty minutes, he'd been thumbing through *Sports Illustrated*, and it wasn't even the swimsuit issue. She longed to say,

"Get to work, lazybones," but that would sound too much like her mother.

"Other than the injury to the neck, Charles had no bruises or lacerations," she said.

"Uh-huh."

Sounded bored. When was he going to roll up his sleeves, dig into the file?

"That's consistent with Katrina's story that Charles consented to being tied up and collared," she said.

"Yeah."

"The toxicology was normal. Blood gases showed—"

"Hey, rookie." He tossed down the magazine. "You're interrupting my train of thought."

"Excuse me. I'm trying to learn the forensics."

"You're wasting your time."

"Really?"

"Pretend you're Pincher. How do you prove the death was a homicide and not an accident?"

"Motive," she said. "Pincher needs a reason Katrina would kill Charles or he can't win a circumstantial case."

"Exactly," he said. "Forget the blood gases. Figure out motive."

"You didn't get anything from Katrina?"

"Nothing besides passion-fruit iced tea."

"Maybe if you hadn't been so busy flirting."

"I was establishing common ground, building a bond. It's what I do."

"Especially with attractive women."

"Not always successfully." He gave her a long look. "Like I told you, she swears she loved her husband with all her heart. They had a perfect marriage. She had no reason to kill good old Charlie."

"And you believe she's telling the truth?"

"Absolutely. I'm the Human Polygraph Machine, and we've got ourselves an innocent client."

Had he been convincing? He had not told Victoria the truth, the whole truth, and nothing but the truth. He knew she badly wanted Katrina to be innocent, needed her to be innocent. A career prosecutor—if you call three trials and two cups of coffee a career—Victoria had never defended any client, much less a murder client. Steve feared her demeanor could give it away, their client's guilt written all over *her* face. He doubted she'd fight as hard if she thought their client was guilty. Hell, that's when you have to fight harder and be more creative.

Maybe Katrina *was* innocent, but in the real world, the arithmetic was against it. How many lost souls, swallowed by the so-called justice system, were truly innocent? Five percent? Less?

Best was to have a client you liked, a cause that was just, and a check that cleared. One out of three was the norm, he figured.

Yesterday, he'd given his trial team—as he'd come to think of Victoria, Bobby, and Cece—his old key-to-the-jailhouse-door speech. That was true; they had a duty to set Katrina free if they could. But he hadn't revealed how he felt on the ultimate question: Did she kill her husband?

When he was skimming through the magazine, he was replaying those moments alone with Katrina before Victoria arrived. He had tried to rattle Katrina to shake out the truth. It's always a good idea to give your client a dose of cross-examination before the prosecutor has a chance to do it.

Sitting at the table in the courtyard, Katrina's smile had been teasing, her eyes sparkling, her laugh tinkling. As he watched the slit on her skirt slide up her thigh, he wondered: Why so frisky for such a recent widow?

Steve had told her his ground rules for the attorney–client relationship. "Lie to your priest, your spouse, and the IRS, but not to your lawyer. I don't want any surprises at trial, so if there are any skeletons in the cabana . . ."

"Meaning?" Katrina asked, guileless as a child bride.

"Any men in your life besides your husband?"

"Only my masseur, my Pilates instructor, and my plastic surgeon." She laughed and tossed layers of raven hair his way.

"I guess that's a no."

"On the ice tour, we were all young and in great shape. A different hotel every other night, lots of parties, guys with great butts. Some of the guys were even straight, and boy, did they make out like bandits. But when I met Charlie, I quit that scene. I've been faithful to him since the day he proposed."

"And vice versa?"

"Charlie would never stray, I can guarantee you that."

Boasting more about her own abilities than her husband's fidelity, Steve thought. "Anything out there that can embarrass you?"

"There was a party once with about half the Detroit Red Wings, but that's ancient history. And

Charlie knew all that stuff, anyway. He liked hearing about the other men, the group sex, the girl-on-girl. Give Charlie a hot story and leather restraints, he'd be sailing over Viagra Falls."

"Any old boyfriends who are gonna post X-rated video on the Internet?"

Her eyes were clear and cool as a winter rain. "I had lots of X-rated moments, but I didn't let anyone tape them."

"Good."

"I worked a Vegas ice show in a thong and skates. That a problem?"

"Don't think so."

"When you're in a sit spin, the breeze off the ice can really freeze your beav."

For a moment, the only sound in the courtyard was the gurgling fountain of spitting cherubs.

Her tongue seemed to flick across her lips, but she might have just been moistening her gloss. "You un-attached, Steve?"

"Like a piece of driftwood."

"Maybe when this is over . . ."

She let the bait play in the water, but he didn't leap for it.

"Any prenup?" he asked, getting back to business.

"You know a rich old guy who doesn't demand one?"

"I'll need a copy."

"Sure, but I can tell you what it says. If we got divorced, I'd keep what I brought into the marriage."

"Which is what, other than your skates and thongs?"

"What difference does it make? We weren't getting divorced. We were planning a trip to Tuscany in the spring. We were going fishing off Bimini next week. We had a good life."

"It might matter to the State Attorney, so I have to ask."

"Besides my skates and thongs," she said, eyes wary, "if we got divorced, I'd keep my wits. They've always been good to me. As for money, I wouldn't get a dime."

"And if you were married when your husband died, you'd get . . . ?"

"One-third of his estate, the rest goes to his kids from his first marriage."

"If you were unhappy, that might be a motive for murder."

"I wasn't unhappy."

"Or if Charlie planned to divorce you . . ."

"And lose the best blow jobs of his life? Look, we got along. He had his business and his poetry seminars, and I had the club and my friends. Charlie gave me everything I wanted. Why would I risk all that by killing him?"

"Spouses kill each other all the time for the darnedest reasons."

"If I'd killed Charlie," she said, her voice as sharp as a skate blade, "I'd have a better alibi than 'I was sucking his cock and then he strangled.' "

"I wonder if there's a way we might rephrase that for the jury. . . ."

The hazel eyes, which had been sparkling with flirty invitations, had gone cold. "Are you on my side or not?"

"I'm your best friend in the world. I'm here to carry your spear into battle. I just need your help."

"Then hear this, spear carrier: I wasn't fucking around and I didn't kill Charlie. Got it?"

"The way you're looking at me right now . . ."

"What about it?"

"If you're on the witness stand, don't ever look at the jury that way."

"Why not?"

"Because you look angry enough to kill somebody."

Watching Victoria sift through the autopsy and toxicology reports, Steve knew she was wasting her time. Having cross-examined hundreds of witnesses over the years, he'd put his money on his built-in polygraph. It wasn't a matter of respiration, perspiration, or blood pressure. Just a gut feeling.

His gut told him two things. He was fairly certain Katrina Barksdale had been screwing around. As for the other question, he figured it was 75–25 that she'd aced good old contented Charlie. He couldn't articulate exactly why; his gut just told him so.

But that's okay, he thought. If your client is truly innocent, the pressure to win is overwhelming. But a guilty client? Hey, if you lose, justice is done.

He was more troubled about having just lied to his junior partner.

"Okay, so you believe her," Victoria said. "Shouldn't you be working on the case instead of just reading magazines and daydreaming?"

"Relax, Victoria. I'm working even when it doesn't look like it."

"What's your plan? Where's your to-do list?"

"It's all right here." He pointed to his head. "Prep

for the bail hearing, interview our client, talk to the
boat captain, get discovery from Pincher, and come
up with the theme of our case."

"Where do we start?"

Steve looked at his watch. "Lunch."

Sixteen

HOOCHIE-COOCHIE MAN

"Anybody hungry?" a deep voice rumbled, as the door to Steve's office opened. An elderly black man in rimless glasses and a rainbow-colored dashiki walked in, carrying three grocery bags. At his side, Bobby lugged a thermos bottle. Cece Santiago brought up the rear, carrying a Styrofoam cooler.

At her desk, Victoria smelled the sweet, spicy aroma of barbecue sauce.

"Cadillac," Steve said. "Right on time."

"Baby back ribs, Uncle Steve," Bobby said. "Your favorite."

"Plus conch fritters," the old man said. "Bimini bread, ham croquettes, oxtail soup, and my sweet potato pie."

"That's it?" Steve said. "What is this, the South Beach diet?" He grabbed the grocery bags. "Victoria, say hello to Cadillac Johnson. Cook, musician, and friend."

"Hello, Mr. Johnson. I've seen you at the courthouse lunch wagon."

"The Sweet Potato Pie," Cadillac said, smiling. "My kids run it now, but the recipes are still mine."

Thick through the chest, he had a round face with chubby cheeks and a full head of salt-and-pepper hair.

The smells were tantalizing, and Victoria was famished, but if she ate her share, she'd have to take a siesta. Not only that, almost everything violated her vegan principles. Actually, Bruce's vegan principles, she rationalized, thinking . . . *Maybe just one little rib.*

"The Pie wouldn't be there at all, 'cept for Steve," Cadillac told her. "You know about that new zoning ordinance?"

She ran a finger along a baby back rib and sucked off the sauce, tart with vinegar, sweet with brown sugar. "No vendors on public property. How'd you get a variance?"

"Legal quiz, Vic." Steve passed around open cartons, unleashing a mixture of aromas. "Cadillac's been cooking on the courthouse steps for twenty years and the county tries to evict him. How would you argue the case?"

Here we go again, she thought. *Solomon the teacher. Treating me like a schoolgirl.* She nibbled at a rib, the meat falling off the bone, melting in her mouth. "I'd go for a declaratory judgment and an injunction under Section 1983. I'd argue estoppel, due process, equal protection."

"*El bicho,*" Cece said. "Steve don't know that shit."

"Federal litigation?" Steve said, spearing a croquette. "That might work, after about ten years of motions and hearings."

"So what'd you do?" Victoria asked. "Bribe the mayor?"

"And the commissioners," Steve said.

"You didn't!"

"A dozen pulled pork sandwiches and some sweet potato pie."

"You're making this up."

"The law doesn't win cases, Vic. Emotions do. Feelings. The key to every case is finding those emotions and hitting those notes."

"Do I get continuing education credits for your lecture?"

"You get seconds."

Without realizing it, Victoria had wolfed down half a slab of ribs. Okay, Bruce didn't have to know. "Mr. Johnson, these are delicious."

"Thank you, missy," Cadillac said. "Now try some fritters." He sliced a crisp, golden ball. Juicy pieces of conch oozed from the thin fried crust.

"Maybe just one." She dipped the fritter in mango salsa, tasted it, closed her eyes with pleasure.

"Steve's my man," Cadillac said. "He's a fighter. And the price is right."

"Lunch?" she asked, taking a second bite.

"Hell, no. He pays for lunch."

"Guitar lessons." Steve was slicing the pie with a plastic knife. "Cadillac's a helluva musician. Rhythm and blues, early rock."

"Played fish fries, juke joints, bars where you could get your throat sliced for looking at somebody cross-eyed," Cadillac said.

"When you gonna teach me the blues with a shuffle feel?"

"Same day people stop calling you 'Last Out.' "

"Why do they?" Victoria asked.

"Because I'm always the last one out of the library," Steve said.

"*Eso es mentira,*" Cece said. "That's a lie."

"A big fat whopper," Bobby said.

"Steve made the last out in the College World Series," Cadillac said.

"Aw, jeez," Steve said.

"Uncle Steve's a 'Cane," Bobby said. "Played at U of M."

"Couldn't hit a lick," Cadillac said.

Steve winced. "C'mon, guys. I was good at stealing bases."

"And petty cash, if I know you," Victoria said.

"Uncle Steve once scored from first on a single," Bobby said proudly.

"I seem to have a knack for running in circles," Steve said.

"Instead of slowing down rounding second, he speeds up by balancing the centrifugal and centripetal forces," Bobby said.

"So you got thrown out stealing?" Victoria guessed. "That it?"

"Worse," Cadillac said.

"Much worse," Cece said. "Aw, don't be such a baby. Tell her."

Steve sighed. "We're in Omaha, championship game against Texas. Two outs, bottom of the ninth, nobody on base, we're down by a run. We get a triple. I come in as a pinch runner, take a lead . . . and get picked off."

"Oh, dear," Victoria said, not knowing what else to say.

"The thing is, I was safe. It was a bad call."

"Uh-huh."

"Honest. The video proves it. I got in under the tag. My first taste of injustice."

"Some of us seen a lot worse than that," Cadillac said.

Ten minutes later, Victoria sampled her sweet potato pie and listened. Cadillac was telling Steve he'd taught T-Bone Walker to cook catfish, and T-Bone taught him to play bottleneck slide guitar. "And I ended up playing guitar a helluva lot better than T-Bone cooked."

Steve paid rapt attention to the old man, and Victoria wondered just how many people did. Cadillac started telling Muddy Waters stories, and Steve began singing, "I'm your hoochie-coochie man."

Cadillac laughed and slapped his thigh as Steve mangled the lyrics and the tune, completely unfazed. Looking at her, Steve belted out the stanza about a man who could make pretty women jump and shout, but then he forgot the words and started making up his own. Just like he made up his own laws.

She'd better add Cadillac Johnson to the Steve Solomon Fan Club. The old man showed deep affection for him. Leaving her wondering again if she'd been missing something.

What a complicated man you are, Steve Solomon.

Chisel away that purposely obnoxious exterior, there might be a heart and soul buried inside. As she looked at him now, the dark hair falling across his forehead, his eyes bright with pleasure, she let herself see him not as a lawyer but as a man. A man who could round second without slowing down and score

from first on a single. A man who was already a sur-
rogate father and would make a wonderful father to
his own children. A man who—dare she even think
it?—was hot.

If I weren't engaged . . .

Whoa. Where had that come from? She was about
to do the happily-ever-after with Bruce. She was
lucky to have found him. She loved so many things
about him. His honesty and loyalty and levelheaded-
ness. And Solomon? On good days, he could be a
savvy, funny colleague. But on bad days, they still
squabbled and yapped at each other like those dogs
in Judge Gridley's barn.

Whoops. Strike that thought, Counselor.

Those dogs ended up humping on a bale of straw.
Best to banish all thoughts of Steve Solomon and
barking dogs and bales of straw.

But seconds later, her mind, which had, well, a
mind of its own, wandered again: *If I weren't engaged . . .*

Focus, she told herself. Don't think of his arms, his
legs, his hands, his . . .

Omigod. I saw it!

The memory came back to her now. A lost dream
recovered from the foggy mist between sleep and consciousness. When Bruce's alarm clanged her awake
this morning, she was pressed, spoonlike, against
him, feeling his warmth. But the man in her dream
was not Bruce. It was Solomon.

They were walking on a deserted beach, Solomon
wearing nothing but a towel, just like Sunday night at
his house. In the dream, she tore the towel away, revealing his fully aroused . . .

Iron Rod.

Joystick.

Kosher Pickle.

Oh, God, how could she? It was as if she'd cheated on Bruce. She vowed to control her rebellious psyche. Concentrate, she told herself.

Sequester Solomon. Expunge him from every brain cell.

Victoria had no doubt she could, through sheer force of will, remove Solomon from her conscious thoughts. But how, she wondered, stricken with guilt, would she ever control her dreams?

Seventeen

STEALING HOME

Three steps off third base, Steve bounced on his toes, knees flexed, arms relaxed. A wet fog had settled over the field, and he could barely see home plate.

"Steal home," a sweet, seductive voice whispered.

He stayed put. "Who said that?"

The pitcher threw a sizzling fastball that vanished into the mist. "Stee-rike!" an invisible umpire called out.

"Steal home for me," the seductive voice murmured.

Steve turned and squinted through the fog, and there she was. The third base coach. Victoria Lord, and she was not wearing pants! Nothing but skin between her University of Miami jersey and her high-heeled, cork-soled sandals with orange and green straps.

"You're wild and reckless," she said. "That's what I love about you."

"You do?" He was vaguely aware he was dreaming.

Another pitch disappeared into the mist. "Stee-rike two!"

"Please, Steve. Please steal home." A Siren of the base paths.

Steve shivered. It was growing colder, the moisture soaking through his uniform. The pitcher started his windup, and Steve took off. Through the thickening fog, he saw it all unfold in slow motion.

A soft floating pitch.

The catcher turning to shield the plate. That tub of guts, Zinkavich!

The umpire tearing off his mask. Mr. Judgmental himself. His father! Steve slid headfirst, one hand darting beneath Zinkavich's pudgy legs, just as the mitt came down hard, crashing against his temple with a sound of a bowling ball hitting the pins. Pain flared in his skull.

"Out!" Herbert Solomon yelled. "You'll never be the ballplayer ah was, you pantywaist."

"Uncle Steve!" Bobby cried out from somewhere.

"The boy's mine!" Zinkavich thundered. "The boy's mine now!"

"Uncle Steve!" Bobby cried again.

The throbbing in his head grew worse, and now Steve felt a great weight pressing down on his chest.

"Uncle Steve!"

He was coming out of the fog.

Back in his bedroom, but something was wrong. Bobby was on top of him, pushing him into the mattress, clutching at him. Crying, trembling, shouting. "Uncle Steve! Somebody's here!"

"Who? Where?" Steve was wide-awake. Heart racing.

"Outside my window. Looking in!"

"A dream, Bobby. Just a dream."

"No! Someone's here!"

Steve looked at the digital clock on the nightstand: 4:17.

"Don't let them take me," Bobby said.

"No one's taking you. Ever."

Steve reached under the bed, grabbed a metal baseball bat, told Bobby to stay there. Wearing only his Jockeys, he padded to the boy's bedroom. Windows closed, bedsheets tangled. He looked out the window. Nothing but the blackness of the yard. He went into the kitchen, took a flashlight from a drawer, and unlocked the door. Walking barefoot into the yard, the flashlight in one hand, the bat in the other, he looked around. Still nothing.

From a neighbor's yard, he heard the *clack-clack* of a woodpecker hammering a bottlebrush tree. He inhaled the smells of moist earth and jasmine. And something else . . .

Cigarette smoke. Or was it? The smell came and left.

He looked under Bobby's window. No footprints, no cigarette butts.

The poor kid. Bobby couldn't separate reality from his nightmares. But then, Steve wondered, could he?

Two hours later, the sun was just coming up; Bobby was sleeping soundly; and Steve was in the kitchen, slicing a juicy papaya, scooping out the seeds. He left it on the counter with two slices of lime, went into the yard, and checked everything again. No sign of intruders, not even the neighborhood raccoon that turned over garbage cans. Just another nightmare, he thought. If only he could expel the demons from the boy's mind.

Wearing shorts, running shoes, and a Bar Association T-shirt, *"Lawyers Do It in Their Briefs,"* Steve left by the front door and locked up the house. Slipping his Walkman onto his head, he would jog to Tahiti Beach and be back in time to share breakfast with Bobby.

It was a glorious morning of dazzling blue skies and low humidity, the wind gusting from the northwest, signaling an advancing cold front. Steve had already crossed the bridge at the Gables Waterway and hadn't even broken a sweat. On the Walkman, Bob Marley was telling his little darlin' to stir it up. Different music was playing in Steve's mind, Victoria's words from his dream: *"That's what I love about you."*

Now that he thought about it, hadn't she been nicer to him lately? Yesterday, when Cadillac brought lunch, hadn't there been a softer look in her eyes?

So what? She's engaged, fool.

Sure, he could pursue her, but what lay at the end of that road? Heartbreak City. Just what he needed with the Barksdale trial and Bobby's case coming up. He had no time for emotional messiness. Hell, he didn't even have time for a one-night stand.

A solid line of whitecaps broke on the reef offshore. The wind grew stronger; a change in the weather was brewing. Picking up his pace, Steve jogged alongside a county bus that was stopped along Cocoplum Circle, disgorging its cargo of

uniformed maids, on their way to the ritzy waterfront homes where they toiled. A Mercedes convertible sat at the berm, a young man and woman in the
bucket seats, Natalie Cole crooning "Opposites
Attract" on the radio, which made him think of
Victoria once again. She'd been staring at him when
he was talking to Cadillac. Was there some interest
there? Didn't lots of women back out of their engage-
ments?

Dammit. She's here for one case. Then she's gone.
Live with it.

The sweat was flowing now, his breaths coming
hard and fast, his shoes smacking the asphalt with a
rhythmic *slapitty-slap*. Then he hit the zone, and he
was floating. Running effortlessly, feeling strong, able
to leap piles of palm fronds in a single bound. His
mind drifted back to the early morning and to Bobby.
Had someone been at the bedroom window? No way
to tell. But he would take precautions. The burglar
alarm had been on the fritz for years. He would get it
fixed. He would . . .

What the hell!

Pulling out of Mire Flores Avenue, he saw the
muddy green pickup truck. Burning rubber, screeching around the corner, headed toward LeJeune
Road.

Steve strained to see which way the truck would
turn when it reached the intersection. He was running faster than he ever had, faster than he ever
thought possible. Thoughts of Bobby, alone in his
bed, streaked across his mind. When the truck turned
right, Steve was close enough to watch it approach
the Circle.

Please, God, let it go halfway around, straight out Sunset, or farther, straight down Old Cutler.

But it turned right.

And headed across the bridge.

Toward his home.

Eighteen

DORIS FROM INTERCOURSE

When he turned the corner onto Kumquat Avenue, Steve was running out of gas. Drained of adrenaline, feet like slabs of concrete. Winded and scared. Nearing his house, he saw two cars parked in the gravel driveway.

Neither was a muddy green pickup.

One was his old Caddy. The other was a shark-gray, four-door Chrysler with blackwall tires. The bumper sticker read: *"Go ahead and Honk. I'm Reloading."*

Steve walked in a circle around the Chrysler, bent forward, sucking air. His fear was subsiding. He thought he knew who owned the car, and one look through the windows confirmed it. A pair of women's spikes—size ten, he guessed—sat on the front seat, along with gloves and rib pads. In the backseat, several lacrosse sticks, various Ace wraps, adhesive tape, and a jar of a high-protein powder.

Yeah, he knew who was inside, and he was not happy about it. Tucking away thoughts of the green pickup, he sidestepped the overhanging Spanish bayonet leaves on the stone path and stormed into his house.

Dr. Doris Kranchick stood in the middle of his living room, hands on her wide, sturdy hips. The doc wore sensible pumps and a drab gray business suit. Her hair was pulled back so severely, it seemed to tighten her scalp. She was bulky without being fat. Her legs were two stout tree trunks descending to thick ankles. She had a broad, bland face that disguised both her limitless tenacity and a deep reservoir of fury. The white-rimmed remnant of a scythe-shaped scar ran across one cheekbone, a memento of a slashing in a college lacrosse game twenty years earlier.

Despite his best efforts, Steve Solomon had failed to make a dent in Dr. Doris Kranchick. When she was first assigned as Family Services' consultant on Bobby's case, Steve had tried the friendly approach, pitching their common background.

"Hey, we were both athletes in college."

In truth, she'd been far more accomplished, an All-American at Penn State. He knew little about lacrosse but learned that her position, point on defense, was similar to middle linebacker in football, where it helped to be both agile and hostile.

Steve had done his homework. At their first meeting, he had asked Dr. Kranchick about her studies of savant syndrome and frontotemporal dementia, compulsive learning and photographic memory, eidetic imagery and echolalia. He'd even read her article in *Psychology Today:* "Unlocking Your Inner Rain Man." He'd used the lawyer's trick—*you're fascinating; tell me about yourself*—of getting a witness to open up.

Nothing had worked. Doris Kranchick regarded him as she would an opponent advancing on the goal. If she couldn't steal the ball, she'd level him with a cross-body check or an elbow to the spleen.

Now, in the living room, Bobby was huddled in a corner of the sofa. Barefoot and wearing only underpants and a T-shirt, he hugged his knees and rocked silently, his head cocked, his eyes unfocused. Back in his shell. The same look as when Steve had rescued him ten months earlier.

Damn her. Bobby will be a mess for days.

"Everything's okay, kiddo," Steve said, going over to him.

"She's not taking me away?" His voice barely a whimper.

"Of course not. We're just going to talk a bit." Trying not to let his anger show. "Doctor, you should have called."

"Home visits are permitted to be unscheduled," she said.

"This is an invasion of my privacy as guaranteed by Article something-or-other of the Florida Constitution."

"Article One, Section Twenty-three," Bobby whispered.

"How about that? My nephew knows more law than I do."

"I'm sure that's true," the doctor shot back dryly, "but I have other concerns. Just look at the poor child."

Bobby trembled, then turned away, staring off into an unseen corner of the universe.

"You scare him," Steve said. "Hell, you scare me."

Kranchick took off her gray jacket. It looked as if

she planned to stay a while. "Robert should be at Rockland, where there are facilities for his special needs."

"He doesn't need a hospital. I'm hiring a private tutor and a therapist."

"Who?"

"The best people. As soon as I get paid on this big case."

"Right. And just look at this place."

"What's wrong with it?" Steve reflexively straightened the scattered magazines on his surfboard cocktail table. He didn't bother with the empty beer cans and three-day-old pizza boxes. Nearby, a corn plant had died and was shriveling into a drooping skeleton of brown leaves.

"When your sister gave up Robert—"

"Janice didn't give Bobby up. I rescued him."

"The details have always been so vague," Kranchick said. "I can't wait to hear your story under oath."

To Steve, that sounded like a threat. Like something Zinkavich would say. He strained to keep his composure. It wouldn't help if Kranchick's report called him belligerent as well as deficient at dusting.

"I'm sure Robert's mother would want him to have the best care," Kranchick said.

"Janice is a crackhead who doesn't care about anyone but herself. The only one who worries about Bobby is me."

"Then you should want what's best for him."

Steve felt himself heating up, something that almost never happened in court. Arguing your own case was different. Impossible to keep emotion out of it.

"There's no better place than Rockland for high-functioning savants," Kranchick continued. "Robert can learn a vocational skill, and we can learn more about him and others like him."

"I'm not letting you stick electrodes in his brain."

Stay calm. Don't blow it.

"Transcranial magnetic stimulation is noninvasive. And our drug therapy is quite promising."

She walked to Bobby and stroked his cheek: he burrowed even deeper into the sofa.

"Whatever happened to Robert, he has memory abilities rivaling that of the highest functioning autistic savants, but without organic brain damage. Do you realize what a rare opportunity this is?"

"For you or for Bobby?"

"Your intransigence will be noted in my report to the court." She sounded even more like Zinkavich.

"You're supposed to remain neutral, Doctor, not carry Zinkavich's briefcase."

"Do you think forces are conspiring against you? Do you feel persecuted, Mr. Solomon?"

"More like I'm being kicked in the *cajones*."

"Do you have unexplained bouts of anger?"

"Aw, fuck that. You want to write me up as a psycho, Doc, go ahead."

"Your language will also be noted."

"What do you have against me? What have I done to offend you?"

"Nothing," she replied. "My sole concern is Robert's welfare."

In truth, Doris Kranchick loathed everything about Steve Solomon. His city boy cockiness. His manner. Loosey-goosey, her mother, Edna, would have called him. Even the bouncy way he walked. As if he held the key to some secret kingdom, as if every footstep led to some deserved pleasure.

She understood that her own mix of anger and envy was irrational. She had come far from her family's farm in southeastern Pennsylvania, but she knew enough psychology to realize she had never really left behind her low self-esteem. From the clothes she wore to junior high, to her billboard-size forehead, to her dishwater brown hair, there was almost nothing she liked about herself. She still remembered her embarrassment at that high-school all-star lacrosse game when the PA announcer introduced her: "Starting at point, Doris Kranchick, from Intercourse."

"Where's Intercourse?" asked a Pittsburgh girl, laughing.

"A few miles south of Blue Ball," replied a Philadelphia girl, accurately but nastily.

The other girls giggled and *clickety-clacked* their lacrosse sticks. And from that day, they called her "Doris from Intercourse."

The nickname followed her to college, and all the dean's lists and all the forced turnovers could never change it. Seething with anger, she led her team in yellow warning cards and in loneliness.

One lacrosse game stood out in her memory. A joyous game, even though she received seventeen stitches in her face for her efforts. In the Big Ten playoffs, Doris tripped a cute, speedy, ponytailed player from Ohio State. On her way down, the young woman whipped her stick across Doris' cheek, maybe accidentally, maybe not. With blood already spurting, Doris slammed to the ground, aiming her shoulder

squarely at the dimple on Miss Ponytail's chin. A
fractured mandible left the girl eating through a
straw for months. Doris still smiled when she replayed the game in her mind.

Looking back, Doris realized she did little in her
college years but hit the books, hit the sack, and hit
her opponents. But then, in her senior year, she met
Fritz Braeunig, a soccer player from Germany. After a
sports banquet, he took her back to his apartment,
plied her with red wine, and pried her knees apart
with his own well-muscled thighs. Fritz's problem,
she thought, was not taking *nein* for an answer. What
choice did she have? As he maneuvered inside her
thighs, she circled his chest with her lumberjack legs,
locked her ankles behind his back, and snapped three
of his ribs with the sound of a crab shell being shattered by a mallet.

Doris chose Johns Hopkins for medical school because she could help coach the university's famed
lacrosse team. In the winters, she played indoors,
where she was frequently penalized for "boarding
from the rear." Lately, she took out her aggressions
by playing in a men's league near the Florida
International University campus.

Although her life was bereft of companionship and
friends, she did not consider herself unhappy. She
was doing good work for a good cause and had trav-
eled far from the Pennsylvania farm. Employed by
various pharmaceutical companies, she'd worked in
drug research programs in Argentina, Hungary, and
Bulgaria before settling in the more prosaic Ft.
Lauderdale. For the past two years, she'd directed the
pilot autism project at Rockland State Hospital,
where she aggressively pursued new treatments.

Hey, you can't score if you don't shoot.

She could not understand why Steve Solomon refused to share Robert with her. How could anyone be so selfish and shortsighted? She could help the boy, and by extension, many others. And if her research led to more government grants and a profile of her on *60 Minutes,* well, so much the better.

Steve vowed to show his humble side. He'd flatter her while keeping his true feelings in check. "Let's not fight, Dr. Kranchick."

"That's up to you, Mr. Solomon."

"I really admire the work you do."

You are a weird, freaking woman.

"Thank you."

"But if you knew Bobby, you'd see the best place for him is with me."

I wouldn't board a German shepherd with you.

"Raschk korno duchk," Bobby mumbled, his head buried in a pillow.

"What did you say?" Kranchick said.

Bobby lifted his head. "RAKISH CORN DICK!"

Oh, shit, Steve thought. He couldn't let Kranchick know that Bobby was making anagrams of her name.

"When Bobby's nervous, he talks gibberish," Steve said.

"RADISH COCK RINK."

"It could be a form of dementia," Kranchick said, frowning.

"It's more like a game," Steve suggested.

"DRINK SICK ROACH."

She reached inside her jacket, pulled out a pad,

and scribbled a note. "There seems to be a pattern here, but I can't quite get it."

"No pattern," Steve said. "Just random words." Damned if he'd tell her that Bobby associated her name with "dick," "roach," and "cock."

"This just reinforces my beliefs. Bobby needs intensive treatment in a residential facility."

"You're wrong, Doctor. You're so damned wrong."

"You'd have regular visitation rights," she offered.

"Homeschooling's working fine."

"Is it?" She reached under the sofa cushions as if looking for spare change. "Is this what you call schooling? Robert tried to bury the evidence."

"He only reads the articles," Steve said, anticipating a *Playboy* or *Maxim*.

Instead, she held up a black-and-white autopsy photo of Charles Barksdale. An incision ran from ear to ear.

"Oh, that," Steve said, relieved.

"And this?" She grabbed a photo with the skin flaps pulled back from Barksdale's neck, showing the salivary glands and exposed jugular vein.

"Bobby likes autopsies," Steve said. "He can recite the Coroners' Rolls from fourteenth-century England."

" 'Inquest was taken at Middlesex,' " Bobby said in a British accent, " 'on Monday after the Nativity of Blessed Mary the Virgin in the reign of King Edward the Third. . . .' "

"Parlor games," Kranchick said. "Meaningless until we learn how he does it."

"Hey, lady," Bobby said. "Who lit the fuse on your tampon?"

"What! Is this what you teach the boy?"

"No. No. No." Steve felt an icy fear. "That's a T-shirt or something. Bobby, tell her."

"Bumper sticker on a Toyota SUV."

"A Toyota SUV!" Steve proclaimed, as if Bobby had just turned lead into gold.

"With a bald left rear tire," Bobby said. "License plate 7NJ843, manatee logo."

"See, it's just his memory."

Kranchick grabbed her briefcase from the surf-board coffee table. "Whatever's going on in this house is utterly inappropriate. Obviously, Robert needs guidance that you're unable or unwilling to give."

"Look, Dr. Kranchick, maybe I've given you the wrong impression. If you'd stick around a while, let Bobby relax, you'll see how happy he is, how well-adjusted—"

"My decision's made." Her tone was curt. "I'm going to urge the court to deny your petition, termi-nate your custody forthwith, and make Robert a ward of the state."

Steve's hands felt clammy. He'd gone the full route. Reason. Anger. Insincere flattery. Now full-scale panic. He heard himself begging. "Give me another chance, Doctor. Please. Bobby needs me. And I love him."

"Love" wasn't a word he tossed around easily.

"Bobby's my whole world," he went on.

"Your world? So that's what this is about. Your needs. Shouldn't this be about Robert?"

"He loves me, too. Depends on me. He's made tremendous progress."

She clicked on a cruel smile. "How? By sharing your bed?"

"For two weeks, when he first got here. He was too scared to sleep alone."

"Still," she said. "It looks like one of those Michael Jackson situations."

Is she fucking serious?

"You have a dirty mind, Dr. Kranchick."

"It's my job to turn over every rock, see what's crawling underneath. Frankly, even if Robert had no problems, I'd question your fitness as a custodian. Face it, Mr. Solomon, you're undomesticated."

"Whatever that means, it's just temporary. Just a phase."

"Fine. When you've grown up, petition the court under the change-of-circumstances statute."

"But I'm changing right now." An idea was forming, a way to sway her.

"How so?"

"Getting married's a change, isn't it?"

"It can be, depending . . ."

"Well, I'm engaged. Getting married in a month. To a wonderful woman. She's smart and loving and—"

"An optimist," Dr. Kranchick suggested snidely.

"Stable. A real stabilizer. My fiancée is a stabilizing influence."

"Stable" seeming to be the only characteristic he could latch on to. Winging it now, just like in court. "When I'm with her, I feel more mature. More . . . domesticated."

"Really?" The doctor did not sound convinced.

"Your report isn't complete if you haven't interviewed my fiancée."

"Technically, that's true," she conceded, with reluctance. "Who is she?"

Steve's mind raced. There was Sofia Hernandez, the court reporter. She was fine at reading back testimony, but ad-libbing wasn't her strong suit. There was Gina the model, who already had an engagement ring, but she was likely to steal the silverware. There were the twins, Lexy and Rexy, but neither one's IQ matched the temperature on a warm day. And there was Cece, but her tattoos and piercings might be offputting, to say nothing of her rap sheet.

"I'll want to meet her as soon as possible." Kranchick was pulling out her daily calendar. "How's the day after tomorrow?"

"Perfect! Let's make it dinner."

"So what's the woman's name? This stabilizing influence?"

There was only one choice. "Victoria Lord," he said. "You'll just love her."

Nineteen

PROVING LOVE

Heading into Les Mannequins the next morning, Steve vowed to be on his best behavior with Victoria. After all, he had a huge favor to ask.

"Will you marry me? Or at least pretend to?"

Steve knew he desperately needed her help. A lousy report from Kranchick combined with Zinkavich's vicious attacks, and he'd have no chance in court. He'd promised Kranchick that she'd meet his fiancée tomorrow night. So he had to pop the question—on bent knee, if necessary—and teach Victoria the one lawyer skill she so clearly lacked: lying with a straight face.

He left Bobby in the waiting room, where he could spot for Cece on the bench press, the only way to keep her from disappearing for an afternoon at the gym. Opening the door to his office, he instantly sensed that something was wrong.

It was too bright, for one thing, sunlight blasting through the windows. Then there was the smell of ammonia. And all the papers on his desk were stacked in neat piles next to a vase of fresh violets.

Violets?

He shot a look at Victoria, who was sitting at her desk, reading a stack of appellate cases. "What the hell happened in here?"

"I tidied up," Victoria said.

"Like Sherman tidied up Georgia. Why's it so bright?"

"I cleaned the windows."

"Big mistake. Dirty windows are nature's way of keeping us cool."

She continued reading, using a yellow marker to highlight the key points of an appellate opinion. As if the law ever won a case.

He went to his lobster tank, crumbled a stale bagel, and began tossing pieces into the water. He was stalling, trying to figure just how to ask Victoria to be his fiancée-for-a-day. He could predict her first reaction.

"I won't do that. It's unethical."

Despite his best efforts at corrupting her, Victoria stubbornly clung to her rigid standards. Just yesterday, he'd been interviewing a potential client, a guy who wanted to sue Budweiser for false advertising. The guy drank the beer but still couldn't pick up women in bars. Steve thought the case had potential, but Victoria vetoed it.

"You ready to prep for the bail hearing?" she asked, without looking up from her photocopies.

"Sure, sure, we'll prep all you want."

He knew that Katrina Barksdale was sitting unhappily in the Women's Detention Center, which lacked the basics of her Gables Estates home. No Jacuzzi, no pool deck, no monthly pest control. They needed to convince Judge Alvin Schwartz, an eighty-one-year-old misanthrope, to allow her to return home, pending trial. Not an easy task in a capital case, but possible.

"Under *State v. Arthur,* we have a chance," Victoria said.

"Yeah."

"It's the state's burden to deny bail."

"I know."

She glanced up at him. "How do you get along with Judge Schwartz?"

"He hates me."

"Oh."

"But he's senile and sometimes forgets."

"Great."

"He's fond of young women lawyers in miniskirts."

"Forget it."

Steve walked to the window and stared across the alley, squinting against the glare.

"Are you okay?" she asked. "You seem a little distant."

"There's something I need to ask you."

C'mon, say it. Tell her you need her help. Tell her that losing Bobby would be worse than losing one of your limbs.

"Did you Shepardize *Arthur*?" he asked, meekly.

"Of course. It's still the law."

He looked at her as she continued thumbing through her appellate cases. With no court appearances today, she was dressed down. Black capri pants, a man's white shirt—Bigby's, Steve figured—tied at the waist, scuffed flats. No makeup, and it looked as if she hadn't bothered to run a brush through her hair. To Steve, she was sexy in a natural and wholly unintentional way. Maybe that was the problem. Maybe if he didn't have these feelings for her, it would be easier to ask for her help. He could wheedle, plead, beg, grovel. But now he just couldn't. Groveling would have to wait.

"How do you want to handle the hearing?" she asked.

"You take the law, I'll take the facts."

"The facts being that Charles was kinky, Katrina went along for the sake of the marriage, and the death was an unfortunate accident?"

"Yeah." Through the open window, he watched a garbage truck hoisting the Dumpster. "We also stress the theme of our case."

"Which is . . . ?"

"I have no idea. But whatever it is, we need to pound the theme into the public consciousness starting at the bail hearing. We need to write the headline in the *Herald* with it."

She wrinkled her forehead. "The headline's 'Widow Freed on Bail.' Or not."

"Only if some assistant city editor writes it," Steve said. "Our job's to write it for them. With our theme. So what's the thematic content of the Barksdale marriage? What's the glue that held those two together?"

"The state will say it's money."

"Exactly. But what do we say?"

"Love."

"Love," Steve avowed, "is a many-splendored defense. What is love? And how do we prove it?"

"Love is a rational, synergistic coupling of two people with mutual interests and similar values."

"A little clinical for my tastes." Was that how it was with Bigby and her? *A rational, synergistic coupling?* That sounded like fun.

"So what's your definition?"

"Two people who just have to be together," he replied without hesitation. "Two people who are not complete when they're apart. They're lovers and best friends, too. There's lust and laughter, and they can't imagine being with anyone else."

"So Steve Solomon believes in romantic love?"

"In theory. I've never really had anything like that."

"And you think Katrina and Charles did?"

"I doubt it, but I'm a lawyer. Give me a thread and I'll tie you a rope."

"Then let me show you something." She bounded from her chair, crouched down, and opened one of the cardboard boxes under her desk. Sitting cross-legged on the floor, looking like a college coed studying for finals, she pulled out a handful of eight-by-ten glossies. "The Barksdales at play."

Steve settled into a catcher's position next to her and started going through the photos. Hand in hand at charity events, Charles in a tux, Katrina in a designer dress, dripping with jewels. Society page shots from various galas. Smiling faces, Charles with his arm around Katrina, what appeared to be genuine warmth in their eyes.

Victoria grabbed more photos from the box. They must have been in love with their own images. St. Tropez, Monaco, waterfront restaurants, boat decks. Charles was still a handsome man with a head of gray hair, and Katrina a born model, doing the toe-point to flatter her legs, a Paris Hilton tilt of the head to accentuate her jawline.

"These are fine, but they're all posed," Steve said. "I could show you some smiling photos of O. J. and

Nicole Simpson. Or Scott and Laci Peterson. Or Hillary and Bill Clinton."

"Hillary hasn't killed Bill."

"Yet," Steve said.

"Look at this." She pulled a greeting card out of the box and handed it to him. On the cover was a Winslow Homer print of a Caribbean beach. "It's dated the day before Charlie died."

He opened the card and read the handwritten note:

> *Dearest Katrina,*
> *No one could have been so good as you have been, from the very first day till now.*
> *Your Charlie*

"I like the 'Dearest,' " Victoria said. "Kind of quaint and Victorian."

"Okay, he still loved her. How do we prove she loved him?"

"When I saw them, Kat always seemed very affectionate toward Charlie. Very caring."

"What else? Give me examples."

"She was always buying him gifts. Watches, cuff links, clothing."

"Keep going. I like it."

Victoria thought it over a moment. "Maybe three months ago, we went to a surprise birthday party Kat threw for Charlie."

"We," he thought. Meaning Bigby and her. Another reminder she was about to marry the stiff, about to make third-person plural a permanent part of her life.

"The cake was shaped like one of his office towers," she continued.

"Cute. Unless the candles were sticks of dynamite."

"At sunset, we all went out on their boat. Music's playing, we're having drinks, eating stone crabs."

"Even Bigby the Vegan?"

"Bruce only ate the salad. That guy we met, Manko, anchored the boat in Hurricane Harbor off Key Biscayne. And just before the sun went down, the clouds were streaked with crimson, the bay's smooth as silk. I mean, how romantic can you get?"

Steve knew she was talking about Katrina and Charles, but his mind worked up the unfortunate image of Bigby and Victoria on deck. Haloed by the setting sun, serenaded by the band, Bigby kissing her. A slug slithering across a rose.

"Then this little plane flies over with one of those advertising banners behind it, like at the beach."

" 'Use Coppertone,' " Steve said.

"This one said, 'Katrina Loves Charles.' She had it made just for the party. It was really touching. Some people even had tears in their eyes."

"We'll make the jury cry, too. And the media will eat it up."

"So you like it?"

"You nailed it. Our theme. 'Katrina loves Charles.' "

"Isn't that a little simplistic?"

"Themes have to be simplistic. Otherwise, the morons don't get it."

"Jurors aren't morons."

"I'm talking about the judges."

Still sitting on the floor, she pulled out her index

cards and started scribbling notes. Steve gazed down at her. Without makeup, there was a sprinkling of freckles across the bridge of her nose. Every new discovery seemed to fascinate him.

"What?" she asked, catching him staring.

His addled brain immediately told him he had three choices. He could say, *"Just thinking about the rules of evidence."* He could say, *"You're incredibly beautiful and wonderfully talented, so don't be a fool and marry Bigby."* But he said: "Victoria, I have a really big favor to ask."

Twenty

A PURPOSE FOR RUNNING

The setting had to be right. The mood had to be right. The moment had to be right. After all, he was going to ask Victoria to marry him.

Rather than do it in the office, with its eye-stinging smell of ammonia and the clamor of the steel band, Steve suggested they take a ride. Now, top down on the old Caddy, crossing the causeway, he considered just what to say. On the radio, Gloria Estefan was promising that the rhythm was gonna get them. He took it as a good sign that, a moment later, they passed the white and pink mansions of Star Island, where Gloria lived.

"How about a pineapple smoothie?" Steve said.

"What's the big favor you want?" Sounding suspicious.

"I'll tell you all about it when we get there."

"Where?"

"You'll see."

"Why so mysterious? Usually, you just plow ahead, go after whatever you want."

"It's about Bobby."

"So tell me."

"Soon."

He pulled the car into the parking lot on Watson Island, and Victoria said: "Parrot Jungle? Why here?"

He parked in the shade beneath a sign that pointed different directions to the Parrot Bowl, Serpentarium, Flamingo Lake, and Everglades Habitat. "There's something I want you to see."

They got out of the car and headed into the park, wending their way through a throng of Japanese tourists. Steve bought two pineapple smoothies at a refreshment stand and led her past a lagoon dappled with white water lilies. He pointed out the herons with S-shaped necks and showed her the pink flamingos and the ruby-eyed roseate spoonbills that are sometimes mistaken for them. They passed snowy white egrets and long-legged storks. Walking through the make-believe rain forest, they were enveloped by a cacophony of birds, a philharmonic orchestra of *caws* and *coos*.

"Okay, what about Bobby?" she asked.

"Bear with me." He was still working up his courage, formulating his plan.

Staying in the shade of the banyan trees, they took a path bordered by blooming birds of paradise, passed an alligator pond and an outdoor theater where a parrot show was under way, a bird grabbing dollar bills from a performer's pocket to polite applause.

"Here we are." Steve nodded toward a sausage tree. Its cylindrical fruit hung down like Hebrew National salamis in a deli.

Perched on a branch, a citron-crested cockatoo eyed them warily.

"Is that who I think it is?" Victoria asked.

"Hello, hot stuff," Mr. Ruffles said.

"Hello, birdbrain." She turned to Steve. "You still gloating over the Pedrosa trial?"

"Absolutely not. You're missing the point."

"Crime pays?"

"Justice was served. My client's not taking up a jail cell. Mr. Ruffles has a good home. And everybody's happy."

"Everybody's happy," Mr. Ruffles said.

"You can rationalize anything."

"The point I'm making, sometimes the ends do justify the means."

"Okay, I get it. This favor you want is illegal, but in your tortuous reasoning, somehow just."

"Do you know how much I love Bobby?"

She stirred her smoothie with the straw. "It's your one redeeming quality."

"I'd do anything for him, the law be damned."

"So where do I fit in?"

"There's this battle-axe named Doris Kranchick, a doctor who says I'm not fit to care for him. She's Zinkavich's star witness."

"I'll testify for you if that's what you want."

"It is, sort of."

"What's the problem, then?"

"I told Kranchick I'm engaged, and she wants to meet my fiancée."

"Why would you say something like that?"

"I was winging it."

"Winging it," Mr. Ruffles said.

"So who's the lucky . . ." Victoria's face paled. "No. You didn't. . . ."

"Just pretend for a couple hours. Drinks, dinner, and dessert, that's it."

"That's unethical. . . ."

Of course that's her first reaction.

"Blatantly illegal . . ."

Second reaction, too.

"A fraud on the court . . ."

Okay, already.

"Maybe grounds for disbarment."

"So you'll do it?" he asked.

"No!" She stomped away from him, heading down a shaded path.

He took off after her. "Victoria, you're my only hope."

"Why me?"

"Catherine Zeta-Jones is taken."

"So am I." She waved her engagement ring in his face. "Anyway, nobody would believe we're engaged."

"I'm not sure, but I think you just insulted me."

"I'm a terrible liar."

"Don't you ever fake orgasms?"

"Maybe the women in your life do."

"They fake it when they're alone. Please, Victoria. I really need you on this."

She wrinkled her forehead the same way she did in court when puzzling through a problem. "Even if I could convince this doctor that I'm your fiancée, I wouldn't do it."

Above them, birds circled the trees and cried to one another in a babel of cheeps and peeps, titters and trills.

"Do you know the main difference between us?" he asked.

"I'm going to end up a judge, and you're going to end up in jail."

"You refuse to question authority."

"I question plenty. I just don't flout."

"Do you think the state should take Bobby from me?"

"Of course not."

"Then help me."

"I cannot and will not break the law."

"Haven't I taught you anything? The law doesn't work. That's why you have to work the law."

"Sorry. Can't do it."

His frustration turned to anger. "I can't fucking believe it. You're still a robot, still an automaton. By now you gotta know Lady Justice takes it doggy style. The law gets bent over a chair like a girl in Kobe Bryant's hotel room."

"And they say you're not a charmer."

They emerged from the path, silence engulfing the space between them, driving them apart. Alongside a pond, a mother was snapping photos of her two little girls, scarlet macaws perched on their shoulders.

They neared the edge of the bay. Crabs no larger than a fingernail scuttled along the wet sand. Feathery terns scoured the beach for snacks. Just across the water, a bell was ringing, and a barrier arm came down. Traffic stopped on the Venetian Causeway drawbridge.

"I need to tell you something about Bobby," he said.

"Nothing you can say will change my mind."

They stopped beneath a gumbo-limbo tree, its small red fruits bunched in clusters. Victoria's face was half in the sun, half in the shade.

"When Bobby was nine," Steve said, "his mother, Janice, moved to this commune up in the Panhandle. The Universal Friends of something-or-other. Freaks and druggies. When Janice was straight, she'd slap Bobby around and scream biblical quotations at him. When she was stoned, she'd lock him in a dog cage. Then she'd go into town for a few hours or a few days."

"Bobby told me about the dog cage. It sounded terrible. Honestly, Steve, I'd love to help, but—"

"He's making progress every day. And once I get him some specialized treatment, he'll do even better. But this creepy doctor wants to take him away and put him in a hospital."

"How can they do that if you're his guardian?"

The drawbridge was up now, and a sloop with its sails furled putt-putted through, cars backing up on the mainland to the west and on Biscayne Island to the east.

"Janice never exactly consented to my taking Bobby, so he's in sort of a legal limbo."

She thought about it for a moment. "You kidnapped him?"

"Rescued him," he corrected. "But I've never told anyone how. Until now."

He told her then. Told her about the night of freezing rain, about Janice delivering cold soup to Bobby in the shed, about his breaking in and finding the boy in the cage. Told her, too, about the mangy man with the heavy stick and how they fought, the crack of the man's skull, his blood pooling on the floor. Told her about the gunshots and how he ran through the woods, carrying Bobby, chased by barking dogs and men with guns.

When he was finished, Victoria studied him, her lips slightly parted, words trying to form. She felt fragile enough to shatter like white china. "I never could have imagined any of this."

"When I was running, Bobby's arms around my neck, I knew they'd never catch me as long as I didn't fall. All my life, I could run. Really run. But it had no purpose. Then it came to me. Like it was all meant to be. I could run like this so that someday, that day, I could carry this poor kid out of hell and give him a life.

"Sometimes, when I'm drifting off to sleep, I hear the floorboards squeak, and I think they're here. Men with torches and sticks, and they're going to kill me and snatch Bobby. Then I wake up and think, if those are my nightmares, what must Bobby's be?"

Eyes welling, he turned away. "So you think I'm gonna let some fat-assed bureaucrats take him away?"

"Look at me," she commanded.

He turned back. With a fingertip, she caught a tear just as it neared the corner of his mouth, then let her finger track across his lips, as if gently shushing him.

Across the bay, the bell rang again, and the causeway bridge jerked down in fits and starts like an old man dropping into his chair.

"Who knew?" she said, removing the finger from his lips.

"Knew what?"

"That you were capable of such love."

He shrugged. "That other stuff. The courtroom. Just a game. This is life."

Her eyes were soft and watery. "So where are we going?"

"Going?"

"On our honeymoon."

It took a second to register. Then Steve smiled broadly. "You're gonna do it? You're gonna be my fiancée?"

"One night only."

"*Ye-s-s-s!*" Tomorrow night. He laughed, a big pealing laugh like rolling thunder. "You're terrific. If there's ever anything you need. Anything."

"If I'm arrested, get me a good lawyer." She pulled out her cell phone. "I was supposed to play tennis with Jackie at Grove Isle tomorrow, have dinner with Bruce at his club. I'll cancel."

"No. Bring them along. In fact, we'll go to Bruce's club."

"Are you serious?"

"I'll ask Bruce to be my best man."

"You really want him there?"

"He'll make a great impression on Kranchick, maybe even pick up the tab. And Jackie can be your bridesmaid or whatever."

"She's my maid of honor."

"Perfect. Is she like you?"

Her tone was playful. "You mean a robot and automaton?"

"That stuff, I take back. I mean, proper, dignified, principled." He swallowed hard and his voice went soft. "And beautiful and smart and sexy and—"

She put her finger back to his lips. "Don't, Solomon."

"But there are things I want to say."

"Please, don't." Her smile was soft and sweet. "But we'll always have Parrot Jungle."

SOLOMON'S LAWS

7. I will never bribe a cop, lie to a judge, or
    sleep with my partner . . . *hasta qué ella
    diga qué sí.*

Twenty-one

COFFEE KLATCH

On the steps of the optimistically named Justice Building, a custodian scraped up a melting vanilla cake with chicken wings popping out of the icing. The cake was the culinary handiwork of a Haitian *santero*, hired by a defendant's family to cast a spell and sweeten a judge's disposition.

Inside the building, at eight-twenty A.M., Steve had just cleared the metal detector and was in desperate need of a cup of coffee when he heard a foghorn behind him. "Oh, Mr. So-lo-mon."

He stopped and turned. Jack Zinkavich was waddling toward him.

"Your witness lists are late," Zinkavich said.

"Sorry, been a little busy."

"And your exhibit list? Pretrial stips. Statement of the case."

"Almost done."

Meaning Steve was almost done *thinking* about them. Complying with deadlines wasn't his strong suit.

"We need to agree on a trial date," Zinkavich persisted.

"Soon as the Barksdale case is over."

"Not acceptable. Every day Robert is with you is an invitation to disaster."

Steve wrestled his temper under control. He'd promised his father he'd play nice, even though he doubted that Zinkavich was on the level. His old man had a more sanguine view of human nature.

As for Zinkavich, sure he had a shitty childhood and sure he'd been saved by the system, an event as rare as snow in Miami. But unlike his old man, Steve didn't think that Zinkavich had turned into the Galahad of Juvenile Court. To Steve, he was just one of Pincher's flunkies, a careerist with a mean streak. Still, since nothing else was working, he'd try a new and unfamiliar strategy: kissing ass.

Steve said: "We got off on the wrong foot, Jack. Okay if I call you Jack?"

"No."

"I just want to apologize. I said some inappropriate things, and I never should have grabbed you."

"Uh-huh."

"I have a great deal of respect for you, Mr. Zinkavich."

"Sure you do."

"I mean it. I know your background. Losing your mother like that. Being in foster care. So I know how you must feel about children at risk."

"Are you patronizing me, Mr. Solomon?"

"No, I'm just trying to relate to what you went through and—"

"Leave my personal life out of this."

"All I'm saying—"

"You condescending piece of shit."

"Aw, jeez."

"You think you can hide your violent streak under this phony veneer?"

"I don't have a violent streak. I'm actually quite cowardly."

"You're a menace. I know what you did that night in the commune, and I've got the evidence."

Oh, shit.

Was it true? Did Zinkavich have the guy he'd clobbered? Or was the bastard bluffing?

"You're not just going to lose your nephew," Zinkavich bulldozed on. "You're going to prison."

He took off down the corridor, leaving Steve standing there. Alone and alarmed.

The Courthouse Gang was holding up the cafeteria line, pinching bagels, sniffing Danishes, kibitzing about their aches and pains. Marvin the Maven in a navy blue double-breasted blazer, Cadillac Johnson in a bright dashiki, and Teresa Toraño in a dark tweed suit with a simple strand of pearls.

"C'mon, Marvin," Steve said from the back of the line. "Keep moving."

Steve couldn't be late for court. He tried to focus on the upcoming bail hearing, but Zinkavich's threat still rattled around in his brain.

"You're not just going to lose your nephew. You're going to prison."

Just what evidence did Zinkavich have? There wasn't even time to think about it. He needed a jolt of caffeine to jump-start his brain so he could race upstairs to the courtroom. But here he was, trapped behind his pals, who had nowhere to go and lots of time to get there.

"What's your hurry, boychik?" Marvin said.

"Bail hearing in ten minutes. Victoria's waiting for me."

"So, you *shtupping* her or what?" Marvin's voice carried across the cafeteria.

"Hey, none of that. It's all business."

"She shot you down, that it, Steverino?"

"Marvin, you know me. I'll never bribe a cop, lie to a judge, or sleep with my partner."

"Three lies in one sentence. That a record, Cadillac?"

"Not for Steve." Cadillac Johnson mixed half a cup of decaf with half a cup of regular, then poured nondairy creamer on top and added four Equals. Taking his sweet time.

"I believe our Stephen," Teresa Toraño said.

"Thank you, Teresa," Steve said. "My first client and last friend."

"You'll never sleep with Ms. Lord, *hasta qué ella diga qué sí.* Until she says yes."

Marvin coughed a laugh and exchanged high fives with Cadillac, or as high as their arthritis permitted.

"C'mon, guys, she's engaged," Steve protested.

"Since when do legal technicalities bother you?" Marvin shot back.

Steve checked his watch. In eight minutes, either his ass would be planted in front of Judge Alvin Schwartz or he'd be in contempt for tardiness.

"Have you seen the way he looks at her?" Marvin asked his cronies. "He's got it bad."

"Reminds me of this lady in K.C." Cadillac slurped coffee. "Tore out my heart, fed it to the catfish." He sang: *"Kansas City woman. Oh-h-h, what you done to me . . ."*

Marvin was at the register, fishing change from a pocket.

Steve called out: "Put it all on my tab."

"Por Dios!" Teresa said.

Cadillac clutched his chest. "My pacemaker's gonna blow a fuse."

"The big *macher,*" Marvin said. "If I'd known he was paying, I'd have got a bagel."

"Please hurry up," Steve said. "I'm trying to get an innocent woman out on bail."

"I have seen your client, and she is not so innocent," Teresa said.

"A real *paskudnyak,*" Marvin agreed.

"What are you talking about?" Steve said.

"Too much décolletage, very déclassé," Teresa said primly.

Teresa had learned English as a child at Havana's pre-Castro, upper-crust Ruston Academy. When she spoke, Steve could visualize neat feminine handwriting with even spaces between each word. "C'mon, Teresa. Just because you don't like Mrs. Barksdale's taste in clothes doesn't mean she killed her husband."

"Now, Charles Barksdale," Teresa said. "Very classy."

"You knew him?"

"Not really. But I heard him speak at a seminar he sponsored. 'Women Poets, Tortured Souls.' He seemed to be a most sensitive man."

"Especially when wearing a leather penis pouch," Steve said.

"Personally, I think the *puta* killed him," Teresa Toraño said.

Twenty-two

THE SLEEKEST SHARK

"Of all the courtrooms in all the counties of this swampy state, you had to walk into mine," Judge Alvin Schwartz said.

"And good morning to you, Your Honor," Steve said.

Victoria knew the judge's reputation as king of the curmudgeons. She'd appeared twice on his motion calendar and found him to be irascible, impatient, and inattentive. He was also prone to passing gas at sidebar conferences, then blaming it on the stenographer. Old, short, and angry, Judge Schwartz did not particularly like male lawyers who were young, tall, and happy. He had survived three attempts to remove him from the bench for intemperate comments, sexual harassment, and sleeping through trials.

"I know all about your shenanigans, Mr. Solomon."

"Thank you very much, Your Honor," Steve said, as if he'd been named Kiwanis Man of the Year.

At the prosecution table, Ray Pincher stifled a smile. Next to Victoria, Katrina squirmed in her chair. She wore a jailhouse orange jumpsuit, instead of her usual Prada.

The judge said: "You make any mischief in my courtroom, Mr. Solomon, I'll send you to a place you've never been."

"Already been to jail, sir."

"I'm talking about law school."

Across the aisle, Pincher barked out a little laugh.

"What's going on?" Katrina whispered.

"It's okay," Victoria said, patting her arm. "Steve knows what he's doing."

She was trying to reassure their client. And maybe herself, too.

"That you, Ms. Lord?" The judge peered over the top of his rimless spectacles.

"Yes, Your Honor."

"Aren't you on the wrong side of the courtroom?"

"I'm a defense lawyer now. Cocounsel with Mr. Solomon."

"Last good-looking blonde he brought in here was inflatable." The judge gestured toward Katrina with his gavel. "That the little lady what waxed her husband?"

"Your Honor, I must object," Victoria said.

"Don't get your panties in a bunch. There's no jury here, just those jackals of the press." The judge swung the gavel toward the gallery, where a TV camera whirred and a dozen reporters scribbled notes. "Where's that fellow who wrote I should be impeached?"

Three hands shot up. The judge harrumphed and turned to the prosecution table. "Here are the ground rules, Mr. State Attorney. I don't want to hear any of that ghetto rap. None of that . . ." He turned to his

bailiff, a young black woman with dreadlocks.
"Wanda, what's that turd-brained music called?
Hopscotch?"

"Hip-hop," she said.

"No hip-hop. And no Bubonics."

"Ebonics," Wanda said.

"And who's that kid in the front row?"

"My nephew, Bobby," Steve said.

"I've heard about those word tricks of yours, you
little scamp." The judge dug a pinky into his ear,
rooted around, then called out: "Donald Rumsfeld."

"SELDOM FUND LARD," Bobby shot back.

"I'll be damned."

At that moment, the courtroom door opened, and
three tall young women strutted in. They were
dressed identically, in solid black, from their eyeglasses and wigs to their ultraminis, silk blouses, and
knee-high boots. Their lips were painted a glistening
red and glossed to an obscene shine. Carrying thin
black briefcases, they waltzed through the swinging
gate, hip-swiveled to the front of the bar, and
corkscrewed into their seats, just behind the defense
table. In one fluid motion, all three crossed their legs
in unison and pulled legal pads from their briefcases.
It took Victoria a moment to realize they were Lexy,
Rexy, and Gina, looking like Robert Palmer's girls'
band. What the hell? Then she remembered: *"The
judge likes young women lawyers in miniskirts."*

Was there anything Solomon wouldn't do to win?

"And who, may I ask, are these lovely creatures?"
the judge said, brightening.

"My law clerks," Steve said.

"Always glad to help young scholars." The judge
sat up straighter on the pillow he used to ease his

hemorrhoids. "You gals come on back to chambers anytime you want."

Katrina leaned close to Victoria. "The judge seems a trifle odd. . . ."

Again, Victoria patted her arm. A reassuring gesture, but Victoria was growing worried. How do you deal with such a judge?

"What say the state on the defense motion for bail?" the judge said.

"This is a capital case," Pincher replied. "The state opposes all bail."

"What say the defense?"

Victoria rose and exhaled a long breath. She hoped she didn't appear as nervous as she felt. On her table, five color-coded index cards were fanned out like a poker hand. "Under *State v. Arthur,* the court cannot deny bail unless the state demonstrates that the proof of guilt is evident or the presumption great. We submit the state can do neither. Further, Katrina Barksdale has no prior criminal record and has deep ties to the community. In short, she is an excellent candidate for pretrial release."

"Alrighty-ditey," the judge said. "Mr. State Attorney, let's hear some testimony, and keep it short. My bladder ain't what it used to be."

Pincher started with Medical Examiner Wu-Chi Yang. Dr. Yang was a slim man in his forties, in a brown suit and a yellow bow tie. He'd switched to bow ties years earlier because they didn't flap out of the lab coat and drip into whatever squooshy organ he happened to be dissecting.

In clipped tones, Dr. Yang related his findings. "Performed neck dissection after evisceration and removal of the brain. Dissected the sternocleidomastoid muscles, reflected omohyoid and sternohyoid muscles, incised soft tissue medial to carotid artery."

"And what did you find?" Pincher asked.

"Bruising on muscles of neck and hemorrhages near circoid cartilage, consistent with strangulation. Tardieu's spots on face and eyelids consistent with asphyxia."

As Dr. Yang droned on, Victoria shot a look at Steve. On a legal pad, he was drawing a diagram of a table for five, complete with a seating chart. Doris Kranchick at twelve o'clock, then running clockwise, Victoria, Steve, Jackie, and Bruce.

He's planning dinner, not rebuttal.

How will he handle cross-examination if he's not even listening?

Dr. Yang held up a black leather collar—State Exhibit A—and demonstrated how pulling one end through an open loop would tighten it. He showed the judge a photo of the bruises circling Charles Barksdale's neck. A ruler shown in the photo measured the bruise at eighty-six centimeters high. With his own ruler, Dr. Yang then showed that the collar was exactly the same.

"If the collar fit . . ." Dr. Yang said happily.

"You can't acquit," Pincher finished the thought.

Judge Schwartz shot Pincher an angry look. "You want to wrap up this dog-and-pony show?"

"Your conclusion, Dr. Yang?" Pincher asked.

"The cause of death was asphyxia from strangulation, which resulted from a tightening of the collar that compressed the decedent's neck."

"Defense got anything to say?" Judge Schwartz asked.

Victoria waited for Steve to stand. When he didn't

move, she leapt to her feet. "Yes, Your Honor, just a few questions . . ."

"Which I'll ask," Steve said, easing from his chair. "Good morning, Dr. Yang."

"If you say so," the ME said, warily.

Without asking for permission to approach, Steve walked to the witness stand and reached for the leather collar. "May I?"

Dr. Yang shrugged, then handed it over. "Not mine."

"So it's clear, you just expressed your opinion as to the medical cause of death, not whether that death was a homicide, correct?"

"That is right."

Steve turned and walked back to the defense table. Glided, really, Victoria thought. She remembered the poster on his office wall. The courtroom filled with water, sharks cutting to and fro. Steve was the sleekest shark in the lagoon, and these were his waters. Swimming toward the defense table, he unbuttoned his suit coat and smiled at Victoria. Now what?

"Dr. Yang, if I wanted to force Ms. Lord to wear this collar, what would I do?" Steve asked.

"Don't ask me. She's your partner."

In the gallery, someone chuckled.

"Well, let's find out." Steve circled behind the defense table, barely leaving a wake. He lifted Victoria's hair, wrapped the open collar around her neck, and slid the leather tongue through the loop. "Now, if Ms. Lord wants to stop me from tightening this, let's see what she does."

Victoria reached up with both hands and worked her fingers under the collar. Steve pulled the leather through the loop, trapping her fingers against her

neck. She felt her fingernails digging into her flesh.
She gasped for air and Steve loosened the collar,
bending close enough to her neck that she could feel
his breath.

"Let the record reflect that there are fingernail
marks on Ms. Lord's neck where she attempted to
ward off the collar," he said.

He turned back to the witness. "Doctor, what
about Charles Barksdale? Any sign of a struggle? Any
scratches, bruises, lacerations, skin under his fingernails?"

"That's five questions," Pincher protested.

"Let's hear five answers," the judge said.

"No. No. No. No. And no," Dr. Yang said.

Steve stood behind Victoria, resting a hand on
each of her shoulders. It was an odd sensation, feeling him there but not seeing him. The next sensation
was even stranger. One of his thumbs was stroking
the nape of her neck.

"No evidence of a struggle," Steve said, in case the
judge missed it. "So, apparently, Mr. Barksdale consented to being collared and to having the collar
tightened."

"Tightened up to a point, yes."

She felt both his thumbs kneading her neck, like a
Swedish massage. A pleasant, tingling sensation
moved down her torso, and she squirmed in her seat.

"Isn't the bondage, the choking, the sexual paraphernalia consistent with consensual asphyxiophilia?"

"That is correct. It's in the medical journals."

"And the reason it's in the medical journals is because of the occurrence of accidental death during
these practices?"

"Accidental death is a known risk, yes."

Steve paused. The witness had made an important concession, and a good lawyer lets helpful words hang in the air before chasing them away. Victoria allowed herself a slight smile. Steve was in control, not only of himself, but of the entire courtroom. He'd been right about one thing he'd told her early on: She could learn from him.

But her mind wasn't totally focused on legal lessons. The mini-massage was continuing, and her entire body seemed to be overheating. She wished she could take off her Anne Klein cropped jacket, maybe her silk blouse, too. Did Steve even know what he was doing? She hoped that Katrina, sitting alongside, couldn't see what was going on.

"You cannot rule out the possibility of accidental death, can you, Dr. Yang?" Steve said.

"Could be accident, that's right."

Steve made sure the reporters in the gallery saw him smile. He gave Victoria's neck one last squeeze, released her, and sat down. "Nothing further."

Victoria knew that her face was flushed. She wondered if anyone else noticed. Next to her, Katrina leaned over and whispered. "Before we're done today, do you think he can do that to me, too?"

Dr. Yang had left the courtroom and Homicide Detective Delvin Farnsworth was answering questions by the time Victoria felt her body temperature return to normal. She didn't know Farnsworth but had checked around. A twenty-year veteran with a brush mustache and alert, dark eyes, he had a reputation for honesty and competence. She had read his report, so there no were surprises in his direct testimony.

Paramedics had responded to Mrs. Barksdale's 911 call at 11:39 P.M. on November 16, and after attempts to resuscitate her husband failed, the police were called. When they arrived, Charles Barksdale was naked except for a leather collar and what Farnsworth called a "silver-studded leather testicles pouch with a penile opening." A leather mask with a built-in latex dildo was on the floor nearby.

Mrs. Barksdale told detectives that she had engaged in her customary sex play involving cutting off her husband's air supply to enhance his orgasm, Detective Farnsworth testified. This time, during a break in the action, something happened, and her husband stopped breathing. That occurred when she was nearly twenty feet from the bed in a wet-bar alcove of the master suite, and she apparently did not immediately realize that her husband was in distress. The detective raised his bushy eyebrows when reciting that tidbit.

Crime-scene techs tagged and bagged various erotic paraphernalia, including leather straps and collars, chains, masks, fleece-lined handcuffs, cat-o'-nine-tails, and what an evidence form termed a "battery-operated anal stimulation device."

Steve stood up on cross. "What was Mrs. Barksdale's demeanor when you questioned her?"

"She was crying," Detective Farnsworth said.

"About what you would expect from a woman whose husband just died?"

"Objection, irrelevant," Pincher said.

"Overruled," the judge said.

"I've seen so many reactions, I don't know what to expect anymore," Farnsworth said.

"Just what in your investigation made you conclude that the death of Charles Barksdale was not an accident?"

"The totality of the circumstances."

"That doesn't tell us much."

"Wasn't intended to."

"What was Mrs. Barksdale's motive for killing her husband?"

"Objection," Pincher said. "Improper foundation. Goes beyond scope of direct. And protected by work product."

"I'll be the judge of that," Judge Schwartz said. He seemed to think about it, then added, "In fact, I *am* the judge of that. How'd I rule on the last objection?"

"You overruled it," Pincher said.

"Then this one's sustained."

"Let me ask it this way," Steve said. "Did Katrina Barksdale have any reason to kill her husband?"

"I wouldn't know," the detective said.

"Did he deprive her of food, clothing, trips to the South of France?"

"I'd say he provided for her quite well."

"Quite well," Steve repeated. He opened a large portfolio and pulled out a photo blown up to poster size: the Barksdales in formal attire. "That diamond pendant Katrina's wearing at the Attention Deficit Disorder brunch. Who do you suppose bought her that?"

"Wild guess, her husband," Farnsworth said.

Steve moved closer to the witness stand and held up another photo. "What about the aquamarine and diamond brooch she wore to the Stop Bulimia Now dinner?"

"Same guess."

Steve returned to his table and Victoria handed him a file folder thick with receipts. Neiman Marcus. Getz Jewelers. Bavarian Custom Motorcars.

"The generosity went both ways," Steve said. "Did you know that in the last two months before Charles' unfortunate demise, Mrs. Barksdale bought him a sapphire ring, three Zegna suits, and a Breitling Superocean watch, twenty-five jewels, with the extra-large face?"

"She spent a lot of his money. What of it?"

In the gallery, Bobby squirmed in his seat and gestured toward Steve, who caught the movement but shook his head. "What about in these photos? Katrina and Charles look happy?"

"Objection," Pincher said. "It's irrelevant how they looked in photographs."

"How'd I rule last time?" the judge asked.

"You sustained," Pincher said wearily.

"Overruled."

"Do the Barksdales look happy?" Steve repeated.

"I'm a homicide detective," Farnsworth said. "We're not experts on happiness."

Steve pulled out another poster-size photo. "And this shot from the Save the Manatees dinner?"

"He's kissing her. She's got lots of jewelry. What's your question?"

"Does Katrina look like she's about to kill her husband?"

"Probably not that evening."

"How many pictures do you have?" the judge asked, growing bored.

"Hundreds, Your Honor. The joy of this couple was infinite. But let's wrap it up with this one." Steve turned toward the witness but spoke to the reporters. "Three months before he died, Charles Barksdale turned sixty. For a surprise birthday party, Katrina Barksdale sent the whole world a message. She gathered her husband's friends on their boat. She arranged for a band and a gourmet meal. And finally . . ."

He lowered his voice, using the lawyer's trick of garnering more attention with softer words. "Katrina hired an airplane to tow a banner across the sky."

Victoria glanced at Pincher. Why didn't he object? Steve was testifying, not asking a question. Strictly speaking, all of this was irrelevant to bail. Why was the State Attorney as still as a potted plant?

Steve hoisted the airplane photo into view and waltzed along the bar, making sure the reporters had a good look before turning back to the witness. "What does the banner say, Detective Farnsworth? What did Katrina Barksdale proclaim in letters ten feet tall?"

"Katrina loves Charles," Farnsworth said.

"KATRINA LOVES CHARLES!" Steve blared.

"Would it be impolite," Pincher asked, "to inquire what the point of all this is?"

"The point," Steve said, "is that the prosecution has not shown that the proof of guilt is evident or the presumption great. There's no evidence that the death was even a homicide. Indeed, all that's been proven today is that Katrina Barksdale loved her husband very much. The court must therefore release her, pending trial."

Steve ambled back to his chair, circled the

prosecution table, and grinned at the gallery. His victory lap. Like he'd just scored from first on a single and wanted the moment to linger. Then he sat down, reaching over to squeeze Victoria's hand. As he did, a tiny spark of static electricity jolted them both.

WIDOW FREE ON MILLION-DOLLAR BOND
Sky-High Message: "Katrina Loves Charles"

By Joan Fleischman
Herald *Staff Writer*

Katrina Barksdale, accused of murder in the asphyxiation death of her husband, Charles Barksdale, walked out of the Women's Detention Center today, free on one million dollars bond.

Over the strenuous objections of State Attorney Raymond Pincher, Judge Alvin Schwartz granted bail following a two-hour hearing. "Murderers belong in jail, not free on bail," Pincher said.

Defense lawyers Stephen Solomon and Victoria Lord argued that the state could not even prove Charles Barksdale was murdered, much less that his wife was the guilty party. The defense contends that the 60-year-old construction magnate accidentally suffocated during consensual sex with his 33-year-old wife.

Solomon also introduced a series of photographs of the couple in an attempt to show that they were deeply in love. In one photo, an airplane towed a banner reading, "Katrina Loves Charles."

At a post-hearing press conference, Solomon set the tone for the forthcoming trial. "My client is a woman who loved her husband as much as I love the law," he said.

After turning over a deed to the couple's Gables Estates mansion as security, Katrina Barksdale was released, pending trial.

Twenty-three

HOW BIG IS YOUR BIGBY?

Clothes strewn across his bed, Steve dressed for dinner, trying to choose between a boring brown plaid suit he'd bought on sale years ago and a charcoal gray pinstripe job that would be suitable for an execution. Ordinarily, dinner attire meant khaki shorts and a rugby shirt, but tonight Steve had to convince Dr. Doris Kranchick that he was a solid citizen, a marrying man.

"The brown's friendly and the gray's powerful," Steve said, unable to decide.

"Both are dorky," Bobby said. He was drinking a peanut butter and chocolate shake, one of Steve's concoctions to help the boy gain weight. "Didn't you see me waving at you in court?"

"Yeah, what was that all about?" Steve held the brown plaid jacket up to the mirror. "You know better than to interrupt when I'm rocking."

"I wanted to tell you something—"

"Dr. Kranchick, you look lovely tonight," Steve practiced into the mirror.

"—about that Breitling watch."

"Did I look like I was lying just then?"

"No more than usual. Are you listening, Uncle Steve?"

"Yeah, the watch Katrina bought for Charles. Maybe I should ask Victoria what she's wearing. We could be color-coordinated."

"Then you'd be super dorky." Bobby slurped the shake, a glob of peanut butter stuck in the straw. "What I wanted to tell you, I looked at all the pictures, and Mr. Barksdale had skinny arms and wrists."

"So?"

"All his other watches were thin, but the Breitling Superocean is thick. It's heavy-duty, good to like three thousand feet."

"So it's a dive watch. What of it?"

"In those pictures on the beach and on boats, why wasn't he ever wearing it?"

Steve was looking for a tie to match the brown plaid. "Like you said, it wasn't his style. Maybe he didn't like it."

"So why'd Mrs. Barksdale buy it for him?"

"Because she's a ditz. What difference does it make?"

"Was Mr. Barksdale a scuba diver?"

"I doubt he ever got out of the Jacuzzi. Can you wear a striped tie with a plaid—" Steve stopped. A feeling of dread crept over him. "Are you saying what I think you're saying?"

"If you ask me, Uncle Steve, Mrs. Barksdale bought the watch for somebody who wasn't her husband."

———

At about the same time as Steve was trying to match a plaid suit with a striped tie, Victoria was dressing in Jackie Tuttle's Grove Isle condo. They had played two hours of tennis, Victoria rushing the net whenever possible, and sometimes when it wasn't. Jackie had been content to stand at the baseline and hit a variety of dinks, drops, and dipsy doodles, expending as little energy as possible while talking nonstop. Flying to the net was not only draining, it could also break a girl's nose if she got walloped by one of Victoria's powerful volleys.

Now, after showering and downing a pair of gin and tonics each, they were slipping into their clothes while chattering about work and men and a shoe sale at Bloomingdale's. Jackie had changed into a Roberto Cavalli black spandex top with open shoulders, dripping with gold-tone chains. Examining herself in the mirror, she cupped both hands under her breasts and lifted them. "How do my bazooms look?"

"Big and bodacious," Victoria said.

"That's the idea."

Victoria chose a consignment-shop Ralph Lauren dress, white silk from the waist down, a sexy silver mesh racer's back on top. Like a wrestler's singlet, it was scooped low, leaving her shoulders and most of her back bare.

"You can't wear a bra with that," Jackie said, pouring herself into tight, stretchy black and gold jeans that picked up the gold chain motif.

"Wasn't planning to. Do I look too flat-chested?"

"Not a bit. It's great on you. Really hot. You just don't usually . . ."

"What?"

"Dress like that. But it's terrific."

Victoria borrowed a pair of Jackie's shoes—ankle-wrap champagne sandals with three-inch heels—then spent longer than usual on her makeup, trying the chestnut lip liner before starting over with red chocolate, a perfect match with the naked pink lipstick. Jackie watched, a small smile playing at the corners of her mouth.

"What now?" Victoria demanded.

"Nothing. You just seem different tonight. Less inhibited."

"I'm playing a role, that's all."

"Uh-huh."

"I need to make an impression."

"On the doctor or the Bad Boy?"

"Don't start with that. I'm playing the kind of woman Solomon would marry."

"When you're with Bruce, do you play the kind of woman he'd marry?"

"What's that mean?"

"Don't take this wrong," Jackie said, "because I'm your absolutely best friend and I'm not being catty. But I'm just wondering. Which is the real you?"

An hour later, the two women were sitting at a table for five at the Coconut Grove Yacht Club, a pleasantly aging relic of a more genteel era, just yards from the marina. The sun was just setting over the Everglades, but Victoria and Jacqueline already had downed two martinis each. Knowing how much Steve was depending on her, Victoria was starting to feel the pressure. She also had doubts about her mission: How on earth could she reverse whatever lousy impression Steve already had made? She signaled the waiter. Maybe another drink would settle her nerves.

"This time," Jackie said, "I've really sworn off men. That's why I'm reading *Life Without Dick.*"

"That's a book?" Victoria said.

"In the self-help section, right next to *Slouching Toward Celibacy.*"

"This doesn't sound like you."

"All these years I've been looking for a genius with a penis. Then I figured I'd settle for either one. Now I'm torn between flying solo and muff diving."

"No way."

"You don't think I'd make a good lesbo?"

"Definitely not."

"It's that or nothing. Unless the Bad Boy turns me on."

Two more martinis arrived. Victoria was feeling a pleasant buzz, and the tension started to ease. Sure, she could wow this doctor. Just bring her on. Outside the yacht club windows, the moored sailboats were bathed in a pink glow.

"Tell me more about him," Jackie said.

"Solomon? He's incredibly competitive and hates to lose."

"Gee, who does that sound like?"

"No way."

"In the second set, why'd you smash an overhead right at my big butt?"

"An accident." She sipped at her drink. "Solomon's a loner. Stubborn and independent."

"No wonder you can't stand him. You're just alike."

"I am not a loner."

"Then why won't you play with me in the Christmas tournament?"

"You know why. I don't like doubles."

"Because you hate depending on anyone else."

Victoria thought about it. True, she wanted to win or lose on her own. Preferably win. What's wrong with that?

"Solomon's stubborn, bossy, and never admits he's wrong. And he loves the spotlight. You should have seen him at the press conference after the bail hearing. He's surrounded by these bimbos he says are his law clerks, but they're really South Beach models he's dated."

"Another guy who's a modelizer? Jeez, I gotta lose weight."

"The bimbos are fighting for face time, and Solomon's spouting off about how we're going to kick the prosecution's butt. It was unseemly *and* borderline unethical."

"C'mon, he sounds like a hoot."

Solomon did something else, too, something Victoria didn't mention because she was still processing it. With cameras rolling and questions firing, he'd veered into a soliloquy about the natural law and the sanctity of the marital bedroom and other riffs that none of the reporters cared about or understood. Then he noticed Victoria standing off to the side, out of camera range. He pulled her over and wrapped an arm around her shoulder.

"Don't forget to mention my partner," he told the reporters. "Victoria Lord. Not 'Vickie.' Victoria. She's gonna be the best trial lawyer Miami's ever seen."

Solomon had surprised her again. Sure, he could

be arrogant and a total jerk. But sometimes it seemed that his jerkiness was an act, that the nice guy underneath slipped out when he wasn't looking. The opposite of most men, who worked hard to conceal their truly disagreeable traits.

"In a word, Solomon is maddening," she said.

Jackie nibbled at an olive. "Maddening is first cousin to enchanting."

"Not to me." She vowed to reject any cuddly thoughts of Solomon that might have been brought on by his press conference flattery.

"Does he ride a Harley?" Jackie asked. "I love Harleys." She opened her black satin evening bag and took out her compact. Examining her face in the mirror, she smoothed out the lines in her forehead. "He better show up before we lose that magic hour glow."

"Trust me, Jackie, he's not your type."

"Why not? I won't like him or he won't like me?"

Victoria thought about it and came to a startling conclusion. In all likelihood, they would like each other. They had the same ribald sense of humor, the same breeziness. How could she not have seen it? And now that she had, why was she still reluctant to play matchmaker?

"I don't know, Jackie. It's just hard to fix people up."

"Okay, I'm not gonna beg. But if I can't have the Bad Boy, can you clone Mr. Perfect for me?"

"Sometimes I wonder if I even deserve Bruce." Victoria felt a pang of guilt. She hadn't even thought about her fiancé, Solomon being the prime topic of conversation.

"Stop or I'll hurl." Then Jackie's eyes flickered

with a mischievous look. "I'll bet Bruce really makes your sheets sing."

"It'll take another martini before I go there."

"Waiter!" Jackie called out. "The way I figure, Bruce tries so hard at everything, he's gotta be great in the sack."

Why were her lips going numb? Victoria wondered. "The only thing I'll say, I'm usually sore for two days."

"He's hung, too? I hate you."

Just then, Steve hurried to the table, looked at Victoria, did a double take, and said: "Wow! You look outstanding."

"Solomon, meet my haid of monor, Jackal. I mean, maid of honor, Jackie."

Jackie bounded out of her chair and threw her arms around Steve, running her hands across his back.

"Where is it?" she demanded.

"You think I'm wearing a wire?" Steve said, bewildered.

"Your fin. Where's the damn fin?"

Victoria was laughing so hard she snorted, which caused Jackie to melt into a paroxysm of giggles. The only one not laughing was Steve.

"When did you two start drinking?" He counted the toothpicks, circumstantial evidence of their guzzling. "I can't believe this."

"Uh-oh," Victoria said. "We violated one of Solomon's Laws." She mimicked his voice. "Never imbibe until sundown." Then, hoisting the martini glass: "But just like Katrina said, it's gotta be dark somewhere in the world."

"I didn't expect this from you," he said.

"If the law doesn't work, jerk off the law."

"Where's Bigby?" Steve asked, unamused.

"Trying to fit into his underpants," Jackie said, convulsing in laughter, breasts heaving. She grabbed a baguette from the bread basket, waved it at Steve. "Hey, white shark, how's your package? Are you as big as Bigby?"

"Aw, Jesus," Steve said.

The waiter showed up with a tray of martinis. "Would you like to catch up with the ladies, sir?" he inquired.

"I'd like to horsewhip the ladies."

"Me first," Jackie said.

"Take away the drinks. Bring a pitcher of ice water and a pot of coffee," Steve ordered.

Victoria pouted. "Why so uptight, Solomon?"

"This is important to me, okay?"

"Don't worry, Stevie." Victoria patted his hand. "I can carry this off. And if not, there's nobody I'd rather do jail time with than you."

Twenty-four

HOW GREEN IS MY DAIQUIRI?

Steve spotted Bruce Bigby headed across the dining room.

Suntanned and smiling, Bigby made his rounds, smacking pals on the back, braying "Evening, Commodore" to an older gent, strutting toward their table in a black cashmere blazer, the breast pocket emblazoned with the yacht club seal. He grinned hellos to Jackie and Steve, then turned to Victoria. "Heavens, what's that you're wearing?"

"Do you like it?" she asked, extending her bare arms, swiveling to show off her mesh singlet and nearly naked back. She'd had a glass of ice water and three cups of black coffee, and best Steve could tell, was as sober as a judge. Actually, more sober than most judges he knew.

"It's very . . . very shiny," Bruce stumbled. His tie was black silk with little gold anchors. "Aren't you cold?"

"Not a bit, hon."

"No 'hons' and no 'sweeties' tonight. We might slip up later."

"I'm glad to see someone's taking this seriously,"

Steve said. "Thanks, Bruce. For doing this, for everything."

"Hey, *no problema, amigo.* You're teaching
Victoria some lawyer tricks. I'm happy to help out."

Just then, Dr. Doris Kranchick arrived and intro-
ductions were made. Steve watched as Victoria went
into full charm-school mode. Oh, how she admired
someone who devoted herself to science, and had
the doctor seen that recent article in the *Journal of
Applied Psychology* on acquired savant syndrome?
And what about behavioral therapy versus drug
therapy?

Steve lost track when they began discussing cere-
bral refreshment and triggering stem cells to produce
even more neurons. Just when the conversation grew
impossibly dense, Victoria smoothly turned to lacrosse, starting with the Iroquois warriors who
played the game with human skulls. Steve realized
then that Victoria had prepared for the evening the
way she prepared for court. Research, planning, out-
lines. She probably had alphabetized index cards
in her purse: "*Lacrosse, History of Sport. Native
Americans.*"

When Victoria paused, Bruce unexpectedly
grabbed the baton and ran the next lap. He invited
Kranchick to visit his farm, then cursed the "damned
evil weevil" that attacked his avocado trees. Jackie
jumped aboard with an offer to list the doctor's home
for sale at a reduced commission if she'd be interested
in a fabulous new bayfront condo in Hallandale.

The waiter came by with a tray filled with five
slushy drinks. "I took the liberty of ordering for
everyone," Bruce announced. "We're starting with

frozen avocado daiquiris. Then avocado vichyssoise, smooth as liquid silk."

Steve thought he'd rather drink phlegm.

"Then a tofu salad with herbs and avocados," Bigby continued, "vegetarian chili tamales with a tomatillo-avocado salsa, and sweet avocado mousse for dessert."

"Utterly delightful," Kranchick cooed.

Steve knew Victoria wouldn't be able to eat a thing without breaking out in a rash.

They chatted a while, Victoria making Kranchick the center of attention. Somewhere between the second and third tray of green drinks, Kranchick said: "Ms. Lord, it's absolutely wonderful to meet you. You're nothing like I expected."

Steve wondered if he'd just been dissed, but Victoria smiled and replied, "Thank you."

"And your engagement ring," Kranchick gushed. "Simply spectacular."

"Nothing says love like a big fat diamond," Steve chipped in.

"Mr. Solomon, you grow on people, don't you?"

"Like a fungus," he said.

"Which reminds me of citrus canker," Bigby piped up. "Helluva problem."

"I don't mean to pry, Mr. Bigby," Kranchick said, "but are you and Ms. Tuttle an item?"

Bruce wrapped an arm around Jackie, and she dropped her head onto his shoulder. "We're not as far along as Steve and Victoria, but who knows what the future will bring?"

"*Qué sera, sera,*" the doctor sang.

With Bruce and Jackie cuddling, Steve felt he had no choice. He had to keep up appearances, didn't he?

He slipped an arm around Victoria, but somehow, his hand ended up sliding under the fabric of her mesh top. Her skin was warm and smooth. He waited a moment to see if she would move away or dig a high heel into his ankle. When she didn't, he slowly began stroking her back.

She turned her head to him. A placid, controlled expression that betrayed nothing. Steve wished he knew what she was feeling. Desire? Regret? Anger? He sometimes thought he could read the look in a woman's eyes, but can any man?

"Tell me all about your wedding plans, Mr. Solomon," Kranchick said. "Where's the ceremony going to be?"

"Ah, Temple Beth—"

"Church of the Little Flower," Victoria interrupted.

"How lovely! I know it's a little soon to ask, but are you planning to have children?"

"Four," Victoria said, just as Steve said, "Two."

"Three," they corrected, in unison.

"Four?" Bigby asked, looking at Victoria, eyebrows arched.

"And if you don't mind my asking," Kranchick said, "are you planning on any religious training?"

"Jewish," Steve said.

"Episcopalian," Victoria said.

"Catholic," Bigby said.

"One of each?" Kranchick asked, clearly confused.

"We need to talk about the bridesmaids' dresses." Jackie desperately tried to change the subject. "Empire waists? Canary yellow and sunset orange? I'm gonna look like Kilauea."

"Bruce chose them," Victoria said, then realized she'd made a mistake.

Kranchick's high forehead furrowed. "Mr. Bigby, you outfitted the bridesmaids?"

"Yes, because . . ." Bigby began, then stopped. Stumped.

"Because . . ." Victoria said.

"Because . . ." Jackie said.

"Because Bruce is gay," Steve volunteered.

"Oh, my," Kranchick said.

"*Was* gay," Bigby corrected.

"Until he met me," Jackie said, stroking Bigby's cheek.

They were somewhere between the tofu and the tamales. Bigby was going on about the tragedy of medfly infestation, Kranchick listening as if he were revealing the mystery of Creation. Bigby's arm was still draped over Jackie's shoulder, so why shouldn't Steve keep up his own massage? With Victoria's back growing warmer under his touch, he nuzzled her ear and whispered, "For what it's worth, I think Bruce is the luckiest guy in town."

"Do you mean that?"

"I'm green with envy, as green as my daiquiri."

Leaning toward her, Steve's hand moved farther under the fabric, slipping around her rib cage and coming to rest just below her right breast. A perfectly fine, naturally firm, small but shapely, non-Rudnick breast, which now rested on the top of an index finger. She didn't move away, didn't call a cop, didn't slug him.

For a moment, he was fifteen again, in the balcony

of the theater on Arthur Godfrey Road, wondering what Sarah Gropowitz would do if he cupped her 32A in his hand. As he recalled, he did nothing for so long that his arm fell asleep. The pain had been so severe, he'd thought the evening might end with amputation.

Steve sneaked a glance at Victoria. She was blushing, the color starting at the base of her neck, moving like the incoming tide until her cheeks were ablaze. A moment later, she discreetly reached behind her back, removed his hand, and slid her chair back. "If you'll excuse me a moment . . ."

She bolted from the table, avoiding eye contact with Steve. His eyes were trained on the front of her singlet, where her nipples propped up the silvery mesh like roof shingles in a hurricane. He ordinarily hopped to his feet when a lady left the table. But he couldn't stand up just now, not with his napkin pitched like a tent over his crotch. He shot a nervous look at Bruce, who was offering Kranchick a two-bedroom apartment at Bigby Resort & Villas, lakefront view at no charge. Then a peek at Jackie, who was watching him, eyes keen as talons. Smiling devilishly, she dangled a maraschino cherry by its stem, rolled it on her tongue, and bit into it.

"Mr. Solomon, I must say you have wonderful friends," Kranchick said, breaking away from Bigby's sales pitch, "and your fiancée is both beautiful and charming."

"Sometimes I feel like pinching myself, asking if it's all real."

"It's real, old chap," Bruce said heartily. "And you deserve it all."

Old chap? Maybe it was the yacht club surroundings, or maybe he'd overdosed on daiquiris. Still, Bigby was a decent guy, and for a moment Steve felt guilty about the strange brew of feelings he had for the man's fiancée. The guilt, however, was pretty much drowning in a deep pool of desire. With Victoria still nowhere in sight, Steve excused himself from the table.

He searched the bar area.

No Victoria.

He went to the ladies' rest room, knocked on the door, and called her name.

No Victoria.

He ducked into the kitchen and looked around.

Where was she?

He went onto the patio and followed the path to the pier. And there she was, walking along a row of power boats. He caught up to her next to the *Whiplash,* a Fountain speedster owned by a personal-injury lawyer.

"You okay?" he asked.

"I just needed some air."

She was staring across the bay and wouldn't look at him. He came closer. The only sounds were the clanks and groans of the boats in their moorings and the far-off caw of a seabird. The sun had set, and an evening breeze chilled the air.

"You're cold." Steve took both of her bare arms in his hands and felt the goose bumps.

"What were you doing in there?" Sounding angry. Ready to unload on him. "Just what the hell were you doing?"

"I'm sorry. You're helping me. Big-time. So if I was out of line . . ."

"And in court, massaging my neck?"

"It won't happen again. Scout's honor."

"I'll bet a year's pay you were never a Boy Scout."

"I was till they caught me peeping into the girls' bunkhouse."

"And what are you doing now?"

He hadn't realized it, but his hands were rubbing her upper arms. "Just keeping you warm." But in reality, he simply couldn't keep his hands off her. "I apologize. Really, I would never—"

"Shut up, Solomon." She threw her arms around his neck, pulled him close, and kissed him.

He was so startled that it took him a second to kiss her back. But he did. At first, soft and tender. Then deeper, hungrier. Lips melting, tongues circling, it was a long, sigh-filled, sweet river of a kiss that left them both gasping. He held her close, and for a long moment, neither moved.

He tried to fathom his longings. Why did this feel so different than all the rest? Why did this woman matter?

Suddenly, she pulled back and turned away.

"That didn't happen," she said.

"Yes it did."

"I'm drunk."

"Don't think so."

"Or it's some chemical thing. I'm light-headed from not eating."

"You want the paramedics?"

"Or it's propinquity. We work together every day, so naturally some feelings arise."

"That's gotta be it."

"Or it's reverse chemistry. We really don't like each other, so this is some mutually codependent, destructive urge that manifested itself simultaneously in both of us."

"Or a rational, synergistic coupling," he said, using her own words against her.

"I doubt it." She was hugging herself with both hands.

Steve came to her, put his arms around her from behind. "Whatever it is, why not go with the flow?"

She wheeled to face him. "And where will that take us? Besides your bedroom?"

"I don't know. I just thought—"

"Isn't that just like you, Solomon? Do what feels good and damn the consequences."

"Do what feels *right*. And this feels right. Why fight it?"

"For one thing, I'm engaged." She held up her ring finger.

"A lawyer would notice you didn't say, 'I'm in love with someone else.' "

"That's implicit in 'I'm engaged.' "

"Love's never implicit in anything."

"Okay, I *love* Bruce. I love him a lot. I'm going to marry him. Satisfied?"

"If you are."

"I'm not going to play this game."

Suddenly, a woman's voice sang out of the darkness. "I knew it!" A second later, Jackie showed up. "What'd I miss?"

"Nothing." Victoria raked her hair with her fingertips. "We were just planning trial strategy."

"Sure you were. I saw Bad Boy cop a feel, then you took off without your purse, which you wouldn't do if the place were on fire. Then Bad Boy follows you out here, so I thought maybe, just maybe, you might need your lipstick, which believe me, you do." She handed Victoria her purse.

"Oh, God, Jackie." Victoria opened the purse and fished for a mirror.

"Relax. Bruce is describing the horror of root rot, which he claims is like genital warts. The doctor's enthralled. And what do you have to say for yourself, Bad Boy?"

"Nothing happened out here," Steve said.

"Don't worry. I won't rat you out. Vic's my best friend. But it's not fair."

"What?" Steve asked.

"She has two fiancés," Jackie said, "and I don't have any."

Bruce Kingston Bigby

and

Victoria Lord

request the honour of your presence

at their marriage

on Saturday, the eighth day of January

Two Thousand and Six

at six o'clock in the evening

Church of the Little Flower

2711 Indian Mound Trail

Coral Gables, Florida.

Black tie dinner to follow at the Biltmore Hotel*

*No animals or animal products will be used in food preparation.

Twenty-five

A KISS IS NOT A KISS

Where the hell was she?

It was 10:37 A.M., according to the Miami Dolphins helmet clock on Steve's desk, and Victoria was MIA. Not like her at all. She usually got half a day's work done before most people had finished their Wheaties. Or in his case, a handful of guava *pastalitos* with *café Cubano*.

What if she'd quit? Quit the case and quit him.

No answer at her apartment, no answer on her cell phone. She probably spent the night at Bigby's house, a thought that depressed Steve even more.

Kissing me and sleeping with him. The wench.

Thinking about Bigby made Steve feel devious. Not lawyer devious, that was a given. Personal devious, and that wasn't him. Even as an adolescent, he never bird-dogged other guys' girls, cheated on exams, or boasted of his own conquests. And his lies were always harmless and easily disproved, like exaggerating the size of his penis.

So where the hell was she?

Steve was supposed to be interviewing new clients—the Barksdale publicity had flushed out a few quail—but his heart wasn't in it. He was still thinking about THE KISS. Feeling it. Tasting it. The physical sensation lingering on his lips, sweeping through his body, searing itself on his brain. Or what was left of it.

What the hell's going on?

His mind drifted to other kisses. Two decades ago, he'd planted one on fourteen-year-old Sarah Gropowitz in the theater balcony during the movie *Witness*. He remembered waiting until Harrison Ford got his car started in the barn, and Sam Cooke was singing that he didn't know much about history.

Ford takes Kelly McGillis in his arms, and they dance, a brazen sacrilege, because of her Amish upbringing, to say nothing of her recent widowhood. Young Steve figured this was the kind of scene that turned chicks on, forbidden love and all that. Just as Cooke confessed that he was equally deficient in biology, Steve leaned close to Sarah's Clearasil-spotted face. Puckering up, Steve strafed her like a cruise missile hitting a terrorist camp. For his efforts, he got a mouthful of her jujubes, a cackling laugh, and derision from his peers for weeks to come.

Thinking about the movie deflated him. Harrison Ford didn't get the girl. True to his nature, the hard-boiled cop returned to his city. And true to her roots, Kelly McGillis hooked up with a strapping, blond farmer. Sort of an Amish Bruce Bigby. All of which led Steve to two disheartening conclusions.

Maybe opposites attract, but they don't usually end up together.

And . . .

If Harrison Ford couldn't get the girl, how the hell could he?

———————

"*Qué pasa, jefe?*"

Cece stalked into his office with the morning's mail in one hand, a twenty-five-pound dumbbell in the other. Today, she wore lower-than-low Brazilian jeans and a cropped tee. Trying to look like J-Lo or Shakira or Thalia—Steve couldn't keep them straight.

"Victoria call?" he asked.

"Why should she?"

"Because she's late."

"Slave driver." She dumped the mail on his desk. "Your next customer will be here *ahorita mismo.*"

"*Client,* Cece. We call them clients."

She shrugged, her trapezius muscles fluttering.

"It's not like Victoria to be late."

Cece started doing one-arm curls with the dumbbell. "What's with you today?"

"Nothing. Nothing's happened."

"Didn't say anything happened. Why you wigging out?"

"I'm fine. Everything's fine. We've got a murder trial to prep, that's all."

"So how'd dinner go?"

"Kranchick adores Victoria and wants to run off with Bigby."

"So you snowed the doc?"

"I'm not sure. Vic and I weren't always on the same page."

"What a shock," Cece said, shifting the dumbbell to her other hand.

Steve riffled through the mail. He could hear the steel band warming up across the alley. Either that, or a truck was dumping scrap metal on the asphalt.

"What's this?" Steve was holding a square enve-

lope on fine linen paper. His name and address were
written in calligraphy.

"Open it and find out."

"That's your job, Cece. Open the mail, calendar
hearings, deposit checks."

"What checks?"

Steve opened the envelope and pulled out a wedding invitation. *Bruce Kingston Bigby and Victoria
Lord.* Slipping it back into the envelope, he had the
bizarre notion that he could stop the wedding by pretending the invitation did not exist.

What's going on, anyway? What are these feelings?

He felt like a man with a strange, undiagnosed disease. He felt no pain, but had a sense of impending
doom.

Five minutes later, Cece was back in the waiting
room, free weights clanging, and Steve heard a
buzzing. Looking up, he saw Harry Sachs wheeling
himself through the open door in his motorized chair.
Harry was in his early forties, beady-eyed, jowly,
and paunchy. He wore a gray U.S. Marines T-shirt
with camouflage pants and paratrooper boots. An
American flag flew from back of the chair and a decal
read: *"Help a Grenada Vet."*

"I'm not gonna handle your divorce, Harry," Steve
said.

"Who said anything about a divorce?"

"Every month you come in here saying you want
out. I file the papers, then you and Joanne reconcile."

"She's still busting my balls, but that ain't why I'm
here."

Steve liked Joanne Sachs but knew she could be a

nag, always insisting that Harry give up his chosen profession as a con man.

"Then what is it?" Steve said. "I already told you I won't sue your parents for being ugly."

"Not just for being ugly," Harry said. "For having the chutzpah to procreate."

"Forget it."

"Okay, but I got a new one that'll make us both rich. You know that strip club on the Seventy-ninth Street Causeway? The Beav?"

"Don't think I do."

"That's funny, 'cause two of the girls there recommended you. Not that I'd ever use another lawyer."

"I appreciate it, Harry. Tell me about the case."

"Discrimination. We're talking big bucks here."

"I'm listening and I'm fascinated," Steve said, telling two lies for the price of one. In reality, he was still thinking about the taste of Victoria's lips. And just why couldn't Kelly McGillis end up with Harrison Ford? And if she had, would he have come to the country or would she have gone to the city? That's the rub. Even if he ever got together with Victoria, who would change to accommodate the other? And wasn't it asinine even to be thinking these thoughts? She was about to be married, and in case he'd forgotten, the engraved invitation was there to remind him.

Harry Sachs buzzed his wheelchair closer to Steve's desk. "I been a regular at The Beav for years, ever since the cops shut down Crotches. I got the membership card, you buy ten lap dances, get one free, just like Frappuccinos at Starbucks. But they remodeled, and now the VIP lounge is up three stairs, and I can't get there."

"So?"

"Whadaya mean, 'so'? Equal access to public facilities. I'm talking punitive damages, a class action."

"What's the class, con artists?"

"The disabled. We got a right to get our rocks off. Life, liberty, and"—Harry grabbed his groin—"the pursuit of happiness."

"Not exactly what Thomas Jefferson had in mind."

"Sure it is. Didn't you see the Nick Nolte movie? Anyway, they're violating my rights. Some thanks I get for leaving my blood on foreign soil."

"Harry, the closest you ever got to Grenada was Club Med."

"I got the medals!"

"Off the Internet. C'mon, you were never in the Marines, and your wheelchair's a prop for your homeless-veteran scam."

"Who says?"

"You jog. You Rollerblade. You play volleyball at the topless beach."

"That's my rehab."

Steve was ready to roll Harry Sachs out of his office, but instead said: "These lap dances you get—"

"Used to get."

"You ever kiss the girls?"

"You crazy? I don't even kiss my wife."

Twenty-six

THE LUST FACTOR

Harry was gone. The office was quiet, except for the steel band across the alley, playing some sort of conga that seemed to use hand grenades instead of tambourines. Victoria was still AWOL. If she didn't show up in five minutes, Steve would . . .

What? What will you do, smart guy?

Call the police, the hospitals, the Bigster?

Calm down. She's fine. You're just being neurotic.

Then his mood shifted east to west, like squalls in a thunderstorm. He sensed something positive might be in the air. She might be sitting under a palm tree on the beach, writing a Dear Bruce letter.

"I've met someone else. I hope you'll understand. We can always be friends. And by the way, I hate avocados."

Cheered by that thought, he leaned back in his chair, hands behind his head, feet propped on his desk, eyes closed. Wearing nothing but his Speedos, he was at the wheel of a sailboat on a turquoise sea. Victoria appeared on deck in one of her herringbone trial suits. Leaning against the mast, her hair tossed by the wind, she peeled off her outfit, piece by piece, revealing a black thong bikini. Speedo Steve approached, placed a hand on her bare, sun-warmed hip. They kissed, long and slow, with acres of bare skin against bare skin, and this time, she did not pull away. He tasted her moist lips, listened to the wind fill the sail, felt the bulge in his Speedos. He could hear Bob Marley and the Wailers singing "Waiting in Vain."

A moment later, Steve was vaguely aware that *he* was the one singing: *"I don't wanna wait in vain for your love."*

"Oh, Jesus," Victoria said. Not the bikinied Victoria on the sailboat. The real model, cloaked in a charcoal gray, tweedy pantsuit, carrying her briefcase and a cup of coffee into the office. "Auditioning for *American Idol*?"

"There you are," Steve said, trying to recover his dignity.

"Sorry I'm late."

"No problem." He checked her body language. Spine straight, jaw set, no eye contact. In trial lawyer's lore, if the jury refuses to look you in the eye, they've ruled against you. Along with most such fables, he told himself, it's right half the time.

He vowed to stick to business, not even mention THE KISS. Let her bring it up. Maybe the initial shock and denial had worn off.

Sooner or later, she's gotta break down, gotta admit it was a pulse-pounding moment.

She moved quickly to her desk. Outside the window, the steel band was banging out a Caribbean tune that should have been called "Carnivale Migraine."

"We need to see Katrina today," Steve said, in his most professional tone.

Any second now, she's gonna come over here, jump my bones.

"I was going to work on jury instructions," she said.

"This is more important. Kiss off the instructions for now."

Did I really say, "kiss off"?

She didn't seem to notice. He told her Bobby's theory that Katrina bought the dive watch for a man other than her husband, a thick-wristed, scuba-diving guy who, in Steve's opinion, probably did not require latex dildos and leather restraints to become aroused. Listening, she chewed on a pencil. To Steve, at this moment, she was so naturally beautiful and innocently seductive as to be—what's the word he was searching for?—bewitching. In that same instant, he realized that "bewitching" was a word that had never before worked its way into his brain.

Jeez, I'm starting to sound like a perfume commercial.

"So you're going to ask Kat about the watch?" Victoria said.

Steve shook his head. "I don't want her thinking we've lost faith in her. If she really bought the watch for Charles, it'll still be in the house."

"What are you going to do, ransack the master bedroom?"

"Yep. While you're talking to her downstairs."

"You're not serious!"

"If the watch isn't there, we'll confront her. If it is there, no harm done."

"Invading a client's privacy. This one of Solomon's Laws?"

"Then, when we get back, we need to work on our exhibit list."

"I hope you're leaving off the security video."

"Why would I? It backs Katrina's story."

"How many times did you watch it?"

"Once."

"You watch some old football game half a dozen times on the classics channel, but a murder scene video only once."

"*Accident* scene," he corrected her.

"Has Pincher filed his exhibit list?"

"Not yet."

What was she getting at? Both state and defense had gotten the tapes from the home security system. The house had been wired with hidden cameras. None in the bedrooms, so no porn shots of trussed-up Charlie Barksdale with Katrina riding him, cowgirl style. But a camera was fitted into a picture frame in the corridor just outside the master suite. With the door open, the wide-angle lens had caught a sliver of the wet-bar area, maybe twenty feet from the bed. Steve remembered everything on the tape; there wasn't that much. At 11:37 P.M., according to graphics on the screen, Katrina walked into the frame. She was wearing black leather chaps, crotchless panties, and a laced corset with openings in the bra for her peekaboo nipples. Her Sunday church outfit, no doubt.

As Katrina poured herself a drink, she suddenly turned and headed back toward Charlie. Even though the bed was out of camera range, Steve could argue to the jury that what could be seen corroborated Katrina's story: Standing at the bar, she heard Charlie in distress and ran to him. She tried to loosen the leather collar, but it was too late.

"So what's the problem with the video?" he asked.

Victoria dug into her briefcase, came out with the tape, and slipped it into the VCR on the bookshelf. "Did you watch it in slo-mo?"

"No slo-mo. No instant replay. No Telestrator. So what?"

She turned on the VCR and the TV, and the grainy black-and-white video came on. Thirty seconds of nothing but an empty corridor with a gray granite bar visible in a corner of the room. Then Katrina sashays into the frame. If there'd been audio, Steve figured, he could have heard her leather chaps rustling. She pours what looks like vodka into a glass. Suddenly—well, not that suddenly in slo-mo— her head whips back toward the bed. Steve knew what came next, but now he saw something he hadn't seen before. Just a split second before hurrying to the bed, Katrina's eyes flicked toward the corridor.

Victoria froze the frame. "What's she looking at? Who's in the corridor?"

"No one."

"Keep looking. Against the wall."

"What?"

"Don't you see the shadow?"

Steve blinked twice. There was a shaded area on the wall. Or was there? With the frame frozen, the screen pulsated, maybe creating an optical illusion. "It could be the pattern of the wallpaper. Or a trick of the lighting. Or just something the camera lens does."

"I see the outline of a person," Victoria said.

"And some people see the Virgin Mary in a grilled cheese sandwich."

Victoria hit the PLAY button. The shadow, if that's what it was, seemed to fade away.

"We could take the tape to a photogrammetry expert, have it enhanced," she said.

"So could Pincher."

"Sure, if he sees the shadow. But if he's like you—if he's like most men—he'll miss the details."

"Which is why we make a good team. I see the big picture. You see the shadows. I attack with a saber. You jab with a rapier. I drop the bombs. You . . ."

"Clean up your bird crap."

"Remember, Judge Gridley said we were like Solomon versus Lord. But now . . ."

"Now what, Solomon?"

If she didn't have the guts, he did. "Shouldn't we talk about last night?"

"Nothing to talk about. Chapter closed."

"I thought maybe, with the benefit of a night's sleep, you'd—"

"I didn't sleep."

"All the more reason to talk."

She walked to the window, looked across the alley toward the balcony where the steel band was taking a break and passing around a joint the size of a salami. "We have a case to try. That's all we're going to talk about. And when it's over, I'm out of here."

"What's that mean?"

"After I marry Bruce, I'm going in-house with his company. It's the best move for me."

"You're running away."

"From what?"

"Last night—"

"Never happened, and even if it did, it won't happen again," she said, employing the lawyer's technique of alternative pleading. "Look, I'm sorry if I sent out any signals you misinterpreted."

"You kissed me. How'd I misinterpret that?"

"I've been under a lot of pressure. I cracked. That's all it was."

"So you won't talk about what you're feeling right now? What you're thinking?"

She wheeled around. "I'm thinking I liked you better when you were an insensitive jerk."

"I'm not buying it."

"Don't you get it? I'm unavailable. That makes me more desirable. You're inappropriate. That makes you more desirable. It's a flaw in our genetic code. We can't help ourselves, we're drawn to the flames. It's what makes us the screwed-up human beings we are."

"And that's why you kissed me? And I kissed you back?"

"If you have a better explanation, let's hear it."

"I'm not sure. There's something about you that . . ."

He stopped, unable to continue, and she pounced. "That *what*?"

"That makes me, I don't know . . . I . . . I have these feelings," he stammered.

"C'mon," she prodded. "You're the one who wants to open up. Just how do you feel about me?"

"You had me from 'Get lost.' "

"No I didn't. Can't you be sincere?"

"Only if I fake it."

"I mean it. Either tell me how you feel or just shut up."

He hadn't expected her to challenge him. Suddenly, he was back at Beach High with a huge crush on Renée de Pres, an exchange student from Paris. Even now, he remembered everything about her. Dark hair cut short in that sexy French way. Tight miniskirts with the top three buttons of her blouse left open. An alluring accent that made him want to lick the dewy perspiration from behind her bare knees. He was, after all, seventeen with an achy-breaky heart and a perpetual erection.

Renée had been in the stands when they played Hialeah High for the state baseball championship. In the ninth inning, with the score tied, Steve singled, stole second, then third, and scored on a sacrifice fly, sliding headfirst under the tag. His teammates carried him off the field. It was an ephemeral moment, but in his naivete, he believed it was the first of an endless series of joyous spectacles, drums and bugles announcing every triumph of his life.

Four hours later, Renée introduced him to the wonders of blossoming Gallic womanhood in the backseat of his Jeep, pulled into a mangrove thicket at Matheson Hammock. It was his first time, though not hers, and he completed the act even faster than he had rounded the bases. With her guidance, a second effort was more rewarding, and a third left them breathless. By dawn, he was sure no one had ever felt like this before, and he uttered the three magic words—*I love you*—which made Renée laugh and call him a "silly boy."

For the next two weeks, barely a moment went by that he wasn't touching her or kissing her. Every shared experience—no matter how mundane—miniature golf, pepperoni pizza, Sting's "Every Breath You Take," unleashed torrents of joy. Could this be anything but forever-and-ever love?

Then, a mere 363 hours and 17 minutes—by Steve's deranged calculation—after they had first scrunched up in the backseat of the Jeep, it ended. When Steve tried to join Renée in the cafeteria, she was sitting with Angel Castillo, the burly fullback on the football team. Baseball season was over; spring football practice was starting; and Steve had been discarded like a splintered Louisville Slugger.

In the nearly twenty years since, he had refrained from even once telling a woman that he loved her. How could he? The risk of pain was too great. And now he was standing mute in the face of Victoria's challenging glare.

Victoria resisted the urge to pull him out of his chair and throw her arms around him. He had never looked so hopeless and so huggable. So different from the smart-ass she first met in court. But she steeled herself against showing any emotion other than indifference. She wouldn't reveal what she felt. How could she? She couldn't even define it herself. She didn't know what propelled her toward Solomon. But he had been right about one thing: *I kissed him. I grabbed him and kissed him deeply, passionately . . . dangerously.*

So reckless. So irresponsible. So unlike her. She desperately wished she could take it back.

Or did she? With the boats creaking in their moorings and the moonlit sky swirling above, she'd molded her body to his, a yin-and-yang perfect fit. The kiss had left her disoriented and dizzy and frightened. She wanted to write it off to gin and stress and exhaustion. But in truth, she had no idea what was happening to her. Was she subconsciously trying to sabotage her relationship with Bruce? Did she have a self-esteem problem? Did she feel she didn't deserve someone so right? So damn-near-perfect it could sometimes be daunting just being with him?

Working it over now, she thought she was figuring it out.

I'm in love with Bruce and in lust with Steve.

Thank God she'd been around enough to know all about the lust factor. Relationships built on passion last about as long as the fever that accompanies the flu. When was the last time she had succumbed? Maybe six years ago—a lifetime, it seemed—there'd been Randy, a teaching pro at a tennis club in Boca Raton. Australian. Sun-bleached hair. A laugh like surf crashing on rocks. And a sexual athlete. Thank God her chiropractor's bills were covered by insurance.

She was waiting tables the summer between college and law school . . . and totally in love. Or what she mistook for love. Postadolescent lust was more like it. All those steamy nights in Randy's shoebox apartment with its wheezing air conditioner, mildewed shower curtain, and retro water bed. And one night of tears.

She remembered the pain, finding another woman—a married tennis pupil, of all the lousy clichés—riding the waves in Randy's bedroom. His confession was without guilt or remorse: *"Not my fault the sheilas want to have a naughty with me."*

Thinking back, the men after Randy seemed like a procession of faceless gray suits. Lawyers, CPAs, brokers. Ambitious young men in pinstripes. Impatient men who often pushed the relationship too quickly. She remembered Harlan, a brainy tax accountant, popping the question on their third date. At that moment, they were stuck in a mob at Joe's Stone Crab, waiting for a table. How do you politely reply—*"Are you out of your bean-counting mind?"*—when some tourist is standing on your foot and the maître d' is announcing, 'Grossman, party of five!' "

"Why do you want to get married?" she had asked, befuddled.

"Because I love you," Harlan had replied. Then, sheepishly, "And my firm favors married guys in selecting partners."

"So, I'm sort of a talking point on your résumé?"

Romantic love, she believed, was a myth that preyed on our illogical need to fulfill fantasies. It was, by definition, irrational. Just look where it got her mother. Romantic love was like a vacation suntan. It faded quickly.

What she had with Bruce she called "rational love." It was based on logical factors. Intelligence, kindness, sensitivity, empathy. And one more thing: Bruce was the first man in her life—including her father—who didn't disappoint her in a major way. So, romantic love be damned. She cherished and adored Bruce, but in a different way. It was a love based on so much more than passion, she told herself. Then, just to be sure, she told herself again.

———

"I have to know you can handle this," Victoria said.

"Handle what?"

"Our working together without you getting all moony-eyed."

"Aw, c'mon, I'm a big boy. If you say the kiss didn't mean anything, I'm cool with that."

"You sure?"

"Totally."

"Good. From now on, we're living by Lord's Laws. No touching, no flirting, no kissing. Nothing but business."

"You got it," Steve agreed. He had a sense of loss, which was weird, because how can you lose what you never had?

"Now, let's get down to Gables Estates and let you burglarize our client's closets."

"Ready when you are."

Victoria started packing her briefcase. "So, what do you think of Jackie?"

"Seems nice. Has a good laugh."

"Think she's pretty?"

"Sure." Where was this going?

"She thinks you're hot."

"Yeah?"

"You want her number?"

Steve would not let her see his pain. "Sure. She like stone crabs?"

Victoria laughed. "Jackie says some guys take a girl out for stone crabs and expect a b.j. afterward."

"They wait till after?"

"You two have the same sense of humor. This could work out."

"Great."

"I don't want to push you into anything if you're reluctant."

"No. I'd like to see her," Steve said, knowing it was a lie. "As long as you don't mind."

"I think it'd be great," she lied right back.

Twenty-seven

OUT OF THE CLOSET

The rich *are* different, Steve decided. They have bigger closets.

Katrina Barksdale's wood-paneled two-story coliseum was larger than Steve's bedroom. Strike that. The *shoe section* was larger than his bedroom.

He heard the purr of a dehumidifier and smelled a lavish mixture of aromas. The tang of cedar, the richness of leathers . . . the scent of money. Katrina's closet was a cool and peaceful sanctuary, dripping with silks and linens, minks and wools. Every pair of shoes had its own Plexiglas drawer, tastefully lighted like a sculpture in a museum. Designer clothing hung on a motorized track that circled the room like a toy train. You punched in the key of a designer—Armani, Saint Laurent, de la Renta, Moschino—then a garment code, and the track hummed contentedly as it delivered to your manicured hands a suede jacket or lacy skirt or velvet blazer.

Steve had told Katrina Barksdale he needed to take photos, which was true, as far as it went. He'd left her downstairs with Victoria, sipping wine and preparing for trial. He spent the next twenty minutes in the master suite with a digital camera, creating a 360-degree view, from the four-poster, silk-canopied bed—where Charles had expired, breathless but erect—to the arched entryways of the mammoth his-and-her closets. Then he tackled his other mission, finding the Breitling dive watch.

In a vestibule that led to Charles' closet, Steve came across a teak chest with small drawers like a library's card catalog: Charles Barksdale's jewelry cabinet. Inside were cuff links, rings, and an assortment of watches. Audemars Piguet, Vacheron Constantin, Patek Philippe, Cartier, Rolex, even a Casio G-Shock, named for Jeremy Shockey, the football player. Some were new and some antiques, some solid gold, others stainless steel, still others circled with diamonds.

But no Breitling dive watch.

So maybe Bobby was right. Maybe Katrina Barksdale didn't buy the watch for good old Charlie. But then again, there were other places to keep the watch. He'd have to check out the master stateroom on the *Kat's Meow.*

"What the hell?"

The growl came from behind him, and Steve whirled around, looking guilty as a purse snatcher. There was Chet Manko, the boat captain, wearing a mesh athletic shirt and paint-splattered cargo pants and holding a wood chisel.

"That's amazing," Steve said. "I was just thinking about the boat, and *boom,* there you are."

Manko raised the chisel. Muscles ripped on his bronzed arm. "What the hell you doing?"

"Taking photos." Steve held up the camera as Exhibit A to his innocence. "Getting the lay of the land."

"In Mr. B's jewelry box?"

There was some New England in Manko's voice, Steve thought. Working-class Boston, maybe. "Actually, I was looking for something. Evidence."

"What evidence?" Manko didn't even try to mask his suspicion.

"Afraid that's privileged. What are you doing up here, Manko?"

"Digging dry rot out of the balcony overhang." Again, the chisel came up. "Kat know you're in her bedroom?"

Kat. The hired help was on mighty friendly terms with the lady of the house, Steve thought.

He saw it then, gleaming on Manko's thick left wrist. A Breitling Superocean dive watch, extra-large face, good to three thousand feet.

"Aw, shit," Steve said.

"Tell me in your own words when you noticed Charles was in distress," Victoria said.

In your own words.

A lawyer's verbal tic, she knew. Whose words would Katrina use? Abraham Lincoln's?

"Like I told the cops, like I told Steve, like I told everybody, Charlie's tied up, just like always. I whip him with the cat-o'-nine-tails, then do my custom blow job with a mouthful of hot water. That always drove him nuts. After he shoots his load, I go over to the bar and pour myself a Stoli. I hear something, and when I look over at Charlie, he's flopping up and down, making noises like a goose squawking. Wait a second." She paused, biting her lip. "Now that I think about it, I might have been drinking Grey

Goose. Anyway, I run over there, and he's all blue. His face, not his balls. By the time I get the collar off, he's not flopping anymore."

They were in the living room, seated on a beige sofa Katrina said was custom-made in Rome. She was wearing red silk pants and an embroidered blouse with a Chinese design and had polished off half a bottle of a crisp Chardonnay. Victoria was sticking to club soda as she took Katrina through her story, looking for inconsistencies.

"If you're asking me all these questions a zillion times, I must be testifying, huh?"

"We don't know that yet." Victoria noticed how the grain of each limestone tile lined up with the grain of the adjacent one. "If our cross of the state's witnesses leaves reasonable doubt, we might keep you off the stand."

"Isn't that risky?"

"Not half as risky as lying to your lawyer," Steve said, hustling into the room, with Manko trailing. "Didn't I warn you? Dammit, Katrina, didn't I?"

"What's wrong, Steve?" Victoria asked.

"Our slutty client, for starters."

"You can't talk to her that way," Manko said.

"Fuck you, boat boy," Steve exploded. Red-faced, he wagged a finger at Katrina. "You know what I hate more than a woman who kills her husband? A woman who lies to her lawyer."

Katrina coolly placed her wineglass on the mahogany coffee table. A dainty gesture. "What have you been telling him, Chet?"

"Not a damn thing," Manko said.

Katrina crossed one red silk pant leg over the other. "So what seems to be the problem, Stephen?"

He let his voice go high and mocking: " 'I've been faithful to Charlie since the day he proposed.' "

"Oh, that."

"Yeah, that. How long you been porking Manko here?"

"Does it matter? How long, I mean."

"What matters is that you lied to us. And if you lied about one thing . . ."

"Everything else I told you was true."

"Yeah? Who else you fucking?"

"Steve, must you be so crude?" Victoria said.

"Chet is my only extracurricular activity," Katrina said.

"No golf pros?" Steve said. "Aerobics instructors? Sweaty gardeners you invite in for lemonade and a quick pop?"

"You got no right—" Manko took a step toward Steve.

"Shut up!" Steve jabbed a finger into Manko's chest, surprising the bigger man. "I haven't gotten to you yet."

Victoria watched as Steve took over the room, planting himself like an oak in front of the coffee table, raising his voice, telling Katrina that in all his years of practice, he'd never encountered anyone as foolish, and he should withdraw from the case and let her lie to some other lawyer, and she'd be lucky if the jurors didn't lynch her before rendering a verdict. At first, Victoria thought it was an act, Steve trying to scare their client straight. Then, when he grabbed Manko's arm and ripped off the watch, she decided he was losing control.

Steve waved the watch in Katrina's face. "You let me make a fool of myself with that Katrina Loves

Charles crap. But even worse, you led me into a trap. I put Manko on our witness list, but I can't put him on the stand because I can't subject him to cross. And any chance of your testifying is out because I can't let Pincher get at you, either."

"All because I was screwing Chet?"

"What do you mean, 'was'?" Manko asked.

"Didn't I tell you to shut up?" Steve snarled. "I don't have time for a lovers' spat."

Katrina said: "*Was* screwing, *is* screwing, *might* screw again, what's the big deal?"

"Victoria, tell her," Steve commanded. "Spell it out for her."

"Pincher will use your affair to prove motive," Victoria said.

Katrina laughed. "What motive? To be with Chet? To marry him? *Please.*"

"What's that supposed to mean?" Manko said.

"Chet, you're adorable in your own way, but you're just a sport fuck and we both know it, so don't pull that shit."

Katrina had dropped the mask of the Coral Gables socialite, Victoria thought. It hadn't fit very well, anyway. Now she wrinkled her forehead, proof that she was still a few years from her first Botox injection. "Okay, so I lied about being faithful to Charlie, but I didn't kill him."

"Not by yourself," Steve said.

"What's that supposed to mean?"

Steve's eyes blazed. There was something wild and dangerous about him, Victoria thought.

"When you were standing at the bar, Charles was doing just fine," Steve said. "If he was making any noise, it was to say 'Hey, untie me already.' You shot a look at him, then turned to the corridor, where Manko was plastered to the wall, out of camera range."

"You're nuts," Katrina said.

Manko shifted his weight from one foot to the other. "You can't pin this on me."

"Of course I can't, Einstein." Steve clenched a handful of Manko's mesh shirt and shoved him backwards. "Naming you only implicates my client in a murder conspiracy. But Pincher can nail you, even if I can't."

"The fuck he can," Manko snorted.

"Wanna bet? There's a person's shadow on the security video. Pincher's already told me he's sent the tape to his high-tech forensics guys."

No he hasn't, Victoria thought, but kept quiet.

"They'll be able to tell the height and weight of whoever's there," Steve continued. "What do you want to bet it's a guy about six-three and two hundred pounds with a pea-size brain?"

"Fuck you," Manko said.

"Katrina's glance is the signal to the guy. Now he slithers along the wall because he knows just what the camera sees and what it doesn't. He goes over to the bed, tightens Charles' collar, and strangles him."

"This what you lawyers get paid for, making shit up?" Manko said.

"Just out of curiosity, Manko," Steve said, "do you have a record? 'Cause I'm laying odds you've done time."

"A couple of bullshit A-and-Bs," Manko said. "Bar fights, is all."

"So, welcome to the big time."

———

Victoria drove and Steve leaned back in the passenger seat, one foot propped on the dashboard. They were headed north on Old Cutler Road under the banyan trees. Without asking for permission, Steve fiddled with the buttons on her radio. He stopped at a station where Loudon Wainwright III was proclaiming himself the last man on earth.

"Was that an act back there?" she asked. "When you looked like you might have a stroke."

"I thought I'd get straighter answers if they were afraid I was going to break some glassware, so yeah, it was mostly Drama 101. But a part of me was really pissed."

"Why'd you lie about Pincher?"

"I needed to gauge Manko's reaction. Katrina's, too."

"And . . . ?"

"Katrina's telling the truth. She didn't kill Charlie. Neither did Manko."

"And you base this on what?" Victoria was astounded.

"They passed my human polygraph test."

"Oh, please."

"That first day, I thought she was lying when she denied killing Charles," he said.

"What? You told me you believed her."

"I fudged a little. I was afraid your heart wouldn't be in it if you thought she was a killer."

"That's so insulting. I'm a professional."

Steve leaned back, his eyes closed. On the radio, Pat Benatar was singing about crimes of passion. "Anyway, back then, she *was* lying, but only about being faithful. That's what screwed up my polygraph, made me think she was lying about the murder."

"But like you said in the house, if she lied about one thing . . ."

"You gotta trust me on this. She didn't do it."

"There's no such thing as a human polygraph."

"Okay," he said. "Call it a gut instinct. My gut tells me she doesn't have it in her."

"You can't make decisions like this based on your gut."

"That's how I make all the big ones," Steve said. "You ought to try it sometime."

Twenty-eight

A DEEP, DARK SEA

"Bigby doesn't mind us going out?" Steve asked.

"You think this was a date?" Victoria said.

"We had dinner."

"A *working* dinner."

"Some guys wouldn't want their fiancées even doing that."

"Bruce isn't the jealous type. And he knows I'd never do anything stupid."

Steve didn't like the way that sounded. Like the dumbest thing in the world would be falling for him. He pulled the old Eldo into his driveway, next to Victoria's car. "You want to come in for a drink?"

She shook her head. "I'm bushed."

As they got out of the Eldo, he said: "With Bobby at Teresa's, we've got the place to ourselves."

She flashed her prosecutorial look. "Are you putting the moves on me, Solomon?"

"Me? No. Absolutely not. I just thought . . ."

In a neighbor's tree, a mockingbird was singing an aria. What was it Bobby had told him about the mockers? Oh, yeah, only the bachelors sing at night. Looking for a mate from sundown until dawn. A song came into Steve's head: Jimmy Buffet's "Why Don't We Get Drunk and Screw."

"Just what *did* you think, Solomon?"

He wasn't sure. He knew she wasn't going to jump into his arms. In the office, she'd told him with finality, "Chapter closed." The first kiss was a last kiss. So what the hell was he doing? In the tree, the mockingbird began trilling an octave higher. Was the bachelor bird laughing?

"What's that?" she said, looking past him toward the house.

"What?"

"Did you leave your door open?"

He walked along the chipped flagstones toward the house. The top hinge was smashed; the door was open and cockeyed.

"Oh, shit." He gingerly pulled at the door, but the bottom scraped the flagstone step and stuck.

"Don't go in." Victoria was reaching into her purse for a cell phone. "I'll call the police."

"Whoever did this is long gone. I just hope they didn't get my autographed Barry Bonds ball."

He jiggled the door. The bottom screeched and moved an inch. He thought he heard something—the squeak of rubber soles on tile—and a second later, the door flew off the remaining hinge, striking him across his forehead and the bridge of his nose. A searing pain flashed behind his eyes. As the door fell on top of him, he was vaguely aware of a figure running out of the house, past him.

He heard Victoria yell: "Hey!"

He heard the pounding of shoes on pavement.

He heard boulders bouncing off each other inside his skull.

A moment later, he was on his feet, wobbling in the direction of an invisible man. In the darkness, all Steve could see were the fluorescent stripes of the man's running shoes. The shoes turned the corner at Solana Road and headed south toward Poinciana. Steve followed.

"Steve! No, don't!" Victoria was shouting at him. The sounds echoed: he heard every word twice.

Steve was aware that he was not running in a straight line. He thought he was seeing bright flashes, realized they were thin beams of moonlight speckling the street through a canopy of willow trees. The air smelled of jasmine, and in a few moments, Steve began feeling stronger. The guy was not a great runner, or he would have pulled away by now. By the time Steve reached Malaga, he could see the guy was wearing a dark warm-up suit, and there was something covering his head. What the hell was it?

Somewhere in the distance, a police siren wailed. Steve was thirty yards behind when they crossed LeJeune, dodging between cars. Horns blared. His head throbbed, but his legs had regained their balance, and his lungs felt strong. It was only a matter of time.

"Hey, asshole!" Steve called out. "You can't outrun me."

No response.

They had crossed from Miami into Coral Gables and were on Gerona, in an expensive neighborhood of Mediterranean homes. Not exactly Steve's 'hood. They were headed for a dead end, the Gables Waterway just behind the homes on Riviera. If the guy knew where he was, he'd turn on Riviera. If not, he'd find himself with a channel to swim across.

"You got no chance, shithead!" Steve yelled out.

Again, no response, but now Steve was close enough to see that the guy wore a ski mask. He could hear the man's breathing. "You're dying up there, asshole!"

The man crossed Riviera and hopped the curb, running through the front yard of a sprawling Spanish-style house. He disappeared into a hibiscus hedge.

He doesn't know where he is. He's gonna be trapped at the water.

Steve followed.

Three steps into the darkened yard, he felt his foot catch on something. He flew forward, sliding face-first into the hibiscus hedge.

Dammit, a sprinkler head.

He scrambled to his feet, ducked alongside the house, and emerged in the backyard. Where was the guy?

Spotlights illuminated the tiled patio and cast a yellow glow on the dark water of the channel. A wooden dock extended from a concrete seawall. A thirty-foot sailboat was tied up at the dock. A fiber-glass kayak lay near the stern of the sailboat.

But no guy in bright, shiny sneakers dressed for the ski slopes.

In the waterway, a Boston Whaler churned toward the bay. A man in a ball cap was at the wheel.

"Hey, you see anyone out here?" Steve yelled.

"Hoping to see some snapper," the man called back.

At the dock, the Whaler's wake nudged at the sail-boat, whose lines strained against the cleats on the dock. Steve studied the boat, partially lit by the spots.

The guy could have climbed into the cockpit. He could be hiding there right now.

Steve reached into the kayak and picked up a paddle. Molded plastic, not much heft. He would have preferred a Louisville Slugger, smash the guy with an uppercut as if swinging for the fences. Wielding the paddle, he walked along the dock, the old wooden planks groaning beneath his feet. Somewhere across the waterway, a dog yipped. Unseen insects *cricked* and *clacked* and played their night music.

Just who the hell was this guy, anyway? Steve didn't think it was your friendly neighborhood burglar. But he had a suspect. Just hours earlier, he'd told Manko a videotape would place him at the murder scene. Steve had been winging it. He didn't think Manko and Katrina had killed Barksdale. And he doubted anyone could turn the gray, shadowy video into a *gotcha* piece of evidence. Now Steve wondered if his human polygraph had blown a fuse.

Manko would only want the tape if he was guilty.

But why, Steve wondered, would Manko break into his home? Why not the office? Weirder still, Steve had taken the tape home to watch on a better VCR. But Manko couldn't have known that. It was all too confusing for Steve to decipher, especially with his head feeling like a bucket of wet cement.

Now, on the dock, with the water gently lapping against boat hull, Steve tried to see the running figure in his mind's eye. Was this guy as big as Manko? Chasing a man in the dark doesn't give you much chance for a description. Hell, people in broad daylight have a hard time describing their attackers.

With one hand on the stern rail and the paddle in

the other hand, he squinted into the darkened cockpit.

"You in there, Manko?"

Nothing.

"C'mon out. Let's talk this over."

Still nothing.

Then the faintest sensation of a plank yielding beneath his feet. Steve wheeled around, saw the glint of metal and ducked. Something whooshed over his head. The man in the ski mask was swinging a heavy chrome winch handle that nearly parted Steve's hair. The momentum of the swing threw the man off balance, and he stutter-stepped. Steve pivoted his hips and swung the paddle, aiming for the man's head, but from a crouch, he couldn't get the angle. The paddle caught the man's shoulder, knocking him back but not bringing him down.

"Fucker," the man breathed. He regained his footing and feinted with the winch handle.

Steve brought up the paddle to block the swing that never came. The man laughed, feinted twice more, then swung at Steve's face. Steve blocked the handle with the paddle. *Ouch.* He'd jammed his wrist as if he'd broken his bat against a split-fingered fastball. The paddle flew from his hand.

Shit.

"I owe you, fucker," the man said, the winch handle cocked in his right hand.

"Why don't you take off your mask and we'll resolve this amicably," Steve said, as if they were in mediation on an insurance claim.

"Fuck you, fucker."

Fuck you, fucker? With such a limited vocabulary, no wonder the guy turned to crime.

The man took a step toward Steve, who back-pedaled. One foot slipped off the dock and dangled in space. His arms flailing, trying to regain his balance, he fell backward. He heard glass shatter as his head smashed the stern light of the sailboat, and he tumbled into the black water. He was sure he must have made a splash, but strangely, he never heard the sound and never felt himself go under.

For a moment, all went black, and Steve wondered: If I'm unconscious, how can I be conscious of it?

Sinking into the deep channel, enveloped by the cool water, he was in that grayish state between day and night, consciousness and unconsciousness. Woozy but still coherent enough to be in fear.

Fear of drowning.

Fear of alligators.

Fear that the guy would leap into the water and bash in his skull.

Steve opened his eyes and was surprised to find everything was still black.

Of course it's black. I'm at the bottom of a deep, dark sea.

He was suddenly aware of wanting to take a breath. Wanting it more than he'd ever wanted anything in his life. He felt his feet touch bottom, flexed his knees, and shot upward.

It took an impossibly long time to break the surface. When he finally felt the cool air strike his head, he sucked in a long, sweet breath, then swam to a ladder at the dock. Holding on to a barnacle-encrusted rung, he paused a moment, listening. He didn't want to stick his head above the dock and have his brains splattered.

Silence.

He climbed one rung. Waited. Climbed another.

Peeked his head over the planks of the dock. No one was there.

No one calling him "fucker."

Then a glass door slid open at the rear of the house and a man yelled: "Hey, there's no swimming out here, buddy."

IN THE CIRCUIT COURT OF THE ELEVENTH JUDICIAL CIRCUIT IN AND FOR MIAMI-DADE COUNTY, FLORIDA JUVENILE DIVISION

In re: R.A.S.,
       A minor child   Case No. 05–09375 (Dependency)

CHILD PROTECTION REPORT

1. This report is made in accordance with Chapter 39 of the Florida Statutes, by Doris Kranchick, MD, duly appointed by the Division of Family Services.

2. R.A.S., an eleven-year-old male, is a developmentally challenged child who manifests traits of both autism and profound savant syndrome. The child is in need of specialized testing, treatment, therapy, and an individually tailored educational program.

3. R.A.S. is currently in the temporary custody of his uncle, Stephen Solomon, who has failed to reveal the precise circumstances under which R.A.S. came to reside with him.

4. The boy's mother, Janice Solomon, was recently released from state custody, having been convicted of multiple drug and theft offenses. The identity and whereabouts of the boy's biological father are unknown.

5. Stephen Solomon has petitioned the court for long-term licensed custody of the minor child, pursuant to Section 39.623. The undersigned finds that:

(A)   The homeschooling provided by Mr.
      Solomon consists mainly of unsuper-
      vised reading, including criminal court
      files and autopsy reports unsuitable for
      a child.

(B)   Mr. Solomon has denied the under-
      signed an opportunity to perform med-
      ical tests on the child, including
      repetitive transcranial magnetic stimu-
      lation (RTMS). He further has pre-
      vented the child from taking part in
      therapy programs of the Pilot Autism
      Project at Rockland State Hospital.

(C)   Mr. Solomon maintains a professional
      life that can best be described as
      chaotic. An attorney, he has been jailed
      for contempt of court on numerous oc-
      casions and has earned a reputation for
      bizarre behavior in the courtroom.
      Additionally, although he demonstrates
      obvious affection for R.A.S., Mr.
      Solomon is ill-equipped to serve as cus-
      todian for a child of such special needs.

RECOMMENDATION

The undersigned recommends that Stephen
Solomon's petition for custody be denied and that
R.A.S. be adjudged a ward of the state and placed in
a licensed shelter with mandatory testing and treat-
ment under the auspices of the Division of Family
Services.

                              Respectfully submitted,
                              Doris Kranchick, MD

Twenty-nine

ALL YOU NEED IS LOVE

"What bullshit! What total bullshit!"

Clutching a copy of Kranchick's report in one hand, an ice bag pressed to his temple with the other, Steve paced his office. Tie at half-mast, face flushed, a doorknob-size lump on his forehead. Purplish bruises circled his eyes. He looked like an angry raccoon. Victoria sat at her desk, watching and worrying. Bobby crouched cross-legged in a chair, his head buried in a book.

"Just wait till I get Kranchick in court," Steve said.

"I feel terrible," Victoria said. "Maybe if I hadn't run from the table—"

"Nothing to do with it. She likes you. She says my life's 'chaotic.' Unless you're in a coma, whose life isn't?"

"Maybe you should calm down before you start planning trial strategy."

"I'm calm!"

"Shouldn't we talk about the burglary? Do you really think it was Manko?"

He tossed the ice bag onto his desk. "Who else would it be?"

They'd been over this for hours last night after a soggy and bruised Steve had squished back to the house. The intruder had been in the study. Steve's briefcase had been moved, but nothing was taken from the house. The security video was in the VCR, just where he'd left it. What had the burglar been after? So far, nothing made sense. What good would it do to steal the tape when Pincher had a copy?

"Are you going to confront Manko?" she asked.

"Not without proof."

"Yesterday you accused him of murder even though you thought he was innocent, but today you won't accuse him of a burglary you think he committed?"

"Let's see what happens when the forensics guy goes over the tape." A fly buzzed into the office from the window above the Dumpster, and Steve swung at it with the report. Strike one. He opened the report again and read aloud: " 'A reputation for bizarre behavior in the courtroom.' Kranchick's hated me from day one."

"Because you wouldn't do her," Bobby said, without looking up from his book. "You wouldn't stick your screwdriver in her tool shed."

"Bobby, that's really inappropriate," Victoria said.

"Yeah, stow that shit," Steve said.

"No guy will ride her tunnel of love," Bobby said. "I'm gonna tell the judge that."

"The hell you are," Steve said.

"Dive for a pearl in her bearded clam."

"Bobby, chill!"

"Chomp her carpet burger."

"Cut it out, kiddo. And what's that you're reading?"

Holding up a tattered book, Bobby spoke in perfect French: *"La Pendaison, la Strangulation, la Suffocation, la Submersion."*

"If that's porno, get rid of it."

"Coroner's textbook from the nineteenth century," Bobby said.

"Put it away. It's not suitable for a child."

"Yes it is."

"Kranchick wouldn't agree. You want her to take you away?"

"No!" Bobby yelled, then fell into a chant, "No, no, no, no, no, no, no . . ."

"Aw, jeez, I'm sorry."

The boy was rocking in his chair. Victoria remembered that first night at Steve's house. Bobby had blasted her with the squirt gun, then dashed inside, where he buried himself in the sofa and swayed back and forth, locked into some dark cellar of his mind.

"No, no, no, no, no, no . . ."

The boy was a wreck, she thought. If he acted this way in court, Steve wouldn't have a chance. "Bobby, do you want to play the anagram game?" she asked. Anything to calm him down.

"No, no, no, no, no, no . . ."

Steve walked over to Bobby and tousled his hair. The boy twisted his head so the palm of his uncle's hand caressed his cheek. After a moment Bobby rubbed his face against Steve's hand like a contented kitten. Then he picked up the old French coroner's book and, just like that, started calmly reading again.

Steve resumed pacing, swinging the rolled-up report at an imaginary baseball or an imaginary Kranchick, Victoria didn't know which. She was worried about both Solomon boys. Bobby was regressing, and Steve was far too hair-trigger. Bobby's case required logic and reason, strategy and finesse, but Steve was planning an artillery attack.

"I'll expose that quack," he said. "What are her credentials, anyway? Does she have an ounce of compassion? Does she understand that love is more important than charts and tests?"

"Steve—"

"I took Bobby to her hospital. They tried to give him an IV drip of Valium for some tests, and I said, no fucking way."

"Who are your experts? What's your strategy?"

"Do you know what it smells like in that hospital? Ammonia and laundry starch. If I could bring that stink into court, no judge would give Bobby to the state."

Out of control, she thought. No sense of objectivity. No plan.

"If we lose," Steve said, "I'm packing our bags."

"Give up your Bar license, become a fugitive?"

"If that's what it takes."

"Have you thought about retaining counsel?"

"Who can argue the case better than me?"

"Someone who's not emotionally involved."

"You been talking to Marvin the Maven?" Steve put a little gravel in his voice. " 'The man who represents himself has a *shmendrick* for a client.' "

"Marvin's right."

"Not this time. See, the theme of my case is love conquers all."

"Didn't we just try that?" Victoria asked. " 'Katrina Loves Charles'?"

"That was courtroom blather. Love's not about buying watches and diamonds. It's about putting the other person first. What Bobby needs is someone who'll do anything for him, not doctors who want to publish papers about him. What he needs is me."

"I wonder if that's enough," she said. "To win the case, I mean."

"Did you ever see that English movie *Love Actually*?" he asked.

"Yeah. It put me into glucose overload."

"First scene, we see all these couples meeting at the airport. Lovers hugging, kissing, reuniting. And Hugh Grant's saying it's wrong to think we live in a world that's filled only with hatred and greed."

"Yeah, sure. It's a world of milk and honey."

"What he says is, if you look for it, love actually is all around."

He had a distant and almost blissful look. In the right time and place, like a Barry Manilow concert or a freshman seminar on Kahlil Gibran, the look might be appropriate, Victoria thought. But in the grungy law office over the Dumpster, faced with the reality of losing his nephew, Solomon's spaciness was alarming.

He's losing it.

"I remember the scene," she said. "I was thinking, 'This is gonna be one sugar-glazed donut of a movie.' "

"That's what love is, too. Besides the sacrifice and the caring, I mean. It's a Sinatra song. Moonbeams on the bay. A puppy opening its eyes for the first time."

"Where's the Solomon I know? The guy who teaches birds to shit on opposing counsel?"

"When I see Bobby sleeping, tears come to my

eyes. I'm gonna tell the judge that. I'm gonna translate every emotion into admissible evidence."

Okay, she thought. Turns out the courtroom shark was a hopeless romantic. And like another romantic, he was preparing to tilt at windmills, riding a spavined steed and carrying a rusty lance.

"I'm having a little trouble seeing how this is going to win your case."

"That's the beauty of it. It's right in Chapter Thirty-nine of the statutes." He grabbed a book from his desk. "Look. Section Eight-ten, Subsection Five. The court must consider the 'love, affection, and other emotional ties between the child and the person seeking custody.' If the judge does that, I win."

"What about Kranchick's report?"

"Not to worry. I'm gonna wax the floor with it."

"What about all the other criteria in the statute?"

"I'll deal with them."

Unwilling to budge, unable to see that he was hot asphalt and his opponents were riding the steamroller. She wondered how she could get through to him. He was always so much in control when handling other people's problems. Now he seemed so lost in his own.

"I just wonder if you should talk to a lawyer who specializes in dependency cases," she said, diplomatically. "Maybe work together. Turn negatives into positives. Kranchick thinks you're exposing Bobby to improper influences. But you argue that taking Bobby to the office and court is great for his development."

"I do it mostly because we like to hang together," Steve said.

"That's good," she said. "Most boys would love to spend more time with their fathers."

Steve's face seemed to brighten. "You have a feel for this, Vic. You should represent me."

"I've never handled a guardianship case."

"You're a trial lawyer, an all-purpose utility player. You can play any position without being afraid of any case or any lawyer."

"I'm not afraid," she said. "It's just . . ."

"What?"

"Too much responsibility. I know how important this is to you."

"That's why I need you. I wouldn't trust anyone else the way I trust you."

"If I screwed it up . . ."

"You won't."

"I'm sorry, Steve. I just can't."

Ten minutes later, Steve was considering the puzzling Ms. Victoria Lord. Most lawyers he knew had inflated egos. They weren't nearly as good as they thought they were. With Victoria, it was the opposite. She didn't know how good she could be. Her humility made her even more effective in the courtroom.

But why wouldn't she help him? That he couldn't figure out. He stole a glance across the room. On this chilly day, with gusts rattling the windowpane, Victoria wore a brown knit skirt fringed at the bottom. A matching hooded cardigan and fleece-lined, high-heeled suede boots completed the outfit, which Steve had never seen before. He wondered if he was starting to memorize her wardrobe, as he had done with her features, her every look. There was the furrowed brow with pursed lips when she studied a law book, the triumphant smile when she pounced on a winning point, the mysterious gaze when she stared into space. And another look, too.

He'd seen it once, and only because he opened his own eyes to find hers closed. When their lips had parted during their one and only kiss, she radiated total rapture.

Now he replayed their conversation of just a few minutes ago. He surely knew Victoria well enough to crack her codes. Suggesting he get counsel, she'd been overly polite, overly delicate. Then he said, Fine, *you* represent me. And she said no. Why?

There could be only one reason.

He felt his mood plummet. It's not that she lacked confidence in her own abilities.

She thinks I haven't got a chance. She thinks I'm going to lose.

Thirty

WEDDING BELL BLUES

An hour later, Steve was still stewing about Bobby's case, and Victoria was grinding away on the murder case, reading appellate cases, taking notes in neat lettering on her cards. The intercom buzzed and Cece said: "Yo, Vic. Hottie alert. Beefcake on final approach."

Bruce Bigby, in a double-breasted charcoal suit with a thin chalk stripe, breezed through the doorway, kissed Victoria's cheek, and opened a briefcase, all in one motion.

"Hate to burst in like this, sweetie. Hey, Steve." He did a double take. "Jeez, your face."

"Shaving accident," Steve said.

"Hon, what are you doing here?" Victoria said.

"We've got a thousand things to do." He pulled a file from his briefcase. "Steve, you've got to be more careful."

"I'm fine. Stick to your gourds, Bruce."

"Mind your manners, partner," Victoria warned.

"Avocados aren't gourds, Steve," Bigby said.

"Who gives a shit?"

"Steve!" Victoria glared at him.

"I'm sorry, Bruce," Steve said contritely. "Just having a bad day."

"Not a problem, Steve. I understand."

What a nice guy, Steve thought. So even-keeled. So imperturbable. So irritating. Steve realized he both resented and envied Bigby. Then he felt guilty about it. He owed Bigby for trying to help with Kranchick, even if it hadn't worked. And he wanted to make up for being such a prick just now. Forcing some cheer into his voice, he said: "So what's new on the farm, Bruce?"

"Arctic front's headed our way. We might be burning smudge pots by the weekend."

"If you need any extra hands, I'm there." Steve didn't know which would be worse, freezing his ass off, or watching Bigby make out with Victoria in the glow of a smudge pot. "I mean it. You need the fields set on fire, just call me."

"You burn sugarcane fields, not avocado trees. But a mighty decent offer." Bigby dropped his voice to a whisper. "Say, Vic told me. I'm sorry about the doctor's report." He shot a look at Bobby. "Are we allowed to talk about it in front of—?"

"I'm not deaf, dipshit," Bobby said.

"Bobby!" Steve said.

"My fault," Bigby said. "Robert, I apologize."

"So just why are you here, hon?" Victoria asked.

To Steve, she sounded on edge. Not quite "what the hell are you doing in my office when I've got work to do?" But maybe just a tinge of annoyance.

"The wedding, sweetie," Bigby said. "You do remember?"

"It's all she talks about," Steve said, and Victoria gave him a warning look.

"I'm a little busy right now," she said.

Bigby spread the contents of a file on her desk. "Seating charts, floral arrangements, musical selections, speeches to write. Really, sweetie, we're way behind the curve."

"I'm sorry, Bruce, but it's been hectic here."

"I know. I know. Murder and all, but really . . ."

"Look, I'm gonna take a walk on the beach," Steve said. "You two stay here and pick out place settings." He preferred a colonoscopy with a garden hose to listening to their wedding plans.

"We could use your help with final menu choices," Bigby said.

"I'm partial to barbecue," Steve said.

"Not unless it's made of tofu," Bigby reminded him.

Steve got to his feet. "I'll be at Tenth Street Beach if you need me."

"Isn't that the topless beach?"

"Funny, I never noticed."

"Hang on a sec, Steve. I want to ask you for a favor."

"Anything, Bruce."

"I'd be honored if you'd be one of our ushers."

"Me? I don't have any training."

"You'll learn at the rehearsal."

"I don't know. Somebody trips and falls, they might sue me."

"Just think about it. And do you want to sit on the bride's side or the groom's side of the church?"

"The Jewish side," Steve said.

The intercom buzzed again, and Cece announced that State Attorney Pincher was calling. Steve and Victoria exchanged looks—*What's he want?*—and

Steve hit the speaker button. "Hey, Sugar Ray. Coerce any confessions today?"

"Got that discovery you requested." Faint amusement tickled his voice.

"Great. I'll send my courier over."

"You don't have a courier."

"I forgot. Be a pal and send the stuff over with one of yours."

"Oh, I think you and your partner ought to come over here, pronto."

"Yeah, why's that?" Steve heard laughter in the background. He pictured an office filled with Pincher's flunkies.

" 'Cause I want to see your face when your case goes straight to Hades." Again, the ripple of sycophantic laughter. The phone clicked dead.

Steve turned to Victoria. "Pincher's gonna sandbag us, but I don't know how."

"Then the sooner the better."

"Right. Let's get going."

Victoria gathered some papers, dumped them in a briefcase. No muss, no fuss. Steve admired how she just got down to business, readied for the fight.

"Sorry, hon," she said. "The menus and seating charts will have to wait."

"And the flowers?" Bigby said.

"You choose. Really, Bruce. You're better at it than I am."

"If you say so," Bigby said, disappointed.

"I'm partial to birds of paradise," Steve said, heading for the door.

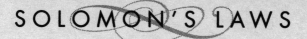

SOLOMON'S LAWS

8.   **There is some shit I will not eat.**

Thirty-one

MY PARTNER

"What happened to your face, Solomon?" Ray Pincher asked. "Your secretary beat you up?"

Steve put on his best Jack Nicholson: "Your wife got excited and crossed her legs a little too quick."

Pincher scowled, but his crew—two female prosecutors and Delvin Farnsworth, the homicide detective—snickered.

"Hated that movie," Pincher said. "Evil prevailed. 'It's Chinatown, Jake.' What kind of crap is that?"

"What do you have for us, Ray?" Steve wasn't being paid enough to listen to Pincher's movie reviews.

"I'm getting there," Pincher said.

Victoria and Steve were sitting on one side of a long rectangular table in Pincher's conference room. There was a nice view from the windows, if you like concrete expressway trestles fifty feet high.

Pincher was wearing a jet black vested suit with a lavender shirt, lavender tie, and lavender kerchief in his pocket. Way too much lavender for Steve's taste. "Solomon is usually a formidable opponent," Pincher said, turning to the detective. "Reprehensible, but formidable. Lately, though, he's been off his game."

"We drove over here for this?" Steve said.

"Maybe it's because this case is out of his league," Pincher continued serenely.

That again, Steve thought. Why had a discovery session turned adversarial before it had even begun?

Sitting next to Pincher, Farnsworth scratched his mustache with a knuckle. Taking notes—or doodling, Steve couldn't tell which—were the two prosecutors, Gloria Mendez and Miranda Cooper. Steve knew both women as competent but skittish in the courtroom. Neither one would give you a decent plea deal, terrified of being upbraided by their boss. Like most young ASAs, they'd made a Faustian bargain. If they could put up with their egomaniacal boss for a few years, laugh at his jokes, remind him of his brilliance, Pincher would pave the way to a deep-carpet firm downtown.

Steve had never been able to make those kind of compromises. He remembered being only eight or nine when his father starting calling him "Olaf," but never told him why. Years later, in English class at Beach High, Steve read the e.e. cummings poem "i sing of Olaf glad and big." And there he was, in iambic tetrameter: *"There is some shit I will not eat."*

It would make a good law, he decided, mindful that Olaf spoke the defiant words while red-hot bayonets were jammed up his ass.

"Solomon completely misread his client," Pincher continued. "Like a sloppy base runner, he gets picked off. That right, Last Out?"

"Let's just get this over with," Steve said, in no mood for Pincher's bullshit.

"My guess, he's preoccupied by his own squabble over in kiddie court."

The son-of-a-bitch. Goading me about Bobby.

"Why don't we just stick to this case?" Victoria said.

"How is that nephew of yours, Solomon?" Pincher asked, ignoring her.

Steve wouldn't take the bait. "Bobby's fine. Thank you for asking."

"Kid's a little weird. But then, with Solomon's family tree, what can you expect?"

Steve felt a hand gripping his forearm. Victoria, urging him to remain calm. He showed her a tight smile he hoped was reassuring, but she looked alarmed.

"Maybe it's genetic," Pincher continued. "Some damaged Solomon gene. I guess they'll figure it out over at Rockland."

Steve felt a hot wave rush over his body, as if he'd just opened the door to a blast furnace. He strained to keep his voice steady. "Unlike these ass wipes of yours, Pincher, I don't have to pretend you're smart or funny or even halfway human. So cut the crap. Give us what you've got."

Pincher pretended not to hear him. Or not to care. "The kid's mother—that'd be Solomon's sister—exchanges sexual favors for intoxicating substances. What do they call that, Del?"

"A coke whore," Farnsworth said.

"Indeed," Pincher agreed. "A harlot so low as to treat her own child worse than barnyard swine. Oh, suffer the little children."

Steve felt beads of sweat on his forehead. He wondered how long it would take him to leap across the conference table and latch on to Pincher's neck. How much time would he have before Farnsworth clubbed him with a gun butt?

"Corruption and carnality run in Solomon's family," Pincher prattled on. "I have always thought of the courthouse as a holy place, but Solomon's own father was a money-changer in the temple."

An image formed in Steve's mind. He was picking up Ray Pincher, throwing him through a window, watching his body explode like a crushed melon on the flagstone courtyard nine stories below.

"There is some shit I will not eat," Steve said, so quietly only Victoria heard it.

He's going to do something really stupid, Victoria knew. She could hear Steve's breath quicken, could sense his muscles tighten.

"As for the weird kid," Pincher said, "the state's gonna put him in a fishbowl . . ."

"There is some shit . . ." Steve's voice, barely a whisper.

". . . stick needles in his brain, and figure out what fucked him up, the Solomon gene or the coke whore's abuse."

". . . I will not eat!"

Steve launched himself across the table and was instantly aware of a strange sensation. Like a steer roped by a cowboy, he was yanked to a sudden stop. He seemed to be suspended in air for a split second, then tumbled back into his chair. Bewildered, he looked down and saw Victoria's hand snagging his belt in a white-knuckled grip. She'd been playing tennis since age four and could crack walnuts in her fist.

"You want to let go?" he said.

"Not yet."

"I was just stretching my legs."

"Stretch them again, Solomon, and I'll tear your pants off."

"Promises, promises."

She laughed. Then so did he. Adrenaline draining, heart rate slowing, he relaxed. She released her grip, and Steve laced his fingers behind his head and leaned back. "Sugar Ray, you're the biggest, baddest lion in the jungle, so you don't have to piss all over the room to mark your territory. Now, I don't know what you're after today, but I figure you'll get around to telling us in your own slippery-ass way. Until then, I'm gonna take a little nap. Victoria, wake me when it's over."

He tilted his chair back and closed his eyes.

He trusts me, Victoria thought. He trusts me not just to keep him from committing an assault, but to go mano a mano with the State Attorney.

"If you have exhibits for us, Mr. Pincher," she said, "I'd appreciate them now. But if all you're going to do is insult my partner, I'll file a motion for sanctions."

"Keep your training bra on," Pincher replied.

Her head snapped back as if hit by a quick jab. "Is that a comment on the size of my breasts?"

"It's a comment on your lack of experience."

"Funny, because it reminds me of a sexist remark I heard you make to Jack Zinkavich about Gloria.

What was it? 'I'd like to eat my lunch off that Cuban butt.' "

Victoria thought she heard Gloria Mendez suck in a breath. Next to her, Miranda Cooper shifted uncomfortably in her chair. Farnsworth clapped a hand over his face, stifling a grin. Pincher opened his mouth as if to say something. Apparently he couldn't think of anything.

"Sure you got that right, Victoria?" Steve asked, opening an eye. "You sure Pincher didn't tell Gloria he'd like to eat his lunch off Zinkavich's butt?"

"Steve, stay out of this," she ordered.

"Yes, ma'am."

"This isn't a joke. Mr. Pincher just committed a violation of federal law. If Gloria wanted to, she could file a complaint with the EEOC and the Ethics Commission, and so could I. So, Mr. Pincher, I advise you to continue your misogynist remarks at your own peril."

"Woweee," Steve yelled, pounding a drumbeat on the table. "Sugar Ray, you can beat the crap out of me all you want. But my partner's tougher than you are. She'll cut off your balls and wear them as earrings."

My partner, Victoria thought. That's what Solomon just called her. *My partner.*

My partner, Steve thought. That's what she'd called him.

"If all you're going to do is insult my partner . . ."

After lashing him to his chair, she had leapt to his defense. Protecting him. Instead of him protecting her. But then, wasn't the lioness more ferocious than the lion?

"All right," Pincher said, recovering his ability to speak. "You two have had your fun." He nodded to Miranda Cooper, who opened a box, pulled out a dozen glossy photos, and slid them across the table.

Steve and Victoria looked at the first photo. A man and a woman on the flying bridge of a huge yacht. The woman was sprawled in the captain's chair, the man standing between her spread legs, both naked. A long-lens shot, the teak steering wheel gleaming in the sun, the woman's dark hair sailing in the wind. Frozen in mid-hump. The woman's face was clearly visible. Katrina Barksdale. The man's back was to the camera. The crack of his ass was in perfect focus.

"What's the jury gonna think when we show them this?" Pincher asked.

"Probably gonna wonder who's driving the boat," Steve said.

The next shot showed the man's face. Chet Manko, no surprise there. His eyes were closed, his hands cupped under Katrina's ass. Then a tutorial of kama sutra positions—Katrina riding Manko cowgirl; him bending her over the rail doggie style; lying on the deck in the good old missionary position. The last photo showed Katrina with a mouth full of Manko.

"Enjoying the show, Solomon?" Pincher asked.

"What's the big deal? They're not breaking any laws, except maybe the ban on offshore drilling."

"What's that you were saying at the bail hearing? 'Katrina loves Charles'? You'll eat those words, Solomon."

"So she was screwing around," Steve said. "That

doesn't mean she killed her husband. Hell, *he's* the one with the motive for murder, not her."

Pincher turned to Farnsworth. "Del, you know what Solomon's thinking right now?"

Farnsworth gestured at a photo that showcased Katrina's shapely ass. "Probably wondering how he can get a piece of that."

"He wants to know how we got the pictures and what else we got."

Steve said: "I figure Charles Barksdale hired a peep, and the peep hired a boat."

"Bingo."

"I also figure he bugged the phones and the bedrooms."

"And what do you think we've got on the tapes?"

Victoria said: "It doesn't matter. All tapes are inadmissible if Katrina didn't know she was being recorded."

"Admissible in the *Miami Herald*," Pincher said. "Your motion to suppress will be heard the day before jury selection. Maybe the judge will keep out the tapes, maybe he won't. Either way, they'll damn sure be on page one of the paper."

"I assume you have transcripts for us," Victoria said.

"Better than that." Pincher nodded to Gloria Mendez, who opened a briefcase and pulled out a portable tape recorder.

"Tape A-twelve," Gloria said. "Barksdale master bedroom suite, eleven-oh-three P.M., two weeks before the murder."

"*Alleged* murder," Victoria corrected her.

Gloria punched the PLAY button. For several seconds, the only sound was Sade singing "Smooth

Operator." Then a sleepy woman's voice: "Wish Charlie would stay away longer."

A man grunted. "Uh."

"You don't know what it's like. He makes my skin crawl."

Katrina Barksdale's voice. No doubt about it.

"Uh-huh." The man graduating to two syllables.

"He thinks he's so smart. All his books. All his poems."

"Poetry's for fags." The man again. Blue-collar Boston in voice. Chet Manko.

"Sometimes I wish he'd just disappear," Katrina said.

"You want Mr. B gone, he's gone."

There was a four-second pause.

"Smo-oo-th operator."

"Bad idea, Chet. If we break up, cops snoop around, you might get nervous and cut a deal."

"You dumping me?"

"I saw it on TV. *Dateline, 60 Minutes,* one of those. The wife's boyfriend nailed her for the murder they did together."

"Why you dumping me?"

"I'm not, Chet. I'm just saying two people is one too many for a murder."

"Smo-oo-th operator."

Silence again, and Gloria Mendez hit the STOP button.

Victoria said: "That's your case? Chet Manko offers to kill Charlie and Katrina says 'no.' "

"Don't be too hasty, Victoria," Steve said. "I think they got her."

"You do?" Incredulous.

"Yeah, it's a crime to play 'Smooth Operator' while having sex."

"You two aren't that dense," Pincher said. "Manko says he'll kill her husband. She says never mind, she'll do it herself."

"She does not," Victoria said.

"It's implied when she says, 'Two people is one too many for a murder.' "

"Typical Pincher case." Steve shook his head. "Conjecture piled on inference topped by innuendo."

But that's not what Steve was thinking. He was thinking about the four-second pause between Manko's offer to kill Charlie and Katrina's semi-rejection of the idea. He put himself in the jury box. He'd expect an innocent woman to say: *"No way, Chet."* And you'd hear the anger in her voice. But the pause made it appear she'd been calmly thinking it over, finally replying, essentially: *"I don't trust you, Chet. If I'm going to kill my husband, I'll do it myself."*

Steve the Juror thought that Katrina was a woman who may have *considered* killing her husband. But Steve the Lawyer still trusted his gut. He didn't think Katrina possessed the kind of evil required to do the job. Sure, she might be shallow and greedy and unfaithful, but a killer? It was a huge leap, and he wasn't making it. Not yet, anyway.

"You've got too many dots to connect, Sugar Ray," Steve said.

"There's stuff you don't know. After he finds out his wife's screwing around, Barksdale goes to his lawyer, tells him to draft divorce papers."

Miranda Cooper handed over a legal document captioned: "Petition for Dissolution of Marriage."

Steve was caught off guard. He'd known about Manko, so the hump-a-rama photos didn't surprise him. But Katrina had never said anything about a divorce.

"There was no divorce petition filed," he said.

"Didn't say there was," Pincher said. "Del, fill him in. It's obvious his client hasn't."

Farnsworth sat up straighter. "Barksdale tells Katrina he knows about Manko and he wants out of the marriage. This is not good news for the lady. Under the prenup, she'll get squat. But if Charlie dies while they're married, she gets a third of his estate."

"That's what we call motive." Pincher's tone was condescending.

"She begs forgiveness," Farnsworth said. "Swears she still loves him. Give her another chance, she'll dump Manko. She lures Barksdale into bed for his favorite kind of kink. Then she kills him."

"In case you're still thinking accident," Pincher added, "take a look at the report from our human-factors expert."

Miranda Cooper pulled out another document.

"It'd be virtually impossible for someone to accidentally strangle in that contraption," Pincher said. "All Barksdale had to do was lean forward to relieve the pressure. But he couldn't do that if she's holding him down."

"So what's your deal?" Victoria said.

"What makes you think I'm offering?" Pincher said.

"Your orientation lecture to new prosecutors. 'Never lay out your case for the defense, unless you're pushing a plea.' "

"Quite right." Pincher turned to Gloria and

Miranda. "I hope you two paid attention the way Ms. Lord did." He took his lavender handkerchief out of his jacket pocket, shook it out, refolded it, slid it back. "Plead to second degree. Twelve-year sentence, out in nine."

Steve put on his poker face. They'd have to talk to their client before responding.

"I remember something else you said in that lecture," Victoria said. " 'You're trial lawyers, not plea bargainers. So try your winners and plead out your losers. Never offer a plea unless your case has a hole in it.' "

"Top of your class, Ms. Lord," Pincher said.

"You're afraid of losing. I don't know why yet, but we'll figure it out. Until we do, you can take your plea and shove it."

Whoa, Steve thought. When did she become a cowboy?

Ray Pincher raised an eyebrow and cocked his head, as if trying to determine if his hearing had failed him. "Solomon, perhaps you should tell your neophyte partner that she might be outsmarting herself here."

"I don't tell her anything, Sugar Ray. She's got better instincts than I do."

Hang tough. Never contradict your partner in front of the enemy.

"I'll hold the offer open until tomorrow at noon." Then, as unruffled as his lavender shirt, Pincher stood and with a mortician's smile said: "I'll escort you out."

Steve and Victoria gathered the discovery documents and walked out of the conference room, with Pincher leading the way to the elevator. Halfway down the institutional corridor of metal walls and industrial carpeting, the State Attorney gestured toward a closed door. "Before you leave, Solomon, there's someone who wants to see you."

A nameplate on the door read:

John B. Zinkavich, Esq.
Division of Family Services

"You got any other doors?" Steve said. "Maybe one with a new car behind it? Or a trip to Acapulco?"

Thirty-two

THE LATE RUFUS THIGPEN

"Did I just hear you turn down a plea without consulting our client?" Steve asked.

"Katrina will do what I tell her," Victoria replied. They were standing at the door to Zinkavich's office.

"That's awfully arrogant."

"Right. Sounds like something you would say."

"Ancient history. I've decided to become more like you."

"Don't get too principled. We've got a murder case to try."

"So?"

"Don't wimp out on me, Steve."

"Jeez, I've created a monster."

"I still have my ethics. I'm just becoming more pragmatic." She rapped twice on the door and turned the knob before anyone said to come in.

Jack Zinkavich, lumpy and disheveled, was slumped in a chair at his regulation gunmetal desk, a box of Krispy Kremes within reach of a pudgy arm. A man in an orange jumpsuit sat in a straight-backed chair, his ankles shackled together.

Along a wall, cardboard boxes overflowed with

Juvenile Court files, the detritus of Miami's endless familial dysfunctions. On the windowsill sat a dozen stuffed animals, playthings for the young witnesses who trooped in with social workers, guardians ad litem, and cops.

"Look who's here," Zinkavich called out, grabbing a glazed Krispy Kreme. "The weasel and the princess."

"What's up?" Steve asked. "We've got work to do."

"You know this guy, Solomon?" Zinkavich pointed the donut toward the man in the jumpsuit.

Steve glanced at the prisoner. Late thirties. Shaved head. Jailhouse pallor and an ugly scowl. "Never saw him before. What'd he do?"

"Cocaine trafficking. Picked up yesterday. History of auto theft, B-and-E, domestic violence." Zinkavich chomped on the donut, spoke with his mouth full. "What about you, Thigpen? Recognize this asshole?"

The man in the orange jumpsuit stirred. "That's the heathen," he said.

Zinkavich licked a sugar slick from his lips. "I got good news and bad news for you, Solomon. The good news is, Rufus Thigpen ain't dead. The bad news is, he can testify against you."

"For what? I don't know this guy."

Thigpen raised his unshackled arm and turned his head. A purplish scar ran like a polluted stream from the crown of his skull to the top of an ear. "You busted my head, fuckface. The night you took the kid."

Steve remembered him now: the psychotic shepherd with the curved stick. He'd had a beard and shoulder-length hair and smelled like a wet beagle.

What was it his father always said? *"Our past clings to us like mud on cleated boots."*

"Mr. Thigpen is a victim of your violent behavior," Zinkavich said. "And quite a compelling witness."

"Steve Solomon is not a violent man," Victoria said.

My trusty partner. Leaping to my defense.

"You don't know him well, Ms. Lord," Zinkavich said. "Not so long ago, he viciously assaulted me in the courthouse. And when he kidnapped the child—"

"I rescued Bobby," Steve said.

"Quiet," Victoria told him. "I'll handle this."

"Regardless of Solomon's motives," Zinkavich continued, "he committed an aggravated assault, fracturing Mr. Thigpen's skull. It's only a matter of time before he unleashes his temper on the boy."

"That's bullshit!" Steve took half a step toward Zinkavich, but Victoria elbowed him in the ribs, and he stopped.

"Just look at that temper." Zinkavich wagged a sugary finger at Steve. "You present an imminent threat to your nephew. You refuse medical treatment for him. You drag him to autopsies. Your idea of homeschooling is a subscription to *Playboy*." A smirk creased his blubbery cheeks. "Frankly, Solomon, I think you'd have a hard time adopting a poodle, much less a child."

Steve seethed, but followed his partner's orders. He would keep his big mouth shut. But he couldn't help wondering why Zinkavich was laying out his case. Just like Pincher. The two cases were unrelated, but this seemed oddly orchestrated.

"Before you leave, Solomon, there's someone who wants to see you."

"Steve Solomon is an excellent parent to Bobby," Victoria said. "I can attest to that."

"And I have a rebuttal witness who will give damning testimony as to Mr. Solomon's fitness," Zinkavich shot back.

"Who?" Victoria asked.

Zinkavich snickered. "Under the rules, I'm not required to tell you."

"If you know your rebuttal witness in advance, the courteous practice is to disclose," Victoria said.

"Courteous practice? Aren't you the newbie?" Zinkavich giggled and his belly shifted, straining the buttons on his white shirt. "We don't wear velvet gloves here, Ms. Lord. We go for the jugular."

"If that's all, we'll be going," Victoria said.

"Not quite all," Zinkavich said, hitting a button on his intercom. A moment later, a uniformed cop came into the room and helped Thigpen out of his chair.

"I owe you, fucker," Thigpen muttered, glaring at Steve, as he shuffled out, shackles clanking.

Zinkavich grabbed another Krispy Kreme, chocolate glazed with candy sprinkles. To Steve, a donut purist, that was overdoing it, like painting lipstick on Mona Lisa. "Due to the exigent circumstances of young Robert living in such a dangerous environment," Zinkavich said, "I've secured an emergency trial date. Next Monday."

"Not possible," Steve said, breaking his vow of silence. "We filed a motion to fast-track Barksdale. That's the day we start trial."

"That's why we'll go from six P.M. to ten P.M. each night."

"Doesn't work. I need the evenings to prepare for the next day in court."

"Not if you plead out the murder case. I have it on good authority that Mr. Pincher has made a generous offer."

"So that's the game. What do I get in return for selling out Katrina?"

Zinkavich shook his head in feigned disbelief. "If you're suggesting there's a quid pro quo—"

"C'mon, what is it? Bobby? Are we swapping Katrina for Bobby?"

Zinkavich chose his words as carefully as a jeweler chooses his diamonds. "I might be inclined to propose temporary shared custody with you as guardian."

"What the hell's that mean?"

"Weekdays in a state facility, weekends with you. After a few months of testing and treatment, Robert could live with you full-time."

"I thought I was too dangerous," Steve said.

"There'd be anger management counseling and home visits by Family Services, but nothing too intrusive."

"What a crock."

"There's something for everybody here," Zinkavich said. "Mr. Pincher gets his victory in Barksdale and you get your nephew."

"I was right about you, Zinkavich."

"Steve, don't," Victoria warned.

"I had you pegged as a phony from day one," Steve said, plowing ahead. "A political hack. Somebody who shines Pincher's shoes and reminds him to zip his fly. You don't give a shit about Bobby."

"Steve, let's go," Victoria said.

"No, you don't get it, Vic. My old man thought this prick was the real deal. But my instincts were better. My gut was right. Old Herbert was wrong. Do you know how happy that makes me?"

"I'm so pleased you're resolving your father-son issues," Zinkavich said dryly. "Now, may I assume you're turning down my proposal?"

"You bet your fat ass I am."

"Fine. Frankly, I would prefer to see you go down hard, which you will. You'll be indicted for aggravated assault, criminal trespass, and kidnapping in Calhoun County. You'll lose your license, your nephew, and what's left of your reputation."

"Some people are ashamed of their hypocrisy, Fink, but you wear yours like a medal."

"If there's nothing else, Mr. Zinkavich," Victoria said, "we'll see you in Juvenile Court next Monday."

"*We?*" Zinkavich said.

"I'll be representing Mr. Solomon."

Steve gave her a look. What happened to *"I've never handled a guardianship case"*?

"Have you ever tried a juvie case?" Zinkavich asked.

"I'm a trial lawyer, an all-purpose utility player," she said, echoing Steve's words. "I can play any position, and I'm not afraid of any case or any lawyer."

Steve felt a strange brew of emotions. Gratitude to Victoria and despair about Bobby. She was coming aboard, but was it a sinking ship? If she had any idea how to win the case, he'd love to hear it, because he had nothing. The two of them would be trying the murder case every day, the guardianship every night, and as far as he could tell, they'd be getting their asses kicked in both.

There was something else strange going on, he thought. Victoria was starting to sound like him, and he was starting to think like her.

"Aligning yourself with Solomon can do you great damage, Ms. Lord," Zinkavich said.

"Thanks for the career advice," she said.

"You'll never be a success in this town if people think of you as Solomon's lawyer, or even worse, his partner."

"I don't care what people think," she said. "I won't compromise my ideals to achieve someone else's definition of success." Then she turned to Steve and smiled. "Right, partner?"

Steve's To-Do List

1. Thank Victoria. (Don't overdo it.)
2. Discredit Kranchick. *HOW????*
3. Neutralize Thigpen. *HOW????*
4. Zinkavich's rebuttal witness. *WHO????*
5. Interview Barksdale's divorce lawyer.
6. Buy prosciutto (from Parma).
7. Confront Katrina with her own words: "Two people is one too many for a murder."
8. Pay Cece. (Postdate check.)
9. Tell Bobby you love him (every day).
10. ~~Tell Victoria how you feel about her.~~

Thirty-three

A REAL ROMANTIC

"Did you get the report back from the photogramme-try expert?" Victoria said into her cell phone.

"Called yesterday," Steve said into his. "Told me the shadow was blurry and crossed two planes."

"Meaning?"

"Without triangular points, he couldn't do the trig equation."

"So no height and weight?"

"He can't even say for sure it's a person."

"So Katrina wasn't signaling someone to come into the bedroom."

"More like Pincher can't *prove* she was," Steve said.

It was the day after their meetings with Pincher and Zinkavich, and they were in separate cars, driving toward the mainland in adjacent lanes on the MacArthur Causeway.

Victoria had spent the morning combing through evidence files and Steve had been on the phone, inquiring about downtown office space. A real office in a high-rise, not the mildewed second floor of a second-rate modeling agency.

Office space for Solomon & Lord, Attorneys-at-Law.

As if they had already won the Barksdale trial and had collected a big fee.

As if she were going to practice law with him when the case was over.

Never seeming to consider the consequences if they lost. Or worse, if they lost *and* were humiliated in the process. Steve the Slasher and Victoria the Rookie. Already, a smart-ass *Miami Herald* columnist had dissed them: "Those South Beach defense lawyers might just have too much sand in their shoes and too few bullets in their briefs to handle a high-profile murder trial."

If disaster struck, Steve could always go back to his penny-ante cases. But what could she do?

Real estate closings for Bruce, that's what.

With so much work to do and too little time to do it, they were splitting up for the day. Steve would interview Charles Barksdale's divorce lawyer, and Victoria would confront Katrina with the dirty laundry Pincher had been sniffing.

"Thanks for stepping up to the plate on Bobby's case," Steve said.

"You've thanked me ten times."

"Without you, I don't know what I'd do."

"Eleven."

The morning was cool and crisp, the bay flat and still. One of the Norwegian cruise ships was headed out Government Cut on their left, a family of gulls circling above the stern. As their cars passed Parrot Jungle, Steve blurted out: "I'm sorry I was such a jerk when we met."

"You're thinking about Mr. Ruffles, aren't you?

But let me remind you that you never paid my dry-cleaning bill," she added.

The Miami Herald building loomed ahead. Steve would exit the causeway there and head down Biscayne Boulevard to Flagler Street, a murderers' row of lawyers' offices. Victoria would swing south on the expressway to Dixie Highway, then take LeJeune to Old Cutler Road and Katrina's bayfront home.

"Thanks to you," Steve said, "maybe we've got a chance in Bobby's case."

"Twelve."

"I'm really depending on you for strategy. I'm clueless how we're gonna discredit Kranchick, much less what to do with Thigpen."

"We'll work on it together."

Just what he wanted to hear.

"How much do you know about Kranchick's autism project?" Her voice faded in and out over the cell.

"Not much," Steve said. "She told me about some behavioral and drug therapy. Megavitamins and magnesium, that sort of thing."

"In her report to the court, she called it a pilot project."

"Yeah?"

"Last night, I looked it up on every medical database I could find. Not much there except some preliminary papers that are pretty vague."

"What are you getting at?"

"Did you notice the foreign hospitals on Kranchick's CV?" Victoria said.

"I remember something in Argentina."

"Pedro Mallo Hospital in Buenos Aires. Kutvolgyi

Uti in Budapest. State University Hospital in Bulgaria."

"So she likes to travel."

"I ran the hospitals through the databases, too. They all have something in common. Pharmaceutical companies test new drugs in them."

"So what's wrong with that?" he asked.

"Probably nothing. Kranchick's into research and testing, so the foreign venues make sense. It's just that the controls are looser there."

"No FDA peeking over your shoulder."

"Exactly."

"You think something's not kosher at Rockland?"

"No way to tell. If we had the time and money, we'd hire an expert consultant, really go through their records."

"I could get Cadillac Johnson."

"You think you can bribe Kranchick with pulled pork sandwiches?"

"Cadillac's got other talents."

"Unless he's an endocrinologist, I don't see how he can help."

"Trust me on this. I'm gonna stop by the Sweet Potato Pie on the way home."

"What for?"

"A couple slabs of baby-backs."

"I stopped eating meat."

"Liar, liar, briefs on fire."

"Okay. Half a slab, extra sauce. But tell Bruce and I'll have to hurt you."

"Our secret."

"So what are you going to ask Cadillac to do?"

"Got a bad connection here," he said, even though he could hear her perfectly.

"We have a deal, remember? Everything by the book."

"Losing you," he said, clicking off. He was working on an idea, and it didn't require an endocrinologist. Just someone with people skills and a measure of courage. The ability to pick a lock might come in handy, too.

Steve knew that Cadillac had played guitar in places where performers sometimes got knifed instead of paid. He'd sold encyclopedias door-to-door. He'd dealt blackjack in a riverboat casino. He was perfect for the job.

If Steve's plan worked, he could tell Victoria all about it when they went to court. If it didn't work, he'd take the fall, not her.

Fifteen minutes later, Steve was sitting in a richly upholstered chair, trying not to spill his Cuban coffee. He was in the office of Bluestein, Dominguez, Greenberg, & Vazquez. The late Charles Barksdale's law firm. Perched on the fifty-third floor of a bank building at Flagler Street and Biscayne Boulevard, Steve could see all the way to Bimini.

Unless a turkey buzzard was in his line of sight.

Which it was.

Steve's glance shifted from the red-faced buzzard with the curved beak to the bald lawyer with the half-glasses. The buzzard was balanced on an outside window ledge covered with shit, the lawyer on the corner of a teak desk covered with files.

"Charlie Barksdale was a real romantic," said Sam Greenberg, the lawyer.

"*Screech,*" said the buzzard.

"Romantic, how?" Steve said.

"The sorry son-of-a-bitch really believed in love."

Greenberg ran his firm's family law division, a euphemism for cutthroat divorces and killer custody wars. He was in his late forties, pale and overweight, conservatively dressed in banker's gray wool. Steve thought he had the look of someone who billed twenty-five-hundred hours a year at five hundred bucks per hour. A tired but wealthy look.

"So Charlie loved Katrina?" Steve said.

"He was nuts about her," Greenberg said.

The buzzard kept its beak shut.

"Plus he liked having a trophy wife," Greenberg continued. "Gave him self-worth."

"His net worth not doing the job?"

"Some guys need trinkets on their arm. Me, I've been married to the same woman for twenty-two years. She's fatter than I am and a wicked scold, but I wouldn't trade her in. Hell, I couldn't afford to."

Steve studied the photo on the credenza. A plump, smiling wife and three kids, one of college age, two younger ones with full sets of gleaming orthodonture.

Greenberg peered over his half-glasses and lowered his voice. "Hot sex, too."

"Congratulations."

"Not me. Charlie. After he met Katrina, he was a walking hard-on. 'Nobody ever got my pecker so hard,' blah-blah-blah. I had to bust his chops to make him do the prenup. He said it violated his principles, ruined the romance."

"When did he tell you he wanted a divorce?"

"A few days before he died. He's sitting right in that chair where you are now. Pissing and moaning. 'The bitch is fucking my boat captain. I'm gonna

divorce her ass.' The usual stuff. But really suffering.
I'm dictating the petition, and he gets sick, goes to the
rest room and barfs. I tell him to come back the next
day, all the papers will be ready to sign."

"But he never showed up?"

"Nope." Greenberg slid off his desk, settled into
his high-backed brown leather chair. On the window
ledge, the buzzard hopped a step, spread its wings,
tucked them in again. Smart birds, the scavengers
winter in Miami, feasting on discarded burgers, *media noches,* and the occasional drug dealer stuffed
into a garbage bag. They fly endless circles over the
downtown courthouse, roosting on the ledges of the
high-rise law firms, providing the source of endless
lawyer jokes.

"I called Charlie when he missed the appointment," Greenberg said. "He said he wasn't feeling so
hot, he'd come in in a couple days. When he didn't, I
sent the petition by courier to his office. Instead of
signing it, he scribbled some nonsense on the ad
damnum clause and sent it back."

"What nonsense?"

"A poem or haiku or something."

"Mind if I see it?" There'd been no handwriting
on the photocopy of the petition provided by Pincher.

Greenberg walked to a teak file cabinet. "Charlie
fancied himself an artiste, not just a guy who built
condos on zero lot lines. When he'd pay my bill, he'd
usually write a poem on the check."

Outside, the wind rattled the windowpane, and
the buzzard hopped off the ledge and soared down
Flagler Street. In flight, with its Yao Ming wingspan,
the black bird seemed as large as an airplane.

Greenberg drew a thin file from the drawer and

handed it to Steve, who quickly found the original Petition for Dissolution. He turned to the last page, saw the formal legal language: "Wherefore Petitioner Prays that the Court Enter a Final Judgment of Dissolution of Marriage."

Scrawled over the printed clause was a handwritten note:

> Hide a few contretemps
> Defer a competent wish
> Cement a spit-fed whore

"What's it mean?" Steve said, thoroughly confused.

"Beats me. But like I said, Charlie—"

"Was a real romantic, I know."

Steve looked at the poem again. What the hell was it? And why write it on the divorce petition? He wished Victoria were here. Maybe she could figure it out.

"Did you ask Barksdale about it?" he said.

"I phoned the next day," Greenberg said. "But Charlie wasn't taking any calls. He was dead."

Sitting in the Barksdale living room, Victoria watched Katrina flip through the glossy photos of her wrestling match with Chet Manko.

"If I'd known they were taking pictures, I'd have gotten a bikini wax," Katrina said, making a face.

Victoria slipped a cassette into a portable tape recorder. "Frankly, we're more concerned about the audiotapes."

Sade was singing "Smooth Operator," but Katrina

was still studying the photos. "Jesus, I look all washed out. That sun on the bay is brutal."

Victoria refrained from saying that she'd look even worse after a few years at Dade Correctional Institution. "Kat, I really need you to listen to this."

Katrina shrugged and tossed her hair over a shoulder. She wore a crisscross black-and-white halter mini that Victoria had seen at Saks. A Balenciaga design, sixteen hundred fifty dollars. Black ankle-wrap sandals with a hanging brass pendant. Giuseppe Zanotti. Six hundred bucks, at least. After Sade had finished singing about a man with eyes like angels but a heart that's cold, and after Manko had finished soliciting a murder, Katrina shrugged again. "What's the big deal? You heard me. I told Chet to forget it."

"Pincher's going to say the tape shows you were considering Manko's offer, and that later you killed your husband without Chet's help."

"That's ridiculous."

"Did you and Manko talk about killing Charles other times?"

"Sure. Chet wouldn't let it go. He had a whole plan. Next time we crossed the Gulf Stream, he'd dump Charlie overboard and claim it was an accident." She shivered. "Just the thought of Charlie being eaten by a shark freaked me out. I told Chet to shut up, never mention it again."

Victoria tried to evaluate her client. Was Katrina telling the truth? Where was the human polygraph when she needed him?

Her cell phone rang. It was Steve, saying he wouldn't have time to pick up the baby-backs, but he'd stop at the Italian deli on the way back to his place. She said to forget about the food, how'd it go with the divorce lawyer?

" 'Cement a spit-fed whore,' " he replied.

"I beg your pardon."

He read her the poem, which she scribbled down. No, she didn't have any idea what it meant, either.

"Charles Barksdale's telling us something," Steve said. "And we better figure it out before Pincher does."

"What's 'contretemps'?" Katrina asked, after Victoria read her the verse.

"A mistake, an embarrassing mishap."

"Like getting charged with bumping your husband off?"

"More like spilling the soup on your date. You have no idea what Charles could have meant? 'Contretemps'? 'Competent wish'? 'Spit-fed whore'?"

"Better not have been talking about me."

"Think about it, Kat. Had Charles ever said anything like this?"

Another shrug, another hair toss. "Charlie was always quoting books, showing off. And writing stuff he called poetry. He never came out and said what he meant."

"That's what poetry does."

"That's why I never liked it. Me, I just say whatever the hell I'm thinking."

Thirty-four

PROSCIUTTO AND MELON, SALTY AND SWEET

"You're slicing the prosciutto too thin," Victoria said.

"Since when does someone named Lord know anything about prosciutto?" Steve said.

"And what's your name, Solomonte?"

They were standing shoulder to shoulder at his kitchen counter. He was carefully constructing *bruschetta al prosciutto*, and she was supervising.

"Jews and Italians both know food," he said. "This is top-grade prosciutto from Parma. It's supposed to be paper-thin, so it melts on your tongue."

Victoria watched Steve slice the pink, buttery meat with the care of a surgeon. Outside, the sun had set, and the wind slammed palm fronds against the windows.

"When I was a kid, my mother served prosciutto and melon appetizers at her dinner parties," she said.

"Great combination. The salty and the sweet."

Like the two of us, she thought. Then chased the thought away. "How long have you been cooking?"

He gave her a sharp look. "I know what you're doing."

"What?"

"This nurturing shtick. You're trying to take my mind off Bobby's case."

Busted. Does he really know me that well?

"What we should be doing is prepping Bobby for his testimony," he said.

"You sure you want him to testify?"

"He needs to tell the judge he wants to stay with me."

"But it's risky. When Bobby gets nervous, there's no telling what he might say."

Steve peeled a garlic clove with his fingers. "Gotta pull rank on you here. Bobby testifies."

"I can be more objective than you can."

"But I have more at stake, so it's my call. Besides, my gut tells me he'll do fine."

"That again?"

"I keep telling you, listen to your gut."

"Mine says I'm starving." She pointed at the tiny ribbons of white that laced the meat. "Is that fat?"

Again, he gave her a long look.

"I'm not nurturing," she protested. "I'm asking because I watch what I eat."

"Just enough fat for flavor."

Tempted, she grabbed a tiny sliver of the meat, nibbled at it, and closed her eyes in ecstasy. "Mmm, succulent." She took a larger slice, placed it on her tongue, and purred, "So *su-cu-lent*."

"If you say 'succulent' one more time, I'm suing you for sexual harassment."

She placed a fingertip in her mouth, extracted the last bit of flavor, and said, "Suc-cu-lent. So sue me, Solomon." She picked up a wafer of garlic, rubbed it across a slice of ciabatta. "You going to heat the bread?"

"Not heat it, grill it. The panini grill gives it crispness. A good meal is a combination of flavors and textures. Like your mother's prosciutto and melon."

"Opposites sometimes fit together well," she said.

He gave her a look but didn't pick up the ball and run with it. "I take it you and Bruce don't do much cooking."

"I'm lousy in the kitchen, and Bruce is pretty much a yogurt and veggie guy."

"For me, eating's a sensual pleasure. Makes up for the lack of other ones."

"Don't pull that on me, Solomon. How's the court reporter with the Rudnicks, anyway?"

"Sofia? Not seeing her anymore."

"Why not?"

He shrugged. "We didn't have a lot to talk about."

"Talk? Could it be you're maturing before my eyes?"

"Nah. Just a temporary phase."

"Have you called Jackie yet?"

He drizzled olive oil on the garlicky ciabatta, put it into the panini grill. "I will. When I get some time."

For someone capable of intricate subterfuge in the courtroom, he was a terrible liar in the kitchen.

A minute later, he removed the ciabatta from the grill, added the prosciutto and a few drops more oil. She took a bite, let the flavors envelop her tongue.

"Oh, that is *so* wonderful."

At the same time, Victoria felt guilty. She should have been at Bruce's an hour ago. What would he say if he knew she was wolfing down a piece of meat?

"Animal flesh! You ate animal flesh?"

Okay, Bruce could be a little dogmatic, she thought. A little controlling, if you got right down to it.

"Don't fill up on the appetizers," Steve said. "You're invited for dinner."

"Sorry, can't."

"Linguine with shrimp and scallops in a puttanesca sauce."

"Ooh. With anchovies?"

"And capers and olives."

"Sounds great, but I promised Bruce . . ."

"Hey, no problem."

But she could see the disappointment in his eyes. "Bruce is so worried about the cold front. Freeze is supposed to hit tomorrow." Embarrassed now. Like she owed Solomon a reason why she was going to her fiancé's house.

"I understand. No big deal."

She used a napkin to wipe all traces of the prosciutto from her lips. She'd pop a couple Tic Tacs before kissing Bruce. "You gonna be okay?"

"Actually, I'm having a personal crisis. I don't know what to get you for a wedding present."

"Ri-ght."

"Mr. and Mrs. Guacamole, the couple that has everything."

"Are you getting passive-aggressive on me?"

"I was shooting for just aggressive."

"I'm worried about you, sandwich man."

"It's not about me." He made a show out of slicing fresh figs to decorate the plate of bruschetta. "You shouldn't become a real estate lawyer."

"I'll take it under advisement." Such a baby, she thought. Why didn't he just say it: *Don't marry*

Bruce. How did Steve ever score all those runs if he was so afraid of failure? Or was stealing home easier than stealing a heart?

"Glass of wine before you go?" he said. "There's a nice Chardonnay in the fridge."

She opened the refrigerator, spotted a bottle, and read aloud. " 'Arnaud Ente Puligny Montrachet Les Referts.' Golly, Solly. That's good stuff. You surprise me."

"I have a client who brings it in from France."

"A wine importer. Great client."

"More like a longshoreman at the Port of Miami."

"So it's stolen?"

"Technically, lost in transit."

She pulled out the bottle and saw something else behind it. An unopened container of coleslaw and a sweet potato pie, both from Cadillac's lunch wagon. She checked the date stamp on the coleslaw container.

Made today!

Steve had told her he didn't have time to see Cadillac. Why would he lie? She tried to think like Solomon, wend her way down the serpentine path he walked.

Because he's planning something illegal.

She closed the refrigerator, found a corkscrew in a drawer, and went to work on the bottle. "That rule of yours, the one about telling your lawyer the truth . . ."

"What about it?"

"I'm *your* lawyer. What are you cooking up with the cook?"

"Cadillac? Nothing."

"Not buying it, Solomon."

"You're just going to have to trust me on this."

"Problem is, I don't. Look, I want to win, but I'd prefer not to be disbarred in the process."

"Which is why you're better off not knowing everything."

Dammit. Does he really expect me to look the other way?

"All I'm doing is leveling the playing field," he continued.

"With a rake? Or a bulldozer?"

"C'mon, ease up, Victoria."

"You c'mon. You can't hide things from me. I won't put up with it."

Just then, Bobby walked into the kitchen. She'd have to grill Solomon later.

"Hey, guys," Bobby said, heading for the counter and picking up a slice of prosciutto. He was wearing his regular uniform, baggy shorts and a Miami Heat T-shirt with a flaming basketball dropping through a hoop.

"You were supposed to be back before dark," Steve said.

"I'm not a baby," Bobby said.

Victoria popped the cork on the wine bottle. "Bobby, you should have a sweater on. It's cold out."

"Only girls wear sweaters."

"Listen to Victoria, kiddo," Steve said, running water over a colander filled with fresh shrimp. "Where you been?"

"Riding my bike."

"Without a helmet?"

"When you were a kid, did you wear a helmet?"

"Objection, irrelevant," Steve said.

"Sustained." Victoria poured two glasses of wine. "Wear your helmet, Bobby."

"Jeez, why are you two ganging up on me?"

"Because we love you," Victoria said.

She had just astonished herself. Blurting it out like that.

We love you?

As if they were a couple. She put down the wine-glass. "I've got to go. See you tomorrow, guys."

"See you," Bobby said.

She slipped into a tailor-cut black leather jacket. "Steve, we'll work on the poem tomorrow, okay?"

"What poem?" Bobby asked.

"You really believe Katrina doesn't know what it means?" Steve asked her.

"Absolutely. She's not real strong on allegory and metaphor."

"What poem!" Bobby demanded.

Steve took a knife and started deveining the shrimp. "Something Barksdale wrote. Doesn't concern you."

"Why not?"

"Because I'm not supposed to get you involved in my cases."

"Little late for that, Uncle Steve."

Steve glanced at Victoria, who shrugged her okay. Then he recited:

"Hide a few contretemps
Defer a competent wish
Cement a spit-fed whore."

"Cool," Bobby said. "Each line has nineteen letters."

"I didn't notice."

"Then I guess you didn't notice they're all the same letters."

"What!" Steve was stunned. "You're saying it's an anagram?"

"Duh," Bobby said, grabbing another piece of prosciutto.

"Bobby, what else can the letters be arranged to say?" Victoria asked urgently.

Bobby made a show out of it, wrinkling his forehead, closing his eyes: "Lots of things. 'Ferment a cowhide pest.' 'A deft timeworn speech.' 'A west morphine defect.' "

"But there's only one we want," Steve said. "A message to Katrina. Or about Katrina. Something like that."

"It's called the 'source gram,' Uncle Steve. The one he used to make all the others."

"So help us out here, Bobby. What other phrases do you see?"

"Get outta town! There'll be hundreds, maybe thousands."

"C'mon, kiddo."

"I'm hungry. Can we do this later?"

"Bobby, this is important."

"I'll do it for a glass of wine."

"No deal. What else do you see? Any phrase with 'wife' or 'woman' in it?"

Bobby pouted.

"We could get them all with a computer program," Victoria suggested.

"No, no, no, no, no," Bobby singsonged. "I wanna do it."

"Make up your mind," Steve said, letting his frustration come through. "Do you want to help or not?"

"Fuck it!" Bobby yelled.

"Cool it!" Steve said.

"Fuck! Fuck! Fuck!" Bobby grabbed a handful of shrimp and threw them across the kitchen, where they *thwacked* against the cupboards. "You don't care about me! Don't care! Don't care!" He was rocking back and forth, eyes unfocused.

"Aw, jeez," Steve said. "How long since you've eaten?"

"Who cares? Who cares?"

"Your blood sugar's low. You know you're supposed to—"

"Don't care! Don't care!"

"C'mon, Bobby. Calm down."

"Don't care! Don't care!"

"Bobby, you're really, really good at this," Victoria said tenderly, "and we really value your help."

The boy's eyes were welling up. "That all you care about, my helping you?"

"Of course not. You're a wonderful boy. Sensitive and sweet."

"I'm not a wuss." A tear streaked down his face.

"No, you're not. You're all boy, and I want to be around to see the man you become."

"Really?" Bobby used the back of his arm to swipe away a tear.

"Watch this," Steve said, picking up the cue from Victoria. He grabbed a handful of shrimp and tossed them against the cupboard. Two or three stuck, and the rest slithered toward the floor.

"Cool." Bobby picked up a handful of shrimp, hurled them at the wall, and started giggling.

"There are still some left," Steve said.

"Victoria's turn," Bobby said.

She grabbed a few shrimp and lobbed them at the cupboard.

Bobby laughed. "You throw like a girl."

Steve put his hand on the back of the boy's neck, gave him a squeeze. "Know what, kiddo?"

"What?"

"No father ever loved a son any more than I love you."

Bobby put his arms around Steve's waist and hugged. Steve wrapped an arm around the boy's shoulders.

"I think I know the source gram, Uncle Steve."

"Sure you do."

"Wanna know what it is?"

"Nah, I want to hug some more."

"C'mon, Uncle Steve."

"It can wait. Tomorrow. Next week. A year after your Bar Mitzvah."

"Now!"

"Okay, kiddo, shoot."

" 'The woman is perfected,' " Bobby said. "That's your source gram. 'The woman is perfected.' "

Thirty-five

THE RUNNING MAN

Saturday morning the weather guys and gals were all atwitter about the arctic blast that was working its way south. "Freeze Watch!" the announcers screamed.

Steve watched the histrionics while standing at his kitchen counter, slicing a carambola, the yellow star fruit that grew on neighborhood trees. On the screen, Ricardo Sanchez, the Channel 4 weather guru, was garbed in a parka. Standing in front of an irrigation canal, Sanchez held his microphone in a gloved hand and interviewed a handsome, blond man in a bombardier jacket, a white silk scarf tied at his neck. Bruce Bigby, looking like a World War I aviator. The Green Baron, maybe?

In the background, Steve could see farmworkers wrapping palm fronds around the trunks of avocado trees. They wore jeans and T-shirts and didn't seem to be suffering hypothermia, even though most would have been natives of frost-free Caribbean islands.

"Could be the coldest night since the freeze of December 1894," Sanchez said.

"We can battle Mother Nature a lot better now,"

Bigby assured him. "Sprinklers, heaters, wind machines. Plus, I've got an army of two hundred workers."

Not one with a green card, Steve felt certain.

Bigby droned on, explaining the difference between radiation frost and advective frost, then smoothly moving to his favorite topic. "Let me remind your viewers that no matter the weather, the Bigby Resort and Villas' sales office will be open tomorrow, regular hours. Affordable vacation units for a lifetime of enjoyment."

It was only eight A.M., but he'd already had his fill of Bigby. He turned off the TV, and five minutes later, Victoria called.

" 'The woman is perfected,' " she said. "I fell asleep thinking about it."

With Bigby alongside, no doubt.

"Me, too," Steve said. "It's a lot different than saying, " 'The woman is perfect.' But what's it mean?"

"Can we work on it Monday? I'm gonna be stuck on the farm all weekend."

"I saw your guy on the weather forecast. He looked dashing."

"I'm so worried," she whispered. "Bruce is trying to act brave, but inside he's terrified about what might happen."

In the background, Steve heard someone shouting. "Smudge pots, *pronto! Comprende?*"

"You're coming down here tonight, aren't you, Steve?"

"Not if I have to watch the two of you smooching around a campfire."

"We'll be working to save the farm. You know that."

"Look, I wouldn't be much use. Even my weeds die."

"Bruce likes you, Steve."

"Bruce is a lousy judge of character."

"Please, do this for me, Steve."

After that, what choice did he have? He told her he'd be there by sundown to shovel shit or whatever Bigby wanted. She said to dress Bobby in several layers, and for a moment, it sounded very domestic to him, like she was his wife and Bobby their son. But that thought passed when Victoria said she had to go. Bruce was calling her, something about sandwiches and soup for two hundred men.

It was sunny and windy, the temperature plunging when Steve, in cotton sweats, took his run. He followed the usual route through South Grove, across the Gables Waterway bridge, to the end of Cocoplum Circle. Bobby rode his bicycle twenty yards ahead. Bribed with the promise of a papaya smoothie, the kid had pulled a windbreaker over his Marlins jersey.

Steve was hoping to get into the zone, that relaxed place where the body goes on autopilot and the mind relaxes in the La-Z-Boy. Sometimes, zoned out, ideas would pop into his head—new sandwich recipes or trial strategies—and he'd race home and write them down. But today he had only questions.

What did Charles mean? "The woman is perfected."

Steve's gut told him it was the key to the case.

Questions in Bobby's case, too.

How do we discredit Kranchick and Thigpen?

Who's the mystery rebuttal witness? And how the hell do we win?

A question about Victoria, too.

If we'd met before she hooked up with Bigby, would things have turned out differently?

All questions, no answers.

Passing the halfway point, Steve concentrated on his form. Arms relaxed, head still. There wasn't much traffic, just a few real estate brokers chauffeuring clients past waterfront homes. He saw Bobby half a block ahead, carving figure eights on his bike, then swerving back on course.

Steve called out: "Hey, kiddo, wait up!"

The boy turned, waved, then pedaled faster, heading away from him, toward LeJeune Circle.

Where does he get that rebellious streak?

Standing upright on the pedals, Bobby turned right at the circle and disappeared from view.

"Dammit." Steve picked up his pace.

Sometimes Steve thought he was overprotective. When he considered his own childhood, he was sure of it. When he was just a little older than Bobby, he would ride his bike from Miami Beach across the Julia Tuttle Causeway, cars whizzing by, horns blowing. He'd look for pickup baseball games in a park near the Liberty City projects. He was usually the only white kid in the game, but he couldn't remember anyone ever hassling him. At least, not until he started betting five bucks he could beat anyone in a race.

Any race. Around the bases, straight down the foul line, from home plate to deepest center field. They'd laughed at him, skinny Jewish kid from the Beach who thought he was a brother. But he'd won six races in a row, pocketed the cash, then dashed off on his bicycle, a couple of sore losers chasing him with baseball bats.

Now Steve crossed the bridge over the waterway, turned on Edgewater, and headed toward the bay.

Bobby was not in sight.

He'd probably turned up Douglas Road, the quickest route home, Steve figured. Not to worry, right? Still, he sped up.

Edgewater was quiet on a Saturday morning. No cars, no pedestrians, just a chorus line of wood storks. He turned left on Douglas, heading up a slight incline, a hill by Miami standards.

Still no Bobby.

He tried to calculate how far the boy could have gone, pedaling with those legs, as spindly as the wood storks'. He didn't like the answer.

Bobby should be here. He should be in sight.

Then, just past Battersea Road, Steve saw it. Bobby's red Schwinn, on its side, its front wheel poking out of an azalea bush.

"Bobby! Bobby, where are you?"

The only sound was the *caw* of an unseen bird.

"Bobby! C'mon, no screwing around."

He forced himself to remain calm. The boy could have walked down Battersea to the seawall. He could be skipping stones across the flat water of the bay. He's on the rocks at the shoreline, Steve told himself. He had to be.

Halfway down the street, Steve could see all the way to the bay.

"Bobby!"

No answer.

He turned around, got back to Douglas, started

running north. Cars were backed up at the Ingraham intersection, an arts festival in the Grove jamming the traffic all the way to Old Cutler Road. He picked up speed, running along the berm in the shade of palmetto trees, looking into each gridlocked car as he passed. Families in sedans, teens in Jeeps, hotshot guys in convertibles. Horns honked; drivers craned out windows; a man cursed.

Breathing hard, Steve willed himself to stay loose. He knew that tensing up would drain his energy. He had to make a quick decision. Douglas Road split in two. Bear right, you head up Main Highway into the downtown Grove and even worse traffic. Stay straight, and you hit South Dixie Highway. If Bobby had been snatched, the car would head for South Dixie. Once there, it could turn north toward I-95, go straight into the Gables, or turn south and head for Kendall. It could go anywhere.

If the car gets to South Dixie, Bobby's gone.

Steve stayed straight, running full bore. He was at De Garmo when he heard the screech of burning rubber. Ahead of him, one of the cars pulled out of the pack. But it wasn't a car.

A muddy green pickup with oversize tires.

It peeled into the oncoming lane and tore left across traffic onto Leafy Way. Steve was too far away to see into the truck.

Was it Janice?

Or Zinkavich's thugs?

Or some freaking pedophile?

No way to see if Bobby was inside. But there are some things you sense. He *felt* Bobby's presence. His heart raced now, not from the exertion of running but from the fear boiling through his veins.

Steve headed toward Leafy Way, a block ahead. A strange choice if they were looking for a shortcut. The street dead-ended three blocks from the intersection.

He figured he had one minute, at most, before the truck pulled a U-turn at the end of the street and came back out to the intersection. The only sounds now were the pounding of his own heart and the slap of his running shoes against the pavement. For the first time, he was aware of his aching legs.

He pictured Bobby at the park, tossing the ball. Herky-jerky movements, no natural coordination, but the kid loved to play. They would pretend Bobby was a Marlins pitcher; Steve would get in the catcher's crouch and call balls and strikes. *"Stee-rike three! Bobby Solomon, the rookie sensation from Miami, strikes out Barry Bonds to end the Giants' threat."*

That someone could hurt this boy filled Steve with a hot, murderous rage.

Then the spigots opened, the adrenaline poured, and Steve flew. Alongside him, the gridlocked cars were a blur, the faces of motorists featureless smudges. He jumped on the hood of a blue BMW and leapt off on the other side, the driver yelling, *"Ay, cabrón!"* as Steve crossed Douglas and spun into Leafy Way.

Sure enough, the muddy pickup with the bug screen was growling back out, coming straight at him. Now he saw it had a reinforced steel bumper mounted with a recovery hook, waist high. There could have been three people in the cab or three hundred; Steve couldn't see past the windshield glare.

He ran straight at the truck. Playing chicken. The

hook would be the first thing to hit him, entering the stomach, exiting his back. Steve had several seconds to imagine the autopsy photos.

He kept running; the truck kept coming.

The truck's horn blared, a steady blast.

He had maybe five seconds to dive over the curb and into a flower bed.

Suddenly, the truck braked hard, tires squealing. It fishtailed to a stop ten feet from him. Bouncing over the curb into a yard alongside a one-story stucco house, it smashed through a ficus hedge.

Steve chased after it.

From a neighbor's yard, someone yelled, "Hey! Fuck!"

The truck plowed through the property at the rear of the house. Churned up chunks of grass, sideswiped a pool cabana, crunched through a planter made of railroad ties. An elderly man in a bathrobe watering flowers leapt away, screeching something unintelligible.

Looking for a shortcut, Steve ran through an adjacent yard and headed for the next street, El Prado. He was betting the pickup would turn right and make a run for LeJeune, away from the snarled traffic. He headed on an angle to intercept it.

Turn right. Damn you, turn right.

Engine roaring, wheels tearing through the soft grass, the truck bounced into El Prado just as Steve emerged from the yard of an adjacent home.

The truck turned right. He had the angle. If he timed it perfectly . . .

You can do this. You can make it.

Running at full speed, Steve reached out. The rear gate of the truck was inches away. He launched himself, his foot catching on the bumper, his hand grabbing at the gate. He tumbled into the truck bed, sliding on his belly until his head hit the base of a lockbox, jamming his neck into his shoulders.

Shit, that hurts. That really hurts.

Bleary, unable to catch his breath, blood trickling down into his eyes, he scrambled to his feet just as the truck swerved right and tossed him into the left side-rail. Then it swerved hard left, and he was flung into the right side-rail. As he bounced off, he got a fleeting look into the tinted rear window of the cab. A man drove; a woman was in the passenger seat. Sitting between them, looking directly at him, tears streaking his face, eyes wide with fear, was Bobby.

Dizzy, his head throbbing, Steve grabbed the handle of the lockbox and steadied himself. He sensed movement behind him and whirled around. There were two old tires with no tread, a rolled-up tarp, and two cans of paint rolling around.

And a dog.

The dog was trying to get its balance, its tail tucked beneath its hindquarters. A big, mangy brown mutt with matted hair, a mix of Rottweiler and German shepherd, he guessed. The dog growled at him as if he had just swiped its pork chops.

"Hey, fellow," Steve said, extending a hand, showing how friendly he was.

The dog crouched on its haunches. The hair stood up on its neck.

Keeping one eye on the dog, Steve opened the lockbox lid. Hammers. Screwdrivers. A drill. A box wrench maybe two feet long. He would have preferred a baseball bat, but the wrench would do. Behind him, the dog's growl deepened ominously.

There was oncoming traffic now, and the truck had stopped swerving. Turning his back to the dog, Steve leaned over the driver's side of the cab, reaching as far as he could, the wrench in his left hand. Just as his backswing hit its apogee, he heard the sound of claws scratching metal. A second later, he brought the wrench down with all his might, and he felt the dog's teeth sink into his butt.

"Shit!" Steve screamed as the window shattered.

"Shit!" yelled the driver from inside the cab.

The truck swerved right, jumped the curb, flattened a mailbox, and slammed into a jacaranda tree. Steve felt himself flying over the side rail. He landed face-first in a honeysuckle shrub. For a moment, all went black. In the next moment, he was aware of several things at once:

His eyes refused to focus, his butt ached, and his nose was bleeding.

The mangy dog was yelping, running down the street.

A man with glass shards stuck in his forehead was getting out of the driver's side of the pickup, blood streaming down in his face.

Bobby ran to Steve, crying.

An overweight woman in granny glasses hustled after Bobby, yelling his name. She had greasy, dark hair that was pulled back in a ponytail. As she ran, her breasts jiggled under a Grateful Dead T-shirt. Her voice brought back vaguely unpleasant memories. "Jan?"

"It's me, Stevie," Janice Solomon said.

"Then I must have died and gone to hell."

"Not yet," the man said. He was standing ten feet away, a jack handle in his hand. Rufus Thigpen.

Shaved head, scarred skull, and a face as mean as a hungry weasel.

"I thought you were in jail, Thigpen."

"They let me out, shithead. Gave me three hundred dollars and a motel room."

"They teach you how to use indoor plumbing?" Steve struggled to his feet, scooping up a handful of dirt from the honeysuckle bed. He didn't think Thigpen saw him do it; the guy was wiping blood from his eyes. Steve was afraid, but not for himself. He could survive being beaten up; Bobby could not survive being taken away.

Thigpen gestured with the jack handle. "I owe you some major pain, fucker."

"Yeah, yeah. That's the second time you said that to me." What had he said at their meeting in the Fink's office? *I owe you, fucker.* There was something about the phrase . . . And the voice . . . And the way he gripped the jack handle . . . And then it came to him. From some deep, dark place, like a chilly waterway.

"It was *you*, Thigpen. That's what you said to me on the dock. *'I owe you, fucker.'* You're the guy with the winch handle and the potty mouth."

"I should have drowned you when I had the chance," Thigpen said.

"I don't get it. Why break into my house? What did you want?"

"Ask your dumb-ass sister. If you can still talk when I'm through with you."

"Don't hurt him, Rufe," Janice wailed.

"Fuck that. He scrambled my brains."

"How can you tell the difference?" Steve said.

Thigpen took a step toward him. Steve knew he'd

have one chance, that's all. His eyes were starting to focus, but the throbbing in his head had worsened. A hundred pounds of sand shifted inside his skull with every movement.

Thigpen took another step and brought the jack handle back.

Almost there. One more step.

Bobby dived for Thigpen's legs.

"No!" Steve yelled.

Thigpen swatted Bobby across the face and knocked him to the ground.

"Touch him again, I'll rip out your throat," Steve said.

"Try it," Thigpen sneered.

Bobby crouched on his haunches in the dirt, a hand over one eye.

"It's gonna be okay, kiddo," Steve promised. "We'll go home in a minute."

"The fuck you will." Taking one last step, Thigpen swung the jack handle. Steve slid to the side, the handle just missing his ear. He flicked out a hand and tossed the dirt into Thigpen's face, closing his eyes.

"Fuck! Fuck!" Thigpen clawed at his eyes, and Steve kicked him squarely in the groin. Thigpen doubled over, and Steve locked both hands together and swung them up, hard, connecting with the man's nose, breaking it with a satisfying crunch of cartilage and a spray of blood. Thigpen collapsed, moaning, one hand clutching his face, the other his crotch.

Steve limped to the truck and leaned on it for support. "Jan, what the hell?"

"I just wanted to see my Bobby for a little bit. I wouldn't hurt him. . . ."

Bobby ran to Steve, wrapped his arms around him.

"Can we go home, Uncle Steve?" He wouldn't look at his mother.

"You bet, kiddo."

Thigpen got to one knee, mumbled something about the sword of God, collapsed flat in the dirt. In the distance, a police siren wailed.

"I would have brought Bobby back, honest," Janice gabbled. "I woulda had to. Rufe didn't want to take him along."

"Where you going?"

Janice pulled at her ponytail. "Away somewhere. After Bobby's case is over. This lawyer, Zinkavich, got us out of jail for helping him."

"You're the Fink's rebuttal witness?"

"If that's what it's called, guess so."

"What are you going to say, that I lost your Barbie collection playing poker when we were kids?"

"That you're violent and unstable and do drugs. That you beat me up when you kidnapped Bobby. That he'd be better off in state custody."

"Zinkavich believe that shit?"

"I told him I knew your dealer. I could set it up so he could bust you for possession right in the courtroom, real dramatic like."

"How the hell could you manage that?" But even as the words came out, he knew. "Thigpen didn't break into my house to steal anything, did he? He was planting something."

"Crystal meth in the lining of your briefcase. But you came home too early. You fucked it all up."

"Jesus, Janice. This is low. Even for you."

"Which is why I want to make amends now."

The siren grew louder.

"Make 'em quick," Steve said.

She seemed to be trying to form her thoughts. Twenty years of assorted powders, pills, and weeds can play havoc with the brain cells. "I got a deal for you, Stevie. How much is my little Bobby worth to you?"

"Everything I've got plus everything I can beg, borrow, and steal."

"About what I had in mind," Janice Solomon said.

SOLOMON'S LAWS

9. I will never break the law, breach legal
   ethics, or risk jail time . . . *unless it's for
   someone I love.*

Thirty-six

THE MEASURE OF A MAN

A cold wind whistled through the avocado trees, chilling Victoria. She was shivering, even though she wore an ankle-length black leather swing coat over a cashmere sweater and jeans. She hoped Bruce wouldn't say anything about the leather. He should just be happy she hadn't pulled out one of her mother's fox boas or mink hats.

Now, where was he?

She was standing in the farm's staging area, a cleared five-acre parcel between two avocado groves. Tractors growled by, kicking up dust. Trucks filled with straw churned between rows of trees, workers with shovels and pitchforks following, chattering in Spanish. Generators roared as men set up portable lights and heaters. In the adjacent grove, sprinklers with rotating arms fifty feet long turned endless circles. Black smoke from the smudge pots curled into the air, and the whir of giant fans blew hot air into the groves. The sun had set an hour earlier, and the low, scudding clouds were lit a surreal orange from the fires in the smudge pots.

Where are they?

Bruce would be busy all night, and she was looking forward to spending time with the Solomon Boys. Maybe Bobby could work with them on the source gram: "The woman is perfected."

What did Charles Barksdale mean?

Was there something he was saying about Katrina they could pick up?

Over speakers mounted on poles, a song played, something with an upbeat Afro-Cuban beat. It took her a second to remember the name: "Maracaibo Oriental." She was swaying to the music, mostly to keep warm, when she saw Steve and Bobby walking toward her, emerging from the black haze.

"Omigod, Steve, what happened?"

He tried to smile through a swollen lip. Bloody scrapes tracked down his face as if an angry lover had dragged her fingernails from forehead to mouth. Victoria looked at Bobby, saw the welt—the hue of a ripe plum—under his right eye, and abandoned Steve.

"Bobby!"

"We kicked some major ass," the boy said.

Victoria gently cradled his chin, examining the shiner. "Does it hurt?"

"A little." He added hastily: "Nothing I can't handle."

She kissed a fingertip and gently ran it under Bobby's eye. "Better?"

"What about me?" Steve asked. "I've got teeth marks on my butt."

"And not for the first time, I bet." She brushed Bobby's hair out of his eyes. "Now, what major ass did you kick?"

With each one interrupting the other, uncle and

nephew gave her the short version of the snatch, the chase, the wreck, and the combat.

"Nobody ever ran as fast as Uncle Steve," the boy said. "Like a world record."

"Bobby was very brave," Steve said. "If he hadn't tackled Thigpen—"

"I smashed him. Then, *ka-pow!* Uncle Steve kicked him in the nuts."

"Wow," Victoria said.

"When I grow up, I'm gonna be just like Uncle Steve."

With the story winding down, Victoria said: "So it was Thigpen who broke into your house. It had nothing to do with the Barksdale murder or the security video."

"Correct," Steve said.

"Meaning you might have been right all along about Katrina being innocent. Manko, too."

"Don't sound so surprised."

"But we still don't have the proof."

"Last time I checked, the burden of proof was on the prosecution."

She laughed. "When did you start believing the letter of the law? An adulterous wife is in the room when her rich old hubby strangles to death. That pretty much shifts the burden."

" 'The woman is perfected,' " Steve said. "The answer's gotta be there."

"Maybe." Her mind drifted back to Steve's account of chasing down Janice and Thigpen. "So that's all your sister wanted, to see Bobby for a few hours?"

"And to tell me she's Zinkavich's rebuttal witness."

"Did you ask what she's going to say?"

"She's going to bad-mouth me. What more do we need to know?"

Odd that he brushed it off that way, she thought. Something wasn't ringing true. She glanced at Bobby, who turned away. What was going on? What wasn't Steve telling her?

Steve wanted to tell her the truth.

But could she handle the truth?

If he told Victoria about Janice's illegal proposal and his equally illegal response, she'd quit Bobby's case. Probably even report him to the Florida Bar. Was that a look of suspicion a moment ago? Or just his guilty conscience playing tricks?

What he planned to do could cost him his license, if it didn't land him in prison. Not the kind of risk he'd take for just anyone.

Still, this went far beyond trampling legal niceties. He'd never bribed a witness before. But then, he'd never been this desperate. Winning custody of Bobby wasn't a legal skirmish; it was his life.

"So tell me what you want," he had said to his sister as they stood by the smashed truck.

"I hate helping that fuck Zinkavich," she said. "He treats me like I'm some low-life criminal."

"Imagine that."

"So I figured I could screw him over instead of you."

"I'm listening."

"He got me and Rufe out of prison, but we're on parole, so he still could violate us and send us back."

"Not unless you do something stupid."

"They find one joint in our truck, we're back in

the can. Hang out with known felons, same thing. Parole's a bitch. That's why we gotta get away, Rufe and me."

"What's that got to do with me?"

"You gotta give us a hundred thousand dollars."

"I don't have that kind of money. In fact, I don't have any kind."

"What about your big murder trial?"

"My client's money is tied up. I don't get a dime unless we win."

That was the truth. Katrina had agreed to pay them two hundred fifty thousand dollars, but it would be collectible only if she was acquitted. An unfortunate technicality in the law doesn't let homicidal wives inherit their husbands' estates.

"You could hit up Dad."

"Mom's medical bills drained him. He's tapped out, living on his pension."

"There's got to be someone else. Someone who'll lend you the bread."

Who would he ask? He didn't have a clue. "What do I get for my money?"

"Me and Rufe disappear and never testify."

It won't work, Steve thought. Kranchick's testimony would still bury him. "Your leaving town's not good enough. If I pay you, you've got to stay and testify."

"How's that gonna help you?"

"When Zinkavich puts you on the stand, you won't give his answers. You'll give mine."

Victoria was watching Steve, kneeling in the dirt, tying Bobby's shoestrings. There's something he's not telling me, she thought.

His sister is going to sandbag him, and he doesn't seem concerned. Zinkavich already has Kranchick and Thigpen, and now this. Steve should be ranting, cursing, pawing the ground, plotting a counterattack. But he seems nonchalant about the whole thing.

What's he hiding?

As she worked on that dilemma, an open Jeep Wrangler skidded to a stop in front of them. The driver wore a Bigby Farms jacket with the avocado logo. The passenger was his boss, Bruce Bigby, standing tall, holding the roll bar for support, blond hair windblown. Wearing an off-white skier's jumpsuit, he had a bullhorn in one hand, a walkie-talkie clipped to his belt, a digital thermometer zippered on his sleeve, and a revolver holstered on his hip. In that getup, Bruce looked part astronaut, part general, and—she hated to think it—a total dweeb.

"Get those heaters into the hollow!" Bigby yelled into the bullhorn. "Gosh darn it, I told you, the trees in the low areas freeze first!"

"Hi, hon," Victoria said.

"Sweetie." He gave her a brisk salute, then hopped out of the Jeep. The legs of his jumpsuit were bloused over the tops of combat boots. On the speakers, Celia Cruz was singing "Corazon Rebelde," ode to a rebellious heart.

"Hey, Bruce," Steve said.

Bigby's eyes went wide. "Jeez, Steve. Another shaving accident?"

"Family reunion."

"Those are open cuts. Have you taken antibiotics?"

"Does Jack Daniel's count?"

Bigby's walkie-talkie crackled with static. *"Señor Bigby, thirty-three degrees in the north quadrant."*

Bigby hit a button. "Get some heaters over there, Foyo."

"Sí, jefe."

"Nobody sleeps. Hot coffee all night. Rum and Coke at dawn."

"Sí, jefe."

"And that music. Does it have to be that Cuban crapola?"

"Is what the men like."

"Whatever." Bigby clicked off the walkie-talkie. "Bobby, care to ride with me?"

Bobby gripped Steve's hand and shook his head.

"He's a little shaken," Steve said. "We'll catch up with you later."

"You got it."

"What can I do to help?" Steve asked.

"Gonna be a long night," Bigby said. "Will you look after my sweetie for me?"

"To the best of my limited abilities."

"What's with the gun, hon?" Victoria asked.

Bigby lowered his voice to a whisper. "The men expect it. *El jefe* always carries a side arm. It's a Caribbean thing."

"And what does *el jefe* shoot?" she persisted.

"Varmints, trespassers . . ."

Guys sniffing after *jefe's* fiancée? she wondered.

The violent bleat of a siren interrupted them. Startled, Bobby stumbled into Steve's chest, his glasses falling to the ground. "No noise. No noise. No noise."

Steve wrapped his arms around the boy. "It's okay, kiddo. It's okay."

"Not really," Bigby said, grimly. "It means the temperature's just hit thirty-two. If it goes to twenty-nine and stays there, I'm in deep doo-doo, if you'll pardon my French."

Did he really say "deep doo-doo"? Victoria wondered.

"I'm taking Bobby inside for a while," Steve said, picking up the boy's glasses.

"There's hot chocolate in the kitchen," Bigby said, "and a spare bedroom next to the den. Make yourself at home."

Steve and Bobby walked toward the house, the boy ferociously gripping his uncle's arm. When they were out of earshot, Bigby said: "With the grace of God, we'll never have to face that."

"Face what?"

"You know . . . that."

She was startled. "If you mean Bobby, he's a wonderful child."

"I know, sweetie. I know. You're a sucker for the bird with the broken wing."

"It's more than that. I really love the boy."

"Sure you do. But would you rather our son be the captain of the football team at Dartmouth or some oddball who scrambles words in his head?"

"Depends who has the bigger heart."

"Whatever." He peeled the thermometer off his sleeve, checked the readout, and frowned. "Keep the kid out of trouble for me, sweetie. He falls down a well, Solomon will sue me quicker than he can say 'shalom.' "

"Don't think I've ever heard him use the word."

"Figure of speech."

"I know, Bruce. Just one I never expected to hear from you."

"Hey, you know me. Not a prejudiced bone in my body. All my doctors and lawyers are Jews. Heck, I wanted you to work with Solomon for a while, remember? Pick up some of his tricks. They're sharper than we are that way."

"Are they?"

"Oh, come on, don't be so sensitive."

She blinked involuntarily, as if she'd been slapped. *Don't be so sensitive?*

"That's very controlling," she said.

"What? How?"

"C'mon, Bruce. You're not that clueless. You can't tell another person how to feel."

Bigby's walkie-talkie squawked again. "Jefe, veintiocho grados *in the hollow.*"

"Darn! Those lights strung yet?"

"*Almost.* Ya casi termino, jefe."

"Gotta go, sweetie." Bigby straightened the holster on his hip and hopped into the Jeep. John Wayne amid the avocados.

"I could come along," she said.

"Sends the wrong message to the men. Wouldn't want them to think their *jefe*'s pussy-whipped."

"Of course not."

She studied him, smoke swirling around his head, diesel fumes in the air.

"What?" Bruce asked.

"I've never seen you like this."

"In a time of crisis," Bigby intoned, "that's when you can take the full measure of a man."

"So true."

He motioned for the driver to pull away. Still

standing, gripping the roll bar with one hand, he waved to Victoria with the other. "Later, sweetie."

"Later, *jefe*," Victoria said, as the Jeep bumped along the path and disappeared into the black haze of the grove.

Thirty-seven

THE WHISPERING
OF PALM TREES

Steve's butt was sore, and his torn lip flared with pain. Bobby was starting to calm down, asking if he could have marshmallows in his hot chocolate. They were walking on a flagstone path between two rows of cypress trees. Bigby's farmhouse sat on a rise ahead of them.

"Big house for one person," Bobby said.

"Two people," Steve corrected.

The house was a solid three stories of Dade County pine with a wraparound porch and a tin roof. It had been built by Bigby's great-grandfather, who'd also had the good sense to buy two thousand acres of surrounding land nobody wanted at the time. The exterior grounds had been preserved much as they must have been in the reign of Bigby the First, Steve figured. A sugarcane grinder sat under a lean-to; a dinner bell topped a ten-foot-high pole; and firewood was stacked next to a smokehouse, where in earlier days hogs were turned into hams.

Steve spotted some modern additions. A red clay tennis court ringed by coconut palms. A lagoon surrounded by a man-made beach, and a chickee hut with bamboo walls and a roof of dried palm fronds. He visualized Victoria as Lady of Bigby Manor, didn't like the picture, chased it away.

He and Bobby walked inside, where a uniformed housekeeper seemed to be expecting them. Bigby must have called ahead on his cell phone or walkie-talkie, Steve figured, or maybe he sent smoke signals. The maid held a cup of steaming coffee for Steve and a cup of hot chocolate for Bobby. With marshmallows.

The coffee stung Steve's lip. The hot chocolate sent Bobby off on a riff about cocoa beans. He'd read somewhere about the health benefits of flavonoids, and he was repeating the chemical composition to Steve, who wasn't listening. Instead, he was thinking about Bruce Bigby. The man with everything. Including Victoria.

So why don't I hate him?

Maybe because Bigby seemed decent enough. Sure, the guy was irritatingly upbeat and so forthright that irony sailed right by him. Then there was that streak of boosterism, hawking his time-shares like some kind of subtropical Babbitt. But so what? Compared to most people Steve encountered each day—violent criminals, incompetent judges, perjurious witnesses— Bigby was a Boy Scout with shiny merit badges. Besides, it didn't matter what he thought. Victoria loved the guy.

So get over it, chump. She's his.

The interior of the house had been updated recently, Steve thought, as he walked Bobby to a guest bedroom. The walls were sleek mahogany, the floors Italian tile. The artwork—mostly South American and Native American—was expensive, eclectic, and tasteful, if you overlooked the six-foot oil painting of two ripe avocados dangling on a branch like pendulous breasts.

The guest bedroom was a cozy place with Native American baskets, wall hangings, and pottery. Steve tucked Bobby into bed, pulling a comforter up to his chin.

"Don't go till I fall asleep, Uncle Steve."

Steve sat on the edge of the bed. "Not going anywhere, kiddo."

"That was raging today, huh?"

"Raging?"

"When you waxed Mom's friend, you were totally tight."

"Totally," Steve agreed. There was something buzzing around in Bobby's head, Steve knew, but it was having a hard time coming out. "You want to talk about what happened, kiddo?"

Under the comforter, Bobby's thin shoulders shrugged.

"You know the rules. Anything you ask, I answer."

"My mom," Bobby said. "Is she a bad person or is she, like, totally whacked?"

He'd never lied to the boy. He couldn't start now. "A little of both. Maybe a lot of both."

"How come she's bad and you're good?"

"She's not all bad and I'm not all good."

And that was the truth, he thought. Only hours earlier, he'd agreed to pay Janice a bribe. One hundred thousand dollars for her favorable testimony. His only defense was that he didn't have the money to carry out the crime. He would work on that tomorrow. He would try *not* to consider the ethical and moral ramifications of what he had agreed to do. That, he knew, would come another day, and with it, a pain worse than his current headache.

The boy's eyelids were fluttering. "If Mrs. Barksdale murdered her husband, wouldn't she be way bad?"

"Way bad," Steve agreed.

"Not the bad that's good. The bad that's bad."

"Yep."

"The woman is perfected," the boy whispered. "We'll figure it out." A second later, he was asleep.

"You're a wonderful father," a soft voice said.

Steve turned. Victoria stood just inside the bedroom door.

"Thanks. But sometimes I think I get more from him than he does from me."

Victoria walked to the bed, reached down, and stroked Bobby's cheek. He was breathing so heavily he seemed to be purring. "He idolizes you. You should be very proud."

But just now, he wasn't feeling proud at all. Not as a would-be father. Not as a lawyer. Not as a man. He felt more like a felon on the verge of being caught. Hoping to change the subject, he gestured toward a darkened window. "How's it going out there?"

"Temperature's dropping. Bruce is freaking."

"Sorry I'm not more help."

"That's okay. I just thought it would be nice to have you around." She was silent a moment. Then she said: "Do you want to take a walk?"

A three-quarter moon peeked through the orange-tinted clouds, and black smoke curled above the trees. Cuban love songs played on the speakers as Victoria led Steve along a path of coral rocks on a ridge above the grove. Suddenly, thousands of brightly colored lights blinked on, turning the avocado grove into a stand of Christmas trees.

"Wow. Look at that."

"Bruce's idea to heat the trees," Victoria said. "He cleaned out every Wal-Mart of Christmas lights from Orlando to Key West."

"Smart guy, your Bigby."

"He's got nothing on you."

"Just a few million bucks. And you."

"Which do you suppose is more important to Bruce?" she asked.

The question surprised Steve. Discussing her relationship with Bigby had been off-limits. "Can't answer for him. Only for me."

His words hung in the air, trapped like the smoke from the smudge pots. After a moment, she said: "Keep going, Solomon."

"I'm cold. Let's go back."

"This way." She took him by the hand.

"Where?"

She didn't answer, just led him down the path toward the lagoon.

"If you're thinking about skinny-dipping, forget it," he said.

Two flaming torches were stuck in the ground at the entrance to the chickee hut at the water's edge. "Come on in," she said. "It's a good windbreak."

"Yeah, for a Miccosukee hunting party."

He lingered at the entrance, and she ducked inside.

He wondered: Just what the hell's going on? The walk. The hut. Was she coming on to him? Or could he be misreading the signals? No doubt his brain was addled by his dinner of Jack Daniel's, Tylenol with codeine, and peanut butter cups.

"What are you afraid of?" Her voice came from the shadows inside the hut.

"You."

"What do you think's going to happen in here?"

"If we were fifteen, we'd make out. But we're not, so I figure you've got pre-wedding jitters, and because I'm your pal, you want to talk. 'I love this about Bruce,' and 'I don't like this about Bruce.' Frankly, Victoria, I can do without it."

"What if I just wanted to make out?"

"What about *el jefe*? He's packing heat."

"I know you, Solomon. You're not afraid of him. All your fears are self-directed."

Steve was aware of something cold and wet striking his forehead. *What the hell?* He turned back toward the grove. The orange-lit sky was flecked with white. "It's snowing!"

"Impossible."

She hurried out of the hut. Then, to his astonishment, she spun a pirouette and yelped with joy, sticking out her tongue to catch the flakes swirling toward her. "It's fabulous!" Over the speakers, Benny Moré was singing something with a bolero beat. "Magical . . ."

"Temporary," he said, watching the snow melt as it hit the ground.

Benny Moré sang: "*Eres tú flor carnal de mi jardin ideal.*"

"So beautiful." She moved to the music, her long leather coat swinging open, the snow whipping in the wind. "I wish I knew the words."

"You're the sexual flower of my perfect garden," Steve said.

"You talking to me, big boy?"

"The lyric. More or less."

They listened. *"Eres tú la mujer que reina en mi corazón."*

"And you reign in my heart," Steve said.

"The song again?"

"Of course."

"You ever talk that way to a woman?"

"Nah." What could he say to her? That she was beautiful and smart? That he respected her values, her integrity, even her damned rectitude, which he had ridiculed but which deep down, he admired and envied? That he was drawn to her for all the mysterious reasons that drive men mad? "I don't talk like that."

"But you've felt that way?"

"What are we playing here, Vic? Let's watch Steve plunge a knife into his own chest?"

"C'mon. Was there a woman who reigned in your heart? Is there now?"

"Why should I tell you? So we can kiss? And then you can run away again?"

"Who said anything about running?"

"Don't do this." He was a trespasser. On another man's property. With another man's woman.

She spoke softly: "The night we kissed, weren't you the one who said, 'Go with the flow, see where it takes us'?"

"The flow takes us nowhere. You've got other plans."

"You're such a fool, Steve Solomon." She put a

hand behind his neck, pulled him to her, kissed his bruised lower lip.

"Ouch."

"Hurt?"

"More than you know."

"Be brave."

Her kiss was feathery as snowflakes. He did not kiss her back. No way he'd blunder down that path: hope, rejection, pain. She'd gut him as a hunter guts a deer.

Her lips moved, soft as rose petals, across his cheek. He felt her warm breath against his ear, along his neck. She kissed him again, then traced a fingertip across his forehead, around one eye, along the length of his nose. As if she wanted to later draw his likeness.

He felt light-headed, floating in the cold breeze with the snowflakes, his world spinning off its axis. Then, without meaning to, he kissed her back. A soft and longing kiss. If his head throbbed, if his lip stung, he no longer felt the pain.

The flames from the torches warmed them, tossed their shadows against the exterior of the hut. From below, Steve heard Benny Moré singing to them.

"Mi pasión es rumor de un palmar."

As Victoria led him into the hut, Steve murmured: "My passion is the whispering of palm trees."

"The song?"

"Me," he said.

The hut was filled with bales of straw, some of which had spilled across the floor. She had not planned this, Victoria thought, slipping out of the long coat and laying it across the straw. She was, for once, riding with the moment, letting her emotions carry her along. She was drawn to Steve and had stopped questioning why. But look at him, so afraid and confused. She unzipped his parka, knowing she would have to take the lead. She pulled the jacket off him, unbuttoned his shirt, ran her hands up his chest.

"I want you," she breathed, kissing him again.

He whispered something, but his face was alongside her neck, and she couldn't hear. One of his hands was working its way under her sweater, and she felt her bra unsnap, and then his hands were on her breasts. Moments later, her sweater and jeans were tangled somewhere in the straw with his clothes, and she peeled off her low-rise panties, because she couldn't wait for him to do it.

Her breaths came deep and fast as his mouth tracked a path down her neck, circled both breasts, settled on one. She felt him pressed against her, hard and erect, and she stroked him, making him gasp. He touched her gently, insistent, probing. She kissed him again, a feverish, deep, urgent kiss.

"I want you inside me," she breathed into his ear. "Now!"

"Already?"

"We've had weeks of foreplay. Now!"

He entered her, and she wrapped her legs around him. Then she arched back, limber as a cat, her body rising to meet his.

Steve could hear his own heart hammering away, thought he could hear hers. He drank her in with all his senses. The curve of her neck, the path of her spine, the smooth silk of the cul-de-sac below her navel. He kissed her, caressed her, tasted her.

For these moments at least, he was free of the consequences, lost in the eternal ritual. He had always thought that every new encounter echoed with memories of earlier ones. But this one did not. This one was new; this one was different from all the rest.

She came with an explosive force, digging her hands into his scalp, pulling his hair, holding on as if she would fall off the edge of the world. A second later, he exploded, too, just as she felt the aftershocks rock her, mini tremors flowing in hot waves.

And then, still inside her, rocking slowly, sucking each morsel of pleasure for as long as it would last, he said it at long last. "I love you, Victoria. I really, really love you."

Thirty-eight

THE MORNING-AFTER BLUES

"Where are the bagels?" Marvin the Maven asked.

"Don't have any." Steve opened a paper bag and pulled out four crusty Italian rolls. "I bought michettes."

"What *mishegoss* is that?"

"We're talking smoked salmon and *caprino panini*."

"*Feh!* They charge another five bucks, give the lox a fancy name."

On this chilly morning, Marvin wore a herringbone sport coat over a black turtleneck. A stocking cap, looking a bit like a yarmulke, covered his bald head.

They were standing in Steve's kitchen, roughly twelve hours after his altered-state experience in the chickee hut. At least his body was here. In his foggy brain, snow swirled, and he was still curled up with Victoria on the straw. Which is just where he'd been when a voice on the speaker asked Señorita Lord to come to the staging area.

Bigby was looking for her. She dressed quickly, kissed Steve, and ducked out of the hut, glancing back, giving him a look he couldn't decipher. Melancholy? Longing? Regret?

He went back to the farmhouse, gathered Bobby from the bed, and carried him to the car. Home, Steve tucked Bobby in, then stretched out on his sofa with a bottle of Chinaco Blanco tequila and tried to make sense of the night. By dawn, his lips felt numb and there was a ringing in his ears.

When Marvin stopped by—a Sunday morning breakfast ritual—he asked about the scrapes and bruises. Steve said he had tripped while jogging. The Maven seemed to buy it. Now he was whining about the menu change. "Where's the cream cheese?"

"I'm using *caprino*. Goat cheese."

"Fancy-schmancy."

Steve spread the goat cheese on a roll, sprinkled it with capers and chives, then placed sun-dried tomatoes on top.

"What's with the tomatoes, boychik?" Marvin asked. "They're all shriveled up, like my *schmeckel*."

"They're sun-dried."

"Not that anyone's complaining. My *schmeckel*, I mean, not your tomatoes."

Steve stirred lemon juice with olive oil and drizzled the mixture over the *panino*. "Marvin, I need a favor."

"Don't worry. I'm gonna help you pick a jury."

Marvin picked up the *panino,* studied it suspiciously, took a bite. "Hey, not bad. Ain't a bagel and lox, but not bad."

"I'm not talking about jury selection, Marvin. I need a hundred thousand dollars."

Marvin whistled. "That's some serious shekels, boychik."

"A loan, not a gift. If we win Barksdale, I'll pay it back quick. If we lose, I'll pay it back slow."

"I'd like to help, but I don't have that kind of cash."

"I figured, but I thought you might have some ideas."

"What about your father?"

Steve shook his head. "Even if he had it, I couldn't ask."

"You mean you *wouldn't* ask. Isn't it time to forgive and forget?"

"Not now, Marvin. I can't ask him, not on this."

Marvin tugged at a fold of skin on his neck. Marvin the Thinker. "What's the money for, if you don't mind my asking?"

Steve shot a look toward the corridor to his nephew's bedroom. All quiet. The boy either was still asleep or he was beating the computer at chess. "It's for Bobby. That's all I can say."

The old man's eyes lit up. "That's different. For Bobby, anything." He demolished the sandwich in three bites. "Not that I know where I'm gonna get the money, but I got some friends."

"Thanks, Marvin."

"You sleep in a stable last night?"

"Why?"

"You got straw in your hair."

Steve ran a hand over his head, plucked a strand from behind his ear. "Bigby's farm," he said, and left it at that.

"What were you doing there, besides lusting after his fiancée?"

"That about sums it up."

Steve had succeeded in not thinking about Victoria

for the last few minutes, but there it was again. Just before Marvin arrived, Steve had called her cell phone, but there'd been no answer. Where was she this morning? With Bigby? Or taking a long walk through the trees, thinking of Steve?

"I don't know how I'm going to try Barksdale with her," he said. "Or Bobby's case, either."

"Why not? I thought the two of you were getting along these days."

"I'll be sitting close enough to smell her shampoo. Every time she'd give me a document, our hands would touch, and . . ." Steve stopped. He hadn't intended to open up.

Marvin was staring at him. "*Ay, gevalt.* You're in love!"

Now Steve wanted to talk. If he had a closer relationship with his father, this would be the time— "*Hey, Dad, what should I do?*"—but with Herbert, he wouldn't get advice, he'd get criticism. "I need some advice, Marvin."

"Got one word for you. 'Viagra.' "

"Don't need it."

"Neither do I, but in case you're nervous when you and that shiksa goddess do it the first time, it can help."

Steve was silent.

"Ah! You already *shtupped* her?"

This wasn't going to be easy, Steve knew, but he needed to talk. "Marvin, can you be discreet?"

The old man shrugged. "Was Jesus a nice Jewish boy?"

———

Five minutes later, the front door opened and another Sunday morning regular walked in.

"Where are the bagels?" Cadillac said, entering the kitchen.

"Don't got any," Marvin said. "Mr. Fancy Pants bought machetes instead."

"Michettes," Steve said.

"Just as well," Cadillac said. "Poppy seeds stick in my dentures." He looked at Steve. "What happened to your face?"

"I fell jogging."

"I got marked up like that once," Cadillac said. "Tripped over a windowsill."

"How's that possible?" Steve said.

Cadillac sat down at the kitchen table, sighed, propped his feet on a chair. "A jealous husband was coming in the bedroom door with a shotgun, I was going out the window without my pants. Kansas City. Or maybe St. Louis."

"What's with the duds?" Marvin asked. Cadillac was wearing dark blue coveralls with a patch on the chest that read: "Rockland State Hospital."

"Doing a favor for Steve," Cadillac said.

"Everybody he's asking favors these days."

"Cadillac's a helluva PI," Steve said.

"Janitor's more like it," Cadillac said. "Your doc was there last night, by the way."

"So you couldn't snoop?"

"Sure I could. Gimme a sandwich and lemme tell it my way."

Steve put the finishing touches on a *panino* he'd been working on.

"Last couple nights, I been going through her

desk," Cadillac said. "In-box, out-box. Patient records. Test charts. Lot of mumbo-jumbo. Last night, I come into her office around eleven o'clock, pushing my broom, rolling my cart. Only this time she's still there. Big woman with a sour face."

"She say anything to you?"

"Not to me. She was on the phone."

Steve handed Cadillac the *panino*. "So you left?"

"Hell, no." Cadillac took a bite, nodded his approval. "I emptied her wastebasket, dusted the counters, puttered around. She just kept on talking. Old black man pushing a broom. You don't get more invisible than that."

"Who was she talking to?"

"All I know, his name was Carlos, and he was in Mexico."

Steve's look must have asked a question because Cadillac said: " 'What time is it in Guadalajara, Carlos?' That's what she was saying when I walked in. Then she says she wants a thousand units of replen-something."

Steve grabbed a pen and a pad. "Replen . . . ?"

"One of those drug names they make up that don't mean nothing. Like Viagra."

"I don't need it," Marvin said for the second time that morning.

"So that's it?" Steve said.

"Settle down, boy," Cadillac said. "When you write a song, you don't give away the story in the first verse."

"Okay, okay."

"Like all those songs Gordon Jenkins wrote for Sinatra." He started singing softly:

*"Opposites attract, the wise men claim,
Still I wish that we had been a little more the
same,
It might have been a shorter war."*

"Sounds like Steverino and his lady partner," Marvin said.

"Can we get back to Kranchick for a second?" Steve pleaded.

"Then the song throws you a curve." Cadillac resumed singing:

*"She knew much more than I did,
But there was one thing she didn't know,
That I loved her, 'cause I never told her so."*

Cadillac smiled. "There's the surprise. He never had the guts to tell the lady he loved her."

"Just like our friend." Marvin turned to Steve. "Unless you told her last night."

"What happened last night?" Cadillac asked.

"What happened in the *hospital* last night?" Steve countered.

"Steverino *shtupped* his law partner," Marvin said.

"No," Cadillac said.

"The *emmis*. Right under the nose of her fiancé."

"Attaboy," Cadillac said. "Reminds me of the time I was seeing this dancer who was married to a comic. Every night, when he went on the stage—"

"Cadillac! What the hell happened in the damn hospital?"

"All right. Keep your britches on. The doc must not have liked the price. 'Cause she says, 'Forget it, Carlos. You're not gonna fuck me up the ass.' "

"She said that?" Marvin made a *tsk-tsk* sound.

"Reminded me of a foulmouthed little mama I knew in Memphis," Cadillac said.

"Then what?" Steve demanded. "After she argued with Carlos about price?"

"She said something about calling this supplier in Argentina. But Carlos must have lowered the price because she calmed right down and said, fine, she'd wire the money first thing in the morning, and no, she didn't want a receipt. No paper trail. She hangs up and I go out and work the rest of the floor."

"Replen-something," Steve said, mostly to himself. "Replen what?"

"Replengren," Cadillac said.

"How do you know?"

"Because after she left, I came back and emptied her wastebasket a second time. It's my damn job, right?" He reached into his pocket and handed Steve a slip of paper. A crumpled sheet from a notepad with the Rockland State Hospital logo on top, Kranchick's name on the bottom, and what had to be her hand-writing in between.

80 mg Replengren X 1000
San Blas Medico

"So what is it?" Marvin asked.

Steve wrote "Replengren" on his pad followed by three question marks. "Something Kranchick doesn't want anybody to know about, and that's gotta be good. You're beautiful, Cadillac. I love you. You, too, Marvin."

"Forget us," Cadillac said. "Did you tell the lady that you love her?"

"He told her," Marvin said. "She didn't say nothing back, and now the schlemiel wants some advice from the Maven."

"Thanks for being so discreet," Steve said, rubbing both temples. A headache was brewing.

"So what did you tell him?" Cadillac asked Marvin.

"I told him to get off his *tuches*. Love don't come along every day, and if you let her get away, you'll always regret it."

Thirty-nine

SIX-LOVE

The woman is perfected, Victoria brooded.

Which meant what? Made perfect from something less so?

She herself was neither perfect nor perfected. She was, on this Sunday morning, a miserable, lying, self-loathing slut.

She lay in bed trying sort out her feelings. Bruce's bed. With Bruce snoring contentedly beside her.

The avocado crop was saved and Bruce, drained from the night's excitement and a pitcher of rum-and-Coke at dawn, had tumbled face-first into bed, still wearing his jumpsuit and combat boots. The holster and pistol, thankfully, were draped over the railing of a treadmill in the corner of the bedroom.

She woke up angry. At herself.

What have I done?

She had violated her most cherished principles. Honesty, loyalty, fidelity. But why? Did she love Steve Solomon? No, that would be preposterous.

Half the time I can't even stand him.

No way did their relationship fit her well-conceived definition of love. No way was it a rational, synergistic coupling of two people with mutual interests and similar values. This coupling was animalistic, like Judge Gridley's beagles in the barn.

It was irrational. Illogical. Insane.

So why did she do something so hurtful and self-destructive? Bruce deserved better. And Solomon? The poor guy had resisted. For a moment, she wondered if she was guilty of date rape, at least in some philosophical way.

When she left Steve in the chickee hut, she'd felt a mixture of guilt and apprehension. She feared Bruce would see it on her face. But he'd been oblivious, rambling on about the low clouds holding in the heat and the snow being a blessing in disguise. Then he grinned and said: "A blessing in the skies." Okay, so he was a little impaired in the humor department. Could she spend an eternity with a man who couldn't make her laugh?

She slipped out of bed, dressed quietly, and left.

The morning was clear and chilly, the sun still low in the east, as she aimed the Taurus north. She would call Jackie on the cell, roust her from bed. But before she could dial the number, her cell phone rang, and she checked the readout. Solomon. What was there to say? She let it ring.

Traffic was light on South Dixie, and when she reached LeJeune Road in the Gables, she hung a right, even though that wasn't the way to Grove Isle. Why had she turned there? Did the car have a mind of its own? Then a left on Kumquat. She slowed as she approached the bungalow with the Brazilian pepper tree and Spanish dagger shrub.

What am I doing? What stable, mature decision is this?

Running from your fiancé's house to your lover's.
Is that what Solomon is? My lover?

She had never liked the word. It always sounded sleazy.

She stopped the car across the street from Solomon's house. His old Cadillac was parked out front, top up. Another car, too. A Lincoln with a personalized plate: MAVEN-1. Then she remembered: Marvin was a Sunday morning regular for breakfast. As she sat there, a second car pulled up, an old Chevrolet sedan. She watched as Cadillac Johnson got out. He was wearing blue coveralls instead of his usual dashiki.

She thought about walking in, calling out: *"What's cooking?"*

But it would be awkward. She mustn't talk to Solomon until she decided just what the hell she was going to do with her life. And where he fit in. Which he didn't.

She put the car in gear and drove away.

Jackie hit a lazy lob that lacked height, distance, and desire. Victoria, who had been camped at the net, took two steps backward, aimed her left hand skyward as if pointing at a shooting star, then brought the racquet forward in a vicious overhead smash. The ball rocketed toward Jackie, who hopped sideways and yelped as she took a stinging hit on her calf.

"Ow! Jeez."

"Sorry." Victoria walked back to the baseline. They were on a green clay court at Grove Isle. Just on the other side of the windscreened fence, boats were tied up at the dock and the bay rippled with white-caps. "That's six-love. One more set. Your serve."

"Forget it." Jackie was rubbing her calf. "It says 'Wilson' on my leg. What are you mad at me about?"

"Nothing." It wasn't something you just blurted out: *"By the way, Jackie, I never told you before, but I'm really a lascivious slut."*

"So what's going on? You've been taking out your frustrations on that fuzzy ball since we started playing." She walked to the sideline table, grabbed a fleece pullover, and slipped into it.

Victoria joined her, opened a thermos of coffee, poured for both of them. "I'm just a little tense, that's all."

"Pre-wedding jitters."

"That's exactly what Solomon said."

"When's he going to call me, anyway?"

"He's kind of unpredictable, so I wouldn't be sitting by the phone."

"If I didn't know better, I'd think you were seeing that Bad Boy on the side."

Victoria was silent.

"Usually, this is where you say, *'Jac-kie,'* the way Sister Agnes did when I wore stretch pants in seventh grade."

Victoria sipped her coffee.

Jackie studied her. "Fu-ck me! You and the Bad Boy?"

Victoria remained silent.

"C'mon, Vic. What's the use of getting boned if you can't tell your best bud?"

"Last night—" Victoria began, with some trepidation.

"I knew it! I knew the day you met him."

"How? I despised Solomon."

"Exactly. He got you so worked up, I knew something was going to happen." Jackie lowered her voice to a conspiratorial whisper. "How was it?"

"You mean physically?"

"What other way is there?"

"*Jac-kie.*"

"C'mon, tell me, Vic. Did you pop more than once? Did he? Tell me, and I'll tell you about this Honduran coffee baron who can lick his own eyebrows."

Victoria had vowed not to go into detail. She wouldn't describe how Steve pressed all the right buttons, including the button that mattered.

"I'll bet it was great," Jackie said, pumping her.

I won't get down and dirty.

"Was it great?" Jackie said.

I'll keep the discussion on a high plane.

"Between Bruce and Steve, who's the better clit tickler? C'mon, I need play-by-play."

"It was un-fucking-believable," Victoria said, surprising herself with her language. "I was on fire. Burning with fever."

Jackie made a show of fanning herself with an open hand. "Oh, my God."

"When he was inside me, it was like he was touching me everywhere. Like an electrical current. And so intense. One volt more, I swear, I would have passed out."

Jackie made a grunting sound that was close to being obscene.

Victoria lowered her voice. "With my eyes closed, I actually saw sparks."

"No."

"Like a meteor shower."

"I think I'm getting wet."

Victoria took another sip of coffee. "Now I need to figure out why I did it."

"What's to figure? You were horny. Solomon's hot. You got laid."

"It's more complicated than that!"

"Then figure it out the next time he boinks you."

"What next time?"

"C'mon, you gonna give up the greatest sex of your life?"

Victoria felt lost. She yearned for advice, but her best friend was off in sexual fantasyland.

"I'm going home and checking the batteries in Mr. Happy," Jackie said.

Maybe she should call The Queen for advice, Victoria thought. Catch up with her in Switzerland or Rome, or wherever. The Queen had more experience with men. On second thought, Victoria knew exactly what her mother would say. *"I've been unhappy rich and unhappy poor,"* The Queen would say. *"Unhappy rich is better."*

"Maybe I'm afraid of happiness. Maybe I'm trying to sabotage my relationship with Bruce."

"What's the problem? Marry Bruce. Boff Solomon on the side."

"I can't do that!"

"Then do what you lawyers do. Grab a yellow pad. Write down the pluses and minuses of each guy." Jackie handed her a flyer for the Grove Isle Christmas party, turning it over to the blank side. "Start with Bruce. Write down a personality trait you really like, then compare him with Solomon on the same characteristic."

"Does this come from *Cosmo* or did you make it up?" Victoria said, grabbing a pen from her purse and starting to write.

Bruce	Steve
Reliable	Unpredictable
Cautious	Reckless
Anchored	Adrift

Jackie peered over Victoria's shoulder at the list. "No contest. The Bad Boy wins."

"C'mon, Jackie. This is serious."

"Okay, then give Solomon a chance. He's gotta have at least one quality you like."

"He has wonderful parenting skills. You can see that with Bobby. Plus . . ."

Rigid	Flexible
Boring	Fun
Controlling	Easygoing

"Hang on a sec," Jackie said. "Aren't you beating around the bush? No pun intended."

"You mean sex."

"Ye-ah. What about Bruce, other than the fact he's hung like a Clydesdale?"

"He's good. But maybe a trifle mechanical . . ."

"Mechanical is fine for a dishwasher, but from what you said about the Bad Boy . . ."

"Solomon makes me laugh and he makes me lunch. . . ."

"And he makes you come. Combo platter.

Excellent. C'mon. If you had to make a decision, which by the way you do, who's it gonna be?"

"What would you do?"

"Can't help you, Vic. But I might be interested in your discard."

Victoria tried to focus, tried to see through the clouds of indecision. It's fine to celebrate the power of multiple orgasms, but that's surely no reason to spend your life with the perpetrator. . . .

"If you've gotta think this hard," Jackie said, "you're gonna make the wrong decision."

"I can't just go with my emotions. I need to analyze all the factors."

"You're getting a man, not a mutual fund."

Victoria took a deep breath. "Bruce and I have similar interests. Similar values. Our love is perfectly logical. Perfectly rational. I made a commitment to him, a reasoned, thoughtful commitment. He's everything anyone could want. I mean, no one's perfect, right?"

Jackie didn't answer, so Victoria just kept going. "I'm going to marry Bruce. And that's final."

Forty

NO HUGS, NO KISSES,
NO ERRORS

On a quiet Sunday night—Victoria wouldn't return his calls and Bobby was reading the encyclopedia—Steve sat at the kitchen table, snacking on red peppers and goat cheese and drinking Grolsch, the Dutch beer. He turned on the laptop and started Googling.

First, he plugged "Replengren" into the search window, and bingo, a hundred references popped up. A synthetic hormone manufactured in Germany, Replengren regenerated damaged brain cells in rats, but not without side effects, including impaired motor skills. The FDA was considering whether to approve the drug for testing on humans, but so far, no decision had been made.

Holy shit.

Would Kranchick jump the gun with an experimental drug?

He put her name into the search engine and came up with a dozen monographs and research papers she'd written over the years. He'd found these earlier when he did his original homework, coming up with her article "Unlocking Your Inner Rain Man." But this time, he was looking for something specific.

Using the FIND function, he searched everything she'd written for the word "Replengren."

Nothing. She'd never mentioned the drug.

He set about reading Kranchick's papers anyway. He skipped the highly technical studies with charts of acid secretions and diagrams of brain electrical activity. He skimmed the ones speculating on the cause of autism, everything from measles in pregnant women to food additives and PCBs. He spent more time—a two-beer read—on a savant syndrome piece in which Kranchick predicted that transcranial magnetic stimulation would soon produce startling mental feats in both autistic and nonautistic persons.

What he read twice, highlighting with a yellow marker after printing it out—just as Victoria would have done—was the oldest and least technical of all the articles. It was an opinion piece in a medical journal from Kranchick's first year of residency at a Baltimore hospital. He'd read it before but it had meant little then. Now, viewed in the context of Replengren, it took on new meaning. In the article, Kranchick criticized a hospital's decision to fire a researcher who'd purposely induced psychotic episodes in schizophrenics by giving them amphetamines.

"Didn't Edward Jenner inject smallpox into an eight-year-old boy in order to come up with a vaccine?" she wrote. *"Didn't Walter Reed allow infected mosquitos to attack Cuban workers in order to discover the cause of yellow fever? Didn't Louis Pasteur test his rabies vaccine on children even before he tried it on animals?"*

Steve felt his heartbeat quicken. What was the question he'd just asked himself?

Would Kranchick jump the gun with an experimental drug?

Some questions are too easy. Why not ask: *Is Pincher a prick? Is Zinkavich a ton of truffled pork?* He skipped to the last paragraph of Kranchick's article.

"Advances in medicine require courage, vision, and the uncompromising ability to go where others fear to tread. The greater good demands no less."

The greater good.

Steve wanted to ask Kranchick who gave her the right to play God. But that could wait. He had his trial strategy to consider and another Grolsch to drink. How could he prove that Kranchick was giving an unapproved drug to the patients at Rockland? The handwritten note Cadillac snatched from the wastebasket wasn't admissible. And how would he even tell Victoria about it? He could imagine their conversation.

She: *"Dammit, Solomon. What you've done is unethical and illegal."*

He: *"But we learned the truth. When the law doesn't work . . ."*

She: *"Live with it! You can't decide what laws to follow and what to ignore. Who gave you the right to play God?"*

He: *"Touché."*

Even after polishing off another Grolsch, he didn't know what to do.

By Monday, the cold front had pushed out to sea, and the morning was sunny and warm. Parked under the portico at Brickell Townhouse, listening to Bob

Marley ask, "Is this love?" Steve waited for Victoria. He figured he had not seen her in thirty-two hours, nineteen minutes, and forty-six seconds. Roughly.

This morning they would begin selecting a jury in the Barksdale trial, and sometime after dark, they would start taking testimony in Bobby's case. He was up to his ass in Pinchers and Finks. But at the moment, all he could think about was Victoria.

Thirty-two hours and twenty minutes ago—make it *twenty-one*—she had climbed out of the straw, leaving him alone and forlorn. He had dialed her number three times on Sunday; she never picked up, never returned his calls.

She's pretending it didn't happen. Well, he could do the same.

But it wouldn't work. Their lovemaking was playing on an endless loop in what was left of his brain.

A moment later, she came flying out the lobby door in full trial uniform: double-breasted charcoal suit and a simple strand of pearls. Looking serious. Businesslike. And beautiful. She good-morninged the doorman, tossed her briefcase into the backseat, and hopped in. "Sorry I'm late."

No "Good morning, sweetheart." No peck on the cheek. Not even a smile.

"No problem," he said.

Sooner or later, she'd have to confront it. He felt like shouting: *"I told you how I feel. Now you tell me."*

In sullen silence, he drove up Twelfth Avenue toward the Justice Building. This was how it was going to be. No hugs, no kisses, no errors. So much he wanted to say, but the atmosphere was all wrong. The harsh sunlight of day had replaced the flaming torches, the Cuban love songs, the swirling snow. Besides, hadn't he already laid it all out? He'd said he loved her. What else could he do?

"Who's going to handle voir dire?" she asked. A professional tone, one partner to another.

"You do the talking. I'll watch the jurors, take notes."

"Really?"

"You're friendlier. They'll like you more. Hell, they'll fall in love with you."

Love, he thought. He had love on the brain.

The air horn sounded on the drawbridge at the Miami River. Dammit, they'd be stuck a good five minutes. He wouldn't add it to his laws, but it's a good idea not to be late to court the first day of a murder trial. He pulled to a stop, third car in line.

"So?" he said.

"So?"

He couldn't help himself. He couldn't *not* ask. "What's the deal? Is this gonna be another 'it never happened'?"

She stayed quiet. A white egret high-stepped its way up the ascending bridge. On the radio, Jimmy Cliff boasted he could see clearly now.

"It happened," she said finally.

He waited for her to continue, but she didn't. The egret kept going uphill. Jimmy Cliff claimed it was a bright sunshiny day, but it sure didn't feel that way to Steve. "I'm a little on edge here, trying to figure just where I stand."

The bridge had gotten too steep. The egret took off and circled over the river, where a freighter loaded with minivans moved ponderously toward the open ocean.

"I can't think about you right now," she said.

"That's a little cold, isn't it?"

"We have a murder case to try all day, then Bobby's case tonight, then we do it all over again tomorrow. Bruce is breathing down my neck about seating charts for the reception, and he's ordered an avocado tree ice sculpture without asking me. Jackie hates her dress, my period's due tomorrow, and you, Steve Solomon, want me to bat my eyes and tell you how the earth moved, and it's never been that way before, and oh, my God, let's sail off to some island together."

"Did it? The earth move, I mean."

"Oh, Jesus."

"First you blast me because I didn't express my feelings. Now I've put my balls on the chopping block, and what do you do?"

"I'm tabling you."

"Table Bigby and the ice sculpture. Talk to me, dammit."

"Not until both cases are over. When everything's finished, we'll talk." The barrier arm on the bridge was lifting. "Now, let's go win a murder trial."

Forty-one

SEEMS LIKE OLD TIMES

Steve and Victoria climbed the front steps of the Justice Building, just as the Voodoo Squad janitors finished their cleanup. The cakes, candles, and skulls—offerings to various Santeria gods from families of defendants—were tossed into garbage bags, and the accused were left to their fate before mere mortals: judges and jurors.

Katrina would be waiting in the lawyer-client lounge. Victoria hoped she had followed instructions on what to wear. They had spent several hours last night in Katrina's vast closet, Victoria spending a good deal of the time saying, "No."

No to the one-button tuxedo in silk crepe de chine, with the plunging neckline.

No to the metallic cherry red crochet dress with the scoop neck.

No to the shimmering, beaded lace dress with the sheer top.

They had settled on a Carolina Herrera wool flannel skirt suit in pearl gray, a tasteful belt at the waist. Now, on the escalator headed to the courtroom,

Victoria listened to Solomon lecture her on jury selection in that annoying, superior tone.

"Watch the body language. Try to figure who are leaders, who are followers."

"I will."

"Strike all unattractive women, they'll hate our client."

"I know," she said.

"The man who sits with his elbows in his lap is submissive. The guy who encroaches on the next juror's chair is dominant."

"I know. I know."

"See who's carrying hardcover books, who's carrying the *Daily Racing Form*."

"Got it."

"Strike anyone reading a book by Bill O'Reilly."

"Why?"

"They're gonna be obnoxious know-it-alls."

They got off on the second floor and took the escalator to the third floor. "Watch Marvin the Maven in the front row," Steve said. "If he tugs an earlobe—"

"He wants me to steal second base?"

"He wants you to challenge the juror. Another thing: Let the panel know right away that our client's guilty of adultery."

"I'll do it in opening statement."

"Too late. Do it first thing in voir dire. I want to see their reactions, strike anyone who gets uptight."

"If we make too big a deal out of it, it'll look like we're afraid—"

"Look, I don't have time for a tutorial here. Just do what I say."

"I don't *need* a tutorial."

Why's he lashing out like this? she wondered. Because she didn't leap into his arms today?

I should never have slept with him. I'm an idiot!

"I'm worried about the infidelity issue," he said.

You too? she thought.

"We get some religious nuts on the jury, they'll hang her for screwing Manko, no matter what the evidence is on murder. Are you up to speed on cognitive dissonance theory?"

"I studied psychology at Princeton."

"Congratulations. Do you know this corollary? If you can get people to publicly commit to positions they didn't previously agree with, they'll change their behavior to conform to their new commitments."

"I've read all the studies."

"Another thing, don't stand too close to the box. It's intimidating. Be relaxed. Walk back and forth if you want, but maintain eye contact. You're having a conversation with the jurors, not interrogating them."

"Jesus, Steve, I know how to pick a jury."

"But when you're cross-examining, stand sniper still. Let the witness squirm."

"I know how to cross-examine, too."

"If you'd listen, I could make a great lawyer out of you."

"That again? You're so damned overbearing."

"And you're just as frigid as the day we met."

"What!"

"*Rigid.* I meant to say rigid."

"Screw you, Solomon."

"You already did, Lord."

Damn him, the cheap-shot artist.

"I know you're angry," she said, "but could you try to be an adult about this?"

"I'm not angry."

Men are such babies. If he keeps this up, the next week will be hell.

"You wanted all-business," he said. "You got it."

Just like old times, she thought. She'd almost forgotten how caustic he could be. What had she been thinking the other night? Could she even imagine being involved with this petulant child? Nothing but bicker and banter, bicker and banter. She was certain she'd made the right decision. How could she have ever doubted that Bruce was the one for her?

Another correct decision: her delay in giving Solomon the news.

She'd said: *"I'm tabling you."* As if Solomon were a motion taken under advisement. As if she hadn't made up her mind.

A little white lie.

Okay, maybe it's cruel, letting him hang on like that. But they had two cases to try, and this was no time to tell him to get lost.

She didn't know how he would handle it. What if he cracked?

When they reached the fourth floor, the corridor was clogged with reporters and photographers. The questions came fast.

"Any chance of a plea?"

"Will Katrina Barksdale testify?"

"Any surprise witnesses?"

Steve held up a hand to quiet them. "You know I try my cases in the courtroom, not in the media."

"What kind of jury you looking for?" one of the TV guys asked.

"Same as always. Alert and smart."

Right, Victoria thought. Alert enough to stay awake. Smart enough to memorize two words: "not guilty."

"Got any aces up your sleeve?" the guy persisted.

"Don't need tricks when your client's one-hundred-percent innocent."

Are any of us one-hundred-percent innocent? Not me, Victoria thought.

Steve kept gabbing as they hustled down the corridor to the courtroom. Blasting the state's case and singing hosannas to their client, Katrina Barksdale. The world's perfect wife, the real victim here. Blah, blah, blah.

Whistling past the graveyard, as her mother liked to say.

Where did that cockiness come from? How could he always be so sure of his footing when anyone else would be sinking in quicksand?

The Barksdale trial was supposed to lift him out of the low-rent district and launch her career. But what if Steve pulled one of his crazed stunts? It's one thing to be held in contempt in a talking cockatoo trial, but in this case, with the news media camped in the corridors, the slightest peccadillo would make headlines. What if the case turned out to be professional suicide?

Not to mention my personal life.

She'd made a horrific mistake, tumbling into the straw with Steve. Now it seemed he had the potential to lay waste to both her nascent career and her impending marriage.

No. I won't blame Steve for any of that. I can't. Any damage to me is purely self-inflicted.

Forty-two

DEAREST

The carnival started with Ray Pincher telling the panel he wanted to seat a jury that would be fair and impartial, not one that would favor the state. It was the first of numerous lies that will be told in the courtroom today, Steve thought glumly.

The first dozen souls in the box were fairly typical by Miami standards. Three retirees, two homemakers, an unemployed man, and a Protestant minister filed into the box. Then a cross-dressing South Beach party planner, a mime who failed to answer audibly, an exotic dancer noted for wrestling men in tubs of coleslaw, a beauty-salon colorist who specialized in pubic hair, and an elderly Hispanic who described himself as a freedom fighter against that butcher Fidel Castro.

Steve sat at the defense table beside Katrina Barksdale, who was demure in her gray suit, seeming to Steve neither slutty nor homicidal. Pincher sat ramrod straight at the state's table. His bulging eyes were alert and wary.

Standing a perfect six feet from the jury box,

Victoria said: "Now, Reverend Anderson, you're familiar with the Ten Commandments?"

"Every one," the minister avowed.

"The Commandments say, Thou shalt not commit adultery, and Thou shalt not kill. But do you understand, Reverend Anderson, that in this courtroom, we're concerned only with killing?"

"Indeed I do. Judging adultery is in someone else's jurisdiction." The minister pointed skyward.

Steve heard someone whisper his name. When he turned, he saw Marvin gesturing toward the rear of the courtroom. Teresa Toraño, Marvin's lady, stood near the door. Steve gave Marvin a *What's up?* look. The Maven nodded in Teresa's direction. *Go boychik, go.*

Steve rose and walked to the back row of the gallery, where Teresa had taken a seat. Her black hair was pulled back into a bun, and she wore a dark tweed jacket and matching skirt. When he slid into the seat next to her, she reached in her purse and took out an envelope.

"Cashier's check," she whispered.

Steve looked at her blankly.

"One hundred thousand dollars," she said.

"You, Teresa?"

"Me."

"Marvin said something about asking his friends. I didn't think he meant you."

"Something wrong with my money?"

"I'm just a little embarrassed, is all."

"You should be. For not coming straight to me."

"I don't know about this, Teresa." If he was going to take the hundred thousand, he wanted her to know the spot he was in. "If Katrina's convicted, I don't get a fee. It'll take me years to pay you back."

"So you'll work it off."

"The funeral homes still have litigation?"

She smiled and folded the envelope into his hand. "No. But you can learn embalming."

From her position in front of the jury box, Victoria glanced toward him. The glance seemed to ask: *Why the hell are you kibitzing while I'm picking a jury?*

"The money is for Bobby's case, yes?" Teresa whispered.

Steve nodded. "I'd rather not tell you more than that."

"I pray for you to Philomena, Patron Saint of Children."

"Thank you, Teresa. For everything." He slipped the envelope into his suit coat pocket.

Victoria was asking the jurors if they understood that Katrina Barksdale sat before them an innocent woman, and that the state bore the burden of proving her guilty. Eleven jurors chimed variations of "yes," "sure," "yeah," "uh-huh," and "*sí.*" The mime nodded.

Teresa whispered: "So, for you to pay me back before I'm in a rest home, I have to hope you get the *puta* off?"

"Hey, none of that. Katrina's my client, which means she's a saint. Like Philomena."

"*Por Dios.*" Teresa scowled her disapproval.

"The picture of perfection," he said, which brought another line to mind. "The woman is perfected."

" 'Her dead body wears the smile of accomplishment.' "

"What?"

"The second line of the poem," Teresa said.

"Holy shit. It's a real poem?" Several jurors turned his way; he'd raised his voice. Victoria looked toward him and pursed her lips, as if to say, *"Shush."*

" 'Edge' by Sylvia Plath," Teresa said.

Steve's knowledge of poetry was minimal. There was Olaf and the shit he would not eat. There were some brawny verses by Carl Sandburg he'd learned in college. *"Pittsburgh, Youngstown, Gary, they make their steel with men."* And there were little ditties that began: *"There once was a girl from Red China."* He could not name one of Plath's poems, but he knew about her, mainly from seeing the Gwyneth Paltrow movie.

"Sylvia Plath committed suicide, didn't she?" he said.

"Just a few days after writing 'Edge.' "

"Wow," he said. The pieces of the puzzle were coming together. He'd assumed Barksdale had written the line himself. But no. He'd stolen a real poem, then created multiple anagrams. Now Steve remembered the note Barksdale sent his wife the day before his death. Victoria had called it "quaint."

"Teresa, do you know this line? Something like, 'Dearest. Nobody could have been so good, from the beginning to the end'?"

She gave him a kind smile, a patient teacher to a slow student. " 'Dearest . . . No one could have been so good as you have been, from the very first day till now.' "

"That's it! Did Plath write that, too?"

Hoping now. A defense forming.

"No. Sylvia Plath didn't write it."

"Damn." Steve instantly deflated. He thought he'd been onto something. Suicide. But if the "Dearest" line didn't come from Plath, where did that leave him?

"Virginia Woolf wrote it," Teresa said. "It was her suicide note to her husband."

"Yes!" Steve gave her a hug. "You're beautiful, Teresa!"

She laughed. "You are a crazy man, but if I were forty years younger . . ."

"I can answer your question now."

She cocked her head, not quite knowing where he was going.

"I'm going to get the *puta* off," Steve said.

Forty-three

THE MEANING OF SYNERGY

"Charles discovers Katrina's affair, so he kills himself?" Victoria said. "What sense does that make?"

"Victoria's right," Katrina said. "If he was gonna kill anybody, it would have been me."

"Are you two listening to me?" Steve said. "This is a *great* defense."

They were sitting in the empty courtroom. Minutes earlier, the jury had been sworn, standing at attention with hands raised, good little Scouts, promising to determine the case solely on the evidence and the judge's instructions. Steve had taken a peek to see if they had their fingers crossed.

Then Judge Hiram Thornberry cleared his throat and said: "Noting the lateness of the hour, we'll stand in recess until tomorrow morning."

Steve noted the hour was only three-thirty P.M. but His Honor liked to beat the traffic home and play nine holes before dark. After the courtroom emptied, Steve told Victoria and Katrina that Charles had committed suicide. The two women spent the next ten minutes trashing his theory.

"Charlie never did anything without help," Katrina said, "including jerk off."

"You're basing all this on the poem?" Victoria shook her head.

"Charles was a literary guy," Steve argued. "He collected books. He sponsored seminars: 'Women Poets, Tortured Souls.' "

"Extremely flimsy evidence," Victoria said.

"C'mon, Vic. What's the first thing you told me about Charles?"

"That he always had to prove he was the smartest guy at the table."

"Exactly. Don't you see how it all fits together? Charles makes an anagram out of a line Sylvia Plath wrote just days before she took her own life. He quotes Virginia Woolf's suicide note, then strangles himself in a contraption where he could control the pressure on his throat."

Victoria was biting her lower lip, thinking it through. "It doesn't make sense. Charles is furious with Katrina. If he dies while they're still married, she inherits her share of the estate."

"Not if she's convicted of murder," Steve said.

"So Charlie framed me?" Katrina said. Her head was swiveling back and forth watching her lawyers' tennis match.

"That's my guess," Steve said. "Some murderers try to disguise their crimes as suicide. Charles flipped it around. He committed suicide and disguised it as murder."

"Then why write a note that might give it all away?" Victoria said.

"He doesn't exactly give it away. Three anagrams

that lead to a source gram that still has to be connected to a poem. Who would figure it out?"

"Not me," Katrina said with a shrug.

"One last chance to prove he was smarter than everyone else," Steve said. "He's laughing from the grave."

"I'm still not buying it," Victoria said. "No man ends his life just to cheat his wife out of some money."

"That's not *why* he did it. That's just the cream cheese on the bagel."

"And the lox? What's that?"

"Once Katrina broke his heart, Charles had nothing to live for," Steve said. Sending up a trial balloon.

"Charlie wasn't like that," Katrina said, bursting it. "I mean, he'd just divorce me and find someone else."

"Okay, he was suicidal for another reason," Steve said, refusing to give up. "But as long as he was gonna do it, he was gonna nail you."

"*What* reason?" Victoria demanded. "We keep coming back to the same place."

"I don't know! I just know he did it."

"We'll never prove it without a reason he'd kill himself," Victoria said.

"Mental illness, maybe," Steve said. "Bipolar disorder. Depression."

"No way." Katrina shook her head, her dark tresses swaying. "Not good-time Charlie."

"Financial reasons," Steve suggested.

"He was stinking rich," Katrina pointed out.

"Medical problems."

"Not once they invented Viagra."

"Did he abuse drugs?"

Another shake, another hair swoosh. "Nothing without a doctor's prescription, and that includes the painkillers."

"What painkillers?" Victoria said.

"Vicodin. A couple of others. I don't remember their names."

"Why was Charles taking them?"

"A couple of weeks before he died, he came down with a stomach virus."

"They don't give you painkillers for a stomach virus," Victoria said.

Katrina wrinkled her forehead. "That's what Charlie brought home from the doctor. I'm sure of it."

"What doctor?" Steve asked.

Philip Atherton, MD, didn't play a doctor on TV, but he sure looked like one. Handsome, early fifties, salt-and-pepper hair carefully swept back, crisp lab coat with his name stenciled above the pocket, the obligatory stethoscope slung around the neck. There was something proper and vaguely British about him. Victoria expected him to sound like *Masterpiece Theatre*.

"I fucking hate lawyers," Dr. Atherton barked in a harsh New York accent. "Bloodsucking parasites."

"I couldn't agree more," Victoria said. She was determined to find common ground. They needed this guy's help, and quickly. She shot a look at Steve, who was scowling.

They were sitting in Atherton's upscale medical suite just off Miracle Mile in Coral Gables. The office had a marble-floored waiting room with a burbling fountain and vases of fresh lilies on glass pedestals. The seven-story building was earth-toned stucco with orange tile terraces. An architect's attempt to make the place look like a Mediterranean villa instead of home to proctologists, podiatrists, and internists.

It was a few minutes before five o'clock. In an hour, Steve and Victoria were due in kiddie court for the start of Bobby's trial. They had thirty minutes, tops, to get what they needed and hit the road.

"Lawyers are lower than pond scum," the doctor said. "Lower than whale shit."

"It's amazing," Victoria agreed, "the lack of ethics one sees." She forced a smile. Next to her, Steve fidgeted. She could see he hated the guy.

"Some things even a whore won't do for money," Dr. Atherton said. "But lawyers . . ."

"Now, about Charles Barksdale," Victoria purred, feeling the minutes tick away.

"What's black and brown and looks good on a lawyer?" the doctor said.

"A Doberman pinscher." Victoria knew that old chestnut had been roasted long before she went to law school.

"That's bullshit," Steve said.

"Steve, I'll handle this."

"Some of us spend a lot of time working pro bono," Steve said.

"To salve your guilty conscience?" the doctor said.

"When's the last time you took a patient without insurance?"

"Steve, please," she said. *Dammit! Bobby has more self-control.*

"Do you know why my malpractice premiums are six figures?" Dr. Atherton said.

"Because doctors screw up," Steve said.

"Because lawyers are leeches," the doctor said.

"I don't have to listen to this shit."

"Stephen," Victoria said, her irritation showing. "We need Dr. Atherton's help, and we need it now."

"That'll be five hundred dollars for fifteen minutes," the doctor said. "Payment up front. Cash or MasterCard. No American Express."

"Isn't that a little steep for a consultation?" Victoria said.

"You have thirteen minutes left," the doctor said, glancing at his watch.

Steve shot a look at Victoria. "I'm maxed out on the plastic."

Naturally, she thought, opening her purse, as Dr. Atherton buzzed for his bookkeeper.

It only took four minutes, and Dr. Atherton didn't reduce the bill. He said he'd been Charles Barksdale's primary care physician for a dozen years. Never a serious problem. Blood pressure and cholesterol under control, some tennis at the club to stay in reasonable shape. Minor knee surgery two years ago to scrape out some loose cartilage. A few weeks before he died, Charlie came in, complaining of abdominal pain and nausea. He'd been vomiting on and off for a week.

"Stomach virus?" Victoria asked.

"I wish," Atherton said. "A CT scan showed a thickening of the stomach wall. I sent him over to Cedars for an exploratory laparotomy. They did a biopsy. Unresectable gastric carcinoma with carcinomatosis."

"Cancer," Victoria said.

"A really nasty one. Linitis plastica. Advanced, inoperable, and fatal. I gave him some painkillers along with the bad news."

Victoria took a deep breath.

Steve's gut was right.

The Human Polygraph had told her Katrina was innocent, and she'd scoffed. Then he'd said Charles had committed suicide, and she'd scoffed again. But here was Barksdale's motive for taking his own life. So why not cut his unfaithful wife out of the estate while he was at it?

Solomon's really good at this.

"What exactly did you tell Mr. Barksdale?" she asked the doctor.

"That he had six weeks to six months to live, and he should get his affairs in order."

"Starting with paying your bill?" Steve asked.

"Steve, stop it." Victoria turned back to the doctor, who was studying his watch. "What was Mr. Barksdale's reaction to his diagnosis?"

"Quiet. He said I shouldn't tell Katrina if I ran into her at the club. He was going to handle that himself."

"But he never did. Charles lied to her, told her he had a stomach virus."

"So she killed him for nothing," the doctor said, amused. "All she had to do was wait for nature to take its course."

Victoria let that one go. Something was buzzing in her mind, the flutter of a mosquito's wings. What was it? "This tumor," she said. "Would it have been visible to the ME doing the autopsy?"

Dr. Atherton snorted. A little puff of condescension. "If you can identify the cancer through a scope, you sure as hell can see it if you split the guy open from stern to stern."

"Even if the ME isn't an oncologist?" she asked, pressing him.

"Linitis plastica looks like somebody planted sod in your stomach. Long, wavy fibers like blades of grass. Even if the ME was half blind and dumb as a lawyer, he couldn't miss it."

Waiting for the elevator, Steve pounded the DOWN button. They had twenty minutes to get to court in rush-hour traffic.

She said: "Why wasn't the cancer—?"

He said: "In Dr. Yang's autopsy report."

She said: "Yang's competent and honest—"

He said: "Which leaves Sugar Ray Pincher."

"Something's wrong," they said in unison.

Okay, he thought. We're on the same page now.

Okay, she thought. This is the meaning of "synergy."

The elevator door opened. They went in and headed down to the parking garage.

Steve said: "Why would Pincher screw around with the autopsy—?"

"When killing a sick man is just as much murder as killing a healthy man?" she said, completing his thought.

"Damned if I know," Steve said, "but if I'm half the cross-examiner I think I am, Dr. Yang will tell us."

"A bit of advice: Use a rapier instead of a sledge-hammer."

"You're telling me how to cross, Lord?"

"Sweet Jesus," she said, using one of her mother's expressions. You tell a man to use his turn signals, he thinks you're castrating him. "Don't be so touchy, Solomon. You're a terrific lawyer."

"Don't patronize me."

"All I'm saying, sometimes you come on a little strong."

He bristled. "That's my style. I mug the opposition. You hug them."

"Okay, keep doing what you do. I'll do what I do. Maybe that's what makes us a good team."

"You just figuring that out, Victoria? All this time and you're just figuring that out?"

The elevator door opened and he walked out ahead of her, shaking his head.

Forty-four

FESSING UP

Steve was driving and Victoria was in the passenger seat, going over her note cards. They were headed north on Ronald Reagan Avenue, so named because the former President once ate a Cuban sandwich at a *restaurante* there. They would cut over to Coral Way, take Twenty-seventh Avenue, and they'd be at the Juvenile Justice Center with maybe two minutes to spare. Steve knew he was running out of time to fess up.

"There's something about Bobby's case I haven't told you."

"Yeah?" Putting down her cards, sounding worried.

"I've got some evidence that'll totally discredit Kranchick."

"What is it?" Sounding dubious now.

"She's using an illegal drug. Something not approved by the FDA."

"Wow. You sure?"

"Positive. But you can't use the evidence."

"Why not?"

"Because we stole it."

"*We?*"

"Okay. Me. Actually, Cadillac, at my request. He rifled her wastebasket."

"The wastebasket?" She shook her head. "Like the Winnie-the-Pooh case?"

Steve knew the case. The judge dismissed a suit against Disney in part because the plaintiffs went through the company's garbage. "Pretty much. Which is why you've got to be subtle."

"How is one subtle with illegally obtained evidence?"

"Get Kranchick to admit she's using an unapproved drug."

"And just how do I do that?"

"Play on her pride. She really believes what she's doing is right. No matter how unethical it is."

As they crossed the Twenty-seventh Avenue bridge, he told Victoria about the opinion piece, Kranchick expressing support for dangerous medical research that had been condemned by medical ethicists. "She's not afraid of taking unpopular positions, of being out of the mainstream. Her principles are her own, not the FDA's."

"So she's like you?" Victoria said. "She makes up her own laws?"

"Mine don't put people's lives at risk." Steve ran a yellow light, another motorist honking at him. They were less than a block away, passing a run-down strip mall with a discount liquor store, a muffler shop, and a pawnshop—Casa de Empeño. "The key to cracking her is that she's not ashamed. She has a sense of honor about what she does. Which is why I don't think she'll lie."

"Your gut again, right?"

"Yeah. Plus my research. Something you taught me."

He pulled the car into the parking lot, thinking the Juvenile Justice Center resembled a prison more than a courthouse. Concrete block pods were built around a barren concrete terrace that had all the warmth of a prisoners' exercise yard. The building's windowless stucco walls had once been white but were now streaked with permanent rust stains. A grim, impersonal place. Steve wondered how Bobby would react to the unfamiliar surroundings. They would find out tomorrow when they brought him to meet the judge. Tonight, he was with Marvin and Teresa, eating a Cuban sandwich and drinking a mamey milk shake at the Versailles on *Calle Ocho*.

"I don't know if I can pull this off," Victoria said.

"Sure you can."

They got out of the car and headed inside, a jet on final approach to MIA screaming over their heads. She still looked troubled. "We both could go to jail and lose our licenses."

"If you do it right, Kranchick will never know where we got the information."

"And if I do it wrong?"

"We'll both go to jail and lose our licenses," Steve said.

Forty-five

HERBERT SOLOMON'S SON

Standing in front of the bench, Zinkavich announced formally: "Jack Zinkavich for the people of the State of Florida."

Not all of them, Steve thought, as his partner got to her feet.

"Victoria Lord, on behalf of Stephen Solomon."

Just little ole me, Steve thought.

They were in the cramped courtroom of Judge Althea Rolle. The judge was a petite black woman with a streak of gray in her tightly cropped hair. Two teddy bears sat on her desk. Drawings by sixth graders covered the walls. Dozens of snapshots were taped to a blackboard, the judge posing with happy families who had just adopted children. There would be no jury here; Bobby's fate was entirely up to Judge Rolle.

The lives of Juvenile Court judges were schizophrenic, Steve figured. They packed off troubled teens to Youth Hall in delinquency proceedings. They handled the gut-wrenching cases known as TPRs—Termination of Parental Rights—yanking kids away from abusive or neglectful parents. And occasionally they brought joy to families who adopt children no one else wants.

Like Jack Zinkavich, Family Services poster boy.

The judge looked up from her file, studied Steve a moment. "You wouldn't be Herbert Solomon's son, would you?"

"Guilty, Your Honor." Steve was used to the question but never knew what to expect next. Sometimes there would be a sad shake of the head, sometimes a scowl, and sometimes . . .

"What a wonderful man."

Steve eased out a breath.

"A judge with a heart," she continued.

"Ex-judge," Zinkavich piped up, an open box of Krispy Kremes on his table. Steve spotted a *dulce de leche*—a top seller in Miami—a cinnamon twist, and an iced donut, with its dark little rim around the top, like a chocolate yarmulke. Salivating, he realized he'd violated one of his own rules—he'd skipped lunch—and dinner was hours away.

"I was so sorry when I heard about your father's troubles, Mr. Solomon," the judge said. "Would you give him my best wishes?"

"I'll do that, Your Honor," Steve said. "Thank you."

Zinkavich cleared his throat. "Judge Rolle, may I inquire into the extent of your relationship with the Petitioner's father?"

"I never slept with him, if that's what you mean."

Zinkavich's head jerked back, causing his several chins to jiggle. "Of course not. I just meant—"

"But if he'd asked me, I don't know what I'd have done."

"I just wondered how close the two of you were," Zinkavich said.

"How many cases you try before me, Z?"

"Twenty-five or so."

"Am I always fair to you?"

"Yes, ma'am. You usually rule with me."

"Yes, I do, even though you're a royal pain in the butt and a total weenie."

"Yes, ma'am."

"You win, Z, because Family Services almost always has the best interests of the child at heart, and that's my sole consideration."

"I understand, ma'am."

"Now, I've never met Mr. Stephen Solomon and I don't care if his father's the Prince of Wales. You understand that?"

"I think so, Your Honor."

"So while I have a little colloquy with the gentleman, why don't you just stuff your mouth with a double-glazed?" Judge Rolle turned to Steve and softened her tone. "We're a little less formal on this side of the river."

"I see that, Judge."

"Broke my cherry with your father."

"Beg your pardon . . . ?"

"Tried my first case before Herbert Solomon. You never forget your first one."

Or your last, Steve thought.

"Auto accident case," the judge continued. "Ink wasn't dry on my diploma, and I couldn't get a shred of evidence in. Every question, these two snippy insurance lawyers would hop up and object. 'Irrelevant.' 'Hearsay.' 'Improper predicate.' "

"Old trick," Steve said, "to rattle a young lawyer."

"Your daddy kept sustaining their objections in that sweet drawl of his. 'Ah wuz you, Miss Rolle, ah'd rephrase that question.' Finally, he called us up to sidebar. I thought he was gonna ream me out for being incompetent, but instead he turned to those white boys and said, 'Ah'd like to hear the little lady's questions, so y'all crackers shut your traps, 'cuz your next objection lands you in contempt.' That shut 'em up real quick."

"Sounds like Dad," Steve said.

"He didn't always follow the letter of the law but he sure adhered to its spirit. I like to think I do the same." She opened a file, then turned to Zinkavich. "Now, why does the state say the petitioner should not be granted guardianship of his nephew?"

Zinkavich didn't bother standing up. "Because Mr. Solomon is incapable of caring for a special-needs child. Because he has prevented testing and treatment of the child that our experts have determined to be necessary."

The *child*, Steve thought. As impersonal as a lawsuit over *property*. Had he reminded Victoria to refer to Bobby by name?

"Because Mr. Solomon exposes the child to inappropriate adult materials," Zinkavich droned on. "And because he has violent propensities and committed serious crimes when he acquired de facto custody."

"You can prove all of that?" the judge asked. She seemed taken aback, Steve thought. Maybe shocked to learn that Herbert's son might not measure up to his father. She wouldn't be the first to reach that conclusion.

"Every word, Your Honor." Zinkavich seemed to

swagger, even though he was sitting down. "Indeed, we will prove that granting Mr. Solomon guardianship rights would violate both the letter"—he showed a self-satisfied smirk—"and the spirit of the law."

"Don't suck up to me, Z. Ms. Lord, I take it you disagree with the state's characterization of your client."

Victoria stood. To Steve, she looked nervous. On unfamiliar ground. A new judge, new legal issues, and a ton of responsibility.

"Steve Solomon is wonderful with Bobby, Your Honor," she said. "Sensitive, loving, and nurturing. It's true that Bobby has special needs, but he also has special gifts. In the course of the case, you'll hear from Bobby so that you can appreciate the marvelous way his mind works."

Right, Steve thought. How many kids know twenty-six synonyms for "penis" and twenty-six for "vagina," each starting with a different letter?

"You'll see how much Steve cares for Bobby and how much Bobby cares for him," Victoria said. "By the close of our case, I think you'll agree that Steve Solomon is a terrific lover."

"Lover?" the judge said.

"Father," Victoria said, blushing. "I meant 'father,' of course."

"Of course. Okay, Ms. Lord, let's take some testimony."

"Petitioner calls Dr. Doris Kranchick as an adverse witness," Victoria said.

Doris Kranchick stomped through the swinging gate of the courtroom as if advancing on goal. Her hair was pulled back, and her only makeup was a pinkish powder intended to cover the scar than ran down her cheek but only served to accentuate it. She wore plain black flats, a no-nonsense suit, and a white blouse with a frilly white bow that Steve figured was Zinkavich's attempt to soften her appearance. It worked about as well as a tiara on a plowhorse.

Victoria used a friendly, conversational tone, something Steve thought he should try sometime. She asked Kranchick about her educational background, running smoothly through college, medical school, her internship, residency, and fellowships. She complimented the doctor on her stellar academic record and noted how extraordinary it was to also be a champion athlete. The two women spent the next few minutes chatting about lacrosse.

"I still play the sport," Kranchick said proudly. She slipped a hand in each suit pocket and pulled out two yellow balls.

The only balls Doris Kranchick was likely to ever hold, Steve thought.

Victoria moved on to the monographs Kranchick had written, the studies she'd directed, the programs she initiated at Rockland State Hospital. It was all very relaxed, the litigation equivalent of a base runner lulling the pitcher to sleep before stealing a base. Then, the preliminaries over, Victoria asked: "Precisely what is Bobby's medical condition?"

"I can't say *precisely,* because Mr. Solomon won't agree to a complete examination."

Score one for the All-American point on defense, Steve thought.

C'mon, Vic. Don't let her rattle you.

"Then tell us what you can about Bobby's condition."

"Robert is a high-functioning savant with autistic characteristics of unknown origin. He is fearful of strangers, given to episodes of hysteria, and insufficiently socialized. As the cause of autism is unknown, it is impossible to determine the source of Robert's malady. However, we do know that he suffered sensory deprivation and malnutrition while in the custody of his mother." She shot a look at Steve. "That would be Janice Solomon, the Petitioner's sister."

Guilt by blood, Steve thought.

Kranchick dropped the lacrosse balls back into her pockets. "We need to test Robert to determine whether he suffered central nervous system injuries or merely psychological damage that's reversible in therapy. That's the key to understanding the source of the echolalia, the anagrams, the foreign-language skills."

Kranchick turned to Judge Rolle. Enthusiastic now. Witnesses always are when you let them prattle on about their passions. "That's what makes Robert so important, Judge. If his right brain was stimulated without CNS damage, maybe we can duplicate that in others with drugs or hormones. I believe we can unlock the Rain Man in all of us. Can you imagine what it would be like to recall verbatim everything you've ever heard?"

"A lot of what I hear I'd just as soon forget," the judge said, "but I get your point."

"Let's discuss the Child Protection report you filed with the court," Victoria said.

"Gladly," Dr. Kranchick said. On a roll now.

"You make some highly critical comments about Mr. Solomon."

"Not everyone finds him as cuddly as you do."

"What's that mean?" the judge interrupted.

"They're engaged." Kranchick raised her eyebrows, as if she disapproved.

Judge Rolle smiled. "Congratulations. You make a beautiful couple."

Zinkavich put down a glazed cruller: "My condolences, Ms. Lord."

"Actually . . ." Victoria faltered.

"Don't," Steve whispered to her. But he knew too well that she could no more lie to a judge than strangle a kitten.

"We are not engaged," Victoria said.

Damn. Just don't try to explain too much.

"Oh?" The judge seemed confused.

Victoria was blushing. "Anymore. We were. Then. But now we're not."

Ker-flumping. Sure sign of the rookie prevaricator.

"And that big rock on your finger?" the judge asked.

"Now I'm engaged to someone else."

"Proves my point," Kranchick said to the judge. "Mr. Solomon is undomesticated and incapable of sustaining a relationship." She turned to Victoria. "I hope it's Mr. Bigby. I preferred him from the get-go."

"All right, let's get back on track," the judge said sternly. "Doctor, I'm interested in Mr. Solomon's abilities as a potential parent, not a potential spouse."

"Mr. Solomon's utterly ill equipped to care for Robert, Your Honor. The boy needs testing and therapy in a controlled setting. Rockland State Hospital would be ideal for him."

Her cheeks still red, Victoria asked: "Do you perform behavioral therapy at Rockland?"

"A bit. But we really don't have adequate staffing for much of that."

"Even though one-on-one behavioral therapy has proven to be the best treatment for autism."

"Perhaps you could tell that to the governor and get us additional funding. Until then, we'll be content to be in the forefront of the most aggressive new therapies."

"Drug therapies?"

Nice segue. Now go for it.

"Drugs, vitamins, hormones."

"Tell us about them."

"Megadoses of magnesium and vitamin B_6, plus some new synthetic polypeptides."

"And the results?"

"Limited success so far. That's why we continue to work so hard."

"Just so we're clear, what you call 'therapy' really means testing with experimental drugs, doesn't it?"

"When drug therapy succeeds, it turns out to be quite therapeutic," Kranchick said.

Damn. The doc's no pushover.

"And when it fails?" Victoria pounced. "What does that turn out to be?"

"Objection. Argumentative." Zinkavich wiped his cinnamon-coated mouth.

"Overruled," Judge Rolle said.

"Therapy that fails is the first step to finding what succeeds," Kranchick said, not backing down.

She's really good. But you're better, Vic. Go get her.

"What about giving autistic children Replengren?"

That stopped Kranchick. She seemed to give great thought to her answer.

Steve prayed that she wouldn't lie. If she lied, they couldn't disprove it.

"Replengren has not yet been approved by the FDA," Kranchick said evenly.

She didn't lie. She also didn't answer the question. Keep going, Vic.

"It's unapproved because Replengren impaired motor skills in lab rats, correct, Dr. Kranchick?"

"At extremely high doses, far higher than would ever be given to humans."

"Which brings us back to the question: Do you give Replengren to human patients?"

"At Pedro Mallo, in Buenos Aires, we used Replengren in some strictly controlled human tests, with promising results."

She's still not answering. Did you notice that, Judge?

Victoria said: "My question has nothing to do with Buenos Aires. Do you give Replengren to patients at Rockland State Hospital in Fort Lauderdale, where you are bound by FDA rules?"

Kranchick's cheeks turned pale, which seemed to brighten her old lacrosse scar. "In a perfect world, you'd never have experimental drugs. You'd plug data into a computer, and out would come the cure for every disease. In a perfect world, every parent would have the resources for the best medical care. Every autistic child would have one-on-one therapy. But the world's not perfect."

The judge cleared her throat. "Dr. Kranchick, you're not being responsive to the question."

Zinkavich got to his feet so fast, he knocked a

half-eaten cinnamon twist to the floor. "Your Honor, perhaps this is a propitious time for a recess."

Nice move, Fink. Throwing a life preserver to your witness.

"It's a propitious time for you to sit down and clam up," the judge told him.

"Doctors must take risks," Kranchick said, her high forehead beaded with sweat. "Parents should consider the greater good. Sabin gave polio vaccine to prisoners in the 1950s. Some contracted polio, but thousands of children were spared the disease. Same thing with malaria and yellow fever. If it were up to me, all prisoners would be subject to medical tests."

Victoria moved closer to the witness stand. "We're not talking about prisoners. We're talking about an eleven-year-old boy."

"We can learn so much from Robert. Children have duties to society, too." She slipped a hand into a pocket, brought out a lacrosse ball, reached into the other pocket, brought out the second ball. If things heated up any more, Steve figured he should be ready to duck.

"If Solomon weren't so damn selfish, we could have worked something out," Kranchick said. "But he wouldn't hear of it. 'Don't stick needles in little Bobby.' No, he's too precious for that. Stick the needles in someone else. No one wants to take the risk. Everyone just wants the benefits."

Zinkavich fished for an objection, couldn't find one, and said: "Your Honor, could I have a word?"

"Zip it, Z," the judge said.

"I ask you this, Ms. Lord," Kranchick rolled on. "What if a child had rare antibodies in his blood, antibodies that could save lives? Wouldn't there be a duty to give blood? Same thing with Robert. Do you know how rare his condition is? I've never seen a subject like him."

" 'Subject'?" Victoria said. "Like a guinea pig. Like a lab rat."

"That's just semantics. That's what you lawyers do. You sound just like Solomon. Maybe you *should* marry him."

Now both balls were in one hand, banging against each other.

And just who stole the Replengren, Captain Queeg?

"Replengren," Victoria said. "You still haven't answered the question. Do you administer an unapproved drug to the children at Rockland?"

"The FDA could rule at any time. Tomorrow, the next day, the drug could be approved."

"And in the meantime?"

The balls click-clacked against each other. "Where would I even get it?"

One last delay. Fighting to the end, the last defender at the Alamo. And speaking of Mexico . . .

"From Carlos," Victoria said. "From San Blas Medico. Guadalajara, Mexico. Isn't that where you buy the drug?"

Kranchick opened her mouth—a dark, empty cave—but nothing came out.

Judge Rolle cleared her throat. "Doctor, do you understand the question?"

Still nothing.

"Doctor—"

"Yes, goddammit! I use Replengren, and someday they'll thank me for it. Someday they'll call me up to the stage and give me a shiny piece of metal because I had the courage to say the earth was round when all the fools said it was square. I sit with these families. I see the heartbreak, the shattered lives. Does Stephen Solomon give a damn about that?"

"He gives a damn about Bobby," Victoria said.

"You don't get it! He doesn't get it. Those prisoners who took the polio vaccine, the ones who got malaria and yellow fever—they're heroes. Robert could be, too. Most likely with no harm to him at all. He could change thousands of lives. He could be the link we're looking for. That's what I'm after. What's so goddamned wrong with that?"

"What's wrong," Victoria said, "is that you don't get to choose the heroes, Dr. Kranchick. The heroes choose themselves."

Forty-six

LEGAL FICTION

Dr. Wu-Chi Yang's monotone could put the jurors to sleep, Steve thought.

No problem. He'd awaken them later on cross-examination.

Steve was sitting at the defense table, half listening to the ME describe in bloody detail his autopsy of Charles Barksdale. At the same time, Steve was thinking about Bobby's case. Last night, Victoria had been brilliant, melting down Kranchick. But already this morning Zinkavich had launched a counterattack.

On his way into court, Steve had been served with new papers. No longer was the state attempting to place Bobby at Rockland. Now Zinkavich argued that Bobby should be placed in a foster home. The state's written motion listed three foster families with "proven track records in caring for autistic children." Alternatively—lawyers just love alternatives—there was a residential program at Jackson Memorial Hospital that specialized in behavioral therapy. Zinkavich's motion stopped just short of arguing that Bobby would be better off with a roving band of gypsies than living in the bachelor bungalow on Kumquat Avenue.

The son-of-a-bitch wasn't going to roll over and play dead.

When they resumed the guardianship trial tonight, Steve figured he absolutely, positively needed three things to happen.

He had to impress Judge Rolle with his parenting abilities.

Bobby had to stay calm. No freaking out.

Janice had to help him, not Zinkavich.

Steve trusted himself and trusted Bobby. But his sister? He'd paid her the money but still didn't know what she'd do. Not only that, the guilt was getting to him. He tried to rationalize it.

Hey, I'm just paying her to tell the truth.

But that's not the way a Grand Jury would look at it. Or Victoria. He could never tell her.

On the witness stand, Dr. Yang was turning a horrific postmortem procedure into a vanilla milk shake of a lecture. "I made the usual incisions, removed the usual organs," he said, matter-of-factly.

Ray Pincher was taking the ME through the basics, establishing cause of death. In the gallery, a dozen reporters jotted notes. Front row center, Marvin the Maven worked a crossword puzzle, Teresa Toraño surreptitiously fondling his leg beneath the newspaper. Next to them, Cadillac Johnson dozed, sucking at his dentures. At her stenograph machine, Sofia Hernandez clicked away with her aquamarine-lacquered nails.

"I eviscerated and removed the brain, then performed neck dissection." Dr. Yang wore a snazzy blue blazer, a white shirt, and a lemon-yellow paisley bow tie. An old hand on the hot seat, he maintained eye contact with the jury, but there wasn't much he could do about his flat, droning voice.

Victoria, wearing her poker face, took notes. Next to her, Katrina looked pained as the medical examiner described slicing through various organs of her late husband's body. She was following instructions. Steve had told her to sniffle when testimony turned to viscous fluids and gooey tissues. Today she wore basic black. Well, maybe not that basic, a matching flannel jacket and skirt with leather trim and oversize black metal zippers.

On the bench was Judge Hiram Thornberry, a pale, quiet, studious man nearing sixty, with graying hair and a trim mustache. He leaned forward his chair, and appeared to be reading a court file. Steve knew better.

He had appeared before Thornberry a few times but could never quite figure him out. The judge was bright enough but never seemed to be paying complete attention. About a year earlier, Steve solved the puzzle by turning to Sofia, who ratted out her boss. Judge Thornberry was appointed to the Circuit bench while still in his thirties, and now, twenty-five years later, was in the deep doldrums. Ennui to the nth degree. He'd find any excuse to adjourn early and go play golf. Or he'd just retire to chambers with a book and a bottle of brandy. Thoroughly bored with real trials, the judge began to care more about fictional ones. Each day, his judicial assistant would tuck into the court file His Honor's preferred reading. Not the slip opinions of the Third District Court of Appeal. More like Erle Stanley Gardner, John Grisham, or Scott Turow. Or *Mystery Scene Magazine*.

Anything to alleviate the tedium of State of Florida versus X, Y, or Z. Once he learned this, Steve always brushed up on courtroom fiction before trying a case in front of Thornberry.

"I removed and weighed the lungs, then dissected the esophagus off the tracheal bifurcation," Dr. Yang said.

Easy for him to say, Steve thought.

Dr. Yang recounted removing the thyroid gland and the parathyroids, which he said had an attractive café au lait color, reminding Steve that he had missed his second cup of coffee this morning. The ME went on a while about the bruises on the skin of the neck and the rupture of blood vessels on the face, just as he had at the bail hearing. Then there were the bruises on the dissected muscles over the thyroid cartilage and hyoid bone, and small hemorrhages near the cricoid cartilage. He described the leather strap wrapped around Barksdale's neck and other "sexual paraphernalia" in the bedroom. Then he concluded that the cause of death was strangulation by ligature.

Ray Pincher gushed his thank-yous, as if testifying were equivalent to donating a kidney, instead of part of the ME's job. Then Pincher sat down, and Dr. Yang turned his placid face toward Steve Solomon, who got to his feet, buttoned his suit coat, and said, "Let's head a little south of the neck, Doctor."

"South?"

"The stomach."

Dr. Yang didn't flinch, and his hands didn't flutter. Well, what could you expect? The guy had spent fifteen years fending off cagey practitioners of the art of obfuscation.

"Did you examine the stomach?" Steve asked, moving closer to the witness.

"Yes, of course, it's all in here." Dr. Yang gestured with a copy of his report. "Fluids extracted and tested."

"So you must have opened the stomach?"

Dr. Yang fiddled with his bow tie. It wasn't a large gesture. He wasn't sweating or fidgeting or rolling lacrosse balls in his hand. Still, it meant something to Steve, who had questioned the man a dozen times over the years. This was the first nervous tic he'd ever seen from him.

I'm going to nail you.

"Opened the stomach, sure," Dr. Yang said.

"Tell us about it."

Pincher got to his feet. "Objection. Irrelevant."

"How's that?" Appearing irritated, Judge Thornberry tossed down his file. A book flew out, slid across his desk, and was headed for the floor when Steve speared it with one hand like a first baseman grabbing a sinking line drive. He handed the book back to the judge before the jurors could see the title, *The Case of the Sulky Girl.*

"One of my favorite Perry Masons," Steve whispered to the judge.

The judge nodded in agreement but seemed a bit flustered. "State your grounds, Mr. Burger."

"Mr. Burger?" Pincher said.

"Excuse me. Mr. Pincher."

"Charles Barksdale wasn't shot in the stomach," Pincher said. "Charles Barksdale wasn't knifed in the stomach. Charles Barksdale didn't ingest poison. Mr. Solomon is off on a fishing expedition."

"Overruled. I'll allow it."

"I followed the usual routine," Dr. Yang said. "After removing the greater omentum, I cut along the greater curvature of the stomach."

"Take a peek inside?"

"Of course."

"What'd you find?"

"Sushi."

Fishing expedition, indeed, Steve thought. "Sushi?"

"Baby tuna. Crab roll. Ponzu sauce. Last meal about three hours before death, based on decomposition."

"See anything unusual? And I'm not talking about sea urchin."

Dr. Yang's eyes flicked toward Pincher. *Help!* Pincher stayed in his chair, his jaw muscles clenching.

"Everything's in my report," Dr. Yang said.

"Oh, come now, Doctor. Everything's not in your report." Taking a stab at it, just like the ME with his scalpel.

"Objection!" Pincher yelped.

"Again?" The judge sighed and put down his book.

"The question's repetitive," Pincher said. "Asked and answered. Argumentative. And improper predicate."

"That all?" Judge Thornberry said.

Judges were like basketball referees, Steve thought. Some were whistle-blowers, in-your-face activists who jumped on every infraction, no matter how minor. Others just let you play, establish your own limits, create your own rhythms of the game. Judge Thornberry let you play, especially if he was otherwise engaged.

"Improper form, too," Pincher said.

"Overruled," the judge said.

"Everything's in the report," Dr. Yang repeated.

Steve walked to the clerk's table. He picked up the document labeled State Exhibit 3. "This is your report, correct, Dr. Wang?" He waved it like a checkered flag at a NASCAR race.

"My final report, correct."

"Psst." Victoria was trying to get his attention. Steve walked back to the defense table. Victoria's face was flushed, a lioness capturing the scent of the kill. He leaned close enough to feel her breath as she whispered: "Ask him if there's a first draft."

"I'm going to," he whispered back.

"Ask him what was changed between the first and final drafts."

"Gonna do that, too."

"So go. Do it."

"Your Honor, I must protest this starting and stopping of the inquiry," Pincher said. "If the defense has no further questions, the witness should be excused."

"Not so fast," Steve said, turning back to Dr. Yang.

Flipping a page of his novel, the judge grunted at them without looking up. Steve interpreted the sound as: *Keep going, Counselor.* So he moved closer to the witness.

"Dr. Yang, would you reach into your briefcase and give us the first draft of your autopsy report?" Steve said.

"No can do."

"No?"

"We destroy the first drafts when the final drafts are printed out. That way we don't mix them up."

"But surely you have a copy stored in your computer's memory?"

Dr. Yang shook his head. "We overwrite first drafts to keep lawyers like you from picking them apart."

"Why do a second draft at all?"

"Mostly to correct typos. The transcribers misspell medical names, get numbers wrong."

"Who reviewed the first draft of Dr. Barksdale's autopsy?"

"I did."

"Did you show the draft to Mr. Pincher?"

Again, a hand flew to the bow tie, fiddled with the knot. "I think I may have shown the State Attorney. Yes, I believe I did."

"Did Mr. Pincher ask you to change anything?"

"Objection!" Pincher sang out.

"Now what?" Judge Thornberry looked up this time.

"I resent the implication of Mr. Solomon's question," Pincher said.

"This is cross-examination," Steve said. "If the State Attorney didn't resent the implication, I'd be guilty of malpractice."

"Overruled," the judge said.

"I can't recall," Dr. Yang said.

"You can't recall if the State Attorney asked you to change anything in your report?"

"I perform many autopsies," Dr. Yang said. "I talked to Mr. Pincher many times. It's hard to remember everything."

"Of course, there's one way to find out," Steve said with a slight smile. He waited a moment, letting the silence fill the courtroom. "You mentioned a transcriber. You dictated your autopsy report into a tape recorder, didn't you, Dr. Yang?"

The ME's eyes shot to Pincher, then back to Steve. The doc hadn't looked at the jury since Steve stood up. After a long moment, his head bobbed up and down.

"You have to speak audibly so Ms. Hernandez here can take it all down," Steve said, and Sofia gave him a seductive little smile. At the defense table, Victoria rolled her eyes.

"Yes. We make tape recordings."

"And you keep those tapes in a safe in the Records Division of the morgue, don't you?"

"Yes."

Steve turned to the judge. "Your Honor, I request a recess."

The judge seemed startled. "Didn't we already have lunch?"

"Yes, sir, but the state should be made to produce the original tape recording of the autopsy so we can check it against the so-called final report."

"We object," Pincher said. "That tape's confidential."

Victoria, legal eagle, was on her feet. "To the contrary, Your Honor. The tape's covered by Public Records Law."

"This is an untimely request," Pincher said. "Discovery deadlines have passed."

"It's the state's duty to provide all exculpatory evidence, under *Brady v. Maryland,* up to and through the trial," Victoria shot back.

"You're suggesting the tape has exculpatory evidence?" the judge asked. Paying attention now.

"I'm suggesting the State Attorney is guilty of

obstruction of justice," Victoria said, and a ripple of murmurs went through the gallery.

"That's outrageous!" Pincher thundered. "I ask that Counsel be admonished."

Holy shit, Steve thought. Wasn't she the one who said to attack with a rapier, not a sledgehammer?

With a stern look, the judge rapped his gavel and said: "Counsel, in my chambers, now!"

Forty-seven

POETIC JUSTICE

In the corridor, on the way to Judge Thornberry's chambers, Steve whispered: "You keep quiet. I'll take it from here."

"Why?" Her feelings were bruised.

"You were great just now. But this is for the big mojito, so just cheer me on."

"Go, team," she said, peeved.

"C'mon. You know the first rule of arguing to judges?"

"Try to stay out of jail?"

"Know your audience. Play to their interests, fulfill their expectations."

"That's called 'pandering.' "

"Actually, it's called 'lawyering.' "

They settled into leather-upholstered chairs, Pincher scowling at them.

Judge Thornberry said: "The defense has made a serious allegation of prosecutorial misconduct."

"To which I express my outrage," Pincher said.

"And which we'll prove," Steve said.

"Okay, let's get to the bottom of this quick," the judge said. "I want the jury back before they're at one another's throats like in *Twelve Angry Men.*"

"If Your Honor orders the original autopsy tape to be produced," Steve continued, "you'll see how the state altered evidence."

"Keep up the character assassination, I'll sue your ass," Pincher roared.

Troubled, the judge stood and paced in front of a bookshelf, scanning his volumes. Victoria looked, too. Where were the legal books? Just shelves of novels written by lawyers: Turow, Grisham, Scottoline, Martini, Meltzer, Grippando, Latt, Mortimer, Margolin. Dozens more. Victoria wondered if the judge read any law that wasn't fictional.

He reached to a high shelf, fingered a book by Louis Auchincloss, another by Barry Reed, one by Barbara Parker, then pulled down *Kennedy for the Defense* by George V. Higgins. "Are you saying the State Attorney framed Katrina Barksdale?"

"Not intentionally," Steve said. "Mr. Pincher believes my client is guilty."

"You're damn right I do," Pincher said.

"It's Charles Barksdale who framed Katrina Barksdale," Steve said. "The State Attorney only added basil to the bruschetta."

The judge sat down in his high-backed chair. "How'd a dead man frame his wife?"

The judge sounded confused, Victoria thought. Could Steve pull this off?

"Charles Barksdale tells us how," Steve said. "He speaks to us from the grave."

The judge's eyes lit up. "Like Poe."

"Sir?" Steve asked.

"Edgar Allan Poe. *The Tell-Tale Heart.*"

"More like Agatha Christie."

The judge eagerly grabbed a legal pad. "Does it have a double twist? Like *Witness for the Prosecution?*"

"A double twist with a full somersault," Steve assured him.

"Where does the story start?" the judge asked. Eager as a puppy.

"A beautiful young woman marries a rich, older man," Steve said.

"And kills him," Pincher said.

"This is my story, Sugar Ray, not yours. The couple—call them Charlie and Kat—have a very active, very kinky sex life."

"A little sex always spices up the story," the judge said.

"And Charlie really loved her, which is why the next plot point is so painful. He discovers Kat is having an affair with their boat captain."

"Highly cinematic," the judge said, "if they did it on the boat."

Pincher said: "I've got the pictures if you'd like to see them."

"Now comes the conundrum," Steve said, ignoring Pincher.

"Like the missing beer glass in *Presumed Innocent?*" the judge said. "That Turow's a clever fiend."

"Charlie had his lawyer prepare a divorce petition but he never signed it and he never said why. All we have to go on is a three-line poem Charlie wrote on the petition:

'Hide a few contretemps.
Defer a competent wish.
Cement a spit-fed shore.' "

"Odd poem," the judge said.

"It's really an anagram with a message."

"Word games. Arthur Conan Doyle would have loved this."

Now the judge was deep into it, Victoria thought. Okay, so maybe Steve knew his audience. But could he deliver the payoff?

"Unscrambled, the anagram says, 'The woman is perfected,' " Steve continued. "It's from a poem by Sylvia Plath. She committed suicide just a few days after writing it. Then, the day before he dies, Charlie sends a card to Kat. Of all the things he could write— I love you; I hate you; Have a nice day—he steals a line from Virginia Woolf's suicide note."

"I get you," the judge said eagerly, "but just why would Barksdale commit suicide?"

"He was dying of cancer, and there was no time to divorce Katrina and cut her off from his money."

"But suicide doesn't help," the judge said. "The widow would still get her share of the estate."

"Unless—"

"Unless she's convicted of killing him! Outstanding. Perry Mason never came up with anything like this. Not even in *The Case of the Daring Divorcee.*"

"Barksdale wanted Katrina to be charged with his murder. That's why he didn't just take an overdose or drive off a bridge."

"Mr. Solomon has a vivid imagination," Pincher said. "But where's the proof?"

"The anagram," Steve said. "It tells us everything."

Here it comes, Victoria thought. Wrapping it all up in a pretty package. But would the judge buy it?

"When Charles scrambled the line of the Plath poem, he had thousands of choices," Steve said, "but he picked phrases that revealed how he felt about his wife, and what he planned to do. 'Hide a few contretemps.' That's Katrina, keeping her affair secret. 'Defer a competent wish.' That's Charles, wanting revenge, but not being able to live to see it. And 'Cement a spit-fed whore.' That's the biggie. That's Charles sending her to a prison cell, or a tomb, take your pick. That's him framing her for his murder, a murder that never happened."

"Excellent story. The film rights will be worth a bundle. But what's all this got to do with Mr. Pincher and the autopsy report?"

"When Sugar Ray sees the first draft of the autopsy report, he gets a real jolt," Steve answered. "Charles was dying of stomach cancer. No way that's gonna make it into the final draft."

Pincher fixed Steve with a toxic glare.

"Why delete it?" the judge said. "She's still guilty of murder if she strangled him, no matter how sick he was."

"Because—"

"Wait. I figured out *Murder on the Orient Express*. I can get this." The judge took off his glasses, wiped them on his robe, and put them back on. "Give me a clue. Did Charles ever tell Katrina he had cancer?"

"Nope," Steve said. "He died without her knowing."

"Then I've got it! The autopsy would give Katrina a defense. She'd come into court and say she knew Charles was dying all along. Why bump him off if all she had to do was wait a bit and collect her inheritance?"

"Exactly," Steve said. "Sugar Ray assumed she'd lie, and he'd have no way to disprove it."

"I've heard enough," the judge said. "The state will furnish the defense with the original tape recording of the autopsy dictation. I warn you, Mr. Pincher, if Mr. Solomon is correct, I'll make a full report to the Ethics Commission. And the Attorney General's Office."

"This is outrageous!" Pincher said. "We'll appeal."

Victoria cleared her throat and said: "It may not be necessary to produce the tape."

Steve gave her a sharp look but said nothing. She was confident he wouldn't stop her. He'd told her several times about his Sonny Corleone rule: *Never contradict your partner in front of the opposition.*

"Now you don't want the tape?" the judge asked. "Why, Ms. Lord?"

"Because Mr. Pincher is an honorable man. He will do the honorable thing."

"How's that?" the judge asked, bewildered.

"Yeah, this I gotta hear," Steve said.

"Mr. Pincher never would have tampered with the evidence had he believed Katrina Barksdale was innocent," Victoria said. "He thought he was just . . ."

"Adding basil to the bruschetta," the judge said.

"Exactly. Now that Mr. Pincher knows the truth, he can dismiss the case, and there'll be no need for anyone to hear the tape."

Pincher scratched at his chin. "Intriguing suggestion, Counselor."

He's doing the cost-benefit analysis of dumping the case, she thought. And Steve was giving her a sideways glance. He wouldn't do this, she knew. A total advocate, a total warrior, he'd go for the win in front of the jury. She thought there was a safer way to get the same result.

"Wait a second," the judge said. "You can't end a legal thriller by settling a case!"

"It would be best, Your Honor," Victoria said.

"There goes the movie sale," the judge said, sadly.

"I'll need an explanation for the press," Pincher said.

"We have no objection to your taking credit for clearing an innocent woman," Victoria told him.

"Hang on," Steve said. "We should get the credit."

"Steve, the client comes first."

"Since when?"

"Mr. Pincher, give it any spin you want," Victoria said, ignoring Steve, "as long as you dismiss the case against Katrina Barksdale."

"Who made you senior partner?" Steve said. Violating his Sonny Corleone rule.

"I could say that my office has uncovered new evidence," Pincher mused. "Evidence missed by overworked detectives and overlooked by defense counsel."

"Screw that," Steve said. "I didn't overlook anything."

"Quiet, Steve," Victoria said. "Doing justice is credit enough."

"They teach that in the Ivy League?"

"I diligently pursued every lead until justice was

done," Pincher continued, rehearsing his statement to the press.

"Make up your minds, then," the judge said. "Are we going back to trial or not?"

Pincher proclaimed formally: "Judge Thornberry, let's call in the court reporter. The state has an announcement to make."

Forty-eight

MOJITO MAKER

"Go, go, go," Victoria said. "We have an hour to get to Juvie Court."

"I want to talk to the press."

"No way. We'll be late."

She dragged Steve down the corridor. They side-stepped Ray Pincher, who was telling the reporters of his sage and courageous decision to dismiss all charges against Katrina Barksdale.

"Just one little sound bite," Steve pleaded.

"No time."

They shoved their way through the wolf pack of reporters and photographers and hustled to the parking lot.

"You were great today," she said, as they got into his car.

"You, too. Getting Pincher to dismiss. I wouldn't have thought of it."

"And I wouldn't have thought of turning the case into a Perry Mason novel. I've learned a lot from you."

"Ditto." He smiled, forgiving her, she supposed, for taking over at the end.

Twenty minutes later, they were in the bungalow on Kumquat Avenue, where Steve tossed Bobby into the shower, then hastily dressed him in a navy sport coat, gray wool slacks, a white shirt, and a striped tie.

By the time they all piled into the old Caddy, the little preppie's shirttail was out, his glasses were smudged, and his hair was mussed. He sat in the backseat, knees pulled up under his chin, rocking back and forth, looking like the class weirdo genius being carted off to jail for blowing up the science lab.

Steve tuned the radio to the all-news station but punched another button when he heard Pincher saluting himself for uncovering the truth about the death of Charles Barksdale. On the reggae station, Desmond Dekker & the Aces were singing "Israelites," promising a calm after the storm.

Victoria glanced at Bobby and started to worry. He lay on his back, his feet pressed against a window, as if trying to break out of the car. "Maybe we should rethink our strategy for tonight," she said, cryptically.

Translation: I'm scared to death to put Bobby on the witness stand.

"Not your call, cupcake."

"Tell me you didn't just call me 'cupcake.' "

"Don't make some feminist thing out of it. I'm starving, and I'm thinking about the Fink's Krispy Kremes."

She wondered why he couldn't see the danger of having Bobby testify. He knew Bobby always spoke the unvarnished truth. And surely Solomon, of all people, knew that the truth sometimes needs a fresh coat of paint.

"What we're planning could backfire," she said.

"You distract Zinkavich, and I'll go after a couple of glazed crullers."

He's reverted to Irritating Habit Number 396: Ignoring what I say when he doesn't want to deal with it.

She searched for a way to say it was too risky to call Bobby without the boy picking up on it. "Maybe we should reorder our witnesses."

From the backseat, Bobby said: "I'm not scared to talk to the judge."

So much for subterfuge.

"Of course you're not, kiddo," Steve said. "You'll do great." He turned to Victoria. "Bobby testifies. Subject closed."

"You've been telling me to go with my gut, and my gut tells me—"

"Closed."

"Petitioner calls Robert Solomon," Victoria said.

"Objection," Zinkavich said. "The testimony will be tainted by the boy's affinity with his uncle. Not to mention his history of hallucinations."

"We think Your Honor should be the judge of Bobby's competence, not Mr. Zinkavich," Victoria said.

"Does the kid even understand the oath?" Zinkavich asked.

"Do *you*, Fink?" Steve growled, under his breath.

"I heard that, Mr. Solomon," said Judge Althea Rolle, wagging a finger. The judge wore fuchsia robes, a frilly lace rabat at the neck. Her dark eyes were blazing at Steve. "Do you know what we do in Juvie Court when someone acts up?"

"No, ma'am."

"We give them a time-out and they go sit in the corner."

"I apologize to the Court, ma'am."

Meaning, Victoria understood, that he didn't apologize to Zinkavich.

"Now, as for the child's testimony, Ms. Lord, do you really want to do that?"

When a judge asks a leading question, you best head the direction you're being led, Victoria knew. And she agreed with the judge. You never knew when Bobby was going to slip into a screaming fit or burst out that "President Clinton of the USA" can be rearranged to spell, "TO COPULATE HE FINDS INTERNS."

"We believe there can be no better witness than the one most directly affected by this proceeding," Victoria answered. She didn't believe it, but sometimes you do what your client wants, especially when your client is a know-it-all lawyer.

"Here's how it's gonna be," Judge Rolle said. "I'll talk to the boy alone in my chambers. Counsel will sit in the anteroom and listen on the speakers. No coaching from Mr. Solomon and no cross-exam from Mr. Zinkavich. Now, skedaddle, all of you."

Steve paced in front of a set of bookshelves, claustrophobic in the small anteroom. Victoria sat rigidly at a worktable, fingers clutching a pen, poised to take notes. Zinkavich slumped in a cushioned chair, his love handles overflowing the armrests.

"*Would you like something to drink?*" Judge Rolle asked, her voice tinny over the speaker.

"Nope. Uncle Steve made me a papaya smoothie for the ride over." Bobby's voice was high and nervous.

"Sounds healthy."

"Makes me poop," Bobby said.

"Uh-huh."

"Sometimes we get the papayas from the fruit stand on Red Road."

"They have wonderful produce," the judge said.

"Sometimes Uncle Steve just steals them from a neighbor's trees."

"I see."

Yikes. Steve stopped pacing. If he were a smoker, he would light up about now.

"Do you do spend a lot of time with your uncle?" the judge asked.

"Like 24/7," Bobby said. "Except when he, you know . . ."

"When he goes out on dates?"

"Uncle Steve doesn't go on dates. He just has chicks come over, hang out in his bedroom, then split."

"Oh, shit," Steve groaned.

"Do any women ever spend the night?"

"If they've had too many mojitos," Bobby said.

"So I guess your uncle makes more than papaya smoothies," the judge said, a note of sarcasm in her voice.

"I make the mojitos." Bobby said it proudly. "The secret's squeezing fresh guarapo. Sugarcane juice. But not too much, because the rum is already sweet. And the mint leaves gotta be fresh."

Zinkavich said: "We reap what we sow, Solomon."

"Aw, shut up," Steve said.

Over the speaker, the judge said: *"Does it bother you when women sleep over?"*

"No way," Bobby said. *"Sometimes I get to see bare boobs in the morning."*

Steve's throat felt constricted. He doubted he could swallow, wondered if he could even take a breath. He was pretty sure he heard the judge's pen scratching across a notepad.

"And Sofia makes huevos rancheros," the boy continued. *"But Lexy and Rexy don't really cook. They're models, and they eat like a slice of grapefruit and a thimble of yogurt."*

"Models," the judge said, disapproval in her voice. *"Does your uncle see either Lexy or Rexy now?"*

"Not anymore," Bobby said.

Steve felt relieved enough to exhale.

"Used to be, he'd do them both at once."

"Oh, shi-i-i-i-i-t!" Steve wailed.

"They're twins," Bobby explained, helpfully.

Steve whimpered and Zinkavich barked a laugh.

"Quiet, both of you!" Victoria flashed an angry look.

Steve said: "That stuff's ancient history, Vic. Six months ago, at least."

"Please. I'm trying to listen," she said.

Bobby was saying something, and they'd missed part of it.

". . . been a while since Uncle Steve got any trim."

"Trim?"

"You know. Some play. Booty in the bone shack."

"So, no more booty?"

"Lexy, Rexy, Sofia, Gina. They haven't come over since Uncle Steve fell totally in love with Victoria."

"Ms. Lord? His ex-fiancée?"

"Oh, that wasn't real."

"Excuse me?" the judge said, puzzled.

"Being engaged. That was just pretending."

"Whatever for?"

"Uncle Steve didn't want to lose me, and he thought Victoria made him seem more mature."

"I see."

"Not that he wouldn't like to marry her for real."

In the anteroom, Zinkavich laughed so hard, spittle dribbled from the corner of his mouth.

"So now only Ms. Lord comes to the house?" Judge Rolle asked.

"Just to work, not to do Uncle Steve. She's gonna marry this other guy, and Uncle Steve is totally bummed."

God, this was humiliating, Steve thought. Why had no one ever invented a pill that could make you invisible?

"This isn't a court case, it's a soap opera," Zinkavich said.

The judge said: *"Tell me about your homeschooling."*

Yes, tell her, Steve thought. They'd rehearsed this.

"I'm reading the Aeneid *in Latin. Virgil's pretty cool."*

Perfect. Way to go, kiddo.

"And The Iliad in Greek. The battle scenes are totally awesome. Better than that stupid movie Troy."

"That's very impressive," the judge said. *"Did your uncle give you those books?"*

"Yep, plus the fiftieth anniversary edition of Playboy."

Aargh. One step forward, two steps back, Steve thought.

"I thought Stella Stevens was really hot. But she didn't show any cooch."

In the anteroom, Steve banged his head against the bookshelves, knocking a dusty volume of *Corpus Juris Secundum* to the floor. Over the speaker, Judge Rolle seemed to sigh, then said: *"Tell me what you do for fun, Bobby."*

"I play Little League, but I suck bad. Uncle Steve says it doesn't matter, but some kids are mean to me. Once I dropped a fly ball, and one of the dads yells, 'Get that spaz out of there.' "

"That must have hurt your feelings."

"Then I let a ball roll between my legs, and the same guy yells I should be in the Special Olympics."

"Oh, my," the judge said.

"Uncle Steve told the guy to quit talking smack, but he wouldn't. He was, like, humongous, with a fat head, and Uncle Steve yells at him: 'Hey, big mouth, what position did you play, backstop?' And everybody starts laughing, so the guy comes after my uncle, who starts running backwards, and the guy can't catch him. Uncle Steve's saying, 'You're so ugly your first name should be Damn,' and the guy keeps chasing and Uncle Steve keeps backpedaling and says, "If your ass had eyes, you still couldn't see shit.' And the game's stopped because they're on the field and the big guy's swinging at Uncle Steve but missing, and finally the guy stops, out of breath, all red-faced, and bends over and hurls chunks. Right on first base."

"Must have been quite an experience," the judge breathed.

"Later, Uncle Steve told me some people say nasty

things because they're stupid and some because they're mean, and not to let it bother me, because I'm special in a good way."

"I think your uncle's right," the judge said.

"And he said if you're really mad at somebody, beat them with your brains, not your fists."

"You really like your uncle Steve, don't you, Bobby?"

"He's awesome," the boy said.

"How about Victoria?"

"I wish she was my mom."

There was a long pause. Steve wished he could see the judge's face, wanted to know what she was thinking. He glanced at Victoria. She blinked several times, her eyelashes flicking away tears like silver drops of dew.

Forty-nine

MY BIG, FAT STUPID MISTAKE

"I think we recovered nicely at the end," Steve said. Trying to show confidence, knowing Victoria was furious with him.

She shook her head. "Bobby loves you. You love him. But that's not enough to win."

"You're leaving something out. He loves you, too."

"Stop it, Steve. Just stop it. You promised. No more personal stuff."

"You're the one who started crying in there."

"Tears aren't enough to win, either."

They were outside the judge's chambers, taking a thirty-minute dinner recess. A nearby restaurant had delivered sweet fried plantains, chewy palomilla steak, black beans and rice, and enough espresso to keep everybody awake for a week. Bobby was in the judge's chambers, eating with Judge Rolle. Zinkavich was stuffing his face in the anteroom, and Steve and Victoria, famished but too embroiled to eat, were jawing in the corridor.

"I should have gone with my gut, not yours," she said.

"Okay."

"No matter how much he loves you, Bobby made you seem reckless."

"Okay."

"Undisciplined."

"Got it."

"Immature."

"I admit it. I screwed up."

"Like *you're* the one who needs a caregiver."

Why wouldn't she let up? He felt like a marlin attacked by a shark. First a ferocious strike, then the rip of flesh from bone, and finally a quick swallow. Followed by another strike, rip, swallow.

"Enough, already," he said. "From now on, you run the case. I won't interfere."

That stopped her for a moment. "All right. Deal."

Thank God, he thought, he'd finally found a way to quiet her down. "Great. Now let's go over my testimony."

She frowned. "I'm not putting you on the stand."

"What!"

"I'm can't let you be crossed about the night you snatched Bobby."

"I can handle it."

"Only if you admit to a bunch of felonies."

"I'll take the Fifth."

"That'll impress the judge."

"If I don't testify, who will?"

"At your service," announced the suntanned, older man walking toward them. He wore a beige linen suit, and his white hair flowed down the back of his neck. He carried a Panama hat in one hand, an unlit cigar in the other. "How the hell are you, son?" Herbert Solomon said.

"Dad?" Steve was so shocked that for a moment he was disoriented. His father striding down a courthouse corridor? Like he was still a judge, on his way to take the bench. "What are you doing here?"

"Didn't Victoria tell you?" Herbert Solomon said. "Ah'm your star witness."

Steve's shock was turning to anger. What chutzpah. Calling his old man without even asking him. "She must have wanted to surprise me," Steve said, biting off the words.

"Well, ah'm here to help."

"Too late for that."

"C'mon, son. Until all the corn's out of the crib, there's still time."

"Thanks, anyway, but I don't need your help."

"Yes you do," Victoria interposed. "Unlike you, there's nothing your father can be crossed on."

"Really? How about resigning from the bench in disgrace?"

"Judge Rolle already knows about that. Were you listening yesterday? She idolizes your father."

"Ah remember Althea when she was just a pup," Herbert reminisced. "These insurance lawyers were picking on her, and ah—"

"Yeah, yeah, we heard," Steve said. "You're the great white father."

"After every trial, Althea would come back to chambers, ask me why ah did this and that, why ah ruled one way or the other. Always wanting to learn, that little girl. Like to think of her as one of mah protégés."

"You were always so good with strangers." Steve's words were as hard as marbles.

"Don't talk to your father that way," Victoria said.

"Who gave you the right to run my case?"

"You did."

"It was a mistake."

"Then we've both made mistakes lately, haven't we?"

"If you think that," he said, "you're lying to yourself."

"No. I'm finally thinking clearly."

"Our making love was not a mistake."

"What the hell did ah wander into?" Herbert said.

"It was for me," Victoria told Steve. "A big, fat, stupid mistake."

"Bigby, the wedding, real estate closings. Those are your mistakes," Steve told her.

"Y'all are showing way too much of yourselves," Herbert said. "When you go skinny-dipping, you oughta keep close to the willows when you come out."

"I *love* Bruce! I can't wait to marry him. And I'm dying to get out of the courtroom."

"Ah think ah'll head *into* the courtroom," Herbert said, walking away.

"Maybe you *want* to love him," Steve told Victoria. "Maybe you *wish* you loved him. But you *don't* love him!"

"I do!"

"Then what were you doing the other night with me?"

"I don't know!"

"Maybe you better figure that out. Preferably before your honeymoon."

Steve followed his father through the courtroom door.

———

Victoria paced alone in the corridor, hopelessly confused. She thought she'd put all of this to rest.

I used logic and reason, and I chose Bruce.

It made sense. Dealing with Bruce was easy. Comfortable. The way it should be. A mate isn't a sparring partner, right? Dealing with Solomon was impossible. A constant tug-of-war. So why did he still have the power to rattle her?

"There you are!"

Victoria turned to find Bruce striding toward her, carrying a briefcase in one hand and a picnic basket in the other. He was wearing a camel sport coat and dark brown wool slacks and looked like an adorable teddy bear. "Thought you might be hungry, sweetie."

"Hon!" Victoria said. "So thoughtful of you."

He brush-kissed her and opened the basket.

"God, I'm happy to see you." She ran a hand over the luxurious fabric of his coat. It was a sign, she decided, Bruce showing up like this. Confirmation that her choice had been right all along.

"Were you and Solomon arguing again?" he asked.

"The man's exasperating."

"I know, sweetie. I know." He was pulling plastic containers from the basket. "Cucumber avocado soup, bean sprout sandwich with tomato and avocado, and avocado sorbet. You'll feel better after some supper."

Victoria felt her stomach growling but knew she'd break out in splotches after one bite. "Thanks, hon, but I really have to get back into court. It was just so sweet of you to come all the way over here."

"The least I could do."

Her mind drifted to Solomon, the sandwich man. Maybe he'd bring her a mouthwatering prosciutto and ricotta *panino*, but it would grow cold while they squabbled about something or other. Wasn't that the warp and woof of their relationship?

"You look so tired, sweetie," Bruce said.

Startled, Victoria put a hand to her face. "Are my eyes puffy?"

"You just need some sleep."

"Oh." She told herself she appreciated his honesty.

"I hope you can get some rest before the wedding. You don't want to look all haggard in the photo album."

Haggard? On the other hand, honesty is sometimes an overrated quality.

"It's no wonder you're so bushed, having to deal with Solomon day and night."

"That must be it."

"Well, he won't be around aggravating you for long, sweetie." Bigby slipped a file out of his briefcase and handed it to her.

"What's this, Bruce?"

"You've been so busy, I've had to do all the heavy lifting. Menus, seating charts, music selections, honeymoon itinerary. Plus some papers the lawyers want signed."

The words "papers" and "lawyers" struck a somewhat different chord than "menus" and "honeymoon," she thought.

"What papers?"

"Why, the prenuptial agreement, of course," Bruce Bigby said.

———

"Do my eyes deceive me, or is that the Honorable Herbert T. Solomon?" Judge Althea Rolle said. "Even more distinguished and handsome than I recalled."

"Kind of you to say so," Herbert drawled, bowing slightly. "Pleasure to be here, Your Honor." *Yo Ah-nuh.*

"Where you been keeping yourself, Judge?"

Zinkavich cleared his throat, the sound of a growling dog. "Your Honor, I object to your calling the witness 'Judge.' "

"That so?" Judge Rolle said.

"The title is not appropriate for a jurist expelled from the bench. Further, I question the propriety of Ms. Lord even presenting *Mister* Solomon as a witness."

"You do?"

"It's an obvious attempt to curry Your Honor's favor. There are two kinds of lawyers: those who know the law, and those who know the judge."

"No, Z, there's a third kind. Those who don't know shit even when they've stepped in it. *Judge* Solomon is the most decent fellow ever to sit in the Eleventh Judicial Circuit and I'm gonna call him anything I want, and then I'm gonna listen to what he has to say."

"Yes, ma'am," Zinkavich said, meekly.

"And if I come down off the bench and give him a hug and a kiss, you're gonna keep that garbage dump of yours shut. Are we clear?"

"Crystal, ma'am," Zinkavich said.

With a sweet smile, Judge Rolle turned to the witness. "Now, Judge Solomon, what have you been up to?"

"Some fishing, some reading, a lot of thinking," Herbert said.

"Well, it agrees with you. Now, it would give me great pleasure to administer the oath to you myself."

As Herbert Solomon swore to tell the truth, Victoria wondered who was more upset by his presence, Zinkavich or her pouting partner. Solomon had turned away from her in his chair, sitting corkscrew style, sulking. The big baby.

She was confident in her decision to call Herbert Solomon to testify. Strictly speaking, the ex-judge had little relevant information. But when she'd spoken to him on the phone, he'd revealed a deep respect for Steve and how he was nurturing Bobby. This was something worth conveying to the judge.

Hey, Solomon, I'm just following your instructions. "Know your audience."

While thinking these thoughts, she forced herself to compartmentalize. She hadn't even looked at Bruce's seating charts, his musical selections . . . or his prenuptial agreement. What a nice little wedding surprise that was. All things considered, she would have preferred a heart-shaped, diamond-studded pendant.

"Ms. Lord," the judge said.

"Yes, Your Honor?" Victoria responded.

"It's customary at this stage of the proceedings for the lawyer who calls a witness to ask a question or two."

"Sorry, Judge." Victoria got to her feet. "Please state your name and occupation for the record, sir."

"Herbert Solomon. Recovering lawyer." *Re-koven loy-yuh.*

That drew a chuckle from the judge, a scowl from Steve, and a little snort from Zinkavich.

Victoria needed the father to paint a portrait of his son. *Who is this man?* So she asked her questions, and Herbert told his stories, the mellifluous flow of his Savannah drawl as pleasant as a burbling brook.

Herbert talked about Steve and young Janice growing up in the old, rambling house on Pinetree Drive on Miami Beach. He credited Steve's mother, Eleanor, "God rest her soul," for keeping the family together while he was busting his tail as a lawyer, making his name with pro bono work, then on to the bench, eventually becoming chief judge of the circuit, and the first name on the governor's short list for appointment to the Florida Supreme Court.

"That's when my troubles began," Herbert said, "but we're not here to talk about me, except as it relates to Stephen."

He said he regretted all the missed opportunities to spend time with both his children when they were young. Janice took some wrong turns early, running with a bad crowd, using drugs, while Stephen was a jock at Beach High.

"Ah was too in love with mah own ambitions to pay mah children much mind," Herbert said. "Eleanor was sick for years, and there was only so much she could do. The kids grew up pretty much on their own. Ah remember one time ah rushed from court to Tropical Park for the state track meet. Got there too late, just missed Stephen winning the hundred meters. Ah hustled into the stands, and one of the bailiffs from downtown stopped me and said, 'Judge, you must have some of them Negro Israelites in your blood, 'cause white boys don't run like that.'

Later, ah told Stephen how ah watched him win, but he knew ah was fibbing."

"Your Honor." Zinkavich was on his feet. "This is heartwarming, but I object on grounds of relevance."

"Sit down," the judge ordered.

"When Stephen was in college, he started asking me questions about lawyering," Herbert continued. "Just scratching and pecking, not saying what he meant. Eleanor was dying and ah was about to be indicted on false testimony. Ah didn't have the heart to fight, so ah quit the bench and resigned the Bar in return for them dropping the investigation. Stephen was tore up, maybe more than me. That boy never told me straight-out, but ah know the reason he went to law school was to clear mah name. He wanted to ride into court on a big ole white horse, prove ah was innocent. When ah wouldn't let him do it, he got angry at me, too."

Steve squirmed in his chair, Victoria sneaking a peek at him. Painful memories were etched on his face.

"Stephen's got this deep resentment of injustice. Maybe he doesn't always follow every little rule the fat cats come up with, but on things that matter, mah son's got integrity. His principles are more important to him than money. And he's a fine role model for mah grandson."

There was a catch in his throat as he continued. "A man can't help but compare himself to his own son. Me? Ah was caught up in mah own inflated self-importance. Lawyer of the Year? Like being the best rattlesnake in the Okefenokee."

"Don't be so hard on yourself," Judge Rolle said. "You were widely admired. Still are, in my circle."

"Ah'd lost mah way, Althea," Herbert confided, dropping the formalities. "Ah never missed a Bar convention or a Chamber luncheon, and ah'd hang out at the Judiciary receptions till the last shrimp was gone from the bowl. Lord, how ah loved the applause, the slaps on the back, even those damn fool plaques they give you with the little gavels. Stephen doesn't give a rat's *tuchis* about those things. He'd rather spend time with a boy who needs him."

Herbert Solomon turned in the witness chair and looked at Steve head-on. "Mah point is simply this: Ah admire Stephen so much for the man he's become. He puts Bobby first. Before his social life, before his career, before everything. Maybe ah was the better lawyer, but Stephen's the better man."

It was an involuntary movement, what Victoria did then. Placing her hand on top of Steve's, letting her fingers lace through his. He tightened his hand into a fist, pulling Victoria's fingers tight between his, and they remained that way a long moment, his hand warm and firm beneath hers, the two hands wound so closely together as to nearly be one.

Fifty

BASEBALL AND BRIBERY

Steve carried the sleeping Bobby to the car, Herbert walking alongside. Victoria hung back a few steps, giving father and son a moment of privacy.

"You could stay with us tonight, not drive so far," Steve said.

Herbert shook his head. "Ah'm a creature of habit. Need mah hammock on the back porch, mah laughing gulls singing to me."

"What are you doing this weekend?"

"Not a damn thing. You teach Bobby to fish yet?"

"Thought that was your department, Dad."

"Y'all come down to Sugarloaf Saturday, we'll chase the wily bonefish."

"We'd like that."

Victoria listened, realizing this strange, coded conversation was the male dance around edges of emotion. Steve was saying thank you, and Herbert was saying he wanted a closer relationship. Underneath it all, she supposed, father and son were each saying: *"I love you."*

Finally, Herbert reached over and tousled Steve's hair, just as Steve did so often with Bobby. Then

Paul Levine

Herbert got into his rusty Chrysler and pulled out of the parking lot.

Minutes later, Steve was guiding the old Caddy convertible off the Miami Avenue exit of I-95. Bobby was asleep in the backseat. As they neared Victoria's condo, Steve said: "The way I acted when Dad came in . . ."

"Yeah?"

"I was a real horse's ass, to use one of his expressions."

Which she took to mean he was sorry.

"You really turned the case around," he continued.

A thank-you, she translated. "All I did was call your father. He's the one who turned it around."

"It was good lawyering, Vic. Really good."

They sat quietly another moment before she said: "I need your help with Thigpen and your sister."

"Just wing it."

She looked over at him. The lights from the Brickell Avenue condos shadowed his face. What was he thinking?

"*You* might be able to wing it," she said, "but I need to prepare for cross."

"You'll be fine." He turned the Caddy into the driveway of her building, pulled to a stop under the portico. "See you tomorrow, Vic."

"Hey, you."

"What?"

"We won a murder trial today." Wanting to talk. Not wanting the night to end.

"How's it feel?"

She shrugged. "I don't know. I'm exhausted, emotionally drained. And . . ."

"A little let down?"

"Yeah."

"It's always that way. If you win, the high's not high enough. If you lose, the low is lower than you thought possible."

"We should celebrate." Even as she said it, something struck a dissonant note.

Celebrate how? Just the two of us? Invite Bruce? That didn't sound like much fun.

"Sure thing," Steve said.

"Katrina says she'll have a check for us by Friday. A big one."

"Great."

But he didn't sound great, Victoria thought. "Just what you wanted, Steve. A case to put you in the big leagues."

"Yep."

Since when did he become Mr. Monosyllabic?

"And I almost forgot, Katrina's planning a victory party," Victoria said. "Everyone's supposed to dress as cops and convicts."

"You can be the cop."

"Actually, I'll be away. On . . ."

"Your honeymoon."

"Maui."

"Nice."

"Bruce says they have some avocado-growing techniques he'd like to study."

"A tax-deductible honeymoon. The Bigster is one savvy fellow."

That seemed to drain the juice from the conversation. She wanted to ask him to come up, share some tequila, relive their victories. But Bobby was snoozing in the backseat, and it was late, and—an ever bigger reason—this was not the man whose ring she was wearing. Not the man to whom she was betrothed, the man she'd soon promise to love and to cherish till death did them part . . . and the man whose prenuptial agreement she needed to read before morning.

Steve drove home wishing she had asked him to come in for a while. He could have carried Bobby upstairs and put him on the sofa—the kid could sleep in a bowling alley. Steve wanted to talk to Victoria. Not about the two of them. He'd come to accept the fact that she was gone. No, he wanted to talk about what was gnawing at him like rats in the basement. At first, he had vowed never to tell her that he had bribed Janice to flip her testimony in the guardianship case. Now, guilt-stricken, he felt a need to confess. But how could he?

She wouldn't understand. He barely did himself. Why had he paid off his sister? Did he have so little confidence in the system? Or in Victoria? Or in himself? They were winning Bobby's case without cheating. He should have just let it play out. He'd cut corners before, but never anything like this.

An hour ago, Steve had listened as his father spoke so proudly.

"My son's got integrity."

What would his father say if he knew about the bribe? Steve would never be able to face him if the truth came out.

"He's a fine role model for my grandson."

Right, I teach him baseball and bribery, Steve thought. And what about Bobby's testimony? So strange, seeing his life through his nephew's eyes.

Models and mojitos. God, was he really that shallow and immature?

Dark thoughts were swirling in his mind. By the time he swung the car past the Cocowalk shops for the drive down Grand Avenue, the doubts had morphed into borderline paranoia.

What if Janice is setting me up?

She could have been wearing a wire when he gave her the money, their cars parked side by side on the Rickenbacker Causeway. Maybe Pincher and Zinkavich had him under surveillance. Had there been a white van with darkened windows pulled under the trees near the first bridge? He couldn't remember.

When Steve turned onto Kumquat Avenue just before midnight, with a mockingbird hooting in a neighbor's tree, he was certain that disaster would strike tomorrow. A phalanx of police officers would storm the courtroom. He would be led away in handcuffs as Zinkavich gobbled Krispy Kremes and Pincher cackled with laughter.

What was it Pincher had said to him in Judge Gridley's chambers the day of the bird trial? *"I'll have the Florida Bar punch your ticket."*

Yes, of course, they'd set him up. Pincher and Zinkavich must have arranged to snatch Bobby off the street. The whole stinking thing was a setup to entrap him.

He would lose his license.

He'd go to jail.

But worst of all, he'd lose Bobby.

BARKSDALE WIDOW GOES FREE
Suicide, Not Murder, Pincher Delcares

By Joan Fleischman
Herald *Staff Writer*

In a stunning courtroom reversal, murder charges were dismissed yesterday against Katrina Barksdale, the widow accused of strangling her husband, construction magnate Charles Barksdale.

Following a closed-door hearing, State Attorney Raymond Pincher announced in open court that he was dismissing all charges. "The due diligence of my office has uncovered irrefutable proof that Charles Barksdale's death resulted from suicide, not homicide," Pincher said.

Posing for photos on the courthouse steps, Mrs. Barksdale, 33, said she might write a book about her ordeal, but not until she celebrated with a trip to the Bahamas. "That's the way my husband would have wanted it," said the widow. "He was a good-time Charlie, not a gloomy Gus."

At a posttrial press conference, Pincher shrugged off suggestions that his office acted too hastily in securing a murder indictment against Mrs. Barksdale. "Had defense counsel done their job, the case never would have gotten this far," Pincher said. "Because of our tireless efforts, justice has been served."

Defense lawyers Stephen Solomon and Victoria Lord rushed from the courtroom and could not be reached for comment.

Fifty-one

THE HUNDRED-THOUSAND-
DOLLAR QUESTION

His milky gray complexion tinged with pink spots like a poisoned oyster, Jack Zinkavich said: "We have a serious crisis, Judge."

"Is there any other kind?" Judge Althea Rolle said.

Steve sat quietly at the Petitioner's table, letting the little drama play out. Next to him, Victoria watched, notepad in hand.

"What now?" the judge said. She wore baby blue robes, the collar of a white silk blouse visible at the neck. It was just after nine A.M. With the Barksdale case over, they were back on a normal schedule.

"Rufus Thigpen, our first witness, is missing," Zinkavich said.

"Then call your second witness."

"But, Judge, that interrupts my order of proof."

"Don't be so anal, Z."

"I am concerned there may be foul play afoot."

Foul play afoot? Steve thought.

Like Sherlock-fucking-Holmes.

"How so?" the judge asked.

Zinkavich shot a look at Steve, who instantly put

on his angelic Bar Mitzvah boy face. Victoria cast a sideways glance at him, too.

Does she suspect something? Or is it just my guilty conscience?

Victoria seemed tired, he thought, her eyes bloodshot, her hair not quite up to its usual standards. Sleepless night? Not sharing her bed, he didn't know. The fatigue—if that's what it was—softened her edges, made her more vulnerable, and, if possible, even more desirable. She was wearing a brown double-breasted pinstripe jacket with a wide collar and a matching below-the-knee skirt. To Steve, it had an expensive, handmade by nuns in the Swiss Alps look.

Zinkavich said: "I call upon the Petitioner to disclose if he knows the whereabouts of Mr. Rufus Thigpen."

Steve kept quiet. He had a lawyer to take the heat.

"Judging from Mr. Thigpen's rap sheet," Victoria said, "he's probably in jail somewhere."

Yes! Exactly what he would have said, Steve thought, if he were counsel instead of a litigant. He was proud of Victoria. She'd come so far so quickly.

"Just call a witness, Z, so we can move this along," the judge said.

Zinkavich frowned. "In that event, Your Honor, the state calls Janice Solomon."

Hearing his sister's name sent creepy crawlies up Steve's spine. Thigpen's disappearance was part of the bargain, part of what he'd paid for. But Janice could still double-cross him on the witness stand.

His sister frumped her way into the courtroom, avoiding Steve's gaze. She wore a shapeless print dress that stopped just above her ankles and white socks with sandals. She carried a soft leather purse big enough to hold twenty kilos of hash. Her hair was pulled back into a ponytail and was held in place by a psychedelic orange scrunchy. Behind her granny glasses, her dark eyes seemed distant, as if focused on a place her body had left but her mind had lingered. The overall impression, Steve thought, was of a woman who ate too many Cheetos and drank too many Cokes, between bouts of inhaling, injecting, and smoking an array of exotic substances.

After Janice was sworn in, Zinkavich took her through the preliminaries. She was Steve Solomon's sister, two years older. Grew up on Miami Beach, expelled from high school for repeated drug use, attended a combination school-and-dairy-farm for troubled kids in rural Pennsylvania. Tossed out for growing marijuana in an alfalfa field and running a semipro brothel in the barn. Arrested a dozen times for drugs, larceny, and disorderly conduct, plus once for criminal mischief when she squatted on the roof of a police cruiser and peed on the windshield. She didn't really know who fathered Bobby. It could have been this crackhead in Ocala who used to beat the shit out of her. Or this trucker who gave her a lift to Pensacola in return for spreading her legs at a rest stop just off the Loxley exit of the I-10.

Hanging out all the dirty laundry on direct examination. It was the only way to keep your opponent from smearing your witness on cross, Steve knew. Though he was a pompous prick with a vicious mean streak, Zinkavich was not stupid, and so far, he was doing everything right.

Steve stole a glance at Victoria. Ordinarily poker-faced in the courtroom—just as he'd taught her—she seemed both astonished and disgusted at his sister's life story. Judge Rolle never blinked. The judge had heard far worse, Steve figured. But at the same time, he wondered whether some maternity-ward nurse had screwed up thirty-seven years ago. Maybe his real sister was a distinguished researcher with a PhD, working in a lab somewhere, on the verge of curing cancer.

Zinkavich waddled close to the witness stand. "What facilitated your appearance here today?"

"You facilitated my butt out of jail," Janice replied.

"Did I make any promises to you in return for your testimony?"

"You said you could get me time served and early parole."

"On what condition?"

"If I told the truth," Janice said.

Steve tried to relax but could not. Any second, she could torpedo him.

Zinkavich pointed a chubby finger at him: "Does your brother, Stephen Solomon, have a history of violence?"

"A long history," Janice said.

Oh, shit. Here it comes.

She had taken his money. Now she was going to bury him with it.

"Please elaborate, Ms. Solomon," Zinkavich said.

"When I was fourteen, Arnie Lipschitz called me a 'fat whore,' and Stevie kicked the living piss out of him."

"Not quite what I meant."

"I wasn't fat then."

"Forget Arnie Lipschitz. Did your brother ever strike you?"

"He wouldn't have the balls."

Zinkavich seemed surprised. "He never beat you up?"

"I've carried a blade since I was twelve. I woulda circumcised him a second time."

Zinkavich stared a long moment at Janice. This couldn't have been the way they had practiced it. Steve eased out a breath, but just a bit. With Janice, you never knew when the blade would come out.

"What about drug use?" Zinkavich asked. "Did you ever see your brother use illicit drugs?"

"Yeah, sure."

Zinkavich smiled. Back on script. "When was that?"

"About the same time as the deal with Lipschitz. I gave Stevie some pot, and afterward he ate like half a gallon of pistachio ice cream and threw his guts up."

"Anything more recent?"

"Nah. That cured him. He never even smoked a cigarette after that."

Zinkavich's tongue flicked over his upper lip. Something had happened between rehearsal and opening night. "Drawing your attention to last January, Ms. Solomon, were you living on a farm in the Panhandle?"

"A farm?" Her smile displayed stained teeth. "Yeah, me and my friends were growing a cash crop there."

"Did there come a time when your brother removed your son from your care and custody?"

"You mean, did Stevie take Bobby? Yeah."

"And did your brother do so by force and violence?"

Janice shrugged, her fleshy chin jiggling. "I was like totally wasted that night."

Though his feet were planted on the floor, Zinkavich swayed back and forth, like a rabbi praying at the Wailing Wall. "Come now, Ms. Solomon. Are you saying you don't remember that night?"

"I remember it was sleeting that day, froze my ass off."

"And that night, what happened when your brother showed up?"

"I don't know, man. I was in the house doing Ecstasy. You'll have to ask Rufe."

"That would be Rufus Thigpen?"

"Yeah, Rufus the Doofus."

"Where is Mr. Thigpen today?"

"I think he went up to Delray to score some Special K. You know, ketamine."

Zinkavich forced a smile, as if all state witnesses skip court to indulge in illegal activities. "What did Mr. Thigpen tell you about his encounter with your brother that fateful night?"

"Objection, hearsay," Victoria said.

"Sustained," the judge said.

"Your Honor, if I could voir dire the witness," Zinkavich said, "I believe the evidence can come in under the excited utterance exception."

"Knock yourself out," the judge said.

"Ms. Solomon, without telling us what Mr. Thigpen said, what was his condition when you spoke to him that night?"

"Rufe's skull was split open."

"Aha," Zinkavich said. An opening.

"Hasn't made him any smarter, I can tell you that," she continued.

"And you saw Mr. Thigpen in this injured state after his encounter with your brother?"

"Yeah."

"Did Mr. Thigpen speak to you?"

"Yeah."

"And when he spoke, was he excited, agitated, or angry?"

"He was pissed."

"Did he raise his voice?"

"As much as he could. He was bleeding like a stuck pig."

Zinkavich turned toward the judge. "I believe we've met the threshold for the excited utterance exception to the hearsay rule."

Victoria started to object, but Steve placed a hand on her arm. "Let it go," he whispered.

"Why?"

Steve gave her his innocent shrug, but she looked at him with cold suspicion.

"Hearing no objection," Judge Rolle said, "I assume the Petitioner is as curious as the Court to hear the next exchange. Proceed."

Zinkavich lowered his voice into what he must have considered his profound tone. "Just what did Mr. Thigpen say to you, as he lay there, bleeding like a stuck pig?"

"Rufe looked up at me and said, 'You stupid cunt. You locked the kid in the dog cage but never padlocked the shed.' "

Zinkavich's mouth dropped open wide enough to inhale a Krispy Kreme. Judge Rolle cocked her head toward Janice as if listening a second time to something she didn't believe she'd heard the first time. The only sound in the courtroom was the whir of the ventilation system.

No one moved.

Not Victoria.

Or Zinkavich.

Or Judge Rolle.

Steve shot glances at each of them. People with their own lives. Bills to pay, cars to service, doctors to visit. The whole mundane routine of daily life. But in this moment—frozen in time, like a fossil preserved in amber—their minds focused on the same image. An image, he was sure, that would come back to them, as it had to him, time and again.

An innocent child locked in a dog cage in a shed.

Finally, the judge said: "You say there was sleet that day?"

"Turned the yard into a skating rink," Janice said.

The judge chewed on the eraser of her pencil. "How was your son dressed?"

"Underpants and a sweatshirt. I guess." When the judge stared hard at her, Janice added: "I was pretty messed up those days."

"That shed have any heat?"

Janice shook her head.

"Judge, I object to your taking over my questioning," Zinkavich said.

"Sit down and stay down. You're done."

Steve knew that the judge had heard tales of children disciplined with lighted cigarettes, starved in homes with full pantries, and subjected to sexual torture. Judges, cops, medical examiners see horrific wrongs, and after a while, he supposed, their minds create buffers to protect them from psychic pain. But do you ever really lose the ability to be shocked and sickened by cruelty to children?

"Now, cutting through the bullshit," the judge continued, "your brother came to this farm where you were high on drugs and your son was confined like an animal, unclothed and freezing. There was an altercation with Mr. Thigpen, who is also a drug abuser, after which your brother took your son to his home, where he's raising him in apparent comfort and safety."

"Yeah. That's about right."

"Your Honor, I must protest," Zinkavich said.

"Then do it somewhere else." The judge leaned toward Janice. "Ms. Solomon, I want you to put yourself in my place for a moment."

"Not if I have to wear that blue *schmatte* you got on."

"Between making your son a ward of the state or giving your brother guardianship rights, what would you do?"

The question of the day, Steve thought.

The hundred-thousand-dollar question.

Victoria got to her feet. "Your Honor, may we have a brief recess before the witness answers?"

"What?" Steve couldn't believe it. "Let her answer."

"Shut up," Victoria said.

"What seems to be the problem?" the judge asked.

"We just need five minutes, Your Honor."

The judge shrugged and said: "No jive. Back in five."

———

When they reached the corridor, Victoria grabbed Steve by the tie, kicked open the door to the women's rest room, and dragged him inside.

"Hey," he protested.

The harsh, astringent smell of ammonia was in the air.

"You think you can get away with this?" she said.

"With what?" He put on an innocent face that didn't fool her for an instant.

"You tell me. What'd you do, kidnap Thigpen and extort your sister?"

"You're nuts. Let's get back in there. We're one answer away from my winning custody."

"No, we're one answer away from my reporting you to the Bar."

"For what?"

"Whatever you've done is going to backfire. The next time Janice gets arrested, she'll go screaming to Zinkavich. She'll turn on you to save her ass."

"She's got nothing on me."

For someone so shifty, he was a lousy liar. "You're not stealing home on me, Solomon, no matter how fast you think you are."

"Jesus, lighten up."

"I'm giving you ten seconds to come clean."

"Or what?"

"Or I go back inside that courtroom and ask to withdraw as your lawyer and stay the trial until the state investigates your sister's conduct."

"C'mon, Vic. This is the truth: When Janice walked into the courtroom, I didn't know what she was going to say."

"Sure you did. And you knew Thigpen wasn't going to show up. That's why you told me to wing it. You knew exactly what was going to happen."

"I just have good instincts."

"Not that good. What'd you do, bribe them?"

All of Steve's famed instincts told him to keep quiet. He knew how many criminals were tripped up, not by the police, but by their own big mouths. He also knew how self-righteously upright Victoria could be. So he would never understand why, in that moment, he told her. Did he hope that her feelings for him would outweigh her rigid sense of propriety? Was it some test, one she was bound to fail?

"Dammit, Steve," she prodded. "What turned Janice around?"

He blurted it out. "A hundred thousand dollars."

"Oh, no. Oh, no." She was shaking her head. "How could you?"

"I borrowed it."

"Damn you! You know what I mean. How could you suborn perjury?"

"I suborned the *truth*! I paid her *not* to lie. Every word she said in there was true."

"That's a rationalization."

"Yeah, but it's a good one. I was extorted. I'm the victim here."

"Tell that to the disbarment judge. It doesn't matter if Janice told the truth. Paying her is an illegal inducement under the Ethical Rules."

"Then the rules are wrong," Steve argued.

"Damn you!" Her look was anguished and angry. "You're as dirty as Pincher."

"I'm doing justice here. That's a pretty big difference."

"I could have won playing straight."

"I couldn't be sure of that," he said, softly. He moved closer to her, placed his hands on her shoulders, felt her tremble. Any second, she could burst into a rainstorm of tears. Or she could kiss him. Or she could—

Smack. She slapped him hard across the face.

"Ow! What the hell . . . ?"

"I'm required to tell Judge Rolle."

"No way. You ever hear of attorney-client privilege?"

"Doesn't cover fraud on the court. Read *Kneale vs. Williams.*"

"Haven't I taught you anything? When the law doesn't work—"

"There's no wiggle room here. The Ethical Rules are mandatory."

"I'll lose Bobby and go to jail. They'll pull my license."

"I don't have a choice."

"You have the choice to do justice or blindly follow a bad law."

"I warned you when I took the case. I do it strictly by the book."

He slammed his hand into the tile wall. The tile didn't break. He wasn't so sure about his hand. "This makes it easier for you, doesn't it?"

"Makes what easier?"

His hand swelled with pain, and he felt a throbbing in his temples. "My being disbarred, disgraced, out of the picture. It's the proof you needed that you made the right choice."

"I'm marrying Bruce because I love him."

"You haven't changed since that day in the jail cell. You're still the same robot, the same automaton."

"And you're the same unethical lowlife."

"You're bloodless and soulless, Lord. *Sin alma o corazón.*"

"I can't believe I considered being with you for even a second."

"Likewise," he agreed. "We're totally incompatible."

"Polar opposites," she said.

"The cobra and the mongoose."

"Good-bye, Solomon," she said, pushing the door open and heading back to the courtroom.

Fifty-two

LOVE VS. LAW

Victoria knew she had, at most, two minutes before the judge would return to the bench. Sitting with perfect posture at the Petitioner's table, she furiously scribbled notes on a pink index card.

"Your Honor, it is my sad duty under Part 2 of Rule 4, Subsection 3.3 of the Ethical Rules to report an obstruction of justice . . ."

Janice sat on the witness stand, thumbing through one of Judge Rolle's children's magazines, Zinkavich glaring at her from his crumb-covered table. The courtroom door opened, and Steve waltzed in, whistling.

Whistling!

Some upbeat tune. Trying to distract her, Victoria figured, sidetrack her from what the law required her to do.

Steve approached Zinkavich, slapped him on the back: "Jack, my man, let's do lunch sometime, whadaya say?"

"You been drinking?" Zinkavich said.

"Hey, Sis," Steve called out. "Despite everything, I still love you."

"Feeling okay, Stevie?" Janice said.

Victoria watched warily as Steve circled her table, winked at her, and said: "You look absolutely stunning, honey bun."

She tried to ignore him and kept taking notes:

"My partner, Stephen Solomon, has committed a gross violation . . ."

Standing in front of the bench, Steve began singing, "How Deep Is Your Love."

Singing! Like the sappy Bee Gees, only off-key.

Then he glided around the well of the courtroom, swiveling his hips, dancing a rumba with an invisible partner.

Dancing!

Victoria tried not to watch him, but that was impossible. Limber as a snake, he coiled his way from bench to bar, all the while singing. Somewhere between being touched in the pouring rain and living in a world of fools, he slid across her table, his butt scattering her index cards.

"You can stop taking notes, Vic."

"Go away!" She snatched her cards as if they were thousand-dollar bills.

"You probably wonder why I'm so happy."

"I don't care."

"It just occurred to me you're not gonna tell the judge a damn thing. You know why?"

"Get away from me! Now."

She couldn't believe his arrogance. Even after all this, he was still so cocksure of himself.

"Because I know what makes you tick, Vic."

"Hah."

"I know what's important to you. More important than all the rules in all the books."

"Whatever you think you know, Solomon, you're wrong."

He gave her that *gotcha* grin that made her itch to slap him again.

"No matter what you think about me, you love Bobby," Steve said. "I saw it in your face when he was testifying. He said he wished you were his mom. And your look said you wished it, too. You love the kid with all your soul and all your being. And because you know he belongs with me, you couldn't live with yourself if something you did took him away. Just like I always told you, love trumps the law. So tear up your note cards, Victoria, because you can despise me until the end of time, but you won't do this to Bobby."

He slipped off the table and plopped into the chair next to her. Victoria searched for a reply, but before she could say a word, the rear door to the courtroom opened and Judge Althea Rolle hurried in, robes flowing. "Don't bother standing," she said, dropping into her high-backed chair. "We're gonna finish this up real quick."

It had been a performance. Steve wasn't nearly as sure of himself as he tried to appear. But he had taken a shot, aiming for the deepest part of Victoria, the part she kept hidden. He had aimed for her heart.

If it didn't work, if she finked to the Fink and to the judge, he had another option. It would take them several days to crank up the machinery of the criminal justice system. You can't get an indictment overnight. You need subpoenas, affidavits, sworn testimony. Time enough to pack the old Caddy with everything important—some sweats, some John D. MacDonald paperbacks, the *panini* grill—and uncle and nephew would hit the road. To where, he didn't know.

Matamoras, Mexico? Tegucigalpa, Honduras?

He'd never been to either place, just liked the sound of the names.

"Now, Ms. Solomon," the judge began, nailing Janice with a steely look, "my question is this . . ."

Steve sneaked a peek at Victoria. Perched on the edge of her chair, she looked like a bird about to take flight.

"Between the state and your brother," the judge continued, "who would you choose to care for your son?"

"Your Honor, I have something to say," Victoria said.

Damn. Steve wondered if his passport was up-to-date.

"Hold on, Ms. Lord," the judge said. "You'll get your chance. Now, Ms. Solomon—"

"It's important, Your Honor."

"I said, in a minute." Judge Rolle gave Victoria a stern look, then turned back to Janice. "The state or your brother, Ms. Solomon? What's your choice?"

Victoria fidgeted in her chair but kept quiet. For the moment.

"I been in enough state facilities to know the shit that goes down there," Janice said. "Stevie's blood. He's good people. Why not give him a shot?"

"I thought so," the judge said.

Victoria sat at her table, clutching her note cards in a white-knuckled grip.

What's she going to do?

"Does the state have any more witnesses?" the judge asked.

"My cupboard is bare," Zinkavich said, "but I move for a continuance until I can locate Mr. Thigpen."

"Denied."

"Then I ask that the Court withhold ruling until the State Attorney's Office can investigate the veracity of Ms. Solomon's testimony," Zinkavich said, desperately.

"Denied."

"I request for a stay of all proceedings until—"

"Denied. Ms. Lord, please sum up for the Petitioner."

Victoria seemed stunned. "Oh, Your Honor, I'm not ready for closing argument. But there's something I need to disclose—"

"Ms. Lord, if you're half the lawyer I think you are, you already know which way the Court is leaning. So stand up, talk quick, then sit down."

Victoria stood, shakily. "This is difficult. I don't know exactly how to say this."

She was torn, Steve thought. Torn between her heart and those damn rules.

"Ms. Lord, just give me a thought or two about Mr. Solomon, and we'll call it a day, okay?"

Victoria's eyes seemed to focus on a spot on the wall. She sighed. Then she said, "Your Honor, Steve Solomon is the most exasperating man I have ever known."

"That's a start," the judge said. "Go on."

"He has great empathy for people who've got no one to stand up for them. But he's also maddening, impetuous, utterly irrational."

Winging it, Steve thought. But where would she land?

"He has absolutely no respect for the rules," Victoria continued. "He makes up his own. He's witty and fun and smart, but he can do some incredibly stupid, thoughtless things. He—"

"Your Honor," Zinkavich interrupted. "Is this closing argument or couples therapy?"

"Quiet," the judge said. "I want to see where this is going."

"I know this man, Steve Solomon," Victoria said. "Oh, Judge, I know him so well. I've looked deep inside him."

"Objection!" Zinkavich shouted. "Counsel is testifying. It's totally improper to offer personal opinions on the issues."

"Counsel is right," Victoria said, before the judge could rule. "I just crossed the line. It's forbidden by the rules. Frowned on by legal scholars." Her voice took on a sarcastic lilt. "And, oh, how I've always followed the rules."

Her face was flushed now, her eyes flashing with sparks. Running on emotion.

"I got straight A's while working two jobs and playing varsity tennis at Princeton," Victoria said, while unbuttoning her double-breasted jacket. "At Yale, I was the star of the law journal." She tore off her jacket and tossed it at Steve. His hands came up late, and the jacket covered his face before he could whisk it away.

"I was going to make my mark in the public sector," she continued, "spend time in private practice, then go on the bench. All mapped out on color-coded note cards. I planned something else, too. A tall,

handsome, suitable husband and two-point-four perfect children. And I was going to follow all the rules."

Victoria turned, walked back to the table, and
drew back an arm. For a second, Steve thought she
was going to slug him, but instead, she swept an open
palm across the table, knocking her files to the floor
with a crash. "*That's* what I think of the rules!"

Three note cards remained on the table. She
scooped them up and tore them into pieces, showering Steve with confetti. "And that's what I think of
my stupid, color-coded note cards."

Complete meltdown, Steve thought. He had no
idea what she would say next, figured she didn't,
either.

"And I'll tell you something else, Judge."

*Here it is. The end of the line. She was going to
snitch on him.*

"My feet are killing me." She propped one ankle
over a knee, pried off an ankle-strapped Prada pump,
and tossed it to Steve. The second shoe came a moment later. The toss was low, but he scooped it up in
one hand.

Victoria padded toward the bench in her panty-
hosed feet. "Where was I, Your Honor?"

"Somewhere between Mr. Solomon's irresponsible
and irritating conduct and your two-point-four perfect children. And may I compliment you on your
toenail polish? Malibu Sunset?"

"Painted Desert, Your Honor."

Victoria moved back to her table, and for a moment, Steve panicked: the brown taffeta blouse might
be coming off next. "Steve Solomon's taught me so
much," she said. " 'When the law doesn't work,' he
always says, 'you work the law.' At first, it sounded

illegal or at least immoral. But it's not. When used to do good, it's the true meaning of the law. Law tinged with compassion. Law that seeks the truth. Law that protects the innocent. It's the only place where the law and justice truly meet." She turned toward Steve, her eyes glistening with tears. "Otherwise, we're just robots. Unfeeling automatons. Bloodless and soulless. *Sin alma o corazón.*"

She picked up a paper clip from the table, twisted it apart, pricked a finger with a sharp end.

Ouch.

She held up her hand. A drop of blood oozed from a fingertip.

"I'm not a robot. I bleed. I feel pain. And I feel love. So does Steve Solomon. I've never known anyone who loves a child more, who gives more of himself to a child."

She stood there a moment, seemingly dazed, then turned back to the judge. "Your Honor, may I be excused?"

"Go on now," the judge said, with a wave of her hand, "before you bleed on your skirt. Philippe Adec?"

"Zanella."

"Lovely. Wish I was tall enough for the A-line."

Victoria scooped up her purse and headed for the door. Leaving her shoes, her jacket, and her client behind.

"Z, you got anything to add to these proceedings?" the judge asked.

"Only that I wish I'd gone to dental school," Zinkavich said.

Judge Rolle leaned back in her chair and spun a full 360 degrees. When she stopped, she drilled Steve with a steady gaze. "You must be a handful, Mr. Solomon."

"Beg your pardon, Judge?"

"To get a woman like that so hot and bothered." She sighed. "You Solomon men are really something."

"Yes, ma'am," Steve agreed, not knowing what else to say.

"Okay, here's the way it's gonna be." The judge pulled out the court file, made a notation on the cover. "Mr. Solomon's petition is granted. He is awarded full guardianship rights with no limitations other than my request to bring Bobby to chambers for lunch now and then."

She banged her gavel and headed off the bench. Zinkavich gathered his files and left without a word.

Steve sat there alone, shredded pieces of note cards stuck to his jacket.

Holding one of Victoria's shoes, the inside still warm to the touch.

Wondering how it was possible to be so happy and so sad at the same time.

Fifty-three

WHAT A LOSER,
THAT LAWYER

Frank Sinatra was singing, "Bang bang, she shot me down."

"I hate this song," Steve said, punching a button on the car radio.

"Wonder why," Bobby said.

"It's not that. It's just a weak song. Beneath Frank's dignity."

"Uh-huh."

They were driving the old Caddy, top down, across the MacArthur Causeway to Steve's office. Bobby sat cross-legged in the front seat, eating a flaky guava *pastelito*. It was a breezy winter day of picture-postcard beauty. Palm trees swayed, terns hovered over the water, and the gleaming white cruise ships stood out in sharp focus at their berths.

So why am I so miserable?

He figured part of it was simply the adrenaline crash, the letdown after a battle. They'd won the headline-making murder trial. He'd won custody of Bobby. A truly joyous event, more important than any case he ever had or would have. Bobby was already talking about an upcoming fishing trip with his grandfather.

But still, a feeling of emptiness crashed over Steve.

Victoria would be stopping by later to pick up her things. And then she'd be gone.

Win the case, lose the girl.

Not that he ever had her, unless you count a stolen hour on a surreal night of firelight and snow. Had it even really happened? Maybe it was all a dream.

There was no reason to feel down, he told himself. Last night, he'd paid a visit to the Barksdale home. Katrina had kissed him on the cheek and thanked him for his splendid work. Her exact words were: *"You're a fucking great lawyer and you've got one fine ass."*

She was drinking Cristal, which she offered to Steve, and even though he considered champagne carbonated piss, he said, sure, why not. She wore a white, ripply camisole with cabana pants that tied at the waist, or to be accurate, about several inches below her flat and suntanned belly. She kept flinging her dark hair around, repeating how fucking brilliant he was. Soon she was slurring her words, saying he was positively "edible," but probably meaning "incredible," he figured.

She handed Steve a flute of champagne and a cashier's check, her frozen accounts having defrosted after the charges were dismissed. Two hundred fifty thousand dollars to be split evenly with Victoria. After taxes and repaying Teresa the hundred thousand he'd borrowed, Steve figured he'd be about twenty thou in the hole. A few more victories like this, he could declare bankruptcy.

Steve asked where Manko was, and Katrina said

he was preparing the boat for a trip to Bimini, just the two of them.

"You remember, I told you we were all going to go to Bimini, before Charlie croaked?"

"Sure, it was part of our defense—why would you plan a trip with Charlie a week after you were going to kill him."

"Now Chet and I are going. But not Charlie." Giggles burst from her like bubbles of champagne.

"Is there something you want to tell me, Katrina?"

"Nope." Another sip, another giggle. "Unless you want to know a big secret."

He wasn't sure. He wasn't sure if he wanted to hear that his edible and incredible self had cleared a guilty woman of murder. But he had to know. "Go ahead. Tell me a secret."

"No," she said with a little-girl pout. "I shouldn't."

"Let's play a game, Katrina. I'll confess something if you will."

"I like games," she said with a titter. "You first."

"Okay. Remember that security tape?"

"Sure. First you thought there was a shadow of somebody out in the hall. But then your expert said it was nothing."

"That's what I told you. Victoria, too."

"Yeah?"

"I lied."

"Whadaya mean?"

"It was a simple photogrammetry problem, solved with a trig equation. The shadow was a person about six-foot-three, probably over two hundred pounds. Who does that sound like?"

"My Chet," she cooed. She put down her wineglass,

cocked her head coquettishly. "So you knew Chet was there?"

"I knew."

"Why didn't you tell Victoria?"

"I wanted her to work as hard for you as I would."

"Why work so hard if you thought I was guilty?"

"It's my job."

"That's all?"

"That's a lot."

"You still think I killed the old perv?" She seemed to be sobering up.

"You tell me."

"C'mon, you proved Charlie committed suicide."

"I proved Charlie wrote a suicide note. There's a difference. I figure you and Manko killed Charlie before he had a chance to do the job himself."

"You've got it backward, silly. Sure, Chet was gonna kill him, but Charlie beat him to it."

"Is that the truth? You might as well tell me. They can't try you twice for Charlie's death."

"Final jeopardy, right? But it's the truth, I swear. Charlie committed suicide by strangling himself. You should have seen it. His eyes nearly popped out of his head. Gross!"

She seemed totally guileless, and Steve felt a mixture of relief and revulsion. Okay, maybe, she wasn't guilty, but she wasn't exactly innocent, either. Had justice been served? He supposed it had. Katrina had wanted to kill Charlie, but we punish people for what they do, not what they wish. If every woman who wanted to strangle her husband was indicted, criminal defense lawyers would all drive Ferraris. Katrina was morally guilty, of course. If there truly were a judge on a heavenly throne, a real Court of Last Resort, Steve figured she'd face some ultimate justice. But as far as earthly law was concerned, Katrina had been rightfully acquitted. He'd done his job well.

She downed the rest of her champagne. "So, congratulate me."

"For not killing your husband?"

"For marrying Chet."

"Thought you said Chet was just a sport fuck."

"But a good one." She laughed. "We're getting hitched in Bimini."

"Congratulations." Two scorpions on a yacht, he thought. He wondered how long it would take one to sting the other.

"Before we go, there's something I need you to do."

"Yeah?"

"Can you make me one of those prenups?" Katrina asked.

The Caddy was just passing Parrot Jungle when Steve's cell phone rang.

"Althea Rolle called me this morning." Herbert Solomon sounded peeved.

"Oh, shit. I was so drained last night . . ."

"You forgot to tell me some big news."

"I'm sorry, Dad. Really."

Herbert harrumphed into the phone. "Anyway, ah'm glad for you. And Bobby."

It sounded as if forgiveness was forthcoming, so Steve relaxed a bit.

"So if we're on for the weekend, ah'll gas up the boat," Herbert said.

"We're on. Thanks, Dad. For everything."

"You don't know the half of it."

"What's that mean?"

"Where's mah hundred thousand?"

A Saab convertible with its radio blaring salsa passed the Caddy, and Steve wasn't sure he'd heard his father correctly. "What'd you say, Dad?"

"When Marvin paid me a visit, ah was steamed. Hurt, too. Mah own son wouldn't ask me for help."

What the hell? He'd heard right, after all. He just couldn't believe it. "It wasn't Teresa's money?"

"Sweet lady, but she was mah courier, that's all. Ah cashed in mah pension. It's what a man does for his son."

Steve was so astonished he nearly rear-ended an SUV hauling a little runabout on a rickety trailer.

"You still there, son?"

"You gave me all that money without even knowing what it was for?"

"Ah didn't know then. But your sister paid me a visit on her way out of town. Now ah know."

Steve felt a wave of heat roll over him. *So this is what shame feels like.*

"Ah was surprised," Herbert continued.

"I don't know what to say, Dad."

"It was generous of you, son."

"Generous?"

"Paying for Janice's drug rehab like that. A damn fancy place, too."

Drug rehab? Is that what Janice told him the hundred K was for? Or is he just making this easier for me?

"You did the right thing, Stephen. You took care of family. Your sister and your nephew."

Steve couldn't be sure, but he sensed his father knew the truth. What a strange way for the two of them to come together, enmeshed in a family conspiracy. "We gonna catch some fish this weekend, Dad?"

Herbert laughed. "You bring the beer, I'll bring the bait."

Steve slowed the Caddy as a giant Hummer pulled in front of him from the adjacent lane. They were five minutes from the office. The radio was tuned to a sports talk station, a caller complaining that the Dolphin Dolls didn't shake their booties the way the Cowboys' cheerleaders did. Bobby was on his second *pastelito* and had just popped the top on a *Jupiña* pineapple soda. Sugar overload any second.

"Will Victoria still come over to the house?" Bobby said. "You know, after . . ."

"Doubt it, kiddo. Married women hang out with their husbands, at least for a year or so."

Bobby seemed dejected. Which made two of them.

After a moment, Bobby said: "I could light a stink bomb in the church."

There'd been a message on the phone yesterday. Bigby calling to remind him of the rehearsal next Friday. The groom's cheery voice depressed Solomon even more. Why had he agreed to be an usher? He could already hear the comments, could anticipate the torturous death by a thousand compliments.

"Don't they make a lovely couple?"

"She's found herself a real catch."

"Steve, make a toast to the bride and groom."

He'd never get through the reception and dinner. By the time they served avocado vichyssoise, he'd feel like someone was scooping out his vital organs with a soup spoon.

"Turn it up!" Bobby yelled, reaching for the radio.

"What?"

"Hammering Hank's sports quiz."

Their hands both hit the volume at the same time, boosting Hammering Hank Goldberg's bellow into the red zone:

"*Next. Bernie in Surfside. Do you know your U of M sports?*"

"*Yeah, Hank. Shoot.*"

"*Didja hear about that murder trial, the rich babe from Gables Estates?*"

"*I seen it on TV.*"

"*Defense lawyer's a nobody named Steve Solomon. For a* lechon asado *dinner at La Hacienda, what infamous sporting event was Solomon involved in at U of M?*"

"Oh, shit," Steve said.

"Shh," Bobby said.

"*Uh, was he the guy called for pass interference in the end zone against Ohio State?*"

"*Wake up, Bernie! How many Jewish cornerbacks you know?*"

"*Wait a second. Was he that kid got picked off in the College World Series? Last Out Solomon?*"

"*Bernie wins dinner! You eat pork, Bernie?*"

"*Gives me gas, but I eat it.*"

"*Bottom of the ninth, the 'Canes trailing Texas by a run. Two out, Steve Solomon gets picked off third! What a dipstick!*"

"*At least he won the murder trial, Hank.*"

"*Wrong, Bernie. This Solomon couldn't find his*

butt with both hands. The prosecutor solved the case, dismissed the charges. What a loser, that lawyer."

Steve punched a button, picked up the reggae station where Bob Marley was singing "No Woman, No Cry."

"I don't know why, kiddo," Steve said, "but I have a feeling this is gonna be a really bizarre day."

Fifty-four

THE LAST DAY

Steve and Bobby had gotten two steps inside the front door of Les Mannequins when the first wave of infantry attacked.

"Steve, I need you!" Lexy shouted. Her long blond hair, usually ironing-board flat, was poufed up today. She wore hot pink Lycra short shorts with a white shell top.

"Look at me," she commanded, extending a long, bare arm. Her wrist was wrapped in a leather brace.

"I don't do Rollerblade accidents," Steve said, without stopping. If he lingered, he'd pick up half-a-dozen freebie clients before he reached the stairs.

"It's a workers' comp claim," Lexy declared.

"You have a job?" Moving past the front desk now. One stumble, he'd be a wildebeest set upon by lions.

"Part-time. At 1–800–BLOWJOB."

"You're a phone-sex operator?"

The stairs were in sight. A haven as inviting as Key West to Cuban rafters.

"Easy money," Lexy said. "All I do is masturbate."

"Masturbation," Bobby said. "ANATOMIST RUB."

"But if you diddle a dozen times a day, five days a week, you end up with carpal tunnel." Lexy held up the wrist support for show-and-tell.

Steve violated his own rules and stopped at the foot of the stairs. "You really do it? I thought the *oohing* and *aahing* was fake."

"Say, you're not Steve the Stud who calls at three A.M., are you?"

Before Steve could answer, Lexy's twin, Rexy, stepped out of a dressing room in her skyscraper Jimmy Choos. She wore identical short shorts and her hair was piled into an identical pouf. "Steve! They arrested me!"

"Who? Why?"

"DUI, can you believe it? All I had were four or five black Russians. They're like milk shakes, right? Plus they charged me with obstruction of justice."

"Why?"

"For eating my panties."

"You were wearing panties?"

"Just a thong. The cloth is supposed to absorb alcohol and screw up the Breathalyzer, but I still blew a point nine. What should I do?"

"Next time, wear boxers."

Steve started up the stairs and was tugged backwards. Gina had his coattail in one hand and was waving a blue-backed document in the other. "Steve, can you sue a dead guy?"

"If he's got an estate. Why?"

"I was going out with this rich old guy, trying to pull an Anna Nicole Smith."

"And you killed him?"

"No way. He said if I went to bed with him, he'd name me in his will. So I did it, and now, guess what, he's dead."

"Congratulations."

"No. Read it! Paragraph seventeen."

She thrust the document in front of Steve's eyes, and he read aloud. " 'Finally, I promised Ms. Gina Capretto that I would name her in my will. Hello, Gina.' "

The reception room was empty, unless you counted the Pamela Anderson inflatable doll at the desk. Steve and Bobby walked past her and into the inner office.

"Forty-five . . . forty-six . . . Hey, *jefe.*"

Sweating and red-faced, Cece was doing elevated push-ups, her feet on Steve's chair, her arms on the floor, veins throbbing in her neck. She wore denim cutoffs and a chopped T-shirt. Three toes on each bare foot were encircled by faux diamond rings.

"Forty-seven . . . forty-eight . . . Hey, Bobby . . . Brittany Spears."

"SPINY RAT BREAST," Bobby shot back.

"Good one," Cece said. "Forty-nine . . . fifty!" She kicked off the chair into a handstand, pointed her jeweled toes toward the ceiling, lowered into a vertical push-up, then sprang into a front flip and landed on her feet.

Steve glanced at Victoria's desk. The few law books and files she'd brought with her were neatly packed in three cardboard boxes. Though he'd never been married, he imagined this is what it felt like on the verge of divorce. A piece of himself would soon be missing.

Cece grabbed a towel and roped it around Bobby's neck. "Hey, brainiac, I hear you're stuck with your uncle from now on."

"Next year, we're going back to court and he's gonna adopt me," Bobby said. "Then I'll call him 'Dad' instead of 'Uncle Steve.' "

Steve grabbed his calendar from his desk. "Cece, where are my appointments?"

"Don't got any," she said.

"No one's called?"

"MasterCard. You've been canceled."

"I don't get it. Where are the new clients? I just won a big murder trial."

The door opened, and Victoria walked in.

"I mean, *we* just won a big murder trial," he said. "Hey, Vic."

"I need to talk to you," she said.

She wore a glen plaid outfit that reminded him of something. What was it?

That first day. It's what she wore the day we were thrown in jail. And now it's the last day.

Later, when Steve would think about this moment, he would remember her face. Troubled. Eyes puffy. Hair messy. Not much sleep and maybe a crying spell. But just then, he barely noticed. He was too wrapped up in his own punctured dreams of a big-time law practice. "This doesn't make sense. We win a huge case, and this place is like a morgue."

"That's just it," Cece said. "You didn't win Barksdale. At least, people don't think you did. I was in the clerk's office yesterday, and everybody was saying how great it was that Pincher figured out your client was innocent, even if you couldn't. They say he's gonna run for governor as a compassionate prosecutor."

"I don't believe this. Vic, you believe this?"

"Could we talk now? Please."

The phone rang and Steve said, "Maybe that's a new client."

Cece picked it up: "Solomon and Lord, Attorneys at Law . . ."

For a few minutes more, anyway, Steve thought.

"Civil and criminal litigation," Cece continued. "*Hablamos Español.*"

"Steve . . ." Victoria said.

"Yes, Your Honor," Cece said into the phone.

"Hang on," Steve told Victoria, trying to listen. When a judge calls, it was usually not to compliment your lawyering skills.

"Yes, sir. I'll tell him right now, Your Honor," Cece said, then hung up.

"What?" Steve said. "Who was that?"

"Judge Gridley himself. He's pissed 'cause you're late for the Sachses' final hearing."

"What final hearing! You didn't put it on my calendar."

"You expect me to keep track of all the places you're supposed to be?"

"That's your job!"

"Don't yell at me. I'm not your slave."

"Victoria, come on. You've got to represent Harry's wife."

"Why?"

"The Sachses' divorce. Gridley requires both parties be represented, even when it's uncontested. I'll introduce the property settlement agreement. Harry and Joanne will say they signed it, and we'll be out of there in five minutes."

"Then we'll talk?" she asked, but Steve was already hustling her toward the door.

SOLOMON'S LAWS

10.   **We all hold the keys to our own jail cells.**

Fifty-five

SOLOMON'S LAWS

"Y'all think my dog-ass Gators can make the Final Four?" Judge Erwin Gridley asked.

"Tough region," Steve said. "They'll be lucky to get to the Sweet Sixteen."

The judge harrumphed, or maybe the open-jawed alligator head on his desk did. They were in the orange-and-blue chambers of the old Bull Gator himself. Steve sat on one side of the T-bone-shaped conference table, his client, Harry Sachs, alongside. As Harry was not working today—meaning he wasn't pulling one of his numerous cons—he had left the wheelchair at home. He wore jeans and a cammie jacket emblazoned with Marine battle insignia he'd bought on the Internet. Harry was admiring a miniature replica of Ben Hill Griffin Stadium, maybe wondering how much it would bring at a pawnshop. Steve made a mental note to frisk his client before they left chambers.

Directly across the table sat Joanne Sachs, a handsome woman in her mid-forties in wire-framed glasses and a gray wool dress with a white lacy collar. Steve nodded to her, thinking they were a mismatched couple. If he saw Harry and Joanne side by side on the street, he'd figure she was a librarian about to have her purse snatched.

Victoria sat next to Joanne, scanning the Property Settlement Agreement. At the side of the judge's desk, Sofia Hernandez, in a black leather mini and a white blouse, was poised over her stenograph machine. Her long, lacquered nails were emblazoned with silver hearts.

"Mr. Sachs, have you been a resident of Miami-Dade County for six months prior to filing this petition?" the judge asked.

"Yes, sir," Harry said.

"Your marriage irretrievably broken?"

"Like Heidi Fleiss' hymen."

"How's that?"

"He answered in the affirmative," Steve said, giving his client a sharp look.

"Now, this Property Settlement Agreement," Judge Gridley continued, "you agree with its terms?"

"Every word," Harry said fervently.

"You, too, Mrs. Sachs?"

Joanne Sachs started to nod, but Victoria put a hand on her arm and said: "Your Honor, I'm not sure this agreement is entirely fair."

Steve bolted to attention. "What are you doing?"

"Representing my client," Victoria said.

"*Your* client already signed the agreement."

"Without benefit of independent counsel."

"Hey, Lord. Stick to the script, okay?"

"I'm not a potted plant."

"Y'all gonna start up again?" Judge Gridley asked, with interest.

"Judge, it's not fair that Mrs. Sachs gets the eight-year-old Dodge and her husband keeps the new Lexus," Victoria said. "Then there's his pending IRS audit. Mr. Sachs should be required to indemnify and hold his wife harmless from any penalties."

Steve couldn't believe it. The last day of Solomon and Lord, and the woman was mucking up everything. Jesus, why didn't she just clear out already?

"Joanne, fire your lawyer," he said.

"Don't you dare address my client," Victoria said.

"She's not your client. You don't have clients. You have time-shares and green gourds and pretty soon you'll have little green children. I'll tell you something else, Lord. I bought you a really nice wedding present, but to hell with it, I'm giving it to Katrina."

"You're losing it, Solomon," Victoria said.

The judge sighed and said: "I ever tell y'all about those two beagles on my farm, always yapping at each other?"

"Yeah, Judge, you did," Steve said.

"They finally settled it all by humping in the barn," the judge reminded them.

"We tried that, Your Honor," Steve said. "Even had the bales of straw."

"Damn you!" Victoria said. "Your Honor, I move that Mr. Solomon's slanderous statement be stricken from the record."

Sofia Hernandez typed away, a wicked smile on her crimson lips.

"It's only slander if it's false," Steve said. "Are you denying it happened?"

"Calm down, now, both of you," the judge ordered.

"What about my divorce?" Harry Sachs said.

"I'm gonna postpone the hearing and order counseling," the judge said.

"My client doesn't want counseling," Steve said.

"Neither does mine," Victoria said.

"Not for them. For the two of you," the judge said.

"I object," Steve said.

"So do I," Victoria said. "And I insist the Court strike all references to my private life from the transcript."

"Put her under oath," Steve said.

"That's enough," the judge said.

"Ask her if we didn't do it in a chickee hut on a bale of straw," Steve railed on.

"Bastard!" Victoria said.

"Bitch!" Steve said.

"That's by God enough! Y'all just scalded the corn pudding." The judge hit a button on the intercom. "Eloise, send the bailiff in here."

His tie loosened, his jacket crumpled under his head, Steve lay on his back on the molded plastic bench of the holding cell. Victoria paced in the facing cell, the heels of her ankle-strapped Gucci pumps clicking on the concrete floor. For the thirty minutes they'd been locked up, neither had said a word.

"This is ridiculous," she said, finally.

No response.

"Steve, can we talk?"

She couldn't see into the shadows of his cell. Was he asleep? Or just giving her the silent treatment?

"We should never be on opposite sides of a case," she said.

Still no answer. Somewhere inside the walls, the plumbing rattled.

"When we're on the same side," she continued, "no one can beat us. But when we're opposed, we tear each other apart. So, I was thinking . . . maybe we should consider working together."

She heard rustling in the other cell, and in a second, Steve was standing at the bars. "You mean it? Solomon and Lord?"

"Maybe we should give it a try for a while, see how it goes. . . ."

"What's Bruce gonna say?"

"He's unhappy about it."

"You already told him?"

"Last night. When I told him the wedding's off."

"When I told him the wedding's off."

Yeah, she'd said that. But what did "off" mean? To a lawyer, words were crucial.

" 'Off' meaning canceled? Or 'off' meaning postponed?" he asked.

"Canceled. I'm not marrying Bruce."

Steve locked on to the moment. He wanted to preserve the feeling. A cool waterfall, a warm sunset, a full moon on a still bay.

Yes! Yes! Yes!

"What you said in court yesterday was true," she continued. "I do love Bobby. And what I said was true, too. I find you exasperating and maddening. But deep down inside, you're—"

"Wait. Wait a second."

Steve fished in his pocket, pulled out something,

reached through the bars, and unlocked the door to his cell.

"You have a key? You've had a key all this time?"

He swung the door open, walked to her cell, unlocked the door. "Once you've been here a while, they put you on the honor system."

"Why in heaven's name didn't you tell me?"

He walked into her cell, swung the door closed behind him. "You·weren't ready."

"For what?" She put her hands on his shoulders, and he slipped his arms around her waist.

"Law Number Ten: 'We all hold the keys to our own jail cells.' "

"And now I'm ready?"

"You just proved it. You just broke out."

They kissed. Then she placed her head on his shoulder. "Solomon and Lord. I like the sound of it."

"We need a slogan for our ads," he said.

"No we don't. Lawyer advertising is tacky."

" 'The wisdom of Solomon, the strength of the Lord,' " he intoned, like a TV anchorman.

"Blasphemous. *And* tacky."

"Somebody gets hit by a city bus, I want one of us in the ER before the doctor washes his hands," he said.

"No way. We've got to do everything by the book," she said.

"What book is that?"

She cocked her head, studied him. "Is this the way it's going to be?"

"Every day," he promised, pressing his lips to hers.

SOLOMON'S LAWS

1. When the law doesn't work . . . work the law.

2. In law and in life, sometimes you have to wing it.

3. I will never take a drink until ~~sundown . . . two o'clock . . . noon . . .~~ I'm thirsty.

4. I will never carry a pager, drive a Porsche, or flaunt a Phi Beta Kappa key . . . *even if I had one.*

5. I will never compromise my ideals to achieve someone else's definition of success.

6. Lie to your priest, your spouse, and the IRS, but always tell your lawyer the truth.

7. I will never bribe a cop, lie to a judge, or sleep with my partner . . . *hasta qué ella diga qué sí.*

8. There is some shit I will not eat.

9. I will never break the law, breach legal ethics, or risk jail time . . . *unless it's for someone I love.*

10. We all hold the keys to our own jail cells.

ABOUT THE AUTHOR

PAUL LEVINE worked as a newspaper reporter and trial lawyer, practicing law for seventeen years, trying cases in state and federal courts and handling appeals at every level, including the Supreme Court, before becoming a full-time novelist and screenwriter. The winner of the John D. MacDonald fiction award, Levine is the author of the Jake Lassiter novels, which have been published in twenty-three countries. *To Speak for the Dead*, the first Lassiter novel, was a national bestseller and honored as one of the best mysteries of the year by the *Los Angeles Times*. He is also the author of *9 Scorpions*, a thriller set in the U.S. Supreme Court.

He was cocreator and coexecutive producer of the CBS television series *First Monday*, and has written extensively for *JAG*. He lives in California, where he is at work on the second Solomon vs. Lord novel, *The Deep Blue Alibi*. Visit his website at www.paul-levine.com.

Read on for an excerpt of Paul Levine's next Solomon vs. Lord book, *THE DEEP BLUE ALIBI*, coming from Bantam Books in Spring 2006.

THE DEEP BLUE ALIBI

A Solomon vs. Lord Novel

by

PAUL LEVINE

THE DEEP BLUE ALIBI

On sale Spring 2006

"Forget it, Steve. I'm not having sex in the ocean."

"C'mon," he pleaded. "Be adventurous."

"It's undignified and unsanitary," she said. "Maybe even illegal."

"It's the Keys. Nothing's illegal."

Steve Solomon and Victoria Lord were wading in the shallow water just off Sunset Key. At the horizon, the sun sizzled just above the Gulf.

"In this light, you're really magnificent," he said.

"Nice try, hotshot, but the bikini stays on."

Still, she had to admit that there was something erotic about the warm water, the salty breeze, the glow of the setting sun. And Steve looked totally hot, his complexion tinged a reddish bronze, his dark hair slick and lustrous.

If only I didn't have to drop a bombshell on him tonight.

"It'll be great." He grabbed her around the waist. "A saltwater hump-a-rama."

Dear God. Did the man I think I love really say "hump-a-rama"?

"We can't. There are people around."

Twenty yards away, a young couple with that honeymoon look—satiated and clueless—pedaled by on a water bike. On the beach, hotel guests carried drinks in plastic cups along the shoreline. Music floated across the water from the hotel's tiki-hut bar, André Toussaint singing "Island Woman."

Why couldn't Steve see she wasn't in the mood? How can someone so good at picking a jury be so oblivious to the ebb and flow of his lover's emotions?

She pried his hands off her hips. "There's seaweed. And sea lice. And sea urchins." She'd run out of *sea-things.*

"Okay, we can do it in the boring old hotel room."

"So you find our sex life drab without special effects."

"I didn't say that."

She sharpened her voice into cross-exam mode. "Isn't it true that after a few months, all your old girlfriends started to bore you?"

"Not the ones who dumped me."

"Do you realize you have relationship attention disorder?"

"I love our sex life." He pulled her close, and she could feel the bulge in his swim trunks. "Why don't we go in now and get started?"

Get started? Making it sound like cleaning the kitchen.

"You go. Start without me."

She looked toward the horizon where thin ribbons of clouds were streaked the color of a bruised plum. They'd never make it before sunset. No way she was going to miss the orange fireball dip into the sea. She loved the eternal rhythm of day into night, the sun rising from the Atlantic, setting in the Gulf. What dependability. She doubted Steve understood that. If he had his way, the sun would zigzag across the peninsula, stopping for a beer in Islamorada.

She had another reason to stiff-arm his stiff arm.

The bombshell.

She'd been thinking about it all the way to Key West. A pesky mosquito of a thought, buzzing in her brain. She hated to ruin the evening, but she had to tell him soon.

She brought her legs up and floated on her back. As she looked toward the horizon upside down, the sun floated at the waterline, connected to its reflection by a fiery rope.

"Okay, okay, I give up," Steve said. "*Coitus postponus*. What time do we meet your uncle?"

"Eight o'clock. And I told you, he's not really my uncle."

"I know. Good old Hal Griffin. Your father's partner, the guy who bought you fancy presents when you were a spoiled brat."

"Privileged, not spoiled. Uncle Grif's the one who named my mother 'The Queen.' "

"And you 'The Princess.' "

So Steve had been listening after all, she thought. "You think the name fits?"

"Like your Jimmy Choos."

She started swimming the backstroke, heading out to sea, toward the setting sun. Her smooth strokes knifed through the water, now glazed a boiling orange. Steve swam alongside her, struggling to keep up.

"What I don't get is why Griffin's called you after all these years," he said between breaths.

The same question had been puzzling Victoria. She hadn't seen Uncle Grif since her father's funeral when she was twelve. Now, suddenly, a phone call. "All I know is he has some legal work for me."

"You mean for *us*."

"He didn't know about you."

"But you told him, right? Solomon and Lord."

"Of course."

Is this how it begins? A little white lie, followed by bigger, darker ones.

God, she hated this. She had to tell Steve, and quickly. But how?

She could hear him flailing away, kicking up a storm, trying to catch her. Except for swimming—all splash, no speed—Steve was an accomplished athlete. He'd run track in high school and played baseball at the University of Miami, where he was a mediocre hitter but a terrific base runner.

Solomon takes off . . . and steals second!

A good primer for lawyering, Victoria figured.

Conning the pitcher, stealing the catcher's signs, then racing to a base you hadn't otherwise earned. Steve had been particularly adept at spiking opposing fielders and kicking the ball out of their gloves. But like a lot of athletes, he didn't know his limitations. He thought he was good at everything. Poker. Auto repair. Sex. Okay, he was good in bed, very good once she taught him to slow down and stop trying to score from first on a single.

A hundred yards offshore, she started treading water, waiting for him to catch up.

"So where are we eating, Vic?" Puffing hard now.

So very Steve. He could be thinking about dinner while still eating lunch. "Uncle Grif made reservations at Louie's Backyard."

He made an appreciative *hmm*ing sound. "Love their cracked conch. Maybe go with the black grouper for an entrée, mango mousse for dessert."

Sex and food, she thought. Did he ever think about anything else?

"And we'll be back in the room in time for *SportsCenter*," he continued.

Yes, of course he did.

Was it his imagination, or was something bothering Victoria? Steve couldn't tell. She'd been quiet on the drive down the Overseas Highway, occasionally glancing at the red coral heads peeking through the shallow turquoise water. He'd asked how her cases were going—they divided up the workload as *his, hers,* and *theirs*—but she didn't want to talk shop. He sang some old Jimmy Buffet songs. But she didn't join his search for a lost shaker of salt or a cheeseburger in paradise.

Now he told himself that nothing was wrong. After all, he was holding Victoria in his arms as they treaded water. When he'd complimented her, he'd been sincere in his own lusty-hearted way. In the glow of the twilight, she was stunning, her skin blushed, her butterscotch hair pulled back in a ponytail, highlighting her cheekbones. Small breasts, long legs, a firm, trim body. He felt a stirring inside his trunks. The air was rich with salt and coconut oil, and he was with the woman he loved, a woman who for reasons inexplicable, seemed to love him, too.

By his calculations, they still had time to hit the room, make love, and meet Griffin at Louie's. Maybe do it in the shower as they cleaned up for dinner, the Solomon method of multitasking. He just wished the sun would hurry the hell up and call it a day.

Nearby, two windsurfers were catching a final ride, the wind shutting down for the night with the setting sun. Overhead, seabirds dipped and cawed. From the beach, he heard the sound of salsa coming from the bar's speakers, Celia Cruz singing *"Vida Es un Carnaval."*

Damn straight. Steve's life was a carnival, a sun-filled, beach-breezed, beer commercial of an existence. This was better than knocking off State Farm for a seven-figure verdict. Not that he ever had, but he could imagine. Better, too, than stealing home in a college baseball game. That he'd done, against Florida State. Of course, his team lost. But still, a helluva moment.

"Steve, we need to talk," Victoria said.

"Absolutely." He was watching a pink sash of clouds at the horizon turn to gray. A slice of the sun nestled into the water. On the beach, the tourists yelped and cheered, as if they had something to do with this nightly feat. "What do we need to talk about?"

"Us."

Uh-oh.

In Steve's experience, when a woman wanted to talk about *us*, the carnival was about to fold its tent. He quickly ran through his possible misdemeanors. He hadn't left the toilet seat up for two weeks, at least. He hadn't been mean to her mother, even though Her Highness hated him. He hadn't flirted with other women, not even the exotic dancer he was representing in a prickly lewd and lascivious trial.

"So what'd I do?" Sounding defensive.

Victoria put her hands around his neck, twining her fingers, as they treaded water in unison. "You treat me like a law clerk."

"No, I don't. But I am the senior partner."

"That's what I mean. You don't treat me as an equal."

"Cut me a break, Vic. Before you came along, it was my firm."

"What firm? Solomon and *Associates* was false advertising. It was just you. Solomon and *Lord* is a firm."

"Okay, okay. I'll be more sensitive to . . ." What? He'd picked up the phrase from Dr. Phil, or Oprah, or one of the women's magazines at the dentist's office.

"I'll be more sensitive to . . ."

You throw it out when your girlfriend is upset. But it's best if you know what the hell you're talking about. Another problem: He was growing tired treading water. "Your needs," he said, triumphantly. "I'll be more sensitive to your *needs*."

"I'll never grow as an attorney until I have autonomy."

"What are you talking about?"

"Don't get all crazy. It's not going to affect our relationship, but I want to go out on my own."

"Your own what?"

"I want to open my own shop."

"Break up the firm? Trash a winning team?" Stunned, he stopped bicycling and slipped under the water. Popping to the surface, he spit water like a cherub on a fountain. "But we're great partners."

"We're so different. I do things by the book. You burn the book."

"That's our strength, Vic. Our synergy. You kiss 'em on the cheek, I kick 'em in the nuts." Pedaling to stay afloat, he put his arms around her back and pulled her closer. "If you want, I'll change my style."

"You can't change who you are. As long as it's

Solomon and Lord, I'll always be second chair. I need to make a name for myself."

He nearly said it then: *"How about the name, Mrs. Victoria Solomon?"*

But he would have sounded desperate. Besides, neither one was ready for that kind of commitment.

"If it makes you happy," he said brusquely, "go fly solo."

"Are you pouting?"

"No, I'm giving you space." Another phrase he'd picked up somewhere. "I'm giving you space and autonomy and . . ."

What's that noise?

Jet Skis? They ought to ban the damn things. But even as he turned to face the open sea, he realized this sound was different. The roar of giant diesels.

A powerboat roared toward the beach. And, unless it turned, right at them.

From the waterline, it was impossible to judge the size of the boat or its speed. But from the sound—the rolling thunder of an avalanche—Steve knew it was huge and fast. A bruiser of a powerboat good for chasing marlin or sailfish in the deep blue sea. Not for cruising toward a beach of swimmers and paddlers and waders.

Steve forced himself to stay calm. The jerk would turn away at the piling with the no-wake sign, the props whipping a four-foot roller toward the beach. Everyone on board would have a big laugh and a bigger drink.

The boat muscled toward them, riding on a plane, its bowsprit angled toward the sky like a thin patrician nose.

"Steve . . ."

"Don't worry. Just some cowboy showing off."

But it didn't turn and it didn't stop. Now he was worried.

Five hundred yards away, the boat leapt the small chop, splatted down, leapt again. He could see white water cascading high along the hull, streaming over the deck. The roar grew louder, a throaty baritone, like a dozen Ferraris racing their engines. The son-of-a-bitch must be doing forty knots.

Still it came, its bow seemingly aimed straight at them. In twenty seconds, it would be on them. Windsurfers scattered. Swimmers kicked and splashed toward shore. On the beach, people in chaise lounges leapt to their feet and back-pedaled. A lifeguard tooted his whistle, nearly drowned out by the bellow of the diesels.

Squinting into the glare, Steve could see there was no one on the fly bridge. A boat without a driver.

"C'mon!" Victoria cried out, starting to swim parallel to the beach.

Steve grabbed her by an ankle and pulled her back. They didn't have the speed or maneuverability. What they had were five seconds.

"Dive!" Steve ordered.

Wide-eyed, Victoria took a breath.

They dived straight down, kicking hard.

Underwater, Steve heard the props, a high-pitched whine that drowned out the roar of the diesels. Then, a bizarre sensation, a banging in his chest. Was someone smashing his sternum with a ball-peen hammer? A split second later, he heard the *click-click-click* of a bottlenose dolphin, but he knew it was the boat's sonar, bombarding him with invisible waves. Suddenly, the wash of the props tore at him, dragging him up and pushing him down simultaneously. He tumbled head-over-ass, smacked the bottom with a shoulder, and felt his neck twist at a painful angle. Eyes open, he swung around, looking for Victoria, seeing only the cloudy swirl of bottom sand. Then a glimpse of her feet headed for the surface. He kicked off the bottom and followed her, surfacing a second after she did.

They both turned toward the shore just as the boat ramped off the sandy incline, going airborne, props still churning. Steve could hear screams from the beach, could see people scattering as the boat flew over the first row of beach chairs, then grazed the palm frond roof of the tiki-hut bar and crashed through a canvas-topped cabana. The wooden hull split amidships with the sound of a thousand baseball bats splintering, its two halves separating as neatly as a cleanly cracked walnut.

Victoria knew she would reach the beach before him. Her stroke was long and powerful, her kicks deep and fast as a hummingbird's wings.

She ignored Steve's shouts to wait. No, the *senior partner* would have to catch up on his own. She had seen the lettering on the stern as the boat lifted out of the water: *FORCE MAJEURE IV.* She recognized the name, remembered the first one, even after all these years.

How could it be?

In a place where most boats were christened with prosaic puns—*Queasy Rider, Wet Dream*—this craft could only be owned by one man. In the law, a *force majeure* was something that couldn't be controlled. A superior, irresistible force. Like a powerful yacht . . . or its powerful owner.

Steve was still yelling to wait up as she scrambled onto the sand and ran toward the fractured boat. The bridge had separated and was lying on its side in the sand, the chrome wheel pretzeled out of shape. Detritus was scattered in an elliptical pattern around the two halves of the boat. Shards of glass, torn cushions, twisted grab rails, the arm of a radar antenna. The fighting chair, separated from its base, sat upright in the sand, as if waiting for a missing fisherman.

Half-a-dozen Florida lobsters crawled across the sand, a shattered plastic fish box nearby. Something was impaled on one lobster's antenna. It took a second for the bizarre sight to register.

A hundred-dollar bill. The lobster's spiny antenna was sticking right through Ben Franklin's nose.

Then she saw the other bills. A covey of greenbacks, fluttering across the beach, like seabirds caught in a squall.

She heard a man's voice. "This one's breathing, but he's messed up bad."

The hotel lifeguard talking, bent over a middle-aged man in khaki shorts and polo shirt. The man lay on his side, motionless, his limbs splayed at grotesque angles, a broken doll. The lifeguard gently turned the man onto his back, then gasped. A metal spear protruded from the man's chest.

"Jesus!"

The poor man. But thank God, it's not him.

"Another one, over here!" A woman's voice.

Victoria navigated around a thicket of splintered teak decking. A female bartender was crouched in the sand over a thick-bodied man in a white guayabera. Rivulets of blood ran down the man's face from a wide gash on his forehead. "Don't move," the bartender ordered. "We're gonna get you to the hospital."

The man grunted. He appeared to be in his sixties with a thick neck and short, white hair. His eyes were squinted closed, either from pain or the blood running into his eyes.

Victoria came closer, trying to see if it was him. "You should put a compress over the wound."

The man opened his eyes, and Victoria recognized him at once, even after all these years. "Uncle Grif!"

"Hello, Princess." Propping himself on one elbow, grimacing through the pain, Hal Griffin tried to push the bartender aside. "Let me alone. I need to talk to my lawyer."

Carnival Pride^{SM}
April 2 - 9, 2006.

7 Day Exotic Mexican Riviera Itinerary

DAY	PORT	ARRIVE	DEPART
Sun	Los Angeles/Long Beach, CA		4:00 P.M.
Mon	"Book Lover's" Day at Sea		
Tue	"Book Lover's" Day at Sea		
Wed	Puerto Vallarta, Mexico	8:00 A.M.	10:00 P.M.
Thu	Mazatlan, Mexico	9:00 A.M.	6:00 P.M.
Fri	Cabo San Lucas, Mexico	7:00 A.M.	4:00 P.M.
Sat	"Book Lover's" Day at Sea		
Sun	Los Angeles/Long Beach, CA	9:00 A.M.	

ports of call subject to weather conditions

TERMS AND CONDITIONS

PAYMENT SCHEDULE:
50% due upon booking
Full and final payment due by February 10, 2006

Acceptable forms of payment are Visa, MasterCard, American Express, Discover and checks. The cardholder must be one of the passengers traveling. A fee of $25 will apply for all returned checks. Check payments must be made payable to **Advantage International, LLC and sent to: Advantage International, LLC, 195 North Harbor Drive, Suite 4206, Chicago, IL 60601**

CHANGE/CANCELLATION:
Notice of change/cancellation must be made in writing to Advantage International, LLC.

Change:
Changes in cabin category may be requested and can result in increased rate and penalties. A name change is permitted 60 days or more prior to departure and will incur a penalty of $50 per name change. Deviation from the group schedule and package is a cancellation.

Cancellation:

181 days or more prior to departure	$250 per person
121 - 180 days or more prior to departure	50% of the package price
120 - 61 days prior to departure	75% of the package price
60 days or less prior to departure	100% of the package price (nonrefundable)

US and Canadian citizens are required to present a valid passport or the original birth certificate and state issued photo ID (drivers license). All other nationalities must contact the consulate of the various ports that are visited for verification of documentation.

<u>We strongly recommend trip cancellation insurance!</u>

For complete details call 1-877-ADV-NTGE or visit www.AuthorsAtSea.com

---

For booking form and complete information
go to **www.AuthorsAtSea.com** or call **1-877-ADV-NTGE**

Complete coupon and booking form and mail both to:
Advantage International, LLC,
195 North Harbor Drive, Suite 4206, Chicago, IL 60601